Nigel Colborn is a successful country writer and journalist. He appears regularly on BBC Radio 4's *Gardener's Question Time* and contributes widely to the rural press. He is a fellow of the Royal Society of Arts and a member of the Royal Horticultural Society's Committee 'A' judging at major flower shows including Chelsea.

Nigel Colborn has written numerous books on gardening and country living as well as short stories. *Weather of the Heart* is his third novel. He travels extensively and lives with his family in the east of England.

Also by Nigel Colborn

The Congregation

WEATHER OF THE HEART

Nigel Colborn

WARNER BOOKS

A *Warner* Book

First published in Great Britain
by Warner Books in 1997

Copyright © Nigel Colborn 1997

'A process in the weather of the heart'
is taken from *The Poems* by Dylan Thomas.
Reproduced by kind permission of the publisher.

A CIP catalogue record for this book
is available from the British Library.

ISBN 0 7515 2105 1

Typeset by Palimpsest Book Production Limited,
Polmont, Stirlingshire
Printed and bound in Great Britain by
Clays Ltd, St Ives plc.

Warner Books
A Division of
Little, Brown and Company (UK)
Brettenham House
Lancaster Place
London WC2E 7EN

A process in the weather of the heart
Turns damp to dry; the golden shot
Storms in the freezing tomb.
A weather in the quarter of the veins
Turns night to day; blood in their suns
Lights up the living worm.

A process in the eye forwarns
The bones of blindness; and the womb
Drives in a death as life leaks out.

A process in the weather of the heart
Dylan Thomas

PART ONE

DEPARTURES

Chapter One

'I don't want to go,' Anna Morfey told her daughter, '*really*, I don't.' Lisa did not respond, other than to take a hand from the wheel and lay it over her mother's. She squeezed gently, feeling Anna's fist muscles clench under her fingers. Anna stared ahead. I must orientate myself, she thought, I must not lose track of where I am. It is seven months, two weeks and one day since I lost Bernard.

She looked out of the car window but they were travelling too fast to see much – not that there was a lot to see in January. Apart from a dotting of yellow gorse blossom here and there, Hampshire was decked in dreary greys and dirty greens. Ahead, the first signs for Southampton appeared and the nearness of the port made her stomach tense, a beginning of term feeling remembered from her first day at school and before every major move in her life. Lisa, a smooth but nippy driver, tucked in behind an animal feedingstuffs lorry before slipping off the motorway. Within a few minutes, she was able to point out the derricks and shipping of the docks. Anna felt sick. 'I really don't want to—'

'Look, Mummy, there's the *Brisbane*,' Lisa said. 'Goodness, she's *huge*!' The vast white passenger liner dwarfed the quayside buildings, her twin rear funnels rising high above their roofs and issuing a double plume of smoke that curved into the sky, pale grey against the dark clouds of midwinter. Anna stayed silent while Lisa drove past the dockyard checkpoints into the terminal building. There, before pulling herself out of her daughter's expensive but rather bouncy and uncomfortable car, she surveyed the mêlée of confused passengers, cart-trundling porters and unhelpful security officials. 'What a lot of baggage everyone has,' she said, but Lisa had gone to find a porter.

She glanced down at her navy leather handbag, visualising the travel documents within – ship's ticket, traveller's cheques, passport – willing herself not to open it to check, yet again, that everything was there. In her mind she turned the passport pages. The photograph was awful; she was sure she didn't really look as horsy as that. When it had been taken seven years previously she had been disappointed at how much older it had made her look, but when, just before Christmas, she had wanted to make sure the document was still valid for the cruise, its two-inch portrait had surprised her with its youthfulness. Colour of hair, brown; colour of eyes, brown; special distinguishing marks, none. No passport could really describe anyone. Anna's brown hair had been light with a hint of auburn, when she was young, and bleached almost to blonde in warm summers. Now that she was nearly sixty her coiffeuse kept it fair with subtle highlights to disguise the grey. Her eyes were less brown now than they had been, with a touch of milkiness on the rim of the irises, but they remained her best feature: large, and set in her face with a slight downturn on either side so that, when relaxed, her expression suggested sadness, but when she smiled, her whole mien was transformed. Like turning on a light, Verne had said once. 'Jeez, Anna, you smiled!'

Anna had no doubt at all that Lisa had persuaded her to take this world cruise to get rid of her. 'It'll be so therapeutic, Mummy,' she had insisted, showing her the vividly illustrated M&I cruise brochures. 'You'll see new places, meet interesting people, that sort of thing. Besides, three months of sunshine is bound to do you good.' Anna had but glanced at the glossy pages, peppered with photographs of beautiful sun-bronzed people lolling on deck or arriving at exotic destinations. The problem was that she didn't really want to do anything at all. Not any more. But as Lisa had continued her hard sell, Anna had realised that the past few months must have been almost as trying for her daughter as for herself.

'How sick you must be of me,' she had said, and had then regretted being so unkind. Over the preceding weeks, especially at first, only Lisa had kept her from going right over the edge. Only she had tried to supply genuine comfort, had helped with all those irksome practicalities, had been there to give support, had held her tightly during weeping spells, and tucked her up in bed afterwards, holding her hand until the sedative worked and she could sleep. 'Oh, Lisa, darling, do forgive me!' She wished, how she wished she could be kinder to her daughter. Almost as a penance, she had made herself think more carefully about the cruise. She had read the brochure, looked up some of the ports in her antiquated *Encyclopaedia of World Travel* and had even phoned M&I to find out about fares. But she had not been able to kindle any enthusiasm within herself, either for cruising or for anything else. She had talked to Max about it during her next counselling session.

'Your daughter's right. You *should* go,' Max had said, raising two hands and shrugging. 'You can afford my fees, you can afford a world cruise!'

'It's thirteen weeks.'

'Go, have fun!'

'Won't it hurt, missing these therapy sessions?'

'I'll manage,' he had replied. When he said such things with a straight face, she never knew whether he was joking. He had raised his eyebrows twice, quickly, like Groucho Marx. She had tried to smile. I used to have a sense of humour, she had thought. 'As long as you do what I ask,' Max had continued, 'you'll be perfectly all right. Sea air, warm sunshine in winter – you'll benefit, even if your bank balance won't. Those ticket prices, my God!'

Max's approval mattered and when it came she began, at last, to warm to the idea. His task seemed, on the face of it, simple enough. 'I want you to write,' he had said. 'Every day, if you can.' At first she thought he meant letters – she had always been a prolific letter writer – but he wanted her to keep a journal and, if she felt able, to write the story of her life. 'You'll feel really inhibited, at first,' he had said, 'but don't worry. Just keep your pen waggling on the paper. Things will begin to flow and you'll start to feel better.'

'But what sort of things should I write?'

'Anything. About your childhood, about your husband, things you hate, things you love, anything – sex even. If you do it you'll feel better. Trust me, I'm an expert.'

'I don't think I'll bother,' she had told Lisa later that afternoon. 'I'm not even good at writing letters, let alone memoirs. Your father used to say my grammar was awful.' But she booked herself a single cabin on M&I's world cruise, on the *Brisbane* due to sail from Southampton on the sixth of January.

She looked up to see Lisa returning to the car with a porter. She looked agitated.

'Mummy, there's an absolutely *poisonous* security man there who says I can't come on board with you, so I'll have to say goodbye here.' She opened the boot of her car for the porter who began to pile Anna's two suitcases, dressing case, and an old canvas attaché case on to his barrow.

'This all, madam?' he said. Distracted by their imminent parting, neither woman heard.

'But it doesn't sail for hours.' Anna was near tears – not an unusual state for her these days – and stood fiddling with her gloves. 'I thought you'd be able to have tea with me or something.'

'Perhaps it's better this way, Mummy.' Lisa, who had counted the days to her mother's departure, was taken aback by the moment and felt miserable and guilty for having wanted to be rid of her. To add to her shame she felt her own tears welling up. 'I . . . I'll come to the barrier with you.'

'This way, er, ladies,' the porter said, beginning to move his load. 'These 'eavy ones will be delivered to yer cabin. Better keep them little ones with yer.' Within seconds, Lisa was parted from her mother. Security staff at the entrance discouraged lingering, even though there were few other passengers waiting to board at that moment. They snatched Anna's two smaller bags, giving her the briefest moment to kiss her daughter and then making her almost run to retrieve them from the other end of the X-ray tunnel.

'I'll fax you from the office,' Lisa called. 'I've got the *Brisbane*'s number.' But her mother did not hear. Almost in a stupor, she found herself gazing up at the vast white side of the ship before walking across the quay to the gangway. Nothing that big could possibly float. This, logic reminded her, was nonsense, but at least it was far too big to be rocked about by the sea. She would feel safe on it, and perhaps sheltered from the outside world. At a shout, she glanced up in time to be temporarily blinded by a photographer's flash before ascending the clanking gangway stairs. It seemed an incredibly long climb.

At the top of the gangway yet another security man greeted her. She sensed an atmosphere of carpeted warmth inside the ship, but her attention was taken by the parade of Indian stewards lined up on either side of the concourse, every beige and pale blue uniform tunic spotless and pressed with military precision, white gloves on every hand, each brown face alert. One of the older men broke ranks and said, 'Welcome, please, madam. Your cabin number?'

'Oh, I'm not sure.' She had been confused by the faces. Some of the stewards were mere boys, others older men. Most bore an identical expression of alertness, a half smile, not obsequious but not aloof.

'It is on your bag label here, madam.' The steward touched the tag that Anna had herself filled out only yesterday. 'It is A-twelve, madam.' Anna felt more stupid than ever. At the sound of the cabin number, another of the stewards stepped forward.

'May I show you the way?' He took her dressing case and the canvas attaché case. He could hardly be out of his teens, she thought, and she marvelled at the slenderness of his wrists and fingers. Most Asians, she knew, were fine-boned compared to clumsy Europeans, but this boy seemed even more refined, graceful, rather than delicate. Anna tended to notice things like that, and then to remember them. He set off at a brisk pace along a carpeted corridor to a larger concourse where there were lifts. These he indicated with his chin, in case Anna wanted to use one, but she stayed close to him, following him up four flights of stairs and then along another wider corridor. He turned sharp left and she followed him into a widening court with a small seating area and low table at its end, lit by three large portholes. On either side she saw the numbered doors and noted that each cabin had a little window at its corner which looked out into the court. The steward opened the last door for her.

'I am your cabin steward, madam. I am Tony.'

'Thank you, er, Tony.' The English-sounding name seemed incongruous. 'From Pakistan?' Tony looked crestfallen, almost as if she had made an accusation.

'From Goa, madam. All the cabin stewards are from Goa.'

'Oh, of course, how stupid of me.' She wasn't sure where Goa was. The boy smiled again. He seemed to smile a lot, with his eyes as well as his mouth. Anna felt herself warming to his gentle features. 'Thank you for the help.' He nodded and withdrew, closing the door silently.

Anna surveyed the cabin – home for the next thirteen weeks. It was small but well designed, with two varnished wooden doors, one of which opened to a small shower room and lavatory and the other to a roomy wardrobe. The walls were decorated with pale gold emulsion and furnished with a single picture – a print of a sylvan landscape in spring, the undergrowth a haze of bluebells with tufts of pink campion in the foreground. Almost as lovely as the wake-robin woods, she thought. Oceans of white three-petalled trilliums or wake-robin had enchanted her more than thirty years before, in the North American countryside. There was a built-in chest of drawers, more stowage under the single bed and, beneath the porthole, a small dressing table with knee hole and a padded stool. That will be my desk, Anna decided.

She opened her attaché case and took out a large, hardcover notebook. It was expensively bound with maroon oilcloth covers and black leather reinforced corners. The paper – as yet, every page was in virgin condition – was thick and smooth with feint ruled lines. She laid the book on the tiny desk area and then fished in the bag for pens and a six-inch ruler. These she arranged to the side of the book. I ought to write straight away, she thought. Start as you mean to go on. But that made her eyes smart, for some reason, and to wrench her mind off things she peered through the porthole. It was starting to get dark and she could see lights reflected in Southampton Water. A sudden movement startled her, with flashing lights and a scarcely discernible shape travelling past the porthole. A vessel, she assumed; she would not have known the Isle of Wight ferry. She wondered whether to go up on deck or to explore the ship but was afraid of getting lost and being unable to find her cabin again. Instead, she stroked the first creamy page of the book and picked up her pen, but she couldn't think what to write. That elusive first word; the blankness of the page. She had to write something decent, at first, or the whole thing would get off to a bad start.

A tap at the door alarmed her. Her baggage had arrived. She peeped out into the court and saw more suitcases outside A10, the adjacent cabin. These looked expensive but well worn and covered with labels. She assumed that their owners would be experienced travellers and wondered what they would be like. Most people waiting to board seemed quite old but there had been one or two young families with children. She spotted another cabin door opening on the opposite side of the court and retreated into her own before being encountered. She decided to unpack.

Thirty minutes later all her clothes were stowed in drawers or hung on hangers. She assembled a small collection of books – *Persuasion, Middlemarch*, Shakespeare, a couple of Angela Carter novels and John Updike's *Rabbit* tetralogy – on the shelf above her bunk. Bernard had hated *Rabbit, Run* when he read it in sixties America because the hero's weaknesses had set his teeth on edge, and Anna had had to admit Rabbit's attitude to women had rather upset her. But since losing Bernard she had spent a long time looking back, searching for things that had made her happy, trying to find escape from the present pain. America had provided the best and the worst memories and Updike's writing seemed a comforting way to travel into that portion of her past.

Out of her attaché case she fished Lisa's Christmas present, a personal compact disc player. At first this had seemed a pointless extravagance that she would never dream of using. Lisa had also handed her, on Christmas morning, two small but weighty boxes, one containing recordings of all the Mozart piano concerti and the other Puccini's *Madame Butterfly*. And suddenly her periods of insomnia had been made tolerable. Lying in the dark, when terror of the future was her cold companion, she could put on headphones and listen, playing the music as loud as she liked, without disturbing anyone. Not that there had been anyone to disturb during the last six months – apart from Lisa when she was staying at Tonbridge. To Lisa's original discs she had begun to add her own purchases – realising, on her first visit to the record shop and seeing disc prices, just how generous her daughter had been. Now she placed, next to her small library, discs of Chopin, Schubert *Lieder*, Fauré's piano music and Billie Holliday.

She arranged the last of her possessions and, as requested in *Brisbane Today* – the ship's daily newspaper – placed her empty cases outside the cabin door. Simultaneously, the door of A10 opened and Anna heard a male voice say, archly, 'There's no need to be *quite* so venomous this early on the trip.' The occupant erupted into the court, slamming the door behind him and hissing, in a stage whisper, 'Bastard!' Anna stiffened. She hardly felt ready to talk to anyone yet, especially not someone in a temper. She took in his dark, cropped hair, bushy moustache and trim figure, clothed in fashionably baggy twill cotton trousers, patterned shirt and primrose cashmere pullover. He did not even notice her, but walked swiftly out of the court. Before she had time to escape, the door opened again and another male head, this one even closer cropped but blond, peered round the lintel. This time she was noticed.

'Oh dear!' said the head, in a plummy English accent. 'We seem to have made a scene even before this old darling of a rust bucket has untied.' The head was attached to a taller, more ruggedly developed body, clothed in corduroys and a sweatshirt. Anna thought briefly of Verne. 'Are we to be neighbours? How delightful! I'm Cedric.' He stepped forward and stretched out a hand which she took somewhat absently. 'That,' he said, indicating with his chin the direction in which his companion had flounced, 'was Ant.'

'Ant?'

'Ant. His real name is Antony. Spell it with an aitch, though, and he'll sulk. Call him Tony and he'll never speak to you again.'

'My cabin steward is called Tony.'

'He's ours too. I rest my case.' They faced each other for a few more moments, the pause in their conversation becoming uncomfortable as he waited for her to introduce herself. 'And you are . . . ?'

'Anna Morfey.' He seemed to expect more but she felt terribly awkward, unable to expand. She really had done very little socialising in the last six months, though with Bernard their engagement calendar had positively bulged. Right from the beginning there had been university events and dinner parties and, towards the end, huge receptions, public appearances and audiences with royalty. It had been exhausting, but she had loved it. Images from the past began to rear up in her mind. She felt her world – the present world – begin to slip and knew her smile had gone.

'Travelling alone, I presume.' Cedric said. He had detected her bleak attitude within seconds of seeing her and assumed she must be newly widowed. Anna nodded. 'How far do you go?' His archness made the question sound as though there were a double meaning. She had read somewhere that shipboard life could be odd, that cruise liners were full of lonely people hungry for a mate.

'All the way.' The words were out before she realised she had slipped into his trap.

'Ooh, you shameless woman!' he said, but rather lamely, put off by the sadness on her face. 'Oh you mustn't mind us, Anna,' he quickly added. 'We love a joke, Ant and I. Part of the fun of these cruises are the people we meet – we love that bit.' He looked more closely at her and smiled. 'Does that bother you?'

'Of course not,' Anna said, but she rather thought it did. It would certainly have bothered Bernard.

'Excellent! Then we can be friends as well as neighbours.' Anna was about to make her excuses. She felt she'd had enough social encountering for a while but something was worrying her.

'Lifeboat drill,' she said. 'Do we *have* to go?'

'Silly not to,' Cedric said. 'But don't worry, we'll escort you to your muster station. Then we can watch the ship sail at six.'

Anna returned to her cabin, closed the door and sat at her tiny desk. She stared at the first page of her notebook for a full five minutes without moving. She had been trying to sort out her early recollections but it was proving almost impossible. Whenever she conjured up childhood memories later ones pushed them out. What was I doing, she asked herself, by way of an exercise, on this day fifty years ago? But the image of building a snowman in the rectory garden, and shouts of the other children in her mind's ear, transformed to cheers of students sliding down the frozen hill of the American university campus at Purlin on trays they had pinched from the student cafeterias. With moonlight bouncing off the snow, their shapes would be outlined, single boys or pairs, whizzing and whooping down past her, their legs straight out in front of them, arms stretched back for balance; giggling trains of girl students – they called them coeds, for some reason – five or six together, each with arms around the waist of the one in front, buttocks precarious on fragile trays hurtling downwards at speeds that would give you friction burns if you fell off. The bite of frost on her fingers had never been so sharp, in Norfolk, as it was in upstate New York. You had to wear earmuffs whenever you went outdoors, and gloves and thick parka jackets. Even then, you could feel the moisture in your nostrils freeze and tweak the sensitive inner tissues every time you breathed. But I can't write about Purlin until I've done the early stuff, she told herself, and I'm not sure I can write about Verne at all. She picked up the pen and wrote at the top of the page, in block capitals: IN THE BEGINNING. Some minutes later she wrote underneath, in her neatly rounded script:

I was born in Norfolk.

Then she added a tail to the full stop, turning it into a comma, and added:

at Congston Rectory. My father was rector of the three parishes of Congston, Hincham and Sorley. My mother died a year after Charlie, my younger brother, was born.

It seemed so stilted and sparse, and yet there were too many words. She could not remember her mother at all but the sight of Daddy's face, red and bleary from weeping, she could recall without effort. Yet she had been barely three at the time, so how could she possibly remember? I must be recalling someone else's description, she decided – perhaps Dawn's. Dawn was the housekeeper-cum-nanny who, in a

way, she grew to love more than she loved Daddy. She
certainly remembered feeling not quite right about that. And
she adored Charlie. There was a seven-year gap between Anna
and Ralph, her elder brother, so although she was nearly two
years older than Charlie, she felt close. It occurred to her now
for the first time, as she looked at her notebook, that in certain
respects the feelings she had had for Charlie were similar to
those she had first harboured for Bernard. Indeed, it was
Bernard's 'Charlieness' when they met in Cornwall . . .

There was a discreet tap at the door. 'Come in,' Anna
called, shutting her notebook and hoping the ink was dry
enough not to smudge. Cedric came in; Ant hovered by the
door. They were both carrying orange life jackets.

'You'll need one of these,' Cedric said. 'It'll be in your
wardrobe, under the false floor.' As she went to find her life
jacket, Ant came into the room and picked up the notebook.

'This is nice,' he said. 'Are you a writer?' She had
expected an American twang but, though his inflection was
transatlantic, the words sounded British. She disliked seeing
him touch her things; she felt uncomfortable about what these
two were, what they did. Bernard would have had no time for
them at all.

'No,' she said, a little more sharply than was necessary.
Her tone made him act out a little wince and he put the
book down.

'I'm *so*rry.' He straightened it on the desk. 'We don't mean
to pry, do we Cedric?' Cedric caught Anna's eye and winked,
doing a tiny shrug at the same time.

'The fact is, I want to learn to write,' Anna said. Did she?
What on earth made her say that? Just because she hadn't yet
managed to get any coherent thoughts down on paper.

'You do? Oh that's *wonderful*!' they both said.

'You'll have to come to the creative writing sessions,'
Cedric said. 'We've got Jack Pullen on board, and he's
definitely going all the way! *The* Jack Pullen. You know,
October Dance, *Christmas at Margot's* and that . . . thing
they made into a TV mini-series oh, you know, Ant . . .'

'*The Hungerford Connection*,' Ant said, 'it was *dreadful*.'

'Sshhh! Ant!' Cedric's voice went confidential. 'We all know it was absolute crap, but just *think* of the fun we're going to have with his writing classes. I can't wait to see what budding bards he'll attract.'

Anna felt almost happy to be part of their conspiracy, as if the burden on her shoulders had been eased a little, but the feeling afforded only momentary comfort and she released a deep sigh, causing the two men to exchange glances. The ship's whistle blew, heard faintly through the decks, and then bells started ringing. Feeling awkward and rather foolish in her bulky life jacket, Anna found herself being led by Ant and Cedric to her muster station for safety drill.

Two hours later, wrapped in extra cardigan, anorak and a woollen hat pulled down over her ears, she stood at the rail between Cedric and Ant who waved to no one in particular and hurled streamers as the ship was untied. There was a small brass band down on the quay, and a ragged little crowd at the terminal balcony, stamping their feet and rubbing hands in the cold. Couples, on board and ashore, held each other and everyone breathed out puffs of steam. Cedric cried a little when the last mooring lines were cast off and the forty-five thousand tonnes of ocean liner began to edge away from the quay. 'Ridiculous,' Ant muttered, marginally embarrassed as Cedric pulled out a huge red and white spotted handkerchief and wiped his eye. 'Like some damned mother-in-law at a wedding.' He sounded angry, but Anna spotted the affection in his eye. They stayed out on deck until the ship's progress down the Solent created a chilling wind which drove them to seek warmth inside.

'We usually have a drink before getting changed,' Cedric said, 'but it's always a good idea to nip down to the dining room and check up what table we're on.' That was where Anna nearly lost her struggle to fend off an embarrassing breakdown. The head waiter, in spite of being addressed as Angelo, had been baptised 'Cyril' and in spite of having an olive complexion and crisp dark curls, was more English than the Queen. He greeted Ant and Cedric effusively, giving them a speedy rundown of the juiciest of ship's gossip since their last cruise. When he had finally allowed himself to notice Anna, his manner changed. He stiffened, wiped away his smile and nodded curtly. 'Good evening, madam.'

'Angelo,' Cedric said, pronouncing the name with an operatic accent, 'this is Anna Morfey, our neighbour, and our dearest friend so far.'

'And I suppose you want to sit together.'

'Oh yes please,' they both said. Angelo turned to his seating plan. Anna had glanced at both Ant and Cedric. She wasn't at all sure about it really, but felt it would be wrong to say anything else.

'Aha!' Angelo said. 'Might be tricky, Lady Morfey.' Ant and Cedric glanced at each other. 'You see, Captain Maclean has invited you to join his table.'

'Oh, but I . . .' The prospect of social obligations of any kind, this soon after, filled Anna with dread enough, but the prospect of being on duty night after night while the captain and other guests engaged in stilted small talk was intolerable. 'I really don't think . . .'

'You'll just *love* it,' Ant said. 'Such an honour.' Envy gave his tone an edge. He and Cedric had wanted to be on the captain's table for years but, in spite of their buying tickets for a world cruise either on the *Brisbane* or on M&I's other British cruise ship, the *Queen Adelaide*, every winter for the past thirteen, the invitation had never come.

'I really would much rather be with, um, my friends here,' Anna murmured, but she suspected that it might be wise to cooperate with the staff, even though she was the paying passenger. As in so many situations that wanted firmness, or at least a decision of some kind, Anna stood miserable and irresolute.

'The captain does hope you'll accept,' Angelo said. The campiness had evaporated. He was not smiling, but his voice was quiet and kindly. 'Perhaps you'd care to do a spell there and move tables a little later in the cruise. Three months is a long time; besides, there'll be a change of captain at Sydney.' Meekly she accepted the blue card on which her table designation had been written. 'I've put you two on thirty-four,' he told Ant and Cedric. 'It's a four-seater, but I've kept the other places empty, so you can invite friends to join you when you want.' Anna wondered whether it might displease the captain if they invited her, and thought it probably would.

Captain Maclean was not expected to dine on the first evening, but her fellow guests worked dedicatedly through much of the extensive menu which offered appetiser, soup, fish, meat, dessert, cheese, fresh fruit and savoury. Tonight's was called Scotch woodcock, a name for scrambled egg and anchovies that she had always thought was her father's own invention. Seeing the words in print made her blush. The evening twinkled with gold and diamond jewellery, but not with wit. Once the male half of each couple had made certain, turn by turn, that the rest of the group knew how wealthy they were, how talented their children and how extensively they had travelled, awkward silences began to creep into the conversation, and to lengthen. Occasionally a wife giggled or made an empty remark. Faces began to turn to Anna, expecting her to join the competition, but since her comments were modest to the point of self-abasement, and since she kept them to a minimum anyway, they began to lose interest in her and talked, sporadically, among themselves. Time dragged.

At last the others finished their coffee, and she could retire to her cabin. It was too early to think of sleep, but she wanted solitude. Physically, she felt tired. Mentally, grief and satisfaction balanced each other in an ironic mix. The sense of hurt was there – an ugly groundswell that rumbled and ruminated in the pit of her consciousness, ready to erupt at the slightest trigger. But she had made it! She was here, in her cabin – which she loved already – and was embarking on an adventure. The ship, edging round the Isle of Wight and into the open sea, moved with a small but noticeable heave, like a huge sleeping creature taking a light breath, but far from feeling misgivings she felt comforted by the gentle motion. She realised as she sat at the tiny dressing table that coming on this cruise was the first decisive thing she had done since Bernard. Then thoughts of Bernard made the tears come so fast that she was temporarily blinded. She had to have something to cling to. Her hands reached forward for the desk and fell on the cool, textured surface of her journal.

Chapter Two

Anna woke suddenly, in darkness. She wasn't sure what had roused her, but felt her heart beating faster than normal, as if in the aftermath of alarm. The vibration of the ship, which made bulkheads and fittings tick and fidget busily through the hours, had ceased to irritate her. In fact, after her first restless night and the following shattered-feeling morning at sea, she had begun to feel comforted by the noises and by the unfamiliar sensation of the vessel moving through the water. The decks, as Cedric said you must call them, are never quite still and when you walk; your horizon shifts ever so slightly, so that you can't be quite sure whether your sense of balance is faulty or whether the ground beneath your feet has changed. Except that it isn't ground, but merely an inch or two of steel plate separating you from an unimaginable depth of cold, cold sea.

She switched on the small plastic-covered light on the little shelf by her bunk to see what the time was. Its low wattage beam recalled her first holiday away from the family, camping with Bernard in Cornwall. Uncomfortable in single sleeping bag, she had wanted to read herself to sleep in the frail torchlight, but he had begged her to switch off, anxious to conserve the battery. Soon after, they had decided to unzip both sleeping bags and place hers underneath and his over them. The warmth and strength of his body had helped to insulate her from the cold and dark outside, and the hardness of the ground. But we were chaste, she reminded herself. Right up to . . . She blinked several times, looked at her watch – four twenty-seven – and switched off the light, but knew that she would not sleep. Grieving people, she supposed, should be at their lowest ebb about now, in the pre-dawn hour of the wolf, the darkest hour when the moon has set but the sun does not rise – but for her, darkness had become a comforting blanket. Wakeful, but relaxed, she could build up her emotional strength by telling herself things: lucky you're not poor, you need never be uncomfortable. Thank heavens you've got Lisa. And Max. Dear Max – I am sure he really does like you. Surely his manner isn't just laid on as professional comfort. More recently, she had massaged her heartache with thoughts of the forthcoming cruise and now, on her second morning at sea, she told herself that things could be worse and that there had even been moments she had quite enjoyed. Meeting the captain had been a relief, rather than a pleasure, but . . .

'What's Maclean like?' one of the passengers had asked, at that first, tense dinner. 'Anyone sailed with 'im before?' The questioner had been a greengrocer with a chain of shops in South London and Kent. Anna had misheard the name, but secretly called him Mr Cabbage. The response had been silence at first.

'I have,' another man had said at last. He had worryingly dyed black hair and pudgy, mottled hands, like pork sausages, on to which several gold rings had been forced. As far as Anna was able to tell, he had been a property developer in the Newcastle area. She had dubbed him Mr Pig. 'Typical M&I, of course.' He had reflected for a few more seconds. 'Got a beard.' Anna couldn't help conjuring up images of a wild-eyed creature with thorny facial hair and one leg, dot-and-carrying across his quarterdeck, yelling over the storm to a subdued but bloodily mutinous crew. She had suppressed a giggle and distracted herself by pulling her bread roll to pieces.

That first night, although she had not felt sick, she had barely slept because of the noises. At first she had thought that one of her neighbours – Cedric, she suspected – was typing, but then realised that shifting bulkheads caused the irregular ticking and tapping. The ship's slight motion was comforting and, ultimately, so were the noises, but not the light that spilled under the door from the little court outside. She had lain, sighing, turning over, trying to read, trying to listen to music, and then just lying as still as possible, forcing her muscles to relax, and her mind to empty until early morning. Then, jaded, tearful and with an ugly headache, had got up, showered and dressed, put on her watch – the time was five thirty-seven – and had sat at her desk. Through her porthole she had seen occasional flashes of pale foam, and glimpses of the waves looking slick and oily in the pre-dawn blackness. Then she had opened her book and stroked the first page, enjoying its creamy feel beneath her fingertips, and had reread that first lame entry.

> I was born in Norfolk, at Congston Rectory. My father was rector of the three parishes of Congston, Hincham and Sorley. My mother died a year after Charlie, my younger brother, was born.

The words had sounded colder and more stilted than she remembered. But she had picked up her pen and made herself continue.

> We were looked after by Dawn, my father's house-keeper. She was quite fat and, although only eighteen when she started with us, was very grown up. To Charlie and me she seemed huge, and quite often my father would say that she was a lummocking clodhopper, or a true Norfolk dumpling. Her family lived in Congston

village, where her father was a farm worker, but she had her own bedroom in the rectory, so that she could see to our wants.

Writing the words had begun to unlock memories, and with them the imprint of emotions that had made their mark so long ago had come into a sharper focus than she had experienced in years. But the writing still seemed so bald, so uncomfortable. How could she get *real* feelings down on paper?

Dawn, by the world's standards, was an ugly duckling, with her Roman nose and the soft but noticeable moustache on her upper lip. She wheezed when she exerted herself, had massive, dimpled arms whose flesh was blue-marbled in the cold and flushed red in hot weather, and she had carried an animal smell about with her, which may have put off the grown-ups but to Charlie and Anna was warm and milky. With no mother to love them, and a father who, though he adored his brood, felt it improper to display too much affection, Dawn's musky embraces, and her cheap sentimentality were all Charlie and Anna had to sustain their emotional needs. At night she would kiss them – not chastely, on the cheeks, but wetly, on the mouth – and would hug them tight. They would beg her to tell them stories, but often she would read them poems instead, from a ruined copy of Palgrave's *Golden Treasury*, or bits of Shakespeare. Her delivery, in broad Norfolk tones, gave those lines a music and rhythm their writers had never intended. 'T'marra, 'n' t'marra, 'n' t'marra, creep ahn this petty pace from day ter day . . . loife's bu' a walkin' shadder, a pore player . . .'

Dawn did everything. She looked after the children; she cooked on the kerosene stove (Congston had neither mains electricity nor water until the early 1960s); she pumped, by hand, water from the well to the header tank; she fed the pigs and chickens and collected the eggs; she gardened; she picked fruit and she darned and sewed and botched their clothes. She also pumped air into the church organ at

Matins and Evensong for an extra one shilling and sixpence per month.

For Anna and Charlie she poured out affection in equal, unstinting portions. To Anna's father she was respectful, apologising when reprimanded for making mistakes, and turning red and awkward when praised. Ralph, the rector's elder son, was at boarding school, so she knew him less well than the little children, but she still wrote him semi-literate letters, because the family members corresponded, and rejoiced at his homecoming and cried, dutifully, when he left them at the beginning of term. She strongly disapproved of boarding school and was appalled at the prospect of losing the younger children for twelve weeks at a time. But Anna's father assured her that there was no danger of that, since he could barely afford the fees for Ralph, let alone two other children.

Anna completed her education at a small private academy just outside King's Lynn where she learnt much about domestic science and deportment, but Charlie won a place at the King Edward VII Grammar School and went on to Cambridge.

Anna's father always meant to be even-handed, but it was difficult for him to see his daughter in the same light as his sons. He would take both younger children on long nature rambles but Charlie was the one he talked to the most, usually while Anna walked a few paces behind, reluctant to intrude into male conversation. Charlie was the one their father always quizzed about identification of wild flowers; Charlie had to be first to hear the cuckoo and Charlie was the obvious choice to help his father catch butterflies in the flowery byways around the parishes. The rector had been developing his collection since early childhood and Norfolk's dry sunny climate and light sandy soils provided a rich selection of habitats. Both children had a garden plot, tucked away in a corner of the rectory's walled kitchen garden, but Charlie was praised for his early vegetables whereas Anna, being older, was expected to be able to grow flowers without fuss, both for house and altar.

On summer Saturdays, if the weather was fine and the tides right, the rector would take the children to the coast, ten miles away, on shrimping and cockle-raking expeditions. An assortment of tackle was always kept in the capacious boot of the family's ancient black Vauxhall but, apart from a gas cape and wellingtons, it all belonged to the rector and his sons, not to Anna. She was not expected to understand the thrill of sprinting after a silver washed fritillary in full flight, or to delight in lifting a trawl net full of transparent, hopping crustaceans. Sometimes she begged to be allowed to borrow something of the absent Ralph's – a shrimping net, or fishing rod – but the rector would demur. 'Anna, darling, think how awful you'd feel if you happened to break it,' he would say. But he really meant, 'girls don't do that sort of thing.'

She was, however, expected to learn, from Dawn, just how the shrimps should be boiled: preferably in sea water, brought carefully home in an old billy can, and then peeled and covered in molten butter seasoned with pepper, before being left in the cellar to cool. On Dawn's day off, Anna was expected to cope with providing meals, though Charlie and the rector were happy to assist in washing up and clearing away. Even then, they would click together as team members, one washing, the other drying, one holding a cupboard door open while the other bent to place saucepans and tureens inside. As they worked, they would talk, man to man, about cricket, the horrific crowd accident at Bolton Wanderers' football ground, the bombing of the King David Hotel in Jerusalem, and whether Clement Attlee would be able to do any good. Charlie hardly knew who Clement Attlee was, but he would nod and murmur assent at the right places. It was not that her father snubbed her or slighted her intentionally; he simply could not see how a girl could possibly be interested in the same things. The result was that Anna longed to be more like Charlie. She tried everything in her power to please her father, not by doing feminine things, but by trying to be as clever as Charlie, as brave as Charlie and as cheerful.

When the two children were alone together, the relationship

changed. Charlie became both friend and brother. She loved him. Loved him so deeply that when he was away from her for more than an hour or two she would pine. Charlie did not realise how their father's attitude affected her until she was nearly thirteen and he was just eleven, but when, in spite of his tender years, he realised how serious the potential hurt was, he worked hard to make amends. In spite of the age gap, he had come to act more like a male twin or even an older sibling. He always had the ideas, he always led their play, he always planned their adventures deep into the Norfolk countryside. He wore a wristwatch – a Timex, given to him for his ninth birthday, and still miraculously ticking – and would calculate the precise moment at which they would need to start back for home and not be late for a meal or, on Sundays, a service.

About that time, she began to develop an interest in birdwatching. For Charlie's eleventh Christmas, the rector had given him an old pair of ex-army Zeiss binoculars. Anna had received a new workbasket, kitted out with needles, scissors, yarns, buttons and so on, plus a length of gingham cloth, with which to make herself a summer dress. She was grateful, but wanted, very badly, to try Charlie's binoculars. Several times she had ached to pick them up, but did not like to touch them without his invitation. On Boxing Day, she had her first chance.

'Let's go outdoors and see what we can see, sis,' Charlie said, while their father, made drowsy by two glasses of post-lunch port, dozed in the unaccustomed luxury of a midday fire. They pulled on overcoats and boots, and walked through the cold hall of the rectory into the garden where, despite ice on the puddles and a dense crust of white hoar frost on the grass below the yew hedges, the afternoon was bright and sunny with a duck-egg sky.

'Could I borrow them?' Anna said, eyeing the binoculars with ill-concealed envy.

'Whenever you want,' Charlie said, taking the strap from his own neck and carefully lowering it over her head. Their eyes met. Nothing was spoken, but the gratitude in Anna's expression touched Charlie to the extent that his own, similarly dark eyes moistened. He swallowed, and repeated himself: 'When*ever* you want.'

She lifted them to her eyes and immediately the holly on the other side of the rectory lawn was close enough to touch.

'It's a bit fuzzy.'

'You focus by turning this,' Charlie said. She rotated the central wheel slowly until she could see individual clusters of glossy red berries, contrasted with the bottle-green foliage at the top of the tree.

'It's amazing,' she said. 'Oh!' A cock bullfinch had landed on the highest branch and she marvelled at the vivid pink of its breast, the jet black and stark white of the markings on its wings and rump. She could even see the twinkling highlights in its eye. 'Oh! It's so beautiful!'

'Look, sis,' Charlie said, 'why don't you keep them round your neck, whenever we go out together?'

She began to log the number of birds she observed, at first in the rectory garden but later in the surrounding countryside.

'Daddy,' she said one afternoon, running breathlessly into the house. 'Daddy, I think I've just seen a waxwing.'

The rector looked up from his paper. Charlie was sitting at the kitchen table, poring over his Latin prep. 'Really, sis?' He sounded slightly distracted, concentrating on his work.

'Let's look it up,' said the rector. 'Get the bird book.' She ran upstairs and returned, out of breath, with the book open at approximately the right page.

'It's somewhere here, Daddy, look!'

'Now just a minute, young lady,' he said, taking the volume from her grasp and closing it. 'Isn't it more logical to look in the index?' Taking for ever, he found the place and read the description quietly to himself.

'What does it say?' she asked. 'What does it say? Show me the picture!'

'I think you must be mistaken, my dear.' The rector closed the book again. 'Apparently, the waxwing is a rare bird. An occasional visitor.' He glanced over at his son, tossing an imaginary line across the room to hook his support. 'Not the sort of thing a little girl with borrowed field glasses might stumble upon.' Charlie's ears burned red as he concentrated hard on his Latin.

A tap on the cabin door had made her start so violently that her pen had left a stroke of ink on the page.

'Come in!' she had called.

'Good morning, madam. It is eight o'clock.' Tony had held a tray with teapot and cup in one hand but had hesitated, wondering where to put it, since the tiny dressing table was occupied by Anna's open journal. She had snatched up the book and closed it quickly. Writing for more than two hours without stopping had made her right hand feel cramped.

'But it's still dark!' She had put her face to the porthole and peered out on to a cold, grey horizon. The waves had still looked oily black.

'I am too early, madam?' He had seemed regretful, as if he had disturbed her. She had glanced at her watch.

'Not too early. In fact, how much earlier could you bring tea in the mornings?'

'Seven, madam. Earlier if you like.' She had picked up a flicker of doubt on the 'earlier' and wondered what time he came on duty. The crew seemed to work killing hours.

'Seven will be fine. Each day?'

'Certainly madam.' Tony had then withdrawn, closing the door silently, leaving her to skim through what she had written. There had seemed to be such an awful lot of it.

Lack of sleep and the unfamiliarity of the ship had made her feel tired very early in the day. She had got lost several times, but had gradually become familiar with its layout. The nicest bar, she had decided, was the Crow's Nest. This was forward on an upper deck, quite close to her cabin, with a huge semi-circle of picture windows looking out over the bows. The Cricket Club, where Cedric had led her for a lunchtime snifter, was a more folksy bar at the other end of the vessel, decked out like a pavilion with paintings, by Ruskin Spear, of famous cricketers. She and Bernard had known Spear, slightly. There was a biggish theatre, a cinema, several swimming pools and a gloomy lounge, two decks below her cabin. 'We steer well clear of that one,' Cedric had warned her. 'They can give it whatever fancy name they like, but we call it "God's waiting room".' He had indicated the occupants, a small gaggle of octogenarians, all slumbering open-mouthed in deep armchairs.

She had discovered that she could eat breakfast and lunch at a buffet, near the stern, thus avoiding the rest of her table until dinner. During the afternoon she had been to see a film, but could neither understand the plot nor hear much of the dialogue and later had returned to her cabin to find that an invitation to the captain's welcome aboard cocktail party had been slipped under her door. The prospect was so burdensome to her that she had almost wept. How could she face it? She had decided to plead a headache, and to spend the evening in her cabin. Perhaps Tony could be persuaded to bring a sandwich later, or something. But Ant had tapped on her door.

'Couldn't help hearing you'd got back,' he had said. 'Got your party frock ready for *ce soir*?'

'Oh, I don't think I'll go.'

Ant had put on a stagey scandalised look. 'Why ever not? Attendance is positively *required*.'

'I don't really think I feel up to it.'

Ant had gone to his cabin, opened the door and in a stage whisper, said, 'Cedric, dear heart, a word, if you will.' Cedric had emerged and smiled at Anna.

'Hello. Good film?' Anna had shaken her head.

'It's about tonight,' Ant had said, indicating Anna with a jerk of his chin. 'Certain persons expect us to face the banalities of the evening without her to help us through.'

'Oh my God!' Cedric had feigned a swoon. 'What *can* we do?' At that moment, the door of the single cabin opposite Anna's was snatched open and a tall, late-ish-middle-aged man with florid complexion and a bald dome surrounded by a corona of wild, white hair stood swaying for a moment, backlit by his cabin lights.

'Would you people mind keeping it down a bit, please? Some of us are *trying* to sleep.' He had withdrawn again, slamming his door. The three of them had stood frozen with surprise, staring at the closed door. The man had been completely naked.

'Did I imagine that?' Ant had muttered.

'I *knew* it,' Cedric had whispered. 'I had him marked down as a prize beauty the first moment I saw the cut of his jib. Piss artist. Absolute classic case. Been at the sherbet all morning and half the afternoon. I wonder if he'll remember what he did just now, and feel embarrassed.'

'Let's hope so,' Ant had said, then, 'Oh, I say, Anna, are you all right?'

'I think so,' Anna had replied. 'But I'm glad you two were here.'

'Attagirl!' Ant had said. 'And you *will* allow us to take you to the cocktails partail capty?'

'Everyone absolutely *has* to go,' Cedric had added. 'Apart from the serious misfits.' He had indicated the closed door. 'It's quite the most ridiculous thing. We all line up and get presented, like guests at a wedding. You should see some of the retired barrow boys' wives. Positively *dripping* gemstones, *desperate* to make an impression but looking like onion sacks in haute couture.' Anna had felt she had little choice but to acquiesce.

At dinner, Captain Maclean had turned out to be urbane, considerate, humorous and, thought Anna, not wholly unattractive. The beard was a modest, disciplined affair which outlined a chin that would have looked strong enough without adornment. He had twinkling blue eyes, a ready wit and yet seemed to exude calm confidence. Within a very few moments of meeting him, Anna knew that he would be exactly the right person to have in charge in the event of a crisis. At dinner the conversation had been more relaxed and time had passed a little less slowly. 'Calm night ahead of us,' Captain Maclean had said as they finished their coffee, 'but things might get a tad bumpy tomorrow morning.'

'Coming to the show, dear?' Mrs Cabbage had asked. She was rotund and motherly, hopelessly uncomfortable in a bulging, off the shoulder affair of gold lamé and white stilettos which, Anna had noticed when she bent to retrieve her napkin, she had kicked off under the table. 'The singer's ever so good, isn't he Lionel?' Mr Cabbage had beamed and nodded. He had worked conscientiously through every course on the menu, including a final Welsh rarebit, and quaffed his and most of Anna's share of the wine, provided on this special night by Captain Maclean. A dew of perspiration had thrown the tight skin of his cheeks and forehead into soft focus.

'I'd love to,' Anna had said, 'but I had virtually no sleep last night.' She had promised to meet the Boys, as she had begun to call Ant and Cedric to herself, for a *digestif*, but felt too drowsy to want anything other than bed and solitude. On her way out of the dining room, she had paused at their table and made her excuses. They had taken a hand each, squeezed with an earnestness whose sincerity she couldn't quite be sure of, and wished her sweet dreams. She did not realise that she had become one of their projects for the cruise, or that, though they had yet to grow fond of her, they hated to see someone so obviously suffering.

Back in her cabin, she had read her journal again. There were even more words than she realised she had written early that morning. The handwriting was uneven, rushed in some places, neater and more careful in others. In her mind, the writing had zest and fluency, but each time she read her work through it seemed heavier, less natural. She had tried to analyse why she found it so difficult to express her thoughts clearly, and why not being able to bothered her so much. Wanting to do a good job? No, there had to be more, somehow, but blowed if she knew what. Less than ten minutes later, she was in bed with *Rabbit, Run* unopened in her hand. She had glanced at the jacket blurb. 'A small-town tragedy . . . convincing, vivid and awful' – *Times Literary Supplement*. That had done the trick. The last thing she had wanted, at that stage, was to experience something vivid and awful. She had dropped the book on the floor, which Cedric said must always be called a deck, and was asleep within a couple of minutes.

Now, in the intimate darkness of her cabin, she sat up in bed and hugged her knees. Her bladder was full, but she put off the moment, not to prolong the discomfort, but because leaving it a bit longer would use up more time. Time, the enemy, had changed its strategy. In her former life it was always later than she thought; now time was like a tether, holding her back while it dragged out the hours of the night. Morning, her worst period, would approach with numbing slowness, but at last grey light at the window would trigger the change in her mood from resignation to despair. It wasn't that she wanted time to pass more quickly, but rather to find something, anything, to shift the uncomfortable burden of her existence, particularly at this time of day. And if that meant putting off a pee for a quarter of an hour, so be it.

Then the ship moved. This was not the gentle shift of horizons but a decided roll. Her shower-room door flapped open, banged against the wall, which Cedric said must always be called a bulkhead, and then, when the ship rolled the other way, it slammed shut with a loud bang. That was what had woken her up – the ship's movement, the door banging. Deep down, below decks, she fancied she heard a low thud, and then the ship rolled again. By the time she had got out of bed to secure the shower room and cupboard doors, had checked that anything unstable had been 'stowed' as Cedric would have called it, the *Brisbane* was wallowing in a swell that appeared to have conjured itself up from nowhere in no time. It seemed, to her, quite inconceivable that such a vast edifice of metal, bigger than a whole block of buildings, should allow itself to be shifted about like a cork on the waves. She assumed that she would feel seasick. She waited for the first waves of nausea – a feeling vividly recalled from taking a small boat mackerel fishing off Padstow. Bernard had been so solicitous, so sympathetic. 'We'll go back, darling. You're as green as a cabbage.'

'I don't mind, Bernard, really I don't.'

'I'm not having you suffer.' Neither of them had known, that afternoon, that she was already pregnant with William. The word 'William', forming in her mind, brought up a familiar sensation. An increase in heartbeat, a catch in the breath, an ache in the throat. William was gone, Bernard was gone, Lisa was never really much other than gone. Guilt, for thinking anything so unkind after all her daughter had done for her, brought hot tears into her eyes. Now the ship was pitching as well as rolling, soaring up, almost like a fairground ride, plunging down, with a regular but faint booming sound, as the swell pounded against the bows. It was not frightening. She suspected that seasickness was based on fear and, since she had nothing to fear – other than decades of life still to live, alone and with this constant ache – she knew that she would not feel afraid, and therefore not ill. Looking out of her porthole she could see, in the first glimmer of dawn, the waves rearing up like a mountain range constantly on the move. The ship's wild motion, the white foam, the vast scale of the seascape was more majestic, more awesome than anything she had ever seen. The wonder of it held her spellbound at the porthole until she began to feel crampy from standing so still for so long, bent to see out, holding on to the desk to keep her balance. At that point she realised she had not wept. When the familiar grief mechanism had started she had not become immersed in it but rather had looked out of herself into the terrifying, awesome, wonderful vastness of the real, empty world.

At last, she allowed herself into the shower room. Taking care not to stumble and hurt herself in the motion, she slipped her nightdress up, sat on the lavatory and enjoyed the sweet relief.

Chapter Three

Jack Pullen was late for his class. Conversation in the card room on A Deck aft, embarrassed and desultory as it had been from the start, had all but died, but most agreed that, conditions being what they were, he was unlikely to show. The ship was heaving and rolling in a huge Atlantic swell and most of the public rooms, on this second morning at sea, were empty. In the *Brisbane*'s main thoroughfares, plastic bags had been hung over rails and bannisters for those taken short with nausea and unable to reach a lavatory. Near the purser's office, outside the shops and on several of the stairways, Goan stewards were swabbing carpets amid the acidic stench of vomit. Out on deck, even though it was almost impossible to walk upright in the wind and was bitingly cold, figures with greenish-grey faces had wedged themselves into relatively sheltered corners and stood trying to quell their nausea by focusing on distant objects or by gazing out over the ocean.

The eight creative writing students who had evaded sea-sickness were glancing at their watches and wondering whether to give the whole thing up when he erupted into the room. The sudden opening of the door startled Anna who looked up to see a flurry of dark denim – skintight charcoal jeans cinched at the narrow waist with a silver-buckled belt, black shirt, matching denim bum-freezer jacket and round the neck a scarlet bandana. These clothes, though reasonably clean, were scuffed and threadbare, with paler zones of wear on elbow, knee and disgustingly, Anna thought, at the one-sided bulge of the crotch. She noticed that his boots had built-up heels. Inside this outfit the man was small-framed, thin, with a face that showed too many lines even for his age, which Anna would have guessed to be close to seventy had she not known that he was no more than a year older than she. She couldn't decide whether these teenager clothes, obsolete by more than a decade, were a bid for a distinctive appearance or an attempt to recapture lost youth. Either way, it didn't work. He carried a heap of books, a bundle of A4 paper and a small canvas tote bag. These he set down on one of the vacant card tables with such a bang that Anna feared it might collapse. He stood gazing at the group for a full sixty seconds without uttering a word. This was unsettling.

'Come closer!' he said at last, indicating the empty tables nearest the front. The voice was earthy, quiet, but with a penetrating resonance. There was a shuffling spell while the class members did as they were told. Anna found herself nearest to him, with Cedric and Ant taking another two places at her table. The fourth was empty, since its occupant could not have faced the teacher. The only other person she knew in the room was Mrs Cabbage. 'Greetings to you. Congratulations on making it, in spite of the conditions.'

'We wondered what had happened to you,' one of the class members said, a mildly derisory edge to her voice. 'Thought you might have got lost.' Pullen stared at her for several seconds.

'Never apologise. Never explain,' he said. There was another long pause. 'You're all writers. Right?' Silence. 'What do you write about?' More silence. 'Ah yes, I *see*!' Pullen said, overacting like some cheap TV detective. 'We're going to play the old British reticence game. You know, in America, where I lived for several years, it was *de rigueur* at any gathering – and I mean *any* gathering – to go up to the nearest complete stranger and say'—here he adopted a chirrupy accent – '"Well hi there! And how are *you* today?

I'm Jack Pullen."' He stopped and stared at them again. And kept on staring. Something seemed to be expected of them.

'Perhaps you could tell us a little about these classes,' Ant said.

'Perhaps.' Pullen looked at each of the class members in turn. 'But first, why don't we introduce ourselves? I'd like each of you to tell the rest of us a little about yourself. Anything you want: who your favourite authors are, or what your favourite book might be, giving reasons of course. Oh,' he added, 'and while we're about it why don't you tell us what it is that makes you want to be a writer – or, if you think you are one already, what it takes to be one. Let's start over here.' He indicated Mrs Cabbage.

'I'm Sylvia Tanner,' said Mrs Cabbage, comfortably attired this morning in a pink tracksuit, dangly earrings and open-toed, slingback cocktail slippers. 'I'm not really a writer and I don't suppose I read a lot, actually, except when I'm on a cruise like this. I don't really have any favourites. I suppose I like that north country writer best, um, I can't remember her name, Catherine something, but she tells a wonderful story.'

Next to speak was a widow, Elspeth Crampin, who had had several poems published, and who wanted help with developing her poetic skills. The other lone female, Molly Golby, had a husband on board with her, who had encouraged her to come to the classes. 'He says I can write quite well,' she said, 'so I thought I'd have a go.'

'But do *you* think you can write quite well?' Pullen countered. She turned red.

'I don't really know.' She shrugged and went redder. Pullen shrugged also, but whether in sympathy or in parody Anna couldn't tell. Next to go were a couple. Leonard Dicks, a newly retired journalist, wanted to make money writing thrillers. His favourite author was John le Carré. His wife looked at him with pity as he delivered, and then took over with a nicely prepared little speech about how her writing expressed the pain of the female condition. There were terms like 'phallocentric' and 'female castration' in her spiel, which Anna felt were unnecessary, but she was not at all surprised to hear that Mrs Dicks' favourite author was Germaine Greer. Greer was one of the few famous women Anna had really enjoyed meeting. She had been terrified of her intelligence, having watched her annihilate opponents in television debates, but the encounter had been with a gentle, sympathetic woman who had not made her feel stupid at all, even though she knew she was.

The Boys said plenty but gave little away. 'We both absolutely *adore* Jane Austen, don't we, Ant,' Cedric said.

'What about you?' Pullen was now looking directly at Anna. 'Are you a writer?'

'Not yet,' Anna said, 'but I will be. When I've learnt how.' Pullen looked more sharply at her.

'You think I can teach you?'

Anna thought for a moment. 'No,' she said. 'I don't think it *is* something you can teach. But if you can help me just to . . . to . . .' She wanted to say, if you could unlock the door, unpick the ravelled knot, release the sluice so that I can transfer all this, this *feeling* inside me on to paper, and thus get rid of it. If you could just help me to make the words work as well strung together in ink as they seem to do half formed in my mind.

'What writer do you admire?'

'John Updike.' Why did she say that? She had not even started to reread *Rabbit, Run*. Supposing he quizzed her further?'

'Odd choice for a woman,' was all he said. She couldn't be sure, but she suspected that there was something of a sneer on his face as he said it. Then he introduced himself, told them about his methods, explained that they would be expected to write for the benefit of the class as well as themselves, and that they would meet for a couple of hours at the same time every morning that the ship was at sea. 'These are some of my books which you can borrow for a while – or you can buy new copies at the shop.' He arranged them on the table, making a tempting display of rather thumbed copies. 'And on port days,' he said, 'be sure to collect as many exciting experiences as possible. Start to use your eyes and ears. Observe, record, recall, compare, and write, write, write!'

Among the titles Anna noticed *October Dance*, a novel Cedric had mentioned. This she grabbed, while the others browsed, and hurried back to her cabin. Most professional writers, Pullen had said, set themselves a minimum amount of time each day to write. She would do the same. Besides, the cabin was welcoming and soothing after being exposed out there in the ship for so long.

She placed *October Dance* on the shelf with the rest of her books, picked out Updike's *Rabbit, Run* and sat on her bed – made up with cushions to double as a sofa by day – and began to read. The first paragraph – the first line – put her straight there, not just into a back street in urban, eastern America, but right into the characters' heads. She remembered boys playing basketball in the street like that at Purlin. *The scrape and snap of Keds on loose alley pebbles seems to catapult their voices high into the moist March air blue above the wires*. How does he *do* that? She hadn't a clue what Keds were but it didn't matter. And the language? Better English than hers, but how? Why? The second sentence wasn't even a sentence at all. *Legs, shouts.* Her English teacher would not have accepted that. Every sentence had to have subject, verb, object. She reread the first paragraph, caught the rhythm, clocked the images of the handball, rising like exultation to the improvised net, while the players' voices are catapulted up into the sky. And she understood the weight of that last sentence. That really told the whole story and all the subsequent stories, though even Updike couldn't have known how Rabbit would turn out thirty years later, when he wrote: *The kids keep coming, they keep crowding you up.*

A tap at the door made her jump up in alarm. 'Who's there?' she called. Cedric put his head round the door.

'That Pullen creature. Weird, or what?' She gave him a

quarter smile, not so much a sunny spell as a brief thinning of the cloud. 'You were clever, though, Anna.'

'Nonsense!'

'Very clever. I don't think our Mr Pullen knows quite what to make of you. But *I* reckon you're the only one who's going to be absolutely serious about these classes.' He looked at her more closely, with raised eyebrows. 'And yet, the odd thing is, you didn't even know he was going to be on board. Or that there was going to be a creative writing circle at all. Rum, that!'

'Won't you come in?' She had begun to feel uncomfortable with him framed in the doorway. He gave a little bow, and entered the cabin. She gestured to the bunk/sofa. He flopped down on it, throwing his body backwards on to the cushions, somewhat boyishly she thought. Yet again, the ungainliness of his movements, combined with the comeliness of his body, reminded her so sharply of Verne that, for a moment, she felt her expression might give something away.

'The joys of a single existence,' he murmured, looking wistfully around her small but well-ordered quarters.

'Not half so joyful as having a partner,' she muttered.

'No? You should see the mess Ant's left in there today. He just *won't* put anything away. I spend my whole bloody life tidying up after him.' He paused and looked about him again: the books and CDs over the bed, the journal neatly on the desk, not a thing out of place. 'No,' he concluded. 'Not half so joyful.' He stood up. 'I really popped in to see whether you'd like to join us for a pre-lunch bevvy. That poet woman Elizabeth, no, Elspeth Crampin – you know, from Pullen's class – she's joining us, and that couple called Dicks. The view from the Crow's Nest Bar should be pretty spectacular in this weather. Then we could grab a cold buffet, as long as you're feeling up to it.'

'I thought I'd stay here and do some writing.'

'Oh, come on, Anna, we'll have virtually the whole ship to ourselves! It takes a storm like this to clear the faint-hearted out of the way.' He softened his tone. 'It really would be lovely if you could come. Lovely for us, I mean.'

Anna glanced down at her book, eyes greedily snatching a fragment of the text: *The month is March. Love makes the air light. Things start anew; Rabbit tastes through sour aftersmoke the fresh chance in the air* . . . Perhaps that line was auspicious. She sighed.

'All right.'

Later, after a convivial lunch and a tottering walk round the promenade deck, where the wind blew them so hard and the deck was so restless beneath their feet that it was almost impossible to remain upright, Anna left her classmates and returned to her cabin. She had planned to read, but in spite of Updike's magnetism this new hunger had strengthened, a feeling strong enough to compel her to run from the present and wander back through the years into the developing world of her journal. But she forced herself to read on, soon getting hooked into Rabbit's anabasis and following it for page after page, wanting to leave it and return to her own work but unable to extricate herself from the story's grip. Why did unhappy people need to travel so much, to run, run, run? Better to do that than to arrive? At last, a sentence reminded her of the next step in her own story and she put the book on to her bedside shelf, sat at her desk and opened the journal. She decided to write a second heading.

CORNWALL

Every year, for as long as I can remember, we took our family holidays in Cornwall, at Treglase Bay, usually for the first two weeks in September. We stayed at a private hotel run by an enormous, stern landlady called Miss Rook. She was the only woman I knew whose arms were more massive than Dawn's. They were dimpled at the elbow in exactly the same way, and tended to mottle in the cool Atlantic winds. Despite her despotic system – you were in serious trouble if you dared to skip a meal – she was always accommodating to us, probably because of our father's cloth. If we picked blackberries in the cliff-top fields she would make blackberry and apple crumble for us to eat with crusted, yellow clotted cream. She boiled the prawns we netted in the Camel Estuary, she soused the mackerel we caught and she regaled us with wonderful tales of winter storms, drownings and local skulduggeries. Whenever she held forth, she would stand, either framed in her kitchen door or just inside the guests' sitting room, as if she were with us, but not quite *of* us. Charlie, almost every day, volunteered to collect provisions for her from the village shop. I often wondered how she managed the weighty boxes of groceries for the rest of the season when he was not there.

The holidays in Cornwall, year after year, had become such a central part of their lives that it seemed inconceivable to the rector that his young should want to go anywhere else. But the inevitable process of growing up began to pull the children in different directions. When Charlie had completed his first sixth-form year, he had announced that in future summers he would be travelling abroad with his friends. That year, Ralph managed – but only just – to get time off from St Thomas's Hospital, where he had recently qualified as a junior doctor, but Anna had had to take unpaid leave from her job as assistant secretary at Quinton Darbyshire, the King's Lynn solicitors.

Charlie, whose academic prowess had suddenly burgeoned with all the surprise and delight of a June mushroom, had already won a place at Cambridge, subject to good exam results. Anna basked in the reflected light of his glory, even though the rector, who constantly referred to the brilliance of his sons, seldom acknowledged her more modest successes. By her eighteenth birthday, she had managed to become a qualified secretary after attending a full-time course which she had financed by fruit-picking, cleaning and, later, working in the vegetable canning factory – a one-storey asbestos building which sat squatly on the banks of the last muddy tidal reaches of the Great Ouse. When the water was high, the other workers would sit on top of the flood wall during their lunch hour, smoking Park Drive cigarettes and watching ships edging in from the North Sea. But Anna had preferred to be out there alone with the ebbing tide, Charlie's binoculars hanging on her neck, when wading birds – curlew, golden plover, turnstones and, sometimes, rarer species – worked over the grey mudscape and along the receding water margin. Since leaving her small private school, with the minimum necessary exam results and little self-confidence, she had not asked for a penny from her father but had contributed rather more than her fair share of work in running the rectory household.

Getting to work each day was complicated and she often felt she'd be better off in a bedsitter or sharing a flat in King's Lynn, but her father seemed to want her at home and with Ralph gone, and Charlie soon to go, it would have been cruel to leave the old man on his own. Furthermore, she was not at all sure he would feed himself adequately were she not there, each day, to prepare a wholesome evening meal as soon as she got home from work. Nevertheless, there were days, especially in winter, when the early morning walk of almost a mile to Sorley, the bus to Reardon station and the short train ride to Lynn seemed too high a price to pay.

One of the rector's parishioners from the neighbouring village of Hincham drove to his clothing shop in King's Lynn every day, but Anna would not dream of asking him for a lift and, since he had no idea that she was also a commuter, he didn't offer transport. Michael Morfey, High Class Gentlemen's Outfitters, supplied the local gentry and yeomanry with tweedy suiting, heavy twill trousering, dark worsteds for Sundays and durable shirts in dull colours – safe creams, pale greens or rustic checks. His prices were high, but the quality of his clothes impeccable. Many a Morfey suit was handed down from father, or even grandfather, and the question of supplying imported garments, in those days when Bradford and Manchester were still important textile cities, never arose.

Morfey had two sons by two wives. The elder, Edwin, a capable man of almost thirty by the time Anna had begun her first job, was set to take over the shop and allow his father to slip into retirement. There was already talk of a new branch opening in Downham Market and perhaps a third in Norwich. Back in the thirties, when Edwin was just out of nappies, it dawned on his mother that a small child was a more effective and permanent means of imprisonment than manacles or iron bars. The sudden crushing weight of this realisation, unrelieved by her hardworking husband and unheeded by thick-skinned, introverted neighbours, caused her to develop what, in those days, was known as a nervous illness. In deep distress, she abandoned her new family and returned to her parents' home in Dorset where, during a protracted convalescence, she allowed herself to be swept into a romantic vortex by a passionate Italian who loved her for her nervous disposition and who owned a brace of seaside ice cream parlours.

Michael Morfey had been obliged to advertise for a housekeeper-cum-nanny. With King Edward's abdication still fresh in their minds, the chief tattlers of pre-war Hincham, fired by such buzzwords as 'divorce', and 'adultery', assumed, rightly as it happened, that Morfey was living in sin. Partly to quell the gossip, and partly because he did not see how he could do anything else – or anything better for that matter – he divorced Edwin's mother and married his housekeeper. She was already pregnant with Bernard when, with trade-discounted peach satin sleeve resting lightly on charcoal pinstripe cuff, the couple walked into the King's Lynn Register Office.

That Bernard was remarkable soon became clear to the oddly matched couple. His father, a capable solid business-man but with little brain or imagination, could not understand

where the boy got his cleverness from. Bernard could read
before he was four, was capable of abstruse mathematical
problems before his age reached double figures and, by the
time Anna and her family were enjoying their last holiday
together in Cornwall, he had completed a degree with first
class honours in economics at Cambridge and had already
embarked on his doctorate. Since Anna was a girl, and
Charlie five years his junior, Bernard had had little to do
with the rector's children. But when Charlie had won his
place at Cambridge the rector suggested that he should contact
Bernard, who would 'know all the ropes, and could probably
provide a tip or two'. Charlie hadn't made contact, out of
a combination of indolence and reticence – he had always
considered the Morfey family rather distant and formidable
– and the matter had been dropped until now, in Cornwall.
There, walking by himself along the jetty in Padstow while the
three youngsters were surfbathing in Harlyn Bay, the rector
spotted Bernard.

'Young Morfey? It is! How delightful to see a Norfolk face
in this Celtic wilderness!' The rector shook the young man's
hand with clerical enthusiasm, and without preamble invited
him over to Treglase to meet the others. He was about the
same age as Ralph, the rector insisted, but more important,
he should meet Charlie and talk to him about Cambridge.

'Well, I'm not sure. The last thing I want to do is intrude
on your holiday.'

'Nonsense, my dear chap! We'd be *delighted* to have you.
Come and have lunch tomorrow!'

'I return to Cambridge first thing in the morning.'

'Then come today! We're only at Treglase.' The rector
wondered whether Miss Rook would make a scene about
that, but was so taken with the young man. He reminded
him, somewhat, of a more grown-up version of Charlie,
with those dark, intelligent eyes and thick hair brushed
neatly back but ready to rebel and fall forward. The nose
was prominent, aquiline, but not too badly out of propor-
tion to his other features. The mouth, though the lips were

less than full, had a determined set but was mobile, quick to smile.

'I do have someone with me.'

'Fine, bring him along.'

'She's in there.' He indicated the cake shop on the harbour front.

'Aha, well.' The rector was disarmed for a second or two. 'Bring her too, why not? She'll be company for Anna, while we chaps get down to some serious talk.'

Bernard and his friend, Penelope – an English literature graduate from Girton – arrived at Treglase on foot, having walked the coastal footpath from Padstow. They were hot and thirsty, so Anna asked Miss Rook for a large jug of lemon squash and some glasses. This was somewhat risky, since the huge woman had already made a fuss about having to provide two extra lunches at such short notice. 'I quite realise that food rationing is over, rector,' she had said frostily, 'but one does have to plan.'

During lunch, Penelope sat between Charlie and the rector, and the three of them were soon locked into an earnest discussion about the moral issues raised by Hardy's novels. Ralph tended to be taciturn, so Anna found herself in fairly close conversation with Bernard. Not that she minded. She found his looks, his mannerisms, his obvious intelligence so captivating that she quite forgot to eat her steak and kidney pie, allowing it to go cold and congealed. Miss Rook herself came to clear the plates away and tut-tutted about wastage.

'I'm *so* sorry, Miss Rook,' Anna sighed. 'It's absolutely lovely, but I'm really not very hungry all of a sudden,' and she turned her gaze back on Bernard.

'Hmmph!' snorted Miss Rook, giving Bernard a withering look as she snatched up the plate. After a glance at Ralph, who seemed quite happy listening to the chat from the other three, Bernard resumed his close focusing on Anna. He was beginning to be moved by the darkness of her eyes and found that the timbre of her voice struck a resonance deep within himself. She had such a soft, slightly husky tone. If she were musical, which for all he knew she might be, she'd probably sing in the alto line, but he dared bet she could handle the high notes as well.

'Are you up at university?' he asked.

'Lord, no!' Anna laughed at the idea. 'I'm far too thick for that!'

'Who says?' His voice was spiked with a shot of passion and rose a little. 'Who *dares* to say?' Penelope glanced up, distracted temporarily from her absorbing conversation with Charlie. Anna looked in surprise at Bernard. He meant it! No male, other than Charlie, had ever really taken her seriously before. She was flattered.

'I dare to say,' she replied, more serious now. 'I may not be completely stupid, but I'm really not your academic type.'

'Well, then. What do you do?'

'What should a girl do?'

He reflected for a moment. 'Well, *something*. The important thing is never, ever, do nothing.'

'I do work,' Anna said, 'and I help to look after Daddy.' A herring gull dipped over the feathery tamarisk hedge outside the open window, its mewing cry suddenly loud in the dining room. 'And I do quite a lot of birdwatching.' Bernard had little interest in nature but sympathised with anyone obsessive enough to hoard, whether clocks, fine wines or even bird names. He had collected stamps since boyhood but had now changed his emphasis, trading and exchanging, steadily building up the financial value of his collection.

'Do you keep records?'

'Every species,' Anna confirmed. 'All noted down and ticked off. But,' she added, 'I don't just look for rare ones. I love watching them all. They're such wonderful creatures, birds. So bright, so quick and busy, and they have such beauty. The electric blue of a kingfisher's back, flying arrow-straight along the river – there's nothing so gorgeous. Even dull ones: the grey flannel – like a woollen balaclava – on the head of a jackdaw. So charming! Did you know that some jackdaws have blue eyes, or that they mate for life? We watch them on the rectory chimneys, pair by pair, side by side, chuckling in each other's ears, like lovers. Or like old couples, comfortable with each other. When one takes off the other flies up too, and they move through the air together, one never more than a few yards from its mate.'

'When you describe them like that,' Bernard said, 'you make them appeal, even to a Philistine like me.' He touched her hand with the backs of his fingers. 'And for what it's worth, I don't think you're the very remotest bit thick.' Then he caught Penelope's second or third glance and realised that he had become rather too caught up with Anna. He turned deliberately to Ralph and began nudge him into a conversation. Anna saw with a dash of regret that she was now released from his attention for a while. She noticed, at that exact moment, what a large mouth Penelope had in relation to her other features, and how cheese-like and colourless her hair was. It matched her complexion. Even her eyelashes seemed unnaturally blonde.

'I do not see,' Bernard said to Ralph, 'how anyone in your profession can do anything other than abhor the whole concept of a National Health Service.'

'And what is *your* profession,' Ralph asked, in his slow, deliberate drawl, 'that you feel able to pass judgement on how members of mine should think?'

'I'm an economist,' Bernard said, unabashed. 'And all economic theory, whichever model you choose to operate, states that there is no such thing as a free meal. Everything, but everything, has to be paid for, and if you provide the populace with free health care, not only do you burden the taxpayer, you also encourage abuse of the system, malingering among patients and a pampered, nannified society. Furthermore, the means of remunerating the medical profession, willy nilly, becomes inefficient and, inevitably, inadequate.' The words were aggressive but Bernard spoke blithely, with a smile on his face and a gentle, persuasive lilt in his voice. Anna felt some of what he had said made a lot of sense.

'I say, do you mind,' Ralph muttered. 'We're on holiday

and I promised myself I'd keep off shop. And politics for that matter.' Bernard spread his hands and shrugged, making an eloquent but wordless apology.

Putting her pen down and easing her right hand for a few moments, Anna looked back over what she had been writing. Nineteen pages of her journal were now filled with tidy script, the most recent ones curling slightly from the damp pressure of her hands. She added:

> I suppose I did not realise, at that first meeting, that Ralph was as instantly repelled by Bernard as I was instantly attracted. A lot of people felt like Bernard about the Welfare State, and I was as much struck by the passion and conviction with which he spoke as by what he said. He seemed the only truly decisive person around that table, and yet everything he expressed was delivered with such persuasive charm that we would never have suspected we were being seduced by a radical thinker.

The cabin telephone startled her. 'I'm so glad I caught you at home.' Captain Maclean's voice sounded more relaxed than when he made his more public pronouncements. 'I wondered, if you've nothing better to do, whether you'd care to come and have a look at the bridge, and then join me for a cup of tea.'

'Today?'

'In about half an hour, if you'd care to. I'm sorry it's such ridiculously short notice, but the ship is so quiet, and my spies tell me you were out and about with the bravest of seafarers earlier today.' She hesitated. 'Do say you'll come.'

To kill the half hour before going, she took Pullen's *October Dance* from the shelf. On the cover, a soldier – British, she guessed, from the shape of his tin helmet – stood against a battlefield background. Red poppies growing out from the tortured earth told her it was a First World War story. 'Powerful, enigmatic . . .' the blurb proclaimed. 'Pullen at his disturbing best!' She opened the book and glanced at the opening paragraph. *Lousy. Itchy. Private Crabbe was infested. Inside and out, he was verminous. His uniform crawled with living, feasting creatures; lice crept over his scalp, in his armpits, behind his balls; fleas migrated across the skin of his belly; the folds between his toes itched and stank with foot rot. But neither the discomfort of these parasites nor the scalding stream that issued from his rear end at every visit to the field latrine caused half so much pain as the pricking, the gnawing, the constant inner whine of his conscience. Crabbe was filth and he knew it. Worse than the bugs that were eating him. He was lower than the excrement they left on his skin. And the worst of it – or perhaps the best of it – was that only Crabbe knew why.* Anna put the book back on the shelf and fought a sudden swell of queasiness that the storm had failed to produce. She gazed through her porthole, focusing on the most distant waves until it was time to go up.

The view from the bridge gave her an entirely different perspective. Up there you still had the sense of a great ship, an object so massive on the water as to be unbelievable, and yet light and lively enough to respond like a small boat to wind, waves and currents. She looked, first, at the various radar scanning devices, noticing how many blips there were on the screens, each one representing another vessel. 'I had no idea the oceans were so crowded,' she said, but then looked out to an empty horizon.

'The nearest is that one over there.' Captain Maclean pointed to the left horizon, but Anna could still see nothing. 'Almost eight miles away, but it's a huge supertanker and we are on a slightly converging course.' The angry sea looked tamer from all the way up here, but the *Brisbane*'s bows were still rising and dipping in exaggerated movements, occasionally plunging into one of the larger swells so that green water and spray leapt up and washed over the prow. Ahead, though, the sky was clearing and she felt sure the wind had dropped. Captain Maclean introduced her to all the junior officers on duty and began to explain the rudiments of celestial navigation. This she followed for a while, but was soon lost as he described the complications of measuring longitude. 'To find out how far west or east we are of the Greenwich meridian, we need to know the precise time – to the nearest fraction of a second.'

'I'm sorry, but I don't think I've got the brains to understand. I never was any good at maths.'

'When you're back in England,' Captain Maclean said, 'go to Greenwich observatory. They've got examples of early chronometers there, including John Harrison's. He invented the first decent one, you know, back in the seventeen hundreds – the technology will astound you.' He could see that she seemed to have lost what little interest she'd had. Her face had resumed the forlorn, distracted expression that she had worn all through dinner the previous evening, and that had both saddened and attracted him. 'They are also beautiful works of art,' he added, trying to ignite a spark of something – anything – in her. 'One of them looks like nothing more than a huge silver pocket watch, and yet the cunning in the design, and the skill in the construction! Just think how many lives at sea that invention will have saved!'

But Anna had become distracted, remembering a trip to Greenwich during the last summer before Bernard . . . She must stop thinking like this! Her struggle to tear her mind away from such dangerous territory, before this kindly captain detected her distress, sharpened her anguish but did nothing to prevent the images from sneaking back into her brain. Bernard had walked down from the House of Commons to meet her and they had taken a river boat from Charing Cross pier. How they had laughed at the commentator on the boat! Foreign visitors had exchanged glances and shrugged, baffled by his Cockney glottal stops and tortured vowels when he pointed out such landmarks as Cleopatra's Needle, St Paul's Cathedral, Wren's monument to the Great Fire of 1666 and Execution Dock. She and Bernard had behaved like tourists, gazing as if for the first time out over the familiar, busy, brown river. He even went down to the boat's bar and had brought back two mildly sinful mid-afternoon lagers (not very chilled) in disposable plastic glasses. 'We'll be able to do this sort of thing more often once I've retired,' he had said. She had squeezed his hand, so happy to have him to herself for a whole afternoon.

'Once I've retired' – words so full of promise. They had begun to crop up in conversations years before, perhaps even before the fall of Thatcher. 'Once I've retired, we'll be able to think of moving, perhaps to Cornwall,' when she complained about living in the suburbs of Carborough. 'I'll even be able to shop with you, once I've retired,' almost every time she set out for the fortnightly ordeal of trolley-loading at Safeway or Morrisons. 'We could become friends of English National Opera, once I've retired, then we can go all the time,' when he took her to see *Lohengrin* at the London Coliseum. They had been to precisely three operas before that – one for each decade of their marriage.

After visiting the *Cutty Sark* and strolling in Greenwich Park, they had walked through the foot-tunnel under the Thames to the Isle of Dogs and travelled back into town on the newish Docklands Light Railway. How lovely Wren's building had looked from the north side of the river, separated from them by the expanse of water and framed by trees on the rising ground of the park, and by a blue and white sky. And what fun it had been with Bernard on that little railway – as much like a fairground ride as a proper train!

Her equilibrium lurched with the ship's movement. She *had* to tear her mind off this. 'Where is your . . . your . . . ?'

'Our chronometer? Here! But our navigation is all done with radio beams and computers nowadays.' Maclean noticed that something had brought her to the brink of tears. It was clear to him, though nothing had been said, that she was newly bereaved – a lot of his lone female passengers were. 'But we do need to know how to do it with a compass and sextant, anyway. Just in case.' He rubbed his hands together, trying to be brisk and cheerful. 'Now, how about a cuppa?' He ushered

her off the bridge and into his private quarters where a tray
with tiny sandwiches, scones, cream, jam and fancy cakes had
been set down on a large coffee table. It was a fairly modest
room by terrestrial standards, but for captain's quarters on
a ship the accommodation was palatial. Office-like in one
corner, where a desk, chair and filing cabinet stood, the rest of
the room was lined with bookshelves, had large windows with
views on two sides and was furnished with a selection of easy
chairs and sofas all covered in soft black leather. Each ledge
carried a window box in which grew an interesting collection
of house plants including a large lily of some kind with soft
orange flowers. A Clivia, Anna decided, feeling sure she
remembered seeing them in the old temperate house at Kew.
A steward who looked exactly like Tony brought in teapot,
milk and hot water. Anna noticed that there were several
cups and saucers and was a little relieved that she would not
have to have tea alone with Captain Maclean. Not that she
was nervous in his presence, but the pressures of a one to one
conversation could sometimes be hard to bear. Guests began
to arrive at that moment, but her relief was blocked by the
sight of Jack Pullen among them. To avoid him, she joined
a small group that was forming round the chief engineer.

'Seamen don't know they're alive, these days,' he was
saying. 'Imagine being a stoker on an old steamship. Shov-
elling coal day and night, in that filth and heat! Conditions
were unbearable.' She tried to imagine but could not. The
chief caught his captain's eye and changed his tone, obeying
standing orders to circulate at parties. 'Have you met our
doctor yet?' He introduced Anna and a couple of fellow
passengers before moving away. She was chatted to by several
officers and passengers, holding her cup and saucer, refusing
food. Seeing, after a while, that some of the women had
begun to sit down, she moved to Captain Maclean's leather
chesterfield. Jack Pullen walked over and sat beside her.

'Like Patience on a monument.' Pullen beckoned to the
steward, grabbing four sandwiches before he had time to offer
the tray to Anna.

'Sorry?' she said to Pullen.

'Nothing – just Shakespeare.'

'Oh, yes?' She had never understood that speech – the green and yellow melancholy, yes, but who was Patience? And why would she smile at grief? 'Is it *Twelfth Night*?'

'What exactly *are* you writing?' Pullen asked, ignoring her question.

'Well, I've hardly started really. A sort of journal of my past.'

'Memoirs?' He snorted with exaggerated scorn. 'That sort of thing's strictly for amateurs. Politicians, or celebrities – ghost-written, of course. Non-writers, whichever way you look at it.' She was silent. There didn't seem anything to say to that. He went on, 'I mean, I *ask* you, who's going to want to read something like that?'

'What I'm writing is not for public consumption.'

'Aha! Private is it?' He managed a leer that showed yellow teeth.

'Not in the way you think, Mr Pullen.' She was beginning to feel angry with his bullying manner. 'But it cannot possibly be of interest to anyone.'

'Why write it then?'

'I . . . I don't know.' Good question, Anna thought. Because Max told me to? He did, but she knew that the project had become something she needed. To go the whole way back, to open and probe the wounds, searching for glass fragments, shrapnel, any hard objects that would otherwise continue to chafe the flesh and thus aggravate the pain. For healing to begin, she must first extend the injury. 'I feel compelled to.'

'But what's the point?' Pullen persisted. 'You only write if you want to be read.'

'What I'm writing is private.'

'Of course, that's the nature of most people's amateurish introspective ramblings. But don't you see that *all* writing is private? It's a personal thing, between you and your one reader. And the job is to encode those private thoughts, long-ings, feelings, emotions, failures and triumphs into material that's fit for your reader. You can only do that by telling a bloody good story.'

'Probably you're right, but don't you understand that I'm doing this as a kind of therapy?'

'But don't *you* understand that writers, like all artists, are loonies? They feel compelled to express, to communicate – maybe as a soul-bearing exercise, maybe just to grab attention.'

'Are you calling me a loony?'

'No. Because by your own admission you're not yet a writer. But I would count it a greater insult not to be called a loony. Look at the alternatives: shopkeepers, doctors, accountants – if that's sanity who wants it?'

'Most people.'

'Thank God!' The yellow teeth flashed again. 'Leaves more room for some of us to be writers. Christ knows, there's enough competition as it is.' He engulfed the last of his sandwiches, took a slurp of tea and banged the cup and saucer down on the coffee table. 'Now what are we to do about you and your writing?'

'Me?' Anna shrugged. 'Well, nothing different from the other class members.'

'Please yourself.' Pullen got up. 'But they are merely turning up to amuse themselves during the cruise. You showed commitment.'

'Oh, don't overestimate me, Mr Pullen.'

'Jack.'

'Well, don't.'

'What bit of your memoirs are you on right now?' She froze. 'Oh, spare me the details. Just give, say, a year and a place.'

'Nineteen fifty-five. Cornwall.'

'Great. Do me a short story, set in the fifties in the West Country. No real-life characters, unless you want to introduce them. But make me *want* to read it. Right to the end.' He leant a little closer. 'You can slip in a little fucking if you like.'

'Mr Pullen!' How dare he speak so foully.

'I said that on purpose.' He still had his head close to hers. 'If you want to be a writer, *really* want to, you will need to be wholly open and unabashed. How do you suppose a sculptor manages to carve out, centimetre by centimetre, a statue's cock and balls? Warts and all, or it's no damn good! OK?' He straightened up, thanked the captain for tea and strode out. Anna's heart was beating a little faster than she would have liked and she was shaking. Why, she couldn't really understand. She was not easily shocked and bad language, once the surprise element had gone, didn't worry her at all. His bullying aggression, she knew, stemmed from his own weakness and that made it easier to tolerate. But the part that stung was his accurate diagnosis of what was wrong with the way she was writing. She was not being wholly honest as she wrote. She was addressing an assemblage of readers – though she would have died sooner than let anyone see her memoirs – and not communicating her story to one intimate friend.

Her thoughts were disturbed by movement in the room and she realised that everyone except Captain Maclean was leaving.

'I hope that man Pullen wasn't too rude to you,' the captain said as she rose from the chesterfield and prepared to present her thanks. 'He can be quite offensive, but Entertainments insist that he comes on this world cruise every year. He has quite a following among our regulars, you know.'

'So I gather. I'm attending his classes.'

'Well good for you!'

'And thank you for such an interesting afternoon, Captain.'

'Oh not at all! My pleasure!' He held her hand for a moment or two longer than was needed to shake it formally. 'I do hope this cruise will do you some lasting good.' He wanted to find words of greater comfort, but couldn't think what to say.

Chapter Four

Next morning, soon after five, Anna was at her desk. Overnight the sea had calmed and she could detect, through the black of the porthole, a single star. At first, she had put aside her journal and was trying to note down ideas for the story Pullen had assigned, on sheets of typing paper scrounged from the purser's office. She wished she had brought a typewriter, since it was so difficult to write on the plain sheets. The ideas would not form. Every time she tried to think of a character it was either ridiculously unrealistic or turned into someone too real and familiar to be usable. After half an hour, she abandoned the project and pulled the journal towards her again, determined to finish off the 'chapter', as she was calling it now, on Cornwall.

Bernard seemed to be visiting his family at Hincham more frequently than before, now that he had his degree and was working on his doctorate. Often, on a Sunday, he would cycle over to Congston for Matins, after which Daddy would invite him to the rectory for lunch. With Charlie up at Cambridge, I was glad to have his company, and I soon began to miss him when he was not there. I loved the way he talked – he could be so persuasive, and seemed to know so much about so many things – and I loved the way he slipped his hand into mine when we went for Sunday walks between lunch and Evensong.

He was terribly kind to Daddy. He must have been bored silly by him most of the time, but he listened politely, laughed at his jokes, agreed with him loyally and climbed with him on to whatever bandwagon he happened to be riding at the time.

When Bernard was away, Anna pined. She wrote him long, chatty letters almost daily, sometimes typed, for speed, on her boss's typewriter between finishing her day and running for the train. She recounted the Harvest Thanksgiving service blow by blow, not forgetting to describe the appalling stink when Mr Cooper's huge turnips went rotten down by the font. She gave him news of birds she had spotted: the arrival of the first fieldfares and redwings, sped over from their summer homes in Scandinavia by a northeasterly gale which stripped the leaves from the great beech in the rectory garden a month earlier than usual. He wrote back: describing life at Cambridge, mentioning excursions to the London School of Economics and commenting on current affairs – the dock strike, Churchill's rage at Sutherland's unflattering portrait and the troubles in Cyprus. His letters were succinct, witty, sometimes abrasive, but always affectionate.

The winter was long and cold; spring was wet. With it came news of British plans to make a hydrogen bomb, to electrify more railways and to build motorways. At home, Congston and surrounding villages acquired mains electricity, but not water. Bernard arrived unannounced one Saturday afternoon in May, driving an elderly, open-topped Morris Minor. It was the first truly warm day of the year, with cuckoos calling in the trees of the rectory garden and bluebells carpeting the woodland floors. The rector was visiting a parishioner who was dying in King's Lynn hospital, but Anna was in the kitchen garden planting out Brussels sprout seedlings – or rather, holding the watering can while Dawn, grunting with the effort, pushed her dibber into the soft soil to make a planting hole, waited for Anna to fill it with water, and then firmed the young plants into the resulting puddle. At the sound of the car tyres on the gravel of the drive she glanced up. 'Oo-er! 'ere comes your young man,' she said.

'My what?' Anna replied. Since they had met the previous summer, Anna had considered Bernard to be no more than a friend – to the rector, as well as to her. What special feeling she had for him she had kept to herself.

'You 'eard,' Dawn said. 'I've seen yer face when one of 'is letters come in the po-ost.' Bernard saw them in the kitchen garden and walked over. 'A'ternoon, bor!' Dawn muttered. 'Oi suppose yew want me ter get some tea on.'

'Actually, I was going to ask Anna if she'd like to come for a drive.'

'Perhaps when we get back, Dawn,' Anna said. Then to Bernard, 'Give me a minute to tidy up.' She ran towards the house, hesitating a moment and half turning. 'Whose car?' she shouted, before running on.

'Mine. Well, half mine,' he said. 'Dad helped me buy it.'

Within a quarter of an hour, they were driving through the open country. 'Come to Cornwall,' he said.

'What, now?'

'Ridiculous!' He banged the steering wheel with delight. 'Next month. I want to see the sun set over the Atlantic on the longest day – we could stay for a week. I've got a tent and everything, so we could camp.' Anna thought of being with him, and only him, for days on end. She blushed, but the rush of blood was from pleasure, not embarrassment.

'I'd have to ask Father.'

The longest day was cold and rather wet. Bernard and Anna sat on a cliff-top between Harlyn Bay and Trevose Head, huddled together on a groundsheet with their gas capes over their shoulders, their faces bedewed with that fine drizzle in which Cornwall specialises: the billions of droplets are so tiny and so pervasive that vegetation bows under the burden of water, every drop carefully hung on branch, leaf and grass blade, but never a breath of breeze to shake it off. Walk under trees or through fields or moorland and very soon your clothes are saturated. In spite of Charlie's binoculars, it was impossible to see very far, although earlier, peering down into a narrow cove, they had watched guillemots, puffins and razorbills flying to and from the sea. The puffins nested in disused rabbit holes in the short, springy turf of the cliff-top fields among pale yellow flowers of kidney vetch, sea pinks and translucent white sea catchfly. Now Bernard and Anna had moved to a different spot and were waiting for the grey seals, seen earlier that day in the clear water below the cliffs. Under the rustling gas cape, Bernard felt for her hand and said, 'Sorry, but it's turned out to be a bit of a washout.'

'Oh why?' Anna said. 'Aren't you enjoying it?'

'Well, the weather.'

'Oh I don't mind! It always does this in Cornwall.'

He squeezed her hand more firmly. 'Thanks, Anna.'

'Whatever for?'

'Being so decent about it.'

'Bernard,' she said. 'Being . . . here. That's what matters to me, really. Not the weather.' She wanted so much to say, being here with *you*, being anywhere with *you* – that is what really makes me happy, but she couldn't quite make herself utter such frank words. He could be so dismissive sometimes. He held her hand in a hard grip for quite a while but finally released his hold and, rather stiffly, stroked the small of her back.

'Anna.' His voice had developed a rigidity, probably from sitting so stiffly in the damp. 'Might you allow me to . . . to . . .' Now he was rubbing her back in rough, jerky movements, as if trying to force away a lumbar pain.

'Allow you to what?' Not because she disliked his closeness, but because he was beginning to hurt a little, she reached behind her and very gently took his hand away. Instantly, he jumped up.

'Oh, I'm sorry,' he muttered, in a voice almost strangled with mortification. 'I'm *so* sorry!'

'Bernard, whatever's the matter?'

'What? Oh, no . . . it's nothing. Really, nothing!' She got up too, and they resumed their walk in single file along the narrow cliff-top path. She felt miserable and guilty now because she had upset him. He walked fast. She was having to trot a step or two at times, to keep up.

He was tense and nervy for the rest of the afternoon. They had planned to cook themselves a supper of eggs and bacon outside their tent, pitched in the home paddock of a dairy farm on the peninsula, but when they reached its front gate the farmer's wife was watching out for them. As soon as they had walked through her small, walled garden, where pink valerian and clashing red oriental poppies drooped under the weight of water, she poked her head out of the front door.

' 'Tes such terrible weather, m'dears, we wondered whether you might like to 'ave tea with us in the 'ouse.'

'That is really very kind of you, Mrs Petherick, but I'm sure we'll be fine,' Bernard said, rather stiffly.

'My, my, but you'm both soaked through, dears!' They did not need much further persuasion, especially when use of the farmhouse bathroom was added to the offer. One after the other, they bathed and changed into dry clothes before settling down to a large meal of veal and ham pie, lettuce and tomato salad and stewed rhubarb on to which the farmer's wife dropped a large blob of scalt cream. Afterwards, she fetched a piece of local cheddar cheese and set a soft white cottage loaf on the table. 'There's strawberry jam if you'd rather.' While they ate, the drizzle stopped and a northwesterly breeze shifted the clouds enough to allow shafts of late sunshine to highlight dog roses and honeysuckle growing in the slaty banks that served as hedges in those parts.

After tea, replete and calmer, Bernard had suggested another walk, this time to the pub at St Merryn. Neither was very keen on alcohol, and after two half-pints of ale, slowly and thoughtfully sipped, they were ready to walk back in the developing twilight. Without thinking, and without time for self-consciousness, they linked hands and she loved the feel of his strong grip. Physical contact re-established the rapport they had lost and, without thinking, barely knowing what she was saying, Anna murmured, 'I'm glad you're back.' She felt her hand squeezed and her arm swung a little more as they walked.

'This afternoon,' she said, 'when I told you that being here was all that mattered, I . . . that wasn't quite what I meant.'

'You don't need to—'

'What I meant was, well, not just being here but rather, being with you. *That* was what mattered.'

'Oh Anna!' This time he did not wait for permission. He put a hand on each of her cheeks and gently pulled her face up to his. Her lips felt extraordinary on his; an electricity came from her; she was so beautiful she unmanned him, making him feel weak and shaky. 'Anna!'

Back in the tent, she realised how dog-tired she was. They had risen before four that morning and had driven all the way from Congston, across England through Northampton, Oxford, Bath, Exeter and on down the Cornish peninsula. Train journeys, in previous years, even with changes at King's Lynn, Liverpool Street and then Paddington for Bodmin and Padstow, had seemed far less troublesome, especially when you could send your heavy luggage in advance for an extra five shillings and sixpence. The rector used to pack a vast cabin trunk with everything they could possibly need. It had seemed funny to be in Cornwall without the family at first, but now she knew that Bernard was an even better reason to be here, which filled her with a mix of dread and excitement. She slipped into her sleeping bag and, wanting to read, switched on the small battery lamp.

Bernard, as unobtrusively as possible, wormed his long legs into his own sleeping bag beside her in their small tent. 'I say, Anna, the batteries won't last long on that lamp,' he said. With a sigh she switched off and lay there, cold, uncomfortable, miserable to be so near him but not able to touch him. For some time she tried very hard to keep still, but could not prevent the ache in her hip, or the feeling of numbness that crept up whichever side was nearest the ground. Also the night was getting very dark. There were noises – a fox barking, in the distance, scurrying and rustling closer to.

'Bernard,' she whispered, 'I'm a bit frightened.'

'Here, hold my hand.' He reached over and they held hands for a while but her arm began to feel cold and crampy. 'If we unzipped the sides of both bags,' he said, later, 'we could make one into a cover and spread the other out beneath us.' After much unzipping, giggling and reorganising of bodies, she found herself enfolded in his arms. The warmth of his body and the brush of his lips on her neck were enough. With a grateful sigh, happy, she slipped into a deep sleep.

Bernard lay awake for some time. The condition under which Anna's father had given permission for the young couple to travel, unsupervised, was that Bernard would protect his daughter's honour. That the rector should place such trust in him was flattering, but he hoped now that he would be able to resist the temptation to betray that trust.

I was so innocent [Anna wrote, and then altered the last word to ignorant,] that I had no idea what sexual torture it must have been for him lying there with me in his arms, every night for a whole week. How fair and decent he was, even in our most intimate of caresses, to have remained pure. There were times when I felt him pressing hard against my thighs, and I'm sure I sensed his tension, but I simply did not know what I was doing to him. For me, at that time, just being held in his arms was enough. I was blissfully content.

On our last night, I viewed our impending return to East Anglia with a mixture of gloom and elation.

The weather had warmed up considerably; they had decided on a final walk to St Merryn, and to return along the cliff-tops, a long way round, to take a last glance at the rugged coastline. Bernard had been quiet and thoughtful all day, and now he barely spoke. In silence, they prepared for bed. Once in, out of a habit developed over the previous few days, they folded their arms round each other and kissed.

'You are all right, aren't you?' Anna asked.

'Not really, no.' Bernard said. 'At least, I won't be until I've talked something over with you.' He sighed. Anna prodded him.

'Go on then.'

'I don't want to go home.'

'Nor do I.'

'But I know I've got to. More to the point. I don't want to be separated from you. And I know that if you will allow it, I won't have to be.'

''Course you won't. We can see lots of each other.' To her consternation, she felt something drip on her cheek and reached up to feel a tear. His? She held him very tightly.

'I don't intend to be separated from you,' she whispered in his ear, 'because I love you.'

'What I'm driving at,' Bernard said, 'is that I would like us to be married.' Astounded, Anna sat up. Impossible! Impossible that so brilliant a man, so lovely a person could, in his wildest dreams, be serious about someone as ignorant and lowly as herself. She hugged her knees and stared ahead into the darkness of the tent. I'm not worthy, she wanted to say, I'm not nearly good enough. She had loved him, she was sure, since that first time in Padstow last year, but she could not believe that he was *that* serious about her. Now she would worship him! She trembled. She felt her heart beating very hard.

But all she managed to say was: 'Bernard, I'm only nineteen years old.'

Anna had been writing for almost three hours when Tony tapped quietly at her cabin door and came in with her morning tea. She knew she must drink it quickly because Cedric had insisted that they go up on deck to watch the ship coming into port. Earlier, long before daylight, she had seen lights and a dark outline of land, and assumed that by now they should almost be in harbour. But looking out again she was surprised by an uninterrupted view of the open sea.

'That would have been the island of Porto Santo,' Cedric explained in answer to her query. He had seen that she was well wrapped up and had walked with her up to the observation deck, a small area immediately below the bridge, where they stood leaning into the cold breeze as the great ship sliced through the Atlantic. Ant refused to rise before daylight – ever. 'It's the second biggest island in the Madeira archipelago,' Cedric went on. 'The one Zarco first discovered, in fourteen-eighteen. It was a chance discovery, but he managed to get backing from Prince Henry the Navigator to come back and colonise Madeira a year later.'

'What a lot you know!' The sky was pearly, uncluttered except for a single bunch of puffed up clouds on the horizon.

'Zarco is an even bigger hero, on Madeira, than Columbus. You'll see his statue in the middle of Funchal. But there's a heart-rending apocryphal tale of a lovelorn youth called Robert Machin who got here a century earlier, when he eloped from Bristol with his bride, Anne d'Arfet. They planned to go to France, but his ship got swept away in a hurricane and was dashed on to the rocks of Madeira. His lovely bride had died in the storm, and the heartbroken boy had to bury her on the foreshore before he too succumbed to grief and exposure. His crew cut down a cedar tree to fashion a cross for their joint grave before sailing away on a raft.'

'That's terribly sad,' Anna said, genuinely moved. 'How awful if youngsters are forced to elope!' Recent entries in her journal had made this story too apt to hear without an emotional reaction and now her mind wandered back to Norfolk and her youth.

The rector's initial reaction to her news had been effusive. 'My dear, dear boy, I can't tell you how delighted I am! Wait till I tell Charlie! Of *course* you both have my permission, and my blessing as well, with all my heart.'

But that spontaneous joy had begun to fade within moments

of uttering those words. The rector's exultant grin had gradually frozen, revealing the growing fear as he began to realise that he was not to be a part of this new picture. Or if he was, merely as a figure in the background, half lost among the landscape while the couple in the foreground had eyes only for each other.

Now, even though some forty years had passed, Anna could not shed the images so freshly dredged from her memory. The hurt which had appeared on her father's face that afternoon had never really left it until he died. His concern had been understandable at first. She was too young, and Bernard, though full of potential, would be extremely hard up for many years. He had spent the next few weeks constantly asking awkward questons: 'Where will you live? How will continue with your work if a baby arrives?' And worse, 'Did he take advantage of you when you were in Cornwall?' And ultimately, 'Anna, I have to ask, are you doing this because you have to?'

'Father,' she had replied, crimson with rage and embarrassment, 'that question is so unworthy of you that I'll pretend you didn't ask it.' She had known that these questions, even when they amounted to taunts, were not intended to hurt her. They were motivated by fear, not for her – no one could possibly look at the match and feel anything other than confidence in such a splendid man – but for himself. Because of that, his suggestive allegations had hurt less, but his insecurity had undermined her happiness and had made her feel guilty. He has brought me up, she would tell herself, he has given me everything I have. How can I do this to him? How can I sidestep my duty to him? And gradually, the interrogations had changed. At times, he became almost tearful.

'Anna, darling, how will I cope here without you?'

She would reply that he had Dawn. He would be all right. They would not be far away, not at first. There were lots of parishioners who would help out. He was a popular rector, loved, in fact. At the end of their last exchange, he had actually wept and begged her to reconsider, to postpone her marriage until she was older. 'If he loves you, *really* loves you, he will be willing to wait. That's how you can test him.' In her desperation she had even consulted Dawn, although she did not think she would value her advice.

'You follow yer heart, dear,' Dawn had said. 'Love's all that matters, in this world, and love will conquer all, you'll see.'

'But I love Daddy as well as Bernard,' she had replied.

'Then you must choose.' Dawn had caught her in a sweaty embrace. Her musky odour had thrown Anna's mind back to when she was a very little girl, being tucked up in bed with her favourite soft toy, baby Charlie milkily asleep in his cot in the warmest corner of the nursery. 'And o-only you can choose. You do-on't want ter let anyone else choose for yer.'

Now, in mid-Atlantic, almost sixty years old and alone, the scars of these damaging exchanges still smarted, even though her father had eventually been fully reconciled and anyway had been dead for more than a decade.

She looked at Cedric, leaning into the wind made by the ship's speed, mildly surprised at how strong he could appear. 'It's never easy for any parent,' she said. 'If a saint had proposed to me, my father would have found it hard to adjust. Parental opposition can be so annihilating to a young couple's happiness. So unreasonable. And so selfish.'

'Parental opposition?' Cedric uttered a brief laugh, brittle and theatrical. 'And what might you know about that?'

'Plenty, actually.' The veiled scorn in his question did not fail to register.

'Plenty eh? I had the most loving, understanding, liberal-minded, *doting* parents in the business. I was everything to them and vice versa. And I had shared everything with them, every confidence, every problem – almost.' He looked away from her up at the bridge, and then ahead, to the knot of clouds shrouding the mountains of Madeira. 'But you should have clocked their reaction when, at twenty-three, I introduced them to the first real love of my life. They didn't even get as far as shaking hands with him. I didn't see either of them again until my father's funeral in nineteen eighty-seven.'

As the ship neared the island and turned northwards to enter the harbour of Funchal, the sun rose, bringing up the colours: greening the steep volcanic mountains, picking out the red of the clay-tiled roofs, brightening the white stucco walls and energising vivid splashes of flowers – purple bougainvillea, orange flame vine, yellow alamanda. Palms and African tulip trees were visible along the seaside roads and, as the ship edged into her berth on the mole of the small harbour, Anna became aware of a flowery fragrance on the air.

'Mimosa,' Cedric said. 'There are forests of the stuff on Madeira. You can get drunk on the smell.'

Chapter Five

———

'Save changes to CORNWALL before closing?' the machine asked. It was so polite! Even when she did something badly wrong it did no more than flash up a side view of a stern computer face with a speech balloon that told her why it was unable to comply with her request.

She had decided to buy a typewriter – a cheap portable one – in St Thomas or Miami. She had not used a keyboard in years, and had consulted Jack Pullen for advice on the latest makes and models and their prices.

'Typewriters?' He had burst out laughing. 'Serious authors hardly use those nowadays! Oh, I know there are the old stalwarts who still scribble in exercise books with fountain pens and then pay some mug to type it all up for them, but most people, these days, are electronic.'

'I'm not sure I could handle anything as modern as a word processor,' Anna had replied. 'Besides, aren't they terribly expensive?'

'Nah! You can afford a posh cabin on A Deck, you can afford a PC, or better still, a Mac.' She had looked puzzled. 'It's a kind of computer – the kind *you* need. Idiot-proof.'

'Thank you.'

'Oh don't worry, that's the kind I've got, because where computers are concerned I'm a complete eejit, thank God!'

He was anxious to get away at the end of his class and had begun to move to the card room door where, ahead of their time, several bridge enthusiasts were waiting to come in. 'Come to my cabin, I'll show you mine,' he had said, managing to fix the nearest bridge player with his toothy leer. Down on D Deck, Anna was surprised at how much more humble his cabin was than hers. There was no porthole and though it was scarcely bigger than hers, it had a second bunk, covered now with his papers, folders, books and what looked like unwashed laundry. He also had a tiny dressing table on which sat a lap-top computer. It looked no bigger than a box of chocolates and yet, when he opened up the lid and switched it on, she saw the grey screen come to life and was enthralled. He had invited her to sit at its compact keyboard and had shown her how to create a file, and how to save her material. He had demonstrated how she could switch text about, how she could rewrite, tweak, adapt and adjust her work as many times as she wanted; and finally he had switched on the tiny portable printer and let her take away hard evidence of what she had written.

Regardless of cost, she knew that this was her key. This would allow her to arrange stumbling thoughts on the page; would let her churn out long passages – fast, regardless of errors – to read them aloud, and then to play about with the music of the language until it began to develop the right sounds in her head as she read phrase after phrase. Stupid as she was, with this device she would not be required to come up with the most aptly crafted prose on demand. Rather, she could coax it out of the original mess, like the first life forms emerging from the primordial soup, simply by tapping and fiddling on her keyboard. She was sold.

'You can buy one of these pretty cheaply on St Thomas,' Pullen had said, 'even with a small printer. But,' he had added, 'it won't write for you. *That* has to come from your heart, and your head.'

Loading the software, the shop salesman told her, would take a while, so she had wandered the narrow streets of Charlotte Amalie, a little frightened to be by herself, flinching now and then as black youths or men – they seemed so unnervingly muscular and used up so much sidewalk – cruised by. Smiles were plentiful though, especially from the women, and on a street corner she had noticed a pretty girl, presumably in her twenties, with braided hair and a vivid yellow dress, buying objects that resembled boiled chestnuts from a huge female vendor who wore a bright purple top and matching bandana. Her welcoming grin glinted gold in the sun.

'Excuse me,' Anna had dared to ask, 'but can you tell me what those are?'

'Breadnut!' the older woman had said. 'Come from trees like that.' She pointed to a street that inclined sharply upwards. Branches with enormous cut leaves burgeoned from what was obviously a walled garden. Green fruits as big as melons but with roughened skins were visible among the leaves. 'That's breadfruit,' the old woman went on. 'Breadnut fruit looks the same, but these are inside.' The younger girl had been giggling during this exchange, but now she offered the bag.

'Wanna try one?' Her accent was more American than Caribbean.

'I'm afraid I haven't any of the right money,' Anna had said. She wasn't sure what money they took on St Thomas, having paid for her computer with one of her credit cards. Both women had laughed as though she had cracked the funniest joke ever. The vendor had taken a small bag and placed into it three of the nuts, still hot from their recent boiling.

'A gift for you, madame. Welcome to my island!'

'That is so kind. Thank you.' Anna had been about to leave when the younger girl had put a restraining hand on her arm, milk chocolate fingers contrasting with pale European skin. Anna felt a slight frisson of fear.

'No, you try one here. Please?' Anna was confused. One was not supposed to do this. To be distracted by street natives, to risk some horrible food poisoning or even parasites by

eating such things. Yet she had felt obliged. They wanted to
watch her face while she tried the delicacy. The girl showed
her how to peel the tough outer skin from the nut. Anna
had imitated her action on one of the three nuts and bit into
the kernel.

'Mmm!' The taste was perfectly wholesome. Exactly like
a chestnut, though a little more starchy, with a faint aromatic
back-taste. 'It's delicious!' She had uttered a little laugh, and
then, catching sight of the two pairs of kindly eyes, fascinated
by the antics of a tourist, happy to see her sadness transformed
for a few moments, had laughed a little more, but with tears
quite close underneath. Without thinking, she had laid a hand
on the vendor's arm. 'Thank you,' she had said. 'Thank you
so much.'

'You're welcome!' they'd both said in American.

Anna had walked quickly away, wondering what her hurry
was. School was coming out, and she had noticed a phalanx
of small boys walking in pairs, in uniform, first the tinies
– four-year-olds, perhaps even younger, then older ones –
eight-year-olds, she guessed. She had wished she had asked
the nut ladies about their families, about their lives on this
island, and she'd wondered whether one of these little boys
belonged to the girl in the yellow dress. She had noticed that
they wore shoes but not socks, and her mind had edged into
dangerous territory. William's school socks had never stayed
up. His legs, long and thin – just like Bernard's – had simply
been the wrong shape for them.

After walking up the Danish Steps and visiting Government
House which, though originally Danish, gave the impression
of an early American outpost headquarters, she had moved
slowly downhill, back to the computer store.

She had brought a taxi back to the quayside and staggered
on board, loaded down with a series of cardboard boxes
containing computer, leads, mains adaptor, printer and something the shop salesman had explained was her processing
software.

Back on board, she had put the journal into a drawer,

deciding to keep it for only her most private memoirs, and had begun to play with her new acquisition. She realised that it would take some time to learn exactly what it could do but next day was a sea day and, after several exasperated phone calls to Jack Pullen's cabin, and his increasingly testy replies, she had mastered the rudiments. It took several more days to become competent on the word processor, but by the time they had passed through the Panama Canal she was using it as a tool with which to write, rather than as a perplexing but all-absorbing toy.

Now she had several hours before she must change for dinner. The sun outside was far too hot and strong to risk getting burnt, so she had settled down to some serious writing. Over the previous couple of days, she had transcribed all the early material from the hardcover journal to her computer's hard disk, copy typing at first, but then honing and revising as she went. She had rewritten and diluted one section of the memoirs specially for the writing class, and had roughed out two short stories – one a brief anecdote with a predictable twist in its tail; the other a reflective piece where she imagined herself in the shoes of a young girl who is confronted by the prospect of single motherhood. The class had clapped when she read this, but Pullen was obviously unimpressed.

'You can't expect that bloody word processor to write for you,' he had said. 'And you cannot write about something if you know nothing about it.'

'Excuse me,' Vanessa Dicks had said, 'but I think you're being very unfair.' She had glanced round the class to elicit sympathy from the others. 'I think Anna puts the exploitation case very strongly, and I thought her imagery very poignant.'

'Well bully for you,' Pullen had said. 'And perhaps you are right. But let me ask you, Anna. When you were a teenager, did you give birth to an illegitimate child?'

'Of course not!' Anna felt her cheeks burning.

'And did any of your relatives, or even your close friends?'

'No!'

'Precisely my point,' Pullen had sighed. During the first
week of the cruise his class had swollen to fourteen but today
was back to the original eight. 'Pick a subject you know,' he
urged. 'Something you've observed. The most trivial incident
makes a story, *if* you tell it well.'

'Save changes to CORNWALL before closing?' The computer repeated its silent question and she instructed it to get
on with the task. But now the story was moving on and
she wanted to change the name of her document. After a
while, to conserve anonymity, she renamed it M, reopened
the document and began to type.

Daddy got over things, but it took time. At first I was
so happy, being with Bernard, being a *part* of Bernard,
that I could hardly believe anything in my life could
possibly go wrong again. At the wedding itself, Daddy
was heroic, giving all the males hearty back slaps, and
flirting – in his clerical way – with the women. His
laughs and guffaws were louder and more staged than
usual and although I chose not to know at the time,
I really should have seen how much he was hurting.
Charlie got very drunk, which was unlike him, and
was far too boisterous. He was so like Bernard in so
many ways, and I could hardly bear to be leaving him
behind for good. He had had a couple of affairs, one
at Cambridge with a female undergraduate, and one
with a girl from Hunstanton, but both had failed to
last. Friendship was really what Charlie craved, and
the loss of that friendship – something he assumed he
would always have from me – must have cut him up
very badly.

After the wedding, Bernard and I had agreed that
there really wasn't time for much of a honeymoon,
but I had arranged to take a week off work, to be
with him at Cambridge. Before we got on to the train,
at King's Lynn, I went to queue at the ticket office

but Bernard said, 'I've got the tickets.' What a lot that simple sentence meant!

At the time, Anna was grateful that he had relieved her of having to think of something else on top of all the wedding arrangements. It was only later, as the train was puffing away from the platform, that she said, 'How did you know I hadn't already bought my own ticket?' He shrugged and grinned.

'Come over here, Mrs Morfey,' he said. Why on earth is he calling me that? she wondered, and then felt silly, as if she'd queried her own new name aloud. She crossed to the seat adjacent to his. He put his arm round her and squeezed a shoulder. He was bubbling over with some kind of excitement. He kept laughing, in a knowing way, as if he were keeping something back. Outside the carriage window, autumn sunshine lit up fen and river as it sank to the horizon. There was not a hint of mist, despite the low-lying, damp terrain.

'Oh Bernard, look! Ely Cathedral, with the sun setting behind. Isn't that lovely!' For some reason, she found she had tears in her eyes. She squeezed his hand and began to weep more openly. Luckily, their compartment was empty.

'Darling Anna,' Bernard whispered. 'Whatever's the matter?'

'Poor Daddy,' she managed to say at last. 'And Charlie. I'm going to miss them both so much.'

'Shhh. There, there!' Bernard felt awkward, sorry for her unhappiness but worried in case someone came in. The train was steaming slowly to a halt along a platform dotted with passengers, mainly day boys from the King's School, waiting to go home. He could hear the announcer, a female voice like a knife on porcelain: *This – is – Ely.* Suddenly the sliding door to their compartment was pulled open and a clergyman started to walk in but then took in the scene: the worried young man holding a clean handkerchief ready, the girl's face turned away from the door, pretending to be studying the scenery through the window. She would not have realised that her reflection could be seen in the grimy carriage window, a beautiful face made mournful by some urgent grief.

'I do beg your pardon,' the clergyman said, and withdrew before Bernard could thank him. The train moved off. Fifteen minutes later it was slowing down again and the brakes began to grind, ready for the stop at Cambridge. Anna got up and began to gather handbag, gloves, and her small overnight case. Bernard had heaved their two larger suitcases on to the netted luggage rack and would have to get them down himself. But he made no attempt to move.

'I wouldn't bother, my darling,' he said, when she began to look flustered. The train was almost stationary again. 'We're not actually getting out here.'

'What? Why not?' Anna was puzzled

'Because we're going to Paris.' His grin widened. 'Tonight, on the sleeper.' Anna was too astonished to speak. She began to realise that she had entirely the wrong clothes for a trip anywhere, much less for Paris. She wished she had known. Looking forward was such an important part of – of this whole day. She had been looking forward so much, amid the furore of the wedding preparations and the day itself, to snuggling down with him in his flat in Bateman Street. Perhaps they might cross the street for a stroll in the botanic garden next day, and possibly venture out in the evening for a Chinese supper, but otherwise she had imagined just being with him, held close for hours on end. Now this. She needed to plan. She could not do things without thinking first. She was too astonished to speak. 'Don't worry,' he said, 'I've made all the plans.'

'But my passport is at home, in Daddy's study drawer.' He shook his head, still grinning, and tapped his breast pocket. So her father had been in on this conspiracy, and she had not. At that point, the compartment door opened again and two men in brown gabardine raincoats came in, followed soon afterwards by a girl a little older than Anna with mousy hair, a sharp nose and buck teeth. She clutched a cheap hardcover novel with a picture of an embracing couple on its dust jacket and a third face, dark with jealousy, in the background, scowling at the two lovebirds. The title was *Follow your Heart* and the girl was soon lost among its pages, her lips – prinked out in the latest coral pink from Coty – silently mouthing the words. The girl's hands were innocent of rings of any kind. Anna felt surreptitiously for the new gold band on her own finger and heard Dawn's words of advice in her mind's ear, 'You follow yer heart!' She sat in awkward silence all the way to Liverpool Street.

When the other passengers had gone from the compartment, and Bernard had lifted their suitcases down, Anna put her arms round him and said, 'Bernard, darling, this is an absolutely *lovely* idea. I couldn't say, in front of those people, but I do love you so!' The relief and gratitude on his face wiped away all that was left of her vexation. He stopped her from saying anything more with a kiss, planted firmly on the lips. When she felt his tongue, urgent and probing, in her mouth, she almost went back to wishing they could be alone in his Cambridge pad.

Later, in their sleeping compartment, it seemed to Anna that they had been trundling along railway tracks as long as she could remember. They had dined in London before boarding the train, and had undressed in the dark, each shy of the other's scrutiny. She had elected to take the bottom berth, but had begged him to stay in it with her, at least for a while. She had put on a sheer nylon nightdress, and he a pair of pale blue pyjamas with cream piped hems, but in the dark she had thought again, pulled it off her shoulders and slipped quickly between the sheets. He climbed carefully into the cramped bunk, anxious not to bruise her with an elbow or a knee.

'Bernard,' she whispered, as she unbuttoned his pyjama jacket. 'Couldn't you take these off? I want to be as close to you as possible.'

'I don't think this is the best place to start our, you know, our—'

'I don't mind. I just want to feel you near me.' He climbed out of bed, shucked his pyjama trousers and jacket, and got back in. She could feel the roughness of his chest hairs on her breasts, and ran her hand down the strongly muscled back, feeling the small taut buttocks. When she stroked these, below the cleft, with the tips of her fingers, he emitted a low moan of pleasure. They kissed. This time his tongue felt physically hot as it probed the inside of her mouth. He pressed her down with his weight and she loved the feeling – a sweet crushing sensation – and she loved his smell, a muskiness that increased as his excitement grew. But when his hand moved to her sex she felt herself grow tense. Instantly he took his hand back.

'Don't worry, my darling,' he whispered. 'We have all the time in the world.' But she sensed she was disappointing him. She kissed his chest, not sure of the odd feeling of hairiness beneath her lips, and ran a light hand along his flank, hesitating towards his groin, but was then led by curiosity to explore this forbidden area. She was alarmed by his erection; could not imagine anything like that inside her, and yet the way he quivered when she brushed it with her hand excited her.

The next night, in a cheap hotel just off the Place St Michel, their marriage was consummated. The sex itself neither excited nor disappointed her. His nearness was the greatest pleasure, and perceiving his apparent ecstasy, even though it was derived from this unsettling animal thrusting, was reward enough for her. With each bout, during the next few days, it got better. Having him inside her induced a warm glow which increased as he went on, but never as much as it clearly did for him when, gulping for air, and sometimes uttering a hoarse, barking cry, he reached his climax and then subsided, always a little shamefaced, beside her, his temples dewed with sweat. Then followed the spells she loved most. 'Breathing his presence', she came to call them to herself, lying with him, sticky from lovemaking, while his heart rate subsided to normal, and his breathing slowed. He would keep still and hold her in his arms, planting occasional kisses on her temple. Those were the moments she wanted to be endless.

*   *   *

The theatre was not as efficiently air-conditioned as other parts of the ship. When every seat was taken, the auditorium grew hot and the audience soporific. Almost every evening after dinner, the Brisbane Theatre Company was obliged to present a spectacular of some kind. Since most of the passengers were Anna's age or older, nostalgia had to be high on the menu, with old time music hall songs, wartime entertainment and truncated versions of West End musicals that predated the 1970s.

Anna had avoided these events, having a natural aversion to anything theatrical – Bernard had rarely taken her to a play in London – and, since she rose so early in the morning, usually retired soon after dinner. She might stroll on deck with the Boys for a breath of steamy tropical air, but was soon ready for the peace of her cabin. Tonight, however, as the ship sailed from San Francisco, she had been persuaded to come to the show. 'Billy Dudley has come on board,' Ant had explained, 'and his act is such fun. Most ship's comedians are just *ghastly*. They're failures, in the real world, and can only get work at the worst of the clubs, or on ships like this. You must know the sort, Anna, peddling strings of awful jokes, most of them offensive to someone – blacks, queers, the Irish. But this chap is different. He doesn't even tell jokes, really. Not as such.'

'Do say you'll come,' Cedric added. 'Give that infernal machine of yours a rest.'

'Well, I am rather tired,' she had said, but they had sensed that she was weakening. As had become their wont, they very gently took an arm each and reinforced their entreaty. She succumbed.

Minutes later, in the steamy auditorium, she fought sleep while a young female singer dragged herself through an old Vera Lynn number, never quite getting into tune. She felt her head nodding and then Cedric squeezed her hand and she looked up and saw Billy Dudley, a man in his thirties, she guessed, looking dazed, uneasy and hesitant. Even his speech – faintly, unaggressively Lancashire – was hesitant, as if the world was endlessly confusing to him. She even thought he might be forgetting his lines. The audience kept a stony silence.

'I ... er ... I've just got on.' Long pause. 'And I still ... er ... haven't quite got used to leaving the States. I feel a bit like that song, you know' – here he sang in gentle parody – 'I left my heart ... in San Francisco ...' Then slipped into Lancastrian and said, 'Trouble is, I've gone and left my blasted wallet there too.' A faint titter from half a dozen people. 'I haven't actually moved into my cabin yet.' A little more laughter. 'Haven't even *found* it. I didn't know there was a W Deck. It's that far down, they 'ave to issue diving gear to get to it.' Anna could not prevent herself from joining in the laughter, even though the material was so silly and so trivial. Just as Pullen constantly said, it's the way you tell it. As if reading her thoughts, Ant brought his mouth to her ear and said, 'Billy's coming to creative writing tomorrow, as a guest. Give us a few pointers.'

A little further on in his act, when the audience was laughing and applauding every few seconds, a voice from the back shouted loudly, 'Crap!' On stage Billy faltered for the briefest second, but continued. The heckling voice cut in again and was louder. 'Crap and bollocks!'

'My feelings precisely, sir,' Billy retorted, 'but I think the two of us are in the minority.'

'Oh clever,' whispered Ant. 'Didn't Shaw do that?' Heads were turned to the source of the heckling.

'No one should have to stay in this shit hole to hear such utter garbage!' The heckler got to his feet, unsteady, and began to push his way out. Boos and a slow hand clap began. Anna noticed, then, that it was her drunken neighbour and instead of contempt, she felt pity. It was obvious that even the drink failed to dull his senses enough to prevent these howls of anguish. The man turned, near the door, clearly wanting to address the whole theatre, but two crew members put firm hands on his elbows and 'helped' him out. Within moments,

Billy Dudley had won his audience back and when he took his leave, the applause was tumultuous.

Next morning at the writing class, Anna was struck not by his comic genius but by his sadness – or perhaps, she thought, that was how his genius worked. The lost, wistful expression, that she had assumed was the basis of his act, was clearly a permanent part of his nature. And yet while he chatted to the class members in a soft-spoken, hesitant manner, each of them sensed the humour in what he was saying and were soon chuckling. All that wit, Anna decided, was really no more than a product of exasperation. It carried a despairing note relievable only by laughter – even so, people enjoyed laughing. If they didn't, they were lost. The drunk heckler was like that. He had obviously failed to see any sort of funny side and therefore had nothing with which to relieve the pain of his living. Anna wished fervently that, in what her own life had so recently become, she could find something to laugh about.

Chapter Six

———

That Bernard's career would succeed was never questioned. His mind was too original and his personality too confident and energetic for anything but success. In academic circles, his work on economic models for the 1950s had surprised all of his contemporaries. In those days, when the ghost of John Maynard Keynes still walked the corridors not only of power but of almost every economic institution in the civilised world, and where the only alternatives to Keynesian theory seemed to be Communism or Nazi-style fascism – both pretty much the same, when you bothered to analyse the effects they had on society – a philosophy based wholly on unfettered free enterprise found little favour in Europe. Bernard's voice was loud, insistent, too well reasoned and too well presented to be ignored. But it was considered an alternative voice, a voice on the fringe, too radical to be taken seriously during the first two decades of postwar reconstruction, save by a small and as yet not especially powerful minority.

After receiving his doctorate, he decided to drop university life for a while and embark on a spell in the City. He was conscious of a lack of experience in commercial practices and felt unable to understand the financial world as comprehensively as an economist should. He knew that most of the leading firms of stockbrokers would be glad to take on such a keen young brain, and would be prepared to pay a reasonable salary, but he wanted to join a smaller, more aggressive organisation where he could make a bigger mark. Within two years of marrying Anna he had become Economic Adviser to Jasper, Goldstone.

During that wet summer, England triumphed at cricket but the West was looking distinctly wobbly. Jim Laker took nineteen Australian wickets in a single match but in the same year Nasser threw the British out of Suez and the USSR flattened the Hungarian uprising with its tanks.

In the warmth and comfort of their new marriage, snug in their newly acquired and rather heavily mortgaged London flat, Anna set about creating as good a home as she knew how. The location was perfect – just round the corner from University College, where she had landed a part-time secretarial job, and no more than a few seconds' trot from Russell Square tube station. There was a small kitchen, a well-lit sitting room with dining area and two bedrooms. The smaller of these, decorated with cream walls, Cambridge-blue paintwork and a soft beige carpet, Anna decided would make a fine nursery, if one were ever needed.

Within weeks of moving into the flat, at summer's end, they both succumbed to the epidemic of Asian 'flu. On the same day, almost at the same hour, in spite of the mildness of the autumn weather that year, they began to shiver and put themselves to bed where they lay for forty-eight hours, sweating and trembling, each putting off the moment of having to get up to find a drink or to relieve themselves. For the first time since their wedding, they were unable to sleep enfolded in each other's arms – their joints were too stiff, and their bodies too unnaturally sweaty. Bernard had a few days' grace before taking up his post at Jasper, Goldstone and Anna would have leave to catch up on her backlog later. For once, they had the luxury of time and could recover gently over several days. On the third day, Anna walked to the kitchen to find sustenance more solid than hot milk. She scrambled eggs, made coffee and found a couple of tomatoes which she made into a salad. They ate the meal in bed and felt slightly better afterwards.

'I'm having a bath,' Bernard said. His head still ached, but his joints were looser and he felt his strength returning. When he had come out of the bathroom, leaving his sweaty pyjamas on the floor, Anna replaced him and sank gratefully down into his bath water, soaping herself and sponging away the sweat of the virus. She pulled out the plug and then gave her body a final rinse with the shower attachment before drying off. The whole business had exhausted her and she crawled back into bed, also naked. The thought of putting her nightdress back on revolted her, and she wasn't sure she had a clean one ready aired. Bernard was already snoring. It was almost dark outside but not yet five. She lay with the bedside lamp on, listening to his breathing and watching his face. His features were mobile, even in sleep; she kissed his cheek, and then the pulsing vein in his temple.

An hour or two later she woke again, feeling decidedly better and hungry again. He was still snoring. She switched on the radio by their bed, keeping the volume as low as possible, and listened to Jimmy Edwards and June Whitfield in *Take It from Here*, hoping he might wake soon but not wanting to disturb him. Having him there, but asleep, was worse than not having him there at all. He was absent, and she pined for his company. He emitted a louder snore, stirred and opened his eyes. He stretched, smacked his lips in an almost comical manner and then turned to look at her.

'Better!' he said, propping himself up on one elbow. 'I feel much better, don't you?'

'Mmm.'

He noticed that she had shed her nightdress and pulled the sheet away. She felt too tired to protest. He leant forward and very gently took one of her nipples into his mouth. 'Bernard!' she protested, 'we're too ill for that.' But his tongue triggered the network of nerves and blood and tissue that made her whole young body respond.

'Here, come a bit closer.' His presence was so warming. Soon they were enfolded together again.

'Don't let's be too active,' she said. She felt more tense than usual and dry, so that movement felt abrasive. She wanted him near, but did not want to move. 'Just try to keep still.' He lay, inert, and she ran both her hands slowly up and down his back, to his backside, backs of legs, up the insides of his thighs. They were both sweating heavily now, the virus still strong in them, and she could see, when she opened her eyes, that the vein in his temple was bulging with rapid, regular beats. She must keep him still, she did not want him to go away from her but could not bear for him to move inside her at all. As she caressed the back of his balls and cleft of his buttocks, he sighed and let out low, soft groans of pleasure. She pried a little more deeply and felt his legs relax more, palping the most intimate creases and wondering when he would stop her. His groans grew shorter, more ragged as he came. Then he began to withdraw, wanting to catch his breath, but she clamped her hands on his backside and pushed, bringing her knees up a little to keep all of him within her.

'Stay, please stay.' Often, she wished she could be like a man. Their pleasure was so obviously more intense than for women, and there was such a structure to it. No wonder they always wanted sex – she assumed all men were like Bernard. The anticipatory caressing when it was plain enough to see that a man was excited; the act itself, when he would go a little out of his mind as the crisis neared; the catharsis, after which he became so meek and so quiet. That was the moment she savoured. Sometimes she wondered whether there might not be more, something she was missing. But she supposed not. They lay coupled for some time, both dozing.

'Anna, I do love you!' Bernard murmured once, when their eyes met. His penis was still inside her, limp and numb, but she could feel it growing as he gazed into her eyes. Her pupils were dilated in the low light of the bed-side lamp. This time, he initiated a slow, rhythmic action. Lubricated from his previous climax and intoxicated by love for him, she felt relaxed and receptive. The move-ments gave her pleasure, a pleasure that increased with the speed of his thrusts, but still seemed to be leading nowhere, even when he yelped and barked his way through a second ejaculation.

After that they slept. It had been the first time she had not used her diaphragm but she knew that, sooner or later, they would have to start a family. Both wanted children and, now that Bernard was to receive a decent salary, today seemed as good a time as ever to make a start. Anna had not thought for a moment about the full weight of responsibility of having a child; merely that their family would not be complete until she had given birth.

By Christmas, when her period was nearly two months late, she suspected that she must have conceived on the night they had made love in the midst of their bout of flu. She got herself tested, merely to confirm what she already knew by instinct to be true, and then began to attend an antenatal clinic. By early April, her pregnancy was starting to show and her boss at University College asked her what her plans for the future might be. It was an obviously loaded question. There was no maternity leave in those days when employment was fairly full for men but women were, legally, paid less – even for doing identical jobs. It was clear to Anna that she would have to leave sooner or later, so perhaps sooner would be better.

As her pregnancy advanced, changes began to take place in her mind as well as her body. She was surprised to discover new opinions within herself and different attitudes, and began to feel that even the bedrock on which her character had been formed was starting to shift. Back in October when they had both been ill, there had been a horrible fire at the new atomic energy plant at Windscale, in Cumberland. The papers were full of the dangers of radioactive isotopes that had been released and might be found in milk from cows raised in the county – or anywhere else for that matter. Before her pregnancy, terms like iodine 131 and strontium 90 would have given nothing more than a mild frisson of unease – science fiction becoming actuality, but still more fiction-like than real – but now she quaked with terror, literally, as she read the reports. Unborn babies were apparently at risk. The whole idea of nuclear power and nuclear weapons began to obsess her and to terrify her but Bernard would laugh at her concern.

'Of course they're deadly things,' he would say. 'But that's what makes them such a wonderful deterrent. No one, but no one would ever be mad enough to use them.'

William's was a difficult birth, even for a first child. Weeks before, during a soggy, muggy June, Anna's blood pressure soared and she was forced to take bed rest. Pregnancy toxaemia caused her fingers and ankles to swell and nearer to confinement her skin began to tingle and itch. She was restless. She covered herself with lacto-calamine; she rubbed witch hazel on her hands and feet until Bernard was almost nauseated by the hard, metal-edged smell and the abrasive texture of her skin, made flaky with dried calamine. He moved into the single bed in the nursery room. She lost her appetite, living on tiny meals with arrowroot biscuits and lemon barley water to sustain her in between them. From time to time, Bernard ate out before coming home, partly to save her the trouble of having to cook and partly to ensure that he got himself a square meal. It would not have occurred to him to do any serious cooking for himself. As soon as they were married Anna had slipped into the role of housekeeper, and had continued in it, even when she had gone back to work. Now that she was too ill to want to eat much, he found himself with a more or less free hand, but had lost the will – and probably much of the skill he needed – to be able to prepare meals for himself.

Anna spent sixteen days in hospital recovering from her toxaemia. She had lost two stone and was seriously under-weight but her appetite had returned almost overnight, after the birth, and she was afraid that she might gain weight too fast and grow fat.

Now, sitting at her new word-processor, she wrote:

Bernard tried, very hard, to understand about postnatal depression but he found it difficult to cope with. And so did I. For absolutely no reason, I would suddenly find myself weeping. Unable to do a thing. Sometimes, I felt as though my vision was getting narrower and narrower so that my view was restricted by darkening shapes and I was only able see through a hole at the centre. And I felt so tired! Every morning when I woke before six and heard William whimpering for his first feed, I would try to make myself sleep again, willing Bernard to get up first, to change his stinking nappy and clean him up ready for me to nurse in bed. But Bernard never learnt how to change a nappy. Poor lamb, he was doing such killing hours at Jasper, Goldstone he hardly had time for domestic bliss.

I could not bear to breastfeed for long. I found it all so draining. When William was at my breast, I felt my life going out into him, along with my milk, and yet I could not bear being away from him. I was terrified, too, of what later came to be called Cot Death. Ralph had once told me that babies could die in their sleep for no apparent reason and that some of his colleagues, frustrated by an inability to diagnose, proposed a vicious theory that their mothers had smothered them. When he slept, I would hang over his crib for what seemed like hours at a time, making sure he was breathing. Babies can develop a terrifying greenish pallor when they are in deep sleep.

When William was taking his first steps, Anna managed to escape her depression, or, in Bernard's terminology, to 'snap herself out of her moodiness'. She considered returning to work, but by the time the baby was two Bernard's salary was big enough for them to consider buying something in the country.

'I've spotted a cottage,' he announced, arriving home later than usual one Friday evening in June. 'Eighteenth century. It's between Ashford and Maidstone.' They had both been down to Kent several times, partly to look for possible homes, and partly to get out of London at the weekends. Anna loved the bluebell woods in spring because they reminded her of parts of Norfolk, and she enjoyed the scenery further east, where hop gardens, apple orchards and market garden crops made the landscape look like one huge kitchen garden. But they had not made any specific plans, and had only talked about country properties in the loosest terms. As with every previous major move in their married lives, Bernard had taken the initiative. Anna was taken by surprise.

'How do you mean, "spotted"?'

'I took the afternoon off.' He was bubbling. She knew the signs: the restless pacing as he spoke, the absent fiddling with things around the kitchen. 'And I think I've seen exactly what we need. There's half an acre of garden with it, and a stream.'

'A stream?' She was alarmed. 'William could drown!'

'Not he!' He gave her a hug. 'We'll go and see it together, tomorrow. The owners will be away, but they've lent me a spare key.'

He drove them southeast, along the Maidstone road, William asleep in his child seat, in the back of their Austin A30. She was enchanted by the cottage. In Kentish tradition, the upper walls were hung with red tiles above mellowed brick lower walls. Two sash windows flanked the front door and there were two upper windows, slightly smaller, and two dormer windows set into the Kent peg tile roof. The front garden borders were weedy but colourful with summer perennials – lupins, red oriental poppies and cranesbills – and behind the house fruit trees shaded a second lawn, beyond which she spotted a well-ordered kitchen garden where rows of lettuce, potatoes, carrots and peas matured in the gentle sunshine.

'Bernard, it's absolutely *lovely*,' Anna said.

'I knew you'd like it.' He beamed at her. 'That's why I made an offer for it yesterday. It's ours, good as.'

She was taken aback. She was angry. 'Supposing I hadn't liked it?'

'Ah! But I knew you would.'
'But—'
'And you do, don't you?'
And she did. That was what made her so angry.

After San Francisco, the *Brisbane* would be at sea for
several days, steaming across the Pacific to Hawaii. Anna
had taken a while to get used to her computer, but now
felt she was becoming addicted to it. Each time she opened
the chocolate-box lid and looked at the blank screen, she
anticipated the kick it would give. When she pressed the 'on'
button and heard the muted minor chord it played while it
woke up its brain, the sound was as sharp and sweet a source
of pleasure as lighting a cigarette or swallowing the first
evening cocktail. The computer was her gateway, a threshold
that separated present reality from the unique landscape of her
own special past. Yet frequently, travelling the convoluted
highways of her memories made her miserable. Sometimes,
the recollections were so upsetting that she would abandon
her work altogether and sit weeping, as quietly as she could,
with cabin door locked and the blind pulled down over the
corner window. Occasionally, she experienced rage, rather
than sorrow, and then her tears were so bitter and so painful
that they might have been acid scoring furrows in her cheeks.
At other times, she simply felt regret and, as anyone of nearly
sixty with the normal range of human weaknesses, remorse.
Regret for all the wasted time; grief for those she had lost; a
longing – but for what? Her youth back? That was ridiculous,
merely a form of self-pity. For Bernard? Not possible. For
Verne? Not permissible. After such bouts, she would go up
to the Promenade Deck and stride round the length of the
vessel, lap after lap, four times round making one mile.
Once, in fierce heat she tramped three full miles, her face
and body running in sweat. No one seemed to notice her but
she bumped into Mrs Cabbage, as she still privately called
Sylvia Tanner.

'I say, dear, are you all right?'

'Never better,' Anna lied. 'I'm trying to get myself a bit fitter.'

'Well, don't overdo it, dear. You look ever so hot.' Anna had rounded the end of the stern and ducked downstairs, walking the whole length of C Deck before coming up again to her own deck using the stairway nearest to her cabin. The saving grace of a ship the size of the *Brisbane* was that you could run away.

Safely back inside her personal, private quarters, after such a foray, she would make herself switch the computer back on and force herself to edit what she had written, even the parts that had upset her so much. It was like jabbing a toothpick into the cavity of a decaying tooth. The pain was unbearable but when it faded there was a sense of remission. Or was it, she sometimes wondered, simply that aggravating the hurt made a variation, at least, in the constant undertow of misery?

She had to do her work for the writing class. Jack Pullen had warned them that he would expect them to prepare several pieces during this longish spell at sea.

After the first class since San Francisco, Jack Pullen caught up with Anna as she walked towards her cabin.

'How's the Mac doing?'

'Oh, it's wonderful. I'm quite used to it now.'

'Oh good, because I think it would be terrific if you could write me a couple of extra stories – or essays or whatever.'

'Well I'm quite involved with my—'

'Yeah, yeah. The memoirs.' He slowed his pace, forcing her to slow with him. 'But I'd really like it if you would do something.'

'Well, I'm not very inspired. and you seem so . . .'

'So critical?'

She did not reply. She certainly would not admit that his last lambaste would have annihilated her, had she been on the receiving end. He had ridiculed the one poet of their group, Elspeth Crampin, before the whole class. In tears, she had walked out for good and had later complained to the cruise director.

'You're thinking of that Crampin woman?' Anna nodded. 'But you're not like that. She thinks she's a poet. She's not. She's just a silly housewife with too grand a sense of art. You accept that you're not a writer, but you know you can become one. That's what makes you different.'

'I don't think one can *become* anything, at my age.'

'Humbug!' He tapped the papers she was carrying. 'Try something.'

'But I don't know what to write about.'

'Anything! Getting your computer. That must have been a memorable day.' In her mind's eye, Anna sensed a fleeting image, not of the computer store, but of the girl in the yellow dress, who had lain gentle fingers on her forearm, and of the crocodile of obedient schoolchildren. Just then, Ant and Cedric came, side by side, down the wide corridor towards Anna's cabin.

'Sucking up to teacher?' Cedric said. 'No wonder she gets brownie points.' Pullen looked uneasy as they approached

'Make sure you do it, OK?' he said to Anna, and walked briskly away.

'Not one to hang around, is he? Our macho man!' Ant said.

'Mutton dressed as lamb,' Cedric remarked, not bothering to lower his voice.

'Old cock dressed as chicken you mean,' Ant retorted. The departing Pullen may not have heard the remarks, but he certainly heard the raucous laughter and suspected that it was at his expense.

'Why Anna!' Cedric warned, after their mirth had faded, 'you're doing it again!'

'Sorry?' Anna looked concerned and confused.

'You're smiling!'

'Shut up, Cedric!' Ant's voice was sharp. 'Anna, come and have a pre-prandial.'

'No thank you,' Anna said, 'I've just had an idea and I want to jot it down. I'll see you at the buffet at one.'

With her head suddenly full of scenes, smells, sounds and

of the people she had seen in the Caribbean, she went into her cabin, switched on the computer and drummed the desktop with her fingers while she waited for it to boot up. By the time it was ready, the idea was making itself so urgent that her neck hairs were bristling and her fingers trembling. She created a new document which she called BREADNUT. Then she began to write. She had planned merely to note down the skeleton of plot that had half formed in her mind, but it was all so fresh and alive that the words tumbled out as finished prose while her fingers flew across the keyboard.

[BREADNUT]

In that he adored breadnuts, Clayton was exactly like his father; but that was where the resemblance ended. Physically, even at twelve, he was beginning to develop massive shoulders, short, sturdy legs and flat, square hands. His skin had the honey tones of a half-caste – even though Diva herself was pretty dark – and his eyes just the suggestion of an uplift at their corners, making them almost almond shaped. His father was tall, with smooth, purple-black skin, slender legs, arms like a gibbon and the fingers on his hands long and tapering. At cricket he was said to be the terror of the island, bowling slowly but with a viciously unpredictable spin. When he played his guitar, Diva loved to watch his fingers, moving swiftly, brushing across the strings, plucking, stroking as he worked a counterpoint to the blues songs that he sang, improvising words and the melodies.

Happy as she was, with her loving husband and sweet son, Diva was sometimes nagged by this shadow. How? Where did those eyes come from? Whence those chunky shoulders? And how was he made so pale? She stood waiting for her breadnuts at the corner of Church Street and Seneca, watching the islanders in Maintown drift through another day; watching the tourists flagging in the heat of the Caribbean sun, waiting for what? For a taxi back to comfort? For their cruise ships to slip away into the coolness of the turquoise ocean, scattering flying fish in their bow waves? For the rum punches on deck, the thrumming of dance bands under tropic skies? Diva sighed at the thought of all that luxury and wondered why the tourists always looked so unhappy.

At last, the breadnuts were boiled. 'How many you want?' Big Millie glanced up from her streetside stove. Diva raised three fingers. The older woman picked the nuts out deftly, avoiding burning her fingers on their hot skins.

The sound of children's voices – sharp cries, laughs, an underbrush of murmuring. The youngest ones at the head of the procession held hands. Some had forgotten to tuck their little blue shirts into navy shorts. Then the intermediate boys, more streetwise, followed by the elder kids, ready to move up in the world, all the wisdom of double-figure years but not one yet into his teens. Clayton was in the last pair, his face making a pale contrast with the skin of the boy on his right.

Anna glanced at her watch, horrified to see that it was already five past one. Quickly she jotted down the theme for the rest of her story and shut down her computer.

The buffet was rather crowded but she found the Boys, sitting at a table for four with a couple of elderly ladies from the cheaper cabins at the back of the ship. One wore a sun visor which threw a ghastly green shadow over her pancake make-up; the other had her hair in a towelling turban.

'No room! No room!' chorused the Boys.

'There's plenty of room,' said Anna, 'but I don't see the dormouse anywhere.' The old ladies exchanged puzzled glances.

'Well, I suppose you could move a chair over,' one of them said, without attempting to budge up. 'You might be able to squeeze in, just about.' Ant had already risen and snatched a vacant chair deftly from the path of a rotund man who was advancing with a laden tray.

'Excuse me, but I had already spotted that!' the man said, breathless and red, either from carrying so heavy a tray or from wielding his own bulk. 'Do you mind?' Ant held on firmly, ready to dispute possession on Anna's behalf.

'I'm not really very hungry,' she insisted. 'I'll get a fizzy water in a minute, and just perch.' With exaggerated politeness, Ant now placed the chair at the neighbouring table and held it for the man who put his tray down and without another word snatched it, banging it down so that he could sit facing away from them. Ant mouthed a silent kiss at the massive back.

'You missed the dolphins,' Cedric said, when he had returned from the bar, carrying an extra lager for Ant and a mineral water for Anna. He knelt on the deck, insisting that she have his seat. 'We've seen quite a few.'

'Look! Look!' Ant shouted, pointing to a spot in the clear, calm ocean. 'More! Over there.' Anna spotted a white foamy splash and fixed her eyes on the spot. Soon she saw three shapes leaping out of the water in formation, saw their grey tops, yellowish sides and their fins.

'Oh how lovely! I must watch for more. Do you mind if I go to a lower deck, to get closer?' She walked away from them as she asked and went down to the Promenade Deck where, for the next hour, she was fixed as if by bolts to the ship's rail, scanning the surface of the sea until her eyes stung. She had had no idea that there was so much wildlife visible in the oceans. She sighted a large turtle, which she thought was an old cardboard box until she identified four flippers and a carapace marked out in sections like paving. Dolphins came near the ship from time to time, and she was sure there were two different species, but she knew so little about them. She wondered why on earth she hadn't brought Charlie's binoculars. She had, after all, had custody of them for nearly half a century, preferring their chunky, solid feel to the very expensive lightweight pair Bernard had bought her for Christmas the year he got his Big Appointment. Eventually, her eyes could take no more of the glare, nor the salty wind, and she tore herself away from the rail, deciding to visit the ship's library in case there might be a reference book on sea creatures. It came to her, then, that she had not been birdwatching once since losing Bernard, and that, although she had spotted sea birds from time to time, following the ship, she had until now taken little interest.

In the library she found a welter of pulpy novels, several useful works on sea birds, over-designed gardening books by authors who had been guest lecturers on board; among these, obviously misfiled, she unearthed a lavish item that featured the larger sea creatures. Quickly, she flipped through the pages, taking in the huge illustrations and scanning some of the text, which seemed about right for her – neither too technical nor patronisingly simplified. She leafed back to the title page, uttered a little cry of distress that raised one or two heads, half hidden behind wing chairs at the other end of the library, and had to sit down. *Whales, Dolphins and their Allies in Color*, the title proclaimed, and there, in bolder print above the junior contributor's name, was the principal author, Verne Henschke.

There might be an author photograph but she dared not turn to the back fold of the dust jacket. Not in here. In spite of its being marked 'for reference only, please do not remove,' she took the volume to her cabin for closer inspection. It was difficult to tell much from a portrait less than two inches square. He looked different with hair that had not been cropped to the last half-inch but was long enough to allow a boyish wave to hang over the brow, but she recognised the lopsided half grin he used when tense or embarrassed – or being photographed. The picture blurred as her eyes filled with tears, but in her imagination she could hear his voice as clearly as if he were sitting beside her. 'Jeez, Anna, you smiled!'

PART TWO

CROSSING THE LINE

Chapter Seven

—·—

'I've got some rather extraordinary news,' Bernard said when he came home one afternoon in July to find William playing with his best friend, Dave, in the front garden of Forstal Cottage. Like any little boys brought up in the countryside, they were sun-kissed and energetic, William's olive complexion tanning more readily than Dave's fair, freckled skin. William had just celebrated his eighth birthday but his companion, whose dad was a barrister – determined, according to Dave, to become a QC before he hit the Big Four O – had almost a month to wait for his. Dave wasn't quite sure what the Big Four O was, but his dad seemed to spend rather a lot of time talking about it. The boys were enjoying the first day of the summer holidays and now raced each other to the front gate, blond head a whisker behind dark brown.

'Daddy! You're home early!' William said, breathless.

'We're going to live in America,' Bernard said.

'Are we? Can Dave come too?' Dave, the apple of William's eye, went rather red and looked concerned. He wasn't sure his mother would let him do anything like that, though he was pretty sure living in America would be more fun than the boarding school he might be going to in September. Anna had decided that eight was too young for William, who would go when he was nine, or perhaps ten. She was unsure about the whole principle of sending young children away to school but Bernard insisted that it was essential for building character and that, anyway, you couldn't buy a decent education at a day school.

She came out into the garden, startled to see him home during the working day, out of kilter, in his business suit, with the sun and flowers. 'What's all this? It's barely four o'clock.' She peered at his face with growing unease, recognising the signs. He was bubbling, ready to boil over like potatoes on a hob.

'Mummy! Mummy!' William yelled. 'We're going to live in America.'

'Are we?' She stood with her hands by her side, feeling awkward while three pairs of eyes – male eyes, in assertive faces – watched for her reaction. He'd let out something as big as this to their child, to their child's friend, before he had even consulted her. She looked at her garden, noting the results of hour upon hour of loving labour – her labour. Are we? The borders were arranged with bloom and foliage to give lasting delight, winter and summer. She had furnished the house walls, below the hung tiles, with climbing plants: several kinds of clematis, a yellow banksian rose whose button blooms sometimes opened for Easter, honeysuckles and a fragrant summer jasmine. She glanced back, seeing the kitchen garden in her mind's eye, raspberries in mid-harvest, tidy rows of greens maturing for autumn. On the hall table, just inside the front door, a large cut-glass vase held a huge bouquet of sweet peas, their sugary fragrance blending with darker tones of beeswax furniture polish and dried lavender. She could smell those smells, as she stood on the threshold, blending with the scents of the summer garden. She could see the house martins and swallows weaving arcs through the summer sky over the roof ridge. Above them, swifts flew faster, screaming as they hurled themselves through the narrow openings into St Mildred's church tower to feed their young. In a week or two, the swifts would go south, long before the nights became chilly. When Bernard had announced their move from London she had never questioned coming here, had never sought this kind of life, but she had taken to it at once. The village, the soil, the climate all suited her well. She knew that Bernard would want to move on, to move up in the world – he was too clever and too ambitious not to – but so soon? And abroad? To America? That could mean anywhere, from Cape Horn to Baffin Bay. Are we indeed? The hurt of not being part of the decision made her eyes smart. She felt angry and afraid, but she noticed the excitement on the faces of the two little boys. 'Are we, indeed?' she said aloud, making a big effort to brighten her voice.

Bernard was too excited to notice her reaction. 'It's quite amazing,' he said, 'but I've been invited to join the faculty of Purlin University. You know I've been putting feelers out for a professorship, now that I've done my stint in the real world. And, well, as you know, I had lunch with Jocelyn the other day, at Cambridge.'

'Did you? I didn't know.'

'Really? I thought I'd told you.' He paused for a moment. 'I could have sworn I'd told you. Anyway. The deal is: I fly out next week, to finalise things, then if all goes well – which I know it will – we can move out there in August, ready for the beginning of the semester in September.'

'*This* September?'

'What? Well, of course this September.'

'But it's July now.'

'Purlin is absolutely beautiful, I'm told.'

'But what about here?'

'This house? Ooh, sell it, I should think. The market's nice and buoyant now. We could get as much as five thousand for it, five and a half if we found the right buyer.' These words were tossed out, impatiently, before he returned to his news. 'It's a permanent appointment. With tenure, we could be there for the rest of our lives.' He came closer, was surprised by the rigidness of her body and added, more gently, 'But only if we both wanted to.'

*   *   *

The rather imperious woman from land agents Galahad Stamp
had visited Anna to value the property and given what she
hoped was some constructive criticism on her housekeeping
and even her gardening. 'Bung in a few extra bedding plants,
for colour,' she had said, 'and above all, remove every
scrap of evidence that there are children here.' She had
recommended that they hold out for £5,750. Being national,
Galahad Stamp took a bigger commission than local agents
in Maidstone might have done, 'But,' said the woman, who
looked as though she went fox-hunting at least twice a week,
'we have direct access to the *right* people.' A quick sale was
almost assured, she claimed, particularly of a property with
such natural assets. There wasn't time to erect a sign board by
the small wicket gate before the first wave of viewers arrived.
The cottage was sold for its asking price within eleven days
of contacting the agents.

New York was filthy. After the quiet, ordered life in Kent,
Anna felt she had landed in a city that seemed to have lost its
head. People were noisy and rude. Police sirens screamed,
the traffic was frantic, shop windows were tacky and badly
dressed – even those of the famous Fifth Avenue stores –
and the streets felt unsafe. She was too jolted to be able to
see through the frenetic chaos of the city and realise that
out of this neurosis grew a surplus of creative energy; that
among the violence and din was a mind-stretching polyglot
mix of cultures, races, values, religions. All she could sense
was noise and aggression. Kent was picturesque, New York
picaresque. New York was churningly, violently alive; Kent
was gently, genteelly moribund. Her reactions to the first
American city she had experienced, and therefore to the
whole of the USA, were unfavourable, and they were to
stay that way for some time.

Purlin University, founded by Joshua Purlin in 1865, was
considered to be one of the top institutions, comparable with
Harvard, Princeton and Cornell. Purlin, the man, had had the
arrogance typical of his century to think that he could create,

within his lifetime, a university with the stature of Oxford or Cambridge simply by finding the right spot, importing the best ideas from Europe and stocking his libraries with the choicest books. No doubt he confused encrusted traditions with greatness, but unlike those ancient universities, where admissions were based on patronage rather than scholarship, Purlin's entry requirements were almost too simple: potential students needed nothing other than to be in earnest pursuit of academic distinction. A single word, carved into the granite plinth of Joshua Purlin's statue in the central quad of the original campus, represented the essence of those founding aims – 'EXCELLENCE'.

The university, when the Morfeys arrived in 1965, had long since surpassed its European counterparts. In the sciences, particularly medicine, computer technology and atomic research, achievements at Purlin were reshaping the vanguard of world discovery. Some of the most distinguished names in literature and the arts had chairs there and as many potential lawyers wanted to qualify at Purlin as at Harvard.

Architecture, of the earliest buildings, was classical European, with mansard roofs and columned porticoes on the arts quadrangle. Male students resided in a neo-Gothic complex, designed and laid out like Oxford colleges, and there was an undergraduate library that boasted a campanile which added an Italianate touch. The campanile – known as Library Tower – was equipped with a carillon that clanged out melodies every morning, noon and evening. Sometimes these were patriotic tunes: 'America the Beautiful', or 'My Country 't'is of Thee'; sometimes university songs: 'Purlin, we greet Thee!' and occasionally the selection was whimsical. On the dawning of Anna's first day on campus the bells played 'Knees up Mother Brown' followed by something from *La Traviata*.

The campus itself lay close to Lake Kanantuka, a fifty-mile ribbon lake – one of half a dozen similar bodies of water that filled the glaciated valleys, radiating like the fingers of an outstretched hand, their tips thrusting into the high ground of the Allegheny Plateau near the Pennsylvania border, their bases resting on the plains just to the south of Lake Ontario. Each of these lakes carried its own town or city: Watkins Glen, on Seneca, was home of the American Grand Prix; Ithaca, with that other great institution, Cornell University, lay at the finger end of Cayuga and, by Lake Kanantuka, Purlin sat high on the hill above the town of Minorca. Terrain around the campus was rugged, sliced by deep, rocky gorges with tree-clad hills and smaller valleys in between. Rivers were swift, tumbling over falls and rapids in this landscape, but there were low-lying areas too, with smaller lakes, rich green pasturage, swamps and forests. This was dairy country in the sixties, a region where farmsteads were marked by tall, dome-topped tower silos, red Dutch-style hay barns and herds of black-and-white Holstein-Friesian cattle. Farmers who did not milk cows grew apples – not the sharp-tasting, dull-coloured fruits that Anna was used to from Kentish orchards, but vivid red, crisp varieties that snapped when bitten into and whose juice (known locally as cider, even when not fermented) was as sweet as if ready sugared. Country people in upstate New York were slow of speech, calm and deliberate of action with simple tastes, a largely Lutheran respect for God and their fellow folk, but a deep fear of outsiders, most of whom they understood to be Communists.

But the university society, which spilled from the campus into Collegeville and on into downtown Minorca, was wholly different: a blend of frenetic New York City culture with a strong Jewish accent and a range of academic spheres as varied and jumbled as buttons in a dressmaker's workbasket. Nobel Prize-winning physicists, world authorities on genetics and eminent archaeologists would mingle with specialists in agribusiness or professors of hotel administration. Campus chatter was full of science, sex, political posturing – with a surprisingly subversive undercurrent – idealism, pedantry or just plain gossip. All these brainy people lived in a wholly unreal world, removed, literally elevated because of Purlin's altitude, from the rest of life. If you belonged it was a heady, happy existence. You glowed in the heat of so much brain power, despite the terrible weather in such cold, cold country; you drank deeply from the clear-water stream of knowledge that flowed so freely down that hill, and you got drunk on it. But if you did not belong, if you were a wife or a camp follower, it was difficult not to be locked out in the cold. You had to have a subject, or, if you had no subject, you had to find some other reason for your membership of the campus circus. Working in student welfare might do the trick, or having some business or activity that connected you directly with the university. Anna, within days of arriving at Minorca, NY, realised that she did not belong and, worse, could find no way in; but Bernard, fresh, novel and chic with his English accent and crazy ideas, was absorbed into the heart of campus society within hours of his arrival at the economics department.

Remembering how she felt in this strange new environment, Anna wrote:

That autumn seemed to go on forever. Day after leafy day of unbroken sunshine picking out the fall colours – crimson, gold, vermilion – against a sky more blue, more clear than I had ever seen, even in Norfolk. Daytime heat was intense, compared with England, but each night seemed a little colder than the one before until, morning after morning, the grass outside our apartment building was white with frost that wouldn't melt until coffee time.

Compared to Kent, life on campus was busy. There were films to go to and concerts – the world's top artists invariably included Purlin in their itineraries – and almost always a choice of parties. Yet I had never felt so lonely or so isolated.

When the first snows fell at the beginning of November, I thought it a freak occurrence. But snow was to lie on the ground for another seven months, and for four of those seven the outdoor temperature did not rise above freezing point at all, day or night.

Anna had hoped that her Chanel winter coat would suffice for Purlin, but the cold penetrated the durable tweed within minutes of going out into the night air. Cold attacked her knees as she walked. Frosty pincers nipped her ears, making every inch of her cranium ache and the frozen air stung in her nostrils. She realised that she and Bernard would need to equip themselves with heavy ski jackets, hats, scarves, gloves and, most important of all, woollen headbands or muffs that would protect the ears against frostbite. For William, Bernard purchased a little fur-lined leather trapper hat with ear protectors that could be flipped up and secured by laces over the crown. Anna gave him mitts to match.

Rather than queue in the buffet, Anna decided to take breakfast in the dining room. The sound of a vacuum cleaner outside reminded her that Tony would want to come in to tidy up her cabin before his period of duty ended. She emerged at almost exactly the same moment as Cedric and Ant.

'Good morning, Anna dear!' they chimed in chorus, raising their voices above the sound of the vacuum.

'Just look at him.' Cedric jabbed a thumb at Ant, drowsy-eyed, but dressed in tracksuit bottoms and a sweatshirt, a small towel round the neck, tucked in like a comforter. 'Athletic or what?'

'Out of breath already,' Ant muttered. They enacted a slow jogging action, as if they had run for miles.

'Off to gentlemen's keep fit,' Cedric said. 'Fifteen minutes daily exercise – we've signed on for the rest of the cruise.'

'I give it three days!' Ant called, as they both left the court. 'A week, tops.'

While Anna was locking her cabin, the opposite door opened to reveal the drunk, dressed this time in what had once been fashionable beachwear: canary-yellow shorts, grey and yellow shirt – spoilt by food stains down the front – grey cap in matching material. He was obviously crapulous, but whether from the previous night or from an early morning tipple she couldn't be sure. The eyes that regarded her were jaundiced and suffused with shattered blood vessels but behind the rheumy, boozer's stare there was, she was sure, sensitivity and suffering. What was his history? Why did he need to damage himself so? She knew that they shared an unwillingness to take the world at face value. She needed to shun it for long periods, losing herself in her past, because that was more palatable than her future; he needed to soften the abrasive edges of his life with a cushion of alcohol. Bernard had never been a drinking man. She liked her wine at night and occasionally had a lunchtime gin and tonic which she would nurse for as long as possible, telling herself she quite enjoyed the sly feeling of guilt that accompanied the alcoholic flush. How awful that she had been travelling with this man as her neighbour for more than three weeks but didn't even know his name. She tried to compose a smile but couldn't quite manage.

'I have asked you before to keep it down,' he said.

'I don't think we were making an unreasonable noise. It is almost nine-thirty.'

'*I* was trying to sleep.'

'That's what you said last time,' Anna replied. 'But then it was afternoon, and you were somewhat less formally dressed.' She wasn't sure why she said that – possibly as an overture to better understanding – but he turned, without a word, entered his cabin and slammed the door so hard that all the bulkheads on his side of the court shook. Anna wished she had made a more gentle overture.

Down in the dining room she ate a small piece of smoked haddock, a half-slice of toast and drank two cups of coffee before going on deck, determined to walk at least two miles. The blue of the Pacific Ocean, she told herself, was more intense, and more pure than the Atlantic, but it was not half as peaceful as its name implied. They had been travelling into a strongish headwind for two days, since leaving San

Francisco, and although the weather had since calmed there was still enough swell to keep the *Brisbane*'s decks on the move. Aft of the stern rail, soaring, dipping and gliding above the wake of the ship, were several species of sea bird. On their first day out from the American coast, a sizable flock had trailed the ship but, as the distance from land increased, their numbers had diminished, leaving only the strongest flyers to follow the ship for mile after mile. The largest of these was a wandering albatross, a species with a wingspan so vast, but so fragile-looking, that she could not imagine how it could possibly land, or, for that matter, get airborne in the first place. There were smaller, darker species too, but none had the grace of the wandering albatross. When it flew close to the stern rail, she could discern its longish, hooked bill and cruel, searching eyes.

She walked for almost an hour, lingering at the stern on every round to watch the birds, before going back to her computer.

Chapter Eight

The American winter seemed to last for ever. I hoped that when we moved into 604, Tudor Avenue, the weather might have warmed up, but the ground still froze every night, even during April, and I had never before felt so bored or so low. Bernard's enthusiasm for everything made me feel worse for letting him down. Nothing seemed to dim his sparkle, not even the rise of Socialism in Britain.

'The Wilson mob can't last,' Bernard told her. 'They still haven't acknowledged the importance of private capital. Who do they think is going to invest when the rewards are so heavily taxed? And what's the good, if you can't get your money out of the country?' Labour had just been re-elected with an overall majority in the House of Commons of almost a hundred seats. Bernard, considering the country of his birth to have declined beyond redemption, had wanted to move his own capital to New York to help them to buy the modest clapboard house he had spotted just after Christmas on Tudor Avenue, in Collegeville. It had a roomy back yard, about sixty feet by eighty, which he presumed Anna would want to turn into a garden. The front, which sloped sharply down to street level, consisted of a grassed area which ran along the fronts of all the houses and was furnished with specimen trees in small groups. There were hickories, blue cedars, hemlock spruces, a stand of sugar maples and a huge old Indian bean tree. The mummified cylindrical bean fruits were still hanging on its spreading branches when the Morfeys moved into their new home on a bitingly cold Saturday at the beginning of April.

Anna was astounded that the American winter could last so long. The first buds on the big magnolia at Forstal Cottage would be opening now, she thought, looking through her new bedroom window across the snow-covered grass to the salted slush being churned by morning traffic moving up Tudor Avenue to the campus.

North America suited Bernard perfectly. He found the dramatic climate exhilarating and he exulted in the American worship of private enterprise. He had been invited to Purlin to stir up the Economics department, and had been surprised at how old-fashioned some of the thinking had become. Collective wisdom across the country in those days was, he felt, more than thirty years out of date. In a former generation, economists and politicians had tried to find a way out of the trough of depression that had begun so suddenly in 1929, but no one had succeeded until John Maynard Keynes had recommended government spending as the key to renewed growth. Even as late as the sixties, memories of that grinding period of stagnation in Western economies were still too fresh, in American minds, to be discounted. Bernard was convinced that the West had escaped from the spiralling trap of the thirties' Depression for wholly different reasons – largely because of the War, rather than from the Keynesian policies adopted by most of the free world. His mission was to reduce government interference in commerce and to restore the old eighteenth-century model of an 'invisible hand' regulating enterprise by the simple laws of supply and demand. Although the great majority of academics were Democrats and found his views politically to their right, he was, to say the least, a refreshing voice, coming as he did from a continent that seemed to them to be losing its way. He began to receive speaking invitations all over the country and, with his charismatic deliveries and persuasive style, had become quite a celebrity during that first winter. Twice, he appeared on national network television, startling even the most reactionary audiences by deploring the current policies of the Democrats and of Lyndon Johnson, and reminding viewers of their own history.

But Bernard's successes increased Anna's isolation. His work at Purlin was demanding enough, particularly as he was also developing ideas for a new text book, but on top of that he was becoming increasingly committed to travel all over the country. When he was at home, he was so busy he seemed hardly to have time to do more than greet her, eat and sleep. When he'd been away, he returned exhausted and would have a quick shower before crashing out and sleeping from early evening until late next morning.

'I'm going to Washington after the weekend. Why don't you come?' he had asked when he came back to Tudor Avenue, late, from the department. 'I'm told the cherries will be in flower down there.'

'Who will look after William?'

'Other wives travel. They have kids.' Bernard downed his single homecoming Martini and moved to his desk, ready to work through the day's post. 'Dana's coming with me and bringing Evelyn. Their kid stops over with friends when they go away. And vice versa. That's how it works, on campus.'

'William hasn't been here long enough to have many friends yet.'

'Anna, really! If he's been here long enough to grow an American accent, he's had time to make friends.' Every time William called her 'Mom', pronouncing the word with a prolonged, drawling vowel, she felt she had deprived him of his English heritage.

'Darling, don't say "djawanna?" when you mean "do you want to?" Anyway, "would you like to?" sounds better. More polite.'

'But Mom! If I talk like that, the kids'll laugh at me.' He had begged her to exchange his grey British school clothes

for checked, open-necked shirts, denim jeans and a maroon
ski jacket. Finally, after weeks of persuasion, she had given
in and allowed him to have his hair cut like a nail brush, flat
across the top of the scalp, so that when she cuddled him the
bristles felt alien under her hands.

Anna's reticence about travelling with Bernard wasn't
really because of William, but because she was homesick.
In the few weeks since they had moved in, she had tried to
make the small, weatherboarded house on Tudor Avenue as
Kentish as she could. It was her tiny refuge, a little piece of
England abroad, and the idea of leaving it for more than a
short time upset her.

William did have friends, plenty of them. They all called
him Bill, told him he talked like the Beatles, even hero-
worshipped him. Anna would make them heaps of peanut
butter and jelly sandwiches, trying not to gag at the combination, and they'd say, 'Gee, thanks, Mrs Morfey! Do you
have any sodas?'

'Sodas? Um, I'm not sure.'

'They mean fizzy drinks, Mummy, I mean, Mom.'

The first time William brought his chums home and
explained to his mother what they wanted to eat, she put
dairy butter as well as peanut butter on the bread but said she
had not made any jelly that day. This had caused a puzzled
silence among the little boys who knew that you did not make
jelly but that it came in small jars from the supermarket, and
they sat, round-eyed, at the kitchen bench waiting for her
to talk some more so that they could hear her accent until
one said, 'Oh, you mean Jello!' Frequently he came back
from school with a gaggle of them, and as frequently he
trotted from one home to another, around Tudor Avenue
and on the other side of the gorge that sliced Collegeville
in two. There was a foot suspension bridge not far from
the house which bounced and swayed unnervingly as you
crossed, but which had a safe, high railing along either side.
She hoped she could trust him to run about at large on
his own.

Bernard arranged his opened correspondence in neat piles. 'Couldn't he stay over with, what's his name? Buck?'

'Chuck. It means Charles, apparently.' She went into their small kitchen to check on the simmering vegetables and raised her voice fractionally to carry through. 'I don't feel I know Mrs Hartmann well enough to ask.'

'For heaven's sake, she only lives next door but three!' He came into the kitchen. 'She wouldn't hesitate to ask you. It's so much more free and easy over here than at home. Why not give it a go? I'll call Nan Hartmann if you like.' Why did he say 'call' and not 'phone' or 'ring'? And why did he think he could call her Nan when they'd hardly met?

Anna found the casual approach to friendship among adults disconcerting. Within a short time of moving into the house she had received a succession of visits, first from the nearest neighbours, most of whom seemed to be of a similar age and all of whom were dependent upon the university for their income. Later other faculty wives would drop in, take casual coffees in the kitchen, suggest bridge parties, lunch dates and so forth. They found her quiet, a little distrait, incredibly tensed up and reserved, even for an English person. She had begun to dread cocktail parties and dinner engagements – there were many that year, it being the Purlin Centenary. People would walk right up to you and blurt out their names without the slightest hint of deference. They wondered why she seemed so shy at introducing herself, why she tended to stand in the quietest part of the room, if not exactly scowling, at least looking unhappy. So, while Bernard politely flirted with the women and indulged in playful intellectual sparring matches with the men, she would withdraw, or would speak to no more than a couple of guests, giving mechanical answers to their polite questions.

'Maybe I'll come later, Bernard. On another trip.' She was standing not by the stove but in front of the bulletin board reading her chore list for the following day. He stood behind her and put his arms round her waist, and realised that she was not looking at her list but at a small photograph, pinned to the cork with a yellow-headed tack. The picture was of the back of Forstal Cottage, where they had set up a small terrace with outdoor table and chairs. She and William stood, in the picture, by the back door, she holding a bunch of roses, he a freshly picked lettuce, big enough to cover his front from chin to bare, knobbly knee. He must have been six when Bernard had snapped the shot. Bernard turned her, gently, away from the board and kissed her. A pan on the stove boiled over and she had to pull herself away to take it off the heat

'Smells good!' Bernard said.

'Roast lamb. With new potatoes, broccoli and courgettes, except that they call them zucchinis. You can't get purple-sprouting broccoli here, not like . . . well.' The kitchen garden at Forstal Cottage, vivid in her mind, would be luxuriant with emerging spring crops of carrots, spinach and the first radishes. The new occupants might still be picking purple broccoli sprouts, if they had looked after the plants – plants that she had grown, from seed sown the previous April. Anna sighed. 'Could you call William?'

'He likes to be called Bill now.'

'I know. But I can't . . . I just can't . . .' She felt tears coming. She fought them. She really had to stop being so selfish, especially when Bernard was doing so very well and when William seemed so incredibly happy. And as long as she had the two of them, she should not be so . . .

He held her again, kissed the top of her head. 'I know it's difficult for you. I know you're missing home like hell. But you'll come round.' He kissed her again. 'I know you will.'

She stayed still, needing his embrace, smelling the traces of tobacco on his jacket, the slight touch of gin on his breath from his one Martini. His nearness was calming. 'It's this climate. It seems to be so cold for so long. Even the snow's lost its whiteness.'

'Come to Washington.'

'Do you *have* to go?'

He thought for a moment. 'Yes, I'm afraid I do.'

*   *   *

Suddenly it was spring. A few days after Bernard's trip to Washington, Anna opened her curtains to see rain falling and the avenue awash. Areas of green grass had already emerged in front of the house where snow, worn thin and made grey by wind-blown grime, had thawed at speed. She was puzzled by a roaring sound, different in pitch from the usual hiss of traffic-wet streets, and realised that it came from the gorge. Standing on the parapet of the avenue bridge, looking down a hundred feet, she could see the stream at the bottom swollen and yellow-brown with rushing water. An uprooted tree, quite a large one, came tumbling down the river bed as she watched, getting lodged between two rocky outcrops and almost upended on its way to the lake a couple of miles downstream. By the end of the day the rain had stopped, the sun had shone and the snow had melted from all but the most shaded areas. The torrent in the gorge roared all night and all next day.

By the weekend the grass had begun to grow and she noticed tiny wild crocuses emerging in the turf under the maples by their garage. Each night it still froze with sharper frosts than one might expect in a Kentish winter but by lunchtime the weather was warm enough for shirtsleeves, and by mid-afternoon the south-facing grassy slopes of the Purlin campus would be littered with students, stripped off to the waist, showing their winter pallor to the sun. Knee-length madras cotton shorts became campus fashion for both sexes, worn with black loafers and white socks. Bolder students, following the hippy movement, abandoned footwear altogether and wore cut-off jeans ragged with shredded leg-bottoms, untrimmed beards and shoulder-length hair.

Lyndon Johnson was escalating the Vietnam War. Unrest, driven by fear, was growing on every university campus in every state. Draft cards were being burnt. Student rallies and demonstrations were constantly being organised: about the civil rights movement in the Southern states, about apartheid in South Africa, about anti-semitism in the USSR, but above all about the war in Vietnam. They wanted it stopped. As soon as they had their degrees, male students would be called up to serve in the forces, almost certainly to fight in Southeast Asia. At eighteen plus they were expected to die for Uncle Sam, but were not entitled to vote or, in some states, to drink alcohol. Elder generations, fearful of alien domination, were convinced that young minds were being polluted by a huge, unseen, but deeply feared Communist fifth column. Many regarded the young as traitorous or, at the very least, unpatriotic. But the students knew the war to be wholly immoral and unjust, and underpinned their opposition with a healthy dose of the survival instinct.

'Anna, we're invited to a happening,' Bernard said, when he called at the house in the middle of the day to grab a sandwich and collect a couple of books that he'd left behind that morning.

'A happening?'

'A party. Tonight!'

'Tonight?'

'In the English Garden behind the students' union building.'

She decided to wear her woollen plaid skirt, fearing the evening temperature drop, and a cream turtleneck sweater with a simple gold chain on the outside. They were among the first to arrive and were admitted to the garden through a small door – usually locked – in the stone wall that ran up to the students' union building. She had not seen the English Garden before, but had been told of its existence, and had imagined a layout with groomed lawns, formal flower beds and, probably, a summerhouse. But this was more intimate and more charming than she could possibly have imagined. At its northern end was a small area of longish grass, made thin by the shadow of the building on one side, and by tree-thrown shade on the other. The grass bordered some rather chaotic rockwork, planted with alpines, where a serpentine path traced a convoluted route before passing through the trees to return to the green area. A brisk walker would be able to complete the whole route in less than a

minute, but here was a place to linger. Wood anemones –
both blue and white – oxlips, sweet violets and scillas were
flowering in patches here and there, interspersed with North
American woodland flora: brownish trilliums, Dutchman's
breeches and false spikenard. Bernard gave the garden a
perfunctory glance, but was soon locked into an intense
discussion with a graduate student who helped to run the
college radio station. While the other guests arrived, Anna
lingered among the spring flowers beneath the trees, bending
every now and then to look at a bloom more closely, even
trying to stoop low enough to see whether the violets here
were as strongly scented as in the woods in Kent. A voice,
close and just above, startled her.

'When daisies pied and violets blue,' it recited, in warmish
Pennsylvanian tones, 'And lady-smocks all silver-white . . .'
She glanced up and found herself overshadowed by a tall man
with a pale complexion, his hair close-cropped and blond. She
might have been repelled by the lack of colour in his skin and
hair but there was a sensitivity, perhaps a sensuousness, in
his features and a look in his eyes – possibly caused by the
dilation of the pupils in the gathering twilight – that stirred
her. His upper lip was fractionally larger than the lower, and
although it did not pout she found its fullness alluring. In
each large hand he carried a glass of white wine. One he
offered to her. 'Do I go on?' She nodded. With an American
accent, Shakespeare sounded alien. Or did it? The music was
still in the words, even though he said cooh-cooh, instead of
cuckoo. 'And cooh-cooh-buds of yellow hue do paint the
meadows with delight, the cooh-cooh then, on every tree,
mocks married men, for thus sings he . . .' He stopped.
Offered the glass in his right hand. 'You are Anna, I believe,
and this is your favourite tipple.'

'How did you know?' She took the glass.

'The wine?' She shook her head. 'Your name? I asked your
husband over there, and I knew you liked white wine because
I noticed you were drinking it last week, at the Pablo Casals
reception.'

'We didn't meet there. I'm afraid I don't . . .'

'Of course you don't! I'm Verne. Verne Hench Key. H-E-N-S-C-H-K-E.'

'Are you to do with economics?'

'Biology. That's why I came over. Bernie tells me you're a bird fanatic.'

'Bernie? Oh, Bernard!' The correction sounded like a snub. She didn't mean it to. 'Yes, I suppose I am.' As if on cue, there was a strange sound above, like traffic that had suddenly become airborne and was honking quietly as it went. They both looked up. 'Canada geese,' she said. 'Of course! They're really wild here – not like at home.'

'We're on their migration route.' He had noticed how her eyes had lit up. 'They rest on Kanantuka for a day or two at a time, and then move on north, to Canada. They'll have overwintered in Florida.'

'I do so love waterfowl. We had huge flocks of Brent geese near my childhood home in Norfolk. They come flocking into the salt marshes, to feed throughout winter. Then they too go north for summer.'

'So you *are* a birdwatcher,' Verne said.

'From childhood.'

'But that's great!' Verne said. 'And I wanna be the first person to show you our American species. But first,' he took her elbow and nursed her along the last bends of the garden path to the main group of people, 'first I want for you to meet some of the other members of our department.' She wasn't to know, until months later, that when Verne had expressed an interest in her to Bernard, he had suggested that they should get together.

'I'd be so grateful, er, Verne, if you would chat to my wife about birds and things. She's finding it a bit hard to settle here, and needs, you know, sort of bringing out of herself, if you see what I mean.'

Besides talking to Verne that evening she suddenly found herself at the centre of attention. 'Folks,' Verne kept saying. 'You *have* to meet Anna.' He pronounced her name with a fractional lengthening of the first syllable. 'Ah-nna is the bee's knees on Briddish birds!' Several guests, not only members of the biology department, turned out to be keen birdwatchers and some had been to Britain and murmured about memorable trips to Scotland, to the Isles of Scilly and to her native Norfolk. But soon the subject matter broadened, crisscrossing boundary after boundary and this time taking her along with the flow. They were almost the last to leave.

As they walked back across the campus to Collegeville, Bernard was surprised at how animated she was.

'I'm going to do some teaching,' she said.

'You haven't any training.'

'I know. But this is voluntary work. I'm going to teach – or rather, I'm going to coach – children with special needs. It's a voluntary service, organised by Penny Greenbaum.'

'The geologist's wife? Dumpy woman with hair like a haystack?'

'Mmm.'

'Splendid.' Then later, after they had walked on in silence for a while, 'Good party!'

'First one I've enjoyed since we've got here.'

'Are they still as awful as you first thought? Americans, I mean?'

'I never said they were awful.' She tightened her grip on his hand and moved a little closer to him, adjusting her step to his. 'Oh, and that biology chap, Verne. He's going to take me birdwatching next Thursday, to Grackle Wood. You won't mind, will you?'

'Mind? My darling girl of course I won't mind.' Bernard felt the small fingers twitch in his hand. 'I'm just delighted you've found something nice to do.' He was so relieved that she had, at last, shown signs of emerging from months of moody introspection that he failed to pick up the very faintest twinge of unease she had felt in telling him. 'I'll be in Maryland, as you know.'

Chapter Nine

'I *must* work,' Anna declared, alone in her cabin. 'I *must* be
. . . honest.' The first words were almost shouted; the last
were *sotto voce* because of a sudden fear of being overheard
by someone outside. Sometimes she heard whispered voices
in the court and occasionally the smell of cigarette smoke
filtered under her door. She had two more full days at sea
before the *Brisbane* docked at Honolulu. Two days in which
to . . . what? Trivialise her life by tapping down a few
chosen events into her new toy? Her writing, she knew,
was becoming more fluent, her style more relaxed, but she
still felt incapable of getting what she *really* felt down on
disk, to transmogrify the pain, and the joy of experience,
into words on a piece of paper. 'I have to get to grips
with America,' she told herself. Through the porthole, the
sea formed itself into moving ranges of small mountains
and valleys, as dark and blue and sparkling as sapphires,
their summits occasionally capped with white. 'I must be
honest,' she repeated, a whispered commitment that made
her pulse quicken and her breathing accelerate. 'However
difficult that might be. Totally honest.' Her computer had
switched itself off while she mused – it did that sometimes
– and she turned it on again, soothed by the confident chord
it chimed while cranking itself up for work. Transporting
herself back three decades to upstate New York took more

effort, but gradually the present scenery faded and she began to type.

> The walk in Grackle Woods, that spring, opened my eyes to the beauty of the North American landscape. After the scruffy streets of Collegeville, the confined feeling of Minorca's suburban avenues and Purlin's campus, where I had felt so locked out, the countryside had an alluring beauty. The woodland floor was white with wild trilliums, known as 'wake-robin' – thousands of three-petalled blooms, creating a white carpet as far as the eye could see. Here and there, where the bedrock broke the surface, grew columbines – unlike the blue European species, these had red and yellow flowers with long, graceful spurs behind the petals. The first bird I spotted, through Charlie's binoculars, was a cardinal. It seemed impossible for a bird to be so red, so artificial-looking, and yet be a truly wild species. Later we saw the female, dowdy compared with her mate, but with a reddish suffusion in her brown feathers, as if the brilliance might be there, underneath, but had to be kept concealed. The cardinals had built a nest in one of the outermost trees of the wood.

Anna wanted to keep on writing about the natural history of the woodland because she knew that the next part of her narrative was going to be difficult. She played with the computer for a while, making it count words and spell. But at last she typed:

> The ending of that interminable winter may have helped to lift my spirits, but it was really Verne who brought spring into my life.

Anna sat staring at this sentence for a full five minutes while the recollections began to arrange themselves in her mind. She tried to push emotion out of her thought patterns, and to record her story in cold, hard facts. After reading the sentence once more she deleted the passage and began again.

Verne surprised me by arriving alone. He had planned to bring a couple of students – he had several keen birdspotters among his biology majors – but when he arrived, driving an open British sports car, I realised that it would have been well nigh impossible for anyone else to fit into the tiny vehicle.

'Anna!' Instead of opening the door of his Triumph, Verne leapt out as if he were jumping off a boat. Anna had forgotten how tall he was. 'The kids dropped out of the trip. Finals coming up in two weeks has scared them into studying. Dare you go alone with this man into the woods?'

'Do I have a choice?' Was she glad they'd be just two? Why did her warm feeling hide a background of unease, especially with Bernard away in Maryland? He wore pale, drill slacks and a dull greenish-brown shirt made from soft cotton, two buttons open at the neck. His clothes were old, but clean and comfortable, making him look more human than in the professorial tweed sports jacket he had worn at the party in the English Garden. Anna had opted for jeans and one of Bernard's old city shirts which she had once tried to dye maroon, but which had come out a dirty brown – unattractive, but ideal for birdwatching camouflage. She wished, now, that she'd worn something a little less unflattering. Out of habit, she walked to the left-hand side of the car, forgetting that it would not be the passenger seat.

'Oh, do *you* wanna drive? It's a European stick shift but I guess you'd be used to that.'

'Oh, I'm *awfully* sorry,' Anna said, feeling stupid. The idea of driving on the wrong side of the road in an alien land full of oversized cars whose radiators sported lascivious grins, not to mention huge trucks that seemed to stop at nothing, terrified her. She stepped back and almost ran to the true passenger side. Verne opened the door and helped her into her seat, a hand holding her elbow.

Once they had started off, she studied his profile. She noted, for a second time, the way his upper lip rested slightly proud of the lower, the alertness of his eyes and the neatness of his ears. He was very fair, but with skin that tanned rather than freckled. Anna noticed that his forearms and the backs of his hands had a sparse covering of pale, almost downy hair, and had prominent veining which, she thought, made them look strong, but also sensuous. The skin around his eyes seemed almost translucent, and had a tinge of violet.

'Say, you have a kid, don't you?' The question butted into her silent observation.

'William. He's eight.' They continued in silence for a mile or two. She felt awkward and didn't know what to say next. He provided the answers to questions she might have asked, had she felt less shy.

'I do too. Boys. Brad's seven, going on eight, and Peter's five. We should get 'em together. And Bernie too. Have a weekend party when it gets warmer.'

'Oh, we'd love that,' Anna said. Then, 'What does your wife do?' There was a beat, the slightest hesitation, before he answered.

'Anna, she died. In sixty-three.'

'Oh. I'm so sorry.' Anna felt embarrassed, but worse, as she glanced at his profile again and he turned to look at her, she caught the hint of sadness in his grey eyes and felt tears pricking in her own. 'Oh Verne, I really am sorry.' But the moment had passed, and his smile returned. She wondered how she would have managed if Bernard had . . . unthinkable! Would she be able to pass off such a life-shattering event as a mere topic of conversation? And to smile like that so soon after referring to it? But she had caught the moment of grief on his face and knew it concealed more, like glimpsing a fish that turned in dark water, a single brief flash of silver. You saw only one, but you knew there was a shoal down there.

Verne parked and soon they were walking along a wood-land ride, fringed with unscented violets, both blue and yellow, and false spikenard in full flower, downhill towards a swamp.

'What's that pungent smell?' Anna asked.

'Skunk cabbage.'

They saw red-winged blackbirds flying in and out of the reeds and down by the water's edge flocks of birds with a metallic gloss on their necks and shoulders. They reminded Anna of European starlings; certainly they behaved in the same way, swaggering, busy, squabbling in noisy groups, but they were bigger, more crow-like.

'Grackles!' she said, recognising them from an illustration in the bird book she had bought at the College Bookstore. 'So many!'

'That's what gives the wood its name,' Verne said. 'They're common all over, but here is where they like to gather.'

'And that pile of wood. Could that be a beaver dam?'

'Certainly could.' Verne led her through a narrow path. The going was dry, but she was aware of the ground springing round her, a feeling not unlike the movement of the gorge suspension bridge when you walked over it.

'Sphagnum bog,' he said. 'We're on a floating raft of vegetation. There isn't much beneath us.' Insectivorous plants grew among the mosses: pitcher plants with their sinister blood-red blooms and, where he knelt to show her, sundews, whose leaves were covered with reddish hairs, each one tipped with a tiny translucent droplet of glutinous material. Water welled up in the moss at their knees as they knelt. He reached into his pocket for a magnifying lens and plucked a leaf so that she could look more closely at its surface, lifted it to his eye and peered at it through the glass. She spotted for the second time that day the thin lilac-tinged skin of his eyelid, this time magnified through the glass. He looked different with his eyes cast down, studying the sundew. Gently he took her hand and placed the lens in it. She felt her pulse quicken a little at his touch. His hands were moist, but not clammy. Warm.

'There you go,' he said, holding the leaf up to her. Through the lens, she could see the neatly trimmed thumbnail, the pattern of his thumb print, like contour lines, and the fragment of foliage, a green contrast with the flesh tones.

'Isn't that the most beautiful thing?' she whispered. Each droplet glistened with refracted light – red, blue, green, like a minuscule diamond.

'When a teeny insect lands on that, its legs get caught in the sticky dew, then the hairs turn in, holding the little bug more securely while the digestive juices get to work. It may be in microcosm, but it's kinda gory.'

'Poor little bug!'

'Yeah. It's tough at the bottom.' She caught his expression. The same tinge of sadness, even when making a joke. She liked him more for that. Americans, she'd learnt, were quick to show sentimentality but were as capable of callous cruelty as anyone from Europe. Gushing was essential etiquette, but this was less shallow.

They stayed close to the water's edge for just over an hour, close together, talking in whispers so as not to scare the birds. It was natural that he should have placed his hand over hers to draw attention to a Baltimore oriole perching in the poplar that overhung the still water. Natural, too, for her hand to twitch slightly under his, and for him to understand that fragment of body language, to take his hand away quickly, his own heart beginning to beat stronger. She was looking at the bird, and so did not notice the flush that came to his cheeks, or recognise the slightly parted lips or the dilating pupils. All she noticed was the speed with which he snatched his hand away. She registered it as a snub, and to her surprise, and to his mortification, she burst briefly into tears. Startled into inactivity at first, he simply watched her. Quickly she recovered herself. 'Oh goodness! I'm so sorry! I can't think what came over me. All over now.' She simulated briskness, pulling a handkerchief out of her shirt pocket and dabbing.

'Anna! Anna!' His hand was back over hers. 'It isn't all over. And you are not all right.' He looked into her face. 'What's wrong?' But this American frankness was too intrusive.

'No, I'm fine. Really I am.'

'If you say so.' His face was sulky with concern. They moved to another part of the lake edge, walking slowly along the margin path, side by side but a foot or so apart. Soon they came to a tiny promontory of soil bound together by the roots of a huge poplar. Here, partly hidden by the branches which hung down to the surface of the water, they sat on the compacted earth and scanned the pond with field glasses. Neither was concentrating much on the wildlife. Anna was wondering how she could possibly have let her control slip so utterly. Verne was puzzled at what could be making her so obviously miserable. It had to relate to the husband, he decided. It always did. He had found Bernard's bonhomie just a tad too hollow, and the hardness in his eyes too obvious to feel he could ever be much more than a casual acquaintance. The guy was fun at a party, but no way would he want to be stuck with him anywhere.

'Bernie gets around,' Verne said after some minutes of silence.

'He's very busy at the moment.'

'He's popular. Talk of the campus, for now. Everybody knows him.' He paused here and shifted his gaze from the lake to Anna. 'But you? Where do you fit in?' She kept silent. 'Maybe it suits you to be in the shadow.' He began to nod, as if to himself. 'Maybe it does . . . but I don't think so.'

'I don't think that's really your business, do you?'

'No.' He stretched his arms towards her, took both her hands in his. 'But Ah-nna—'

'Why do you Americans persist in lengthening what you regard as foreign "a"s? Mahatma Ga-ahndi! Viet Nahm! My name is Anna – both "a"s are short.'

'Gee, I'm sorry!' His face reddened, but he would not be rebutted. 'When I saw you in the English Garden, staring at those spring blooms, I could *feel* the . . . you know, the vibes, the *aura*. It was clear you were hurting. And then, when we talked, every topic I brought up, you related to England, to your house in Kent.'

'Well . . .' Anna felt her eyes stinging again.

'You're very homesick, aren't you?' Tears flowed. He moved his hands up to her shoulders, to give comfort. 'Don't be,' he murmured. 'Please don't be. There's so much to enjoy over here. So much to . . . I dunno . . . to laugh at, I guess.' And then he kissed her mouth which opened in surprise, which softened at his touch, which clung to his lips with a thirst that had been welling up since he had handed her the chilled white wine in the English Garden. Out of focus, she could see the pale hair on his head and almost out of control she felt her hand wandering to the V formed by the open neck of his shirt. His warm skin felt different from Bernard's. She needed Bernard here, now. She needed to think. Bernard was in Maryland. She stood up quickly, causing the nearest flock of grackles to take off in panic. Their alarm spread across the water and several other birds stirred.

'What are you trying to do?' Her voice was shrill, even though the words were whispered. His eyes downcast, he looked like an adolescent who has stolen a kiss. 'I hardly know you.'

He felt like a teenager. This crazy response – this blend of affront, fear and excitement – even recalled the flavour of his first kiss, the same startled look on Karen Orlbach's spotty face, the soft feel of her angora sweater, the bubblegum pink of it so clear in his mind's eye, and the sense of her body, warm within it. He felt as awkward and as guilty as he had done then, but the hunger he felt for Anna was different. Then, he had reeled under the force of teenage hormones, driven, as a boy is, by an acute lust, sharp-focused in the groin but difficult to understand. Now, the man was driven by more than sexual hunger; now he was responding, body and soul – and especially soul – to a call. He had recognised something about her at the faculty reception, way back in winter, standing erect in a dress that seemed to button up to her chin, looking worried and unhappy in the corner of

the room while some agronomist bored her. He had wanted
to get over to talk, but she and Bernie must have left early
because he had spent the last hour of the party looking out for
her. Then at Spring Weekend in the English Garden he had
received the same signals, not consciously sent but emanating
from her all the same. He had felt drawn to her, tugged out of
his happy complacency by the defenceless look of her back
as she bent to smell the spring flowers.

'Oh boy, Anna. I'm *real* sorry.'

'I think we'd better go home.'

'Sure.'

But all the way back she could still feel the touch of his
lips on her mouth. It tingled and tortured her mind. She tried
to concentrate on Bernard, tried to tell herself what he would
be doing, right now, in Baltimore. She glanced at her watch
– one of Bernard's castoffs which, he had explained, was
gaining almost three seconds a day and was therefore not
accurate enough for his needs – and deduced that he'd be
going over his notes one last time before speaking to the
conference on world trade barriers. She wanted to think
herself into Bernard's head, tried to send thought messages
to him across the ether. Bernard, I *do* love you. I do. I do. But
still her lips tingled, and still she felt, in her mind, the warm
softness of Verne's shirt and the surprising firmness of his
muscles beneath it. Most Americans had struck her as being
flabby, pasty, compared with Europeans, but Verne, though
by no means skinny, was more athletic than Bernard.

'May I come in for a while?' They had arrived back at
Tudor Avenue.

'I think perhaps you'd better not.' He kept his face impas-
sive but the fish turned in the deep water again, flashing
silver. 'And I don't think it would be a good idea if we saw
each other again, do you?' Her words sounded to her, now,
like a sentence on herself. As she spoke, she realised that
she would not be able to go on living in America like this.
Bernard being away so much, everyone seeming so alien, so
involved with their own lives that there was no room for

her to fit in anywhere – until today. She realised that it was Verne's arrival that had brought her to life after that hateful winter, and not the coming of spring.

'OK.' This time she felt his sadness in her own breast, a snag, a catch in the breath. 'Anna, I am truly sorry. It won't happen again.' He held his right hand up, as if about to make an oath. 'I promise.'

'I . . . We mustn't let it.' She was confirming her sentence, standing now at her door, the family home behind her, his concerned face in front of her. On the opposite side of the avenue, visible over his shoulder, a group of lilacs bloomed. She could detect their fragrance, coming in faint waves. An American robin – more like a British thrush with a tan breast than a Christmas-card robin – was rummaging about in the shrubs in front of the house. Even this humdrum avenue was beautiful, in the spring, but it was hard to see how it could stay beautiful without him there.

'But Anna, we can still meet, you know, socially.'

She dithered. Wanting this to end. Wanting it never to end. 'Come to dinner,' she said. 'This Saturday, when Bernard's home. And William, of course.'

'OK.' He looked at her and nodded slowly, as Americans do, head up and down, again and again. Wise expression in eyes, half-fixed smile. 'OK. How about my kids? Do they get to come over?'

'Why surely!' With amazement, Anna heard the words come from her own mouth, the American inflection, even the slight pronouncing of the 'r'. She gave a little laugh in surprise. 'Surely!'

'Jeez, Anna,' Verne said, 'you smiled!'

William took instantly to Brad and Peter. Within minutes of arriving, the three small boys were playing basketball outside, charging for the ball, jumping, pitching for the net which Bernard had fixed for them above the garage door. Inside, while Bernard and Verne talked, Anna organised the dinner in the kitchen. She had invited Dimitra, a Greek Cypriot graduate student studying agricultural economics, to balance the numbers. She half hoped Verne might take an interest, but could not deny her sense of relief when she saw that he was polite and attentive, but that there was no detectable attraction on either side. Dinner went smoothly and although Bernard was very tired from his recent trip he played the host with courtesy and even made them laugh with a couple of anecdotes about his first experiences of Baltimore.

By mid-June, when the university semester had concluded, Verne's visits and joint family activities – usually working round what would be good for the three little boys – had become routine. Anna began to lose her sense of unease in his presence, but could not stop thinking about him. She tried, a couple of times, to talk to Bernard about how she felt, and to get him to understand, but he seemed not to be receptive. She wondered whether he resented her for having been so negative about coming to America. Even in bed she felt that a distance had crept between them.

'Bernard, you're not angry with me, are you?' It was a Sunday morning. They had just made love – furtively and rather quickly, for fear of being disturbed by William – and were lying covered by a sheet in the growing heat of the morning. She noticed how wet with sweat his temples were, after his exertions, and how the small frown he tended to wear was making a permanent line on the side of his brow.

'Angry? Why on earth should I be?'

'I don't know, really.' She shrugged, not sure what to say next.

He raised himself up on one elbow to look at her. Puzzled, but not especially concerned, he touched the side of her face with the backs of his fingers and smiled. 'You're a funny one!' he murmured, and jumped out of bed.

'Must you, so early?'

'Got to. Work to finish.' Wrapping a towel round his naked form, he went out to the bathroom. She gazed at the open door and felt for the warm part of the bed he had just vacated.

Verne was coming over with his boys at lunchtime to pick up William for a fishing trip. She would go with them, but Bernard, she suspected, would have too much work to do and would have to stay home.

Later, just after eleven, Verne phoned. 'Jeez, Anna, I *really* am sorry, but my kids are a no-go area today. Peter has a real nasty stomach upset and I'm pretty sure Brad's headed the same way. A virus, I guess.'

She worked hard to keep the disappointment out of her voice. 'Oh Verne, I *am* sorry.' She remembered that Bernard would be too preoccupied with his own work to give them much time today. 'Maybe next week?' But she remembered that all the boys were going to summer camp so family trips would be off for a while and, with deepening gloom, she recalled that Bernard was due to speak in Chicago on Friday night. She hung up and felt like crying. Bernard came into the kitchen to make coffee, and found her still sitting by the phone.

'What's the matter now?' His voice showed concern, but it was tinged with exasperation.

'Our little trip's off. The Henschke boys have got a tummy upset.'

'Really?' He looked concerned. 'I hope Verne'll be all right for taking them all up to the Adirondacks on Friday morning. I *have* to be in Chicago—'

'I know you do, Bernard. I'm sure they'll be better by then. If not, I'll drive William up there myself.' What was she saying? She had hardly sat behind the wheel in this country before.

'Are you capable?'

'Of *course* I'm capable.' His questioning look stung. 'I can run you to the airport first thing and then go on with William.'

'If you say so.' He waited while she poured water on to instant coffee in his mug. 'It's a longish journey.'

'I'll manage.'

The Henschke boys were well again by Tuesday. On

Thursday night, William was so excited about the summer camp that he could hardly sleep. Verne arrived at their house at eight in the morning to find him waiting by the front door, his kitbag, fishing rod and baseball bat on the step beside him.

'My, you're a keenie,' Verne said. Brad and Peter had been ordered to remain in the back of the station wagon, to avoid delays. 'Say, is Bernie coming with us?' Verne had spotted him carrying a small suitcase through the hall. 'Camp is only for kids, you understand.'

'No such luck,' Bernard said. 'Chicago for me. I'm meeting the great Milton Friedman tonight and staying over till Tuesday. Maybe a while longer.'

'You are?' Verne looked impressed. 'You certainly do get about, Bernie. The biology department sure as hell wouldn't run to so many trips.'

'I'll be the guest of Chicago University, Verne.' Bernard put his case down by the boy's heap of possessions. It looked inscrutable; William's luggage was a child's biography. 'All expenses paid.' Verne whistled to reinforce the conviction that he was impressed.

'So what is Anna going to do this weekend?'

'Oh, I'll garden,' Anna said. 'I must feed and water absolutely everything.'

'On your own?' Verne stopped still in the middle of gathering up William's stuff. 'Anna! Why not come with us? It's a fairish drive each way, but you'll just *love* the scenery.'

'Oh I couldn't possibly,' Anna said, and uttered a short laugh. 'The very idea.'

'Why don't you?' Bernard said, with but the faintest hint of sarcasm. 'You can share the driving.' Anna felt a revival of her earlier anger. She paused a moment and then looked at both men in turn.

'All right. And I *will* share the driving.'

The journey was fun, all the way up. The three little boys wanted to sing, so they ran through a tiresome repertoire of watered-down rugby songs, learnt from William, and then moved through American patriotic songs and finally, after two or three hymns, agreed to button their lips in return for an extra two-dollar bribe apiece. As Verne had promised, the scenery on the way was magnificent. They stopped for a short mid-morning break, and when they returned to the car Verne said, 'Why don't you drive for a spell? I'm kinda tired.'

'OK,' Anna said, trying not to gulp with fear, and before she had had time to worry about it was cruising along the highway while the boys chatted quietly in the back and Verne dozed. Once she got used to the spongy feel of the power steering and the enormous size of the vehicle, compared with her Mini back in Kent, driving proved not only easy but also pleasurable. Fifty miles and a few small towns further and she wondered why she had been so timid about getting behind the wheel in North America.

At the summer camp, she had anticipated difficulty parting from William, but all three boys were so excited that their farewells were perfunctory and soon she and Verne were cruising back towards Minorca. Soon after their visit to Grackle Wood, she might have felt apprehensive about being on her own with him, but after so many weeks of family socialising and such a jolly ride up to the mountains, she felt relaxed. She would miss William – even now, the thought of being in the house without him hurt – but he had been so happy running off with Peter and Brad that she felt happy for him too.

'Why don't we stop somewhere to eat?' Verne said. It was lateish afternoon and they still had a couple of hundred miles to travel.

'Is that wise?'

'What do you have to rush home for? Bernie's in Chicago. You can call him if you're worried.'

'No,' Anna said. She didn't feel an urgent need to talk to Bernard at present. The sting of his scornful remarks the previous weekend had been freshened by the sarcastic tone of his farewell that morning. 'I don't think so.' Verne glanced at her but could read nothing in her features. 'But I am beginning to feel a bit hungry.'

'OK, we'll travel a tad more, and then pull off for a meal.' The Howard Johnson's they stopped at, near Utica, was very quiet. Most of the tables were empty but one or two had couples or single men at them.

'Whaddaya fancy?'

'You choose.'

Verne ordered for both of them. 'Fancy a beer?'

Anna nodded.

'They have rooms here,' Verne said. Anna thought of the miles they had yet to travel. They had spent most of the day in the car and she was not looking forward to the next few hours. But the idea, she knew, was improper.

'I have to be home. In case Bernard phones.' Their food arrived. Frankfurter sausages with a small, rounded pot of baked Boston beans on each plate.

'You're going to love these,' Verne said, dipping his fork into them. 'They're done with molasses.' He chatted for a while but gradually ran out of things to say. Anna stayed quiet. At one point, he reached across the table and placed a large hand over hers – his right over her left. He could feel her wedding ring under his fingers. She tensed.

'Verne, don't. Someone might see.' He laughed but kept his hand in place.

'Anna! We're not doing anything wrong. I just wanted to tell you something.' She pulled her hand away, making him smile and shake his head.

'What?' She waited. The beer was beginning to work on the crampiness in her mind. She loved being with this man. What was wrong with that? But she still had to resist the impulse to look around the tables to check, yet again, that there was no one she knew, no one from campus here. 'What did you want to say?'

'Bernie,' Verne said. The reminder of his name shocked a little. A gooseberry by proxy. 'He gets around. I mean he's away from home one hell of a lot. Does that bug you?'

'Why should it? He has to work very hard.' She put her knife and fork down. Unconsciously her voice took on Bernard's inflection. 'Too many careers are wrecked by wives whining about being left at home.'

'That answer was just a smidge too pat.' He smiled. 'I mean do you – you know – do you ever wonder, when he's away . . . ?'

'Wonder? About what?'

'Sorry. Disregard that. Run the tape back and erase the last eighteen inches.'

Anna smiled now. 'Sometimes,' she said, 'I think there's a bigger language barrier between your country and mine than between us and China.'

'Talking of language reminds me. You know the Purlin Operatic is staging Act one of *Die Walküre* tomorrow?'

'I think I saw a poster somewhere.'

'A couple of my biology majors have been working on me to support them and bring some people. Apparently, the Jewish lobby is calling for a boycott, something to do with Wagner being an anti-semite and God knows what-all else – well, you know what it's like on campus if the Jewish community doesn't approve. But, would *you* care to come along?'

'Isn't Wagner rather loud?' Verne shook his head. 'Bernard says he takes five hours to say what Mozart manages in one.'

'Jeez, Anna, we're all used to hearing Bernie's opinion. But what do *you* think?'

'I, really, I know nothing of Wagner. In fact, I don't really know much about opera at all.'

'But you'll come, hear the kids perform?' She nodded.

'Great! Oh, that's great!'

She insisted on paying her half and they left. Verne dropped her off at Tudor Avenue just after nine. He did not ask to be allowed in. Anna had known that out of politeness she should invite him in for a coffee at the very least, but she was afraid of what might happen.

He preempted her dilemma – she could have hugged him for that – but still felt disappointed when he said, 'Look, er, I'm gonna split, if you don't mind. I still have this morning's breakfast dishes in the sink.'

Chapter Ten

The house at Tudor Avenue was unwelcoming. With neither Bernard nor William to tend to she opted for an early night, hoping to sleep away her feeling of loneliness. But having spent so many hours sitting in the car, sleep would not come. She reached across to Bernard's side of the bed, shivered at the cold feel of the sheets, and pulled his pillow over to hug for comfort. After a whole day in his company, Verne's soft voice was imprinted in her mind's ear and she comforted herself by running over the things he had been saying. Then she realised that the pillow she was hugging represented Verne rather more than Bernard. Bernard was never much of a close cuddler but Verne, she felt sure, would be – he was such a tactile character. She had seen him squeezing the shoulders of his students or clapping the backs of colleagues. He had a habit of doing a little mock head-butt at people he was fond of – not to women, usually, but to male colleagues, even to students.

She felt she had been in bed for hours, lying wide-eyed and alert, but when the bedside phone rang she started so violently that she could feel her heart beating in her throat. She thought it must be well after midnight, but her alarm clock only registered 11.23. She waited a couple more rings to allow her heart to slow down again. It had to be Bernard, phoning this late, and she needed to clear Verne from her mind before she spoke.

'Anna? It's Verne. Say, I hope I didn't wake you.' She felt huge relief at the sound of his voice.

'Are you all right?'

'Never better!' An aping of one of her English expressions. 'But I had this great idea.' She kept silent. He continued. 'I have been meaning to treat myself to discs of Valkyrie. What say I get them early tomorrow, and have you come visit with me, listen to the first act and follow the words.' Anna felt uneasy about going, but felt a warm surge of excitement at the prospect of spending more time with him.

'But we'll be hearing it in the evening.'

'Anna, Anna!' Verne allowed himself a short laugh, not of scorn, but of fond amusement. 'This is such a complex story. You have no idea. One could hear it a hundred times, and still learn new things about it. Whaddaya say?'

'Yes, I'd love to come,' Anna said. 'But I get to do the lunch.'

'OK.'

They talked for ages, Anna lying with the phone crooked by her shoulder, an arm round the pillow, holding it to her side. Eventually, she said, 'Verne, I have to get to sleep. But I'm glad you called. I haven't spent a night alone in this house before and it feels odd. A little scary.'

'Be grateful it's only a couple of nights.'

She slept.

What seemed like minutes later she was woken again by the telephone, but this time sun was streaming through the gap between the curtains.

'Darling?' Bernard's voice sounded odd to her. So English as to be alien. 'I've got together with the team here – Ben Miller, Isaacs, Friedman, of course, and I'm going to need more time. We want to work more on this book project and that means setting up talks with at least one lot of publishers this week. Plus, there's this amazing TV series I might get to be involved in. Will you be OK?'

There was a silence for several seconds while she adjusted her mind. It was going to be another hot day. Already, her neck was sticky with sweat. 'William took to camp like a duck to water.' She had said it to play for a little time, but it sounded like a reproach.

'Oh hell, Anna. I'm sorry, I've been so caught up with this project. Selfish of me.' He breathed out sharply – almost snorted – and continued, 'But I knew he'd be fine. He's such a little extrovert.' Bernard's use of the word often made Anna feel it was an accusation. Extroverts wouldn't let homesickness shut them out of the present; wouldn't have private weeping sessions over tatty snapshots of their former homes. 'You OK, on your own?'

'Fine. I'm going to the Purlin Operatic thing tonight, with Verne Henschke.'

'What? The Wagner?'

'Mmm.' She was about to say that she'd be going to Verne's house for much of the day but he interrupted.

'Sooner you than me! Still, I suppose it'll stop you from being trapped in the house.'

'I wouldn't be trapped anyway. Verne's lending me his station wagon, until you get back – well, until Tuesday morning anyway.'

'He is? Good God!' There was a silence. 'But you don't drive over here.'

'I did more than two hundred miles on the way to Lake Placid yesterday. We shared the driving.'

'Anna that's marvellous news!' He paused. 'I'm so glad you've got over that hurdle – I *knew* you would, in time.' The brightness in his voice tugged. She needed him.

'Bernard, come home.'

'What?'

'I, I don't know. Something's happening. I miss you.'

'Steady, darling! Hang in there! I'll try to get done by Wednesday – Thursday at the absolute latest.'

Verne arrived in the station wagon at ten precisely. She was waiting by the garage door. He held the driver's side door open for her. 'Might as well get used to being in the driver's seat from the start.'

'Bernard phoned. He may not be back until Thursday.'

'That's OK, keep it as long as you like. I've got the Triumph.' He thought for a moment. 'Say, Anna, would you sooner have the sports car?'

'Lord no! That's your precious toy, I wouldn't *dream* of borrowing it.' He attempted, not without skill, to conceal his relief but she read his mind. She drove the station wagon through the small city, somewhat tense at first, but relaxing after they had passed the main drag, and before long had squeezed the large vehicle through his narrow gateway. In the cool of his air-conditioned living room, Verne explained the Ring of the Nibelung and began to unfold the complicated drama – concentrating on *Die Walküre* – with long German quotes, picking out some of the leitmotifs on his upright piano. Anna was impressed with his cleverness, but felt the story of Siegmund and Sieglinde, the hidden sword and the incestuous bond between the twins somewhat unconvincing. Then when the records began she was so enraptured – right from the first stormy bars of the prelude – that she hardly noticed the time go by. Towards the end of the first act, as spring came into Hunding's house and the twins declared their love, Anna felt closer to Verne than she ever had before. If he had kissed her at that moment, the way he had at Grackle Wood, she would not have resisted. But Verne had promised. Why did she regret that? To suppress the guilt that was budding inside her, she forced herself to think about Bernard.

When the first act was over, he collected two beers and some cold chicken portions from the kitchen. 'I said I'd do lunch,' Anna said. 'Let me make a salad, at least.' They returned to the kitchen where she busied herself finding lettuce, cutting up garlic cloves with a paring knife and mixing them with olive oil and fresh lemon juice while he watched, half propped on the kitchen windowsill.

'You could peel and slice that.' She signalled a small onion with her chin.

He found another knife in the drawer and stood beside her,

enjoying the presence of a woman in his kitchen. 'Doesn't the garlic make your fingers stink?'

'You cleanse them with the lemon skins. Look, I'll show you.' She shook some salt into the hollowed-out fruits and then scoured her fingers and thumbs, holding them over the sink. He copied.

'Feels kinda gritty.'

'That's the salt. It scours and the lemon cleans and perfumes. Then we simply rinse them off under the tap.'

'We call that a faucet.' He reached for a towel but instead of giving it to her, he took her hand and began to dry. He held it to his nose. 'Mmm. Lemony, but there's still a trace of garlic. I *like* that.' And he sniffed again, and very gently kissed, and then licked her hand, only briefly, just a darting pink tongue brushing the sensitive area between fore and middle finger. She felt her nerves and tissue responding. He looked up, still holding her hand, his eyes bright, glittering. He brought her hand back to his mouth, this time nuzzling the inside of her wrist. She was unable to prevent a little gasp, barely audible. 'Jesus Christ, Anna!' Verne whispered. 'Jesus Christ!'

'Don't, Verne. Please, don't.' But she could no more take her hand from him than walk upside down on the ceiling. She had never experienced such a need, such a hunger for anyone. All she could keep in her clouded brain was the sense of Verne, the feel of his great size near her, the sensation of his warm skin on her wrist and arm, the fragrance of his body.

'Hey,' his voice was soft and husky. 'Let's get us out of this kitchen.' He led her back through the living room and upstairs. Even though she felt half absent – this was happening to someone else, like in a film, not to her – she registered open doors of the boys' bedrooms, their beds still unmade, toys scattered on the floor, and then the warmth of the sun, flooding his bed, neatly made. He pulled the curtains almost to, but the room stayed light and she registered the warmth of the sun on her skin. Verne kissed her full on the mouth. She expected it. Her lips parted to take his tongue and the sensation was so sweet she could hardly detect his hand undoing buttons. She could not recollect the next moments but found herself still in his arms, with neither of them clothed apart from his undershorts. She felt his tongue probing her ears, felt him kissing her breasts, sensed the soft hairs on his chest and nuzzled them. She was so inflamed with sexual drive by now that her vision was growing misty. She caressed his back while he ran his lips over her neck, breasts, mouth, ears, eyes, everywhere. She tweaked the elastic waistband to get his shorts down. Impatiently, he reached behind him and pulled them off, kneeling up to do so. She sat up and kissed his navel, detecting the maleness in his scent – not unwashed, but musky – and kissed the tip of his penis. She felt him shudder slightly and kissed it again before lying back down and feeling him enter her body with such gentleness that she didn't have to give any guidance or indicate that it was all right. As he increased his pace she felt her own pleasure surging up in waves. She sensed his climax approaching and slowed her own movements, wanting to prolong the moment, but then wanting to give him more pleasure; she began to move again, more vigorously. He cried out, 'Jesus Christ, Anna!'

And it was over. She assumed that he would want to rest now but he stayed with her holding her close with his arms and, now, placing his knees outside hers and locking her legs between his. She could feel his heart hammering beneath his ribs. They were both sweaty but she wanted to be with him, under him for ever so much longer yet. After some minutes, he shifted, replace his legs inside hers and began to move again, this time with a different motion, or with hardly a motion at all, but still stimulating her in a way that was completely new. He worked with his tongue, too, and with his fingers, so that she could feel every nerve ending turn taut and shrill. Deeper waves of sensation, centred on what was happening in her sex, rippled through the rest of her body with increasing intensity. This was a level of pleasure she had never known before and she wanted it to go on for ever. But she could not bear it much longer. It had to go somewhere. She was soaring up and up but to where? And then the great explosion of nerves. She must have grown increasingly silent during the build-up, her muscles tensing, her breath coming in shorter gasps until she stopped breathing altogether, just before the quaking spasms, but all she could recall was the actual explosion. Panting now, while everything began to subside in the afterglow, she clung to him, almost weeping with relief and with a kind of joy that seemed unreal. He made to move over, to ease the weight on her, but she held him tight, making small adjustments to their positions so that they could lie comfortably, breathe, but remain as close as possible.

'That was almost as if you never came before,' Verne murmured. She did not want to speak. Could not trust her voice. Felt on the brink of . . . of what? Eventually she felt able to talk.

'I thought I had,' she swallowed, 'but I don't think I had.'

'Jesus H. Christ,' Verne said. 'I can *not* believe that.' He looked at her. 'Not ever? Not even with Bernie?' The bleakness of her expression warned him to drop the subject.

What did he mean, she wondered, by 'not even with Bernie'? Bernard was the only one, until now. They were silent for some time. Anna's body felt warm and relaxed but in her mind a nauseating mix of emotion brewed and fomented. 'Verne,' she said after a long silence. 'What are we going to do?' She was on the edge of tears. Worse. 'What have we done?' He took hold of her shoulders.

'Anna, I am in love with you.' He held her gaze with a steady look, even though there was a tremor in his voice. 'I've loved you since I saw you at the English Garden. I love you more, even, than I loved . . .' She placed her hand over his lips.

'You can't say that. You mustn't taint your memory of her.' Gently, she edged herself away so that she could sit up. 'This is a thing of the moment. It will pass.'

'I don't think so.'

'It *has* to pass.' She was weeping now. 'It's so wrong. I've got to think of William. Of Bernard.'

Verne sighed and turned away from her. 'That bastard doesn't give a shit about you.'

'You can't possibly know.'

'I know what I've seen.'

'Verne. Stop it!'

'He hasn't even given you an orgasm. What the fuck sort of a marriage is that?'

'Verne, you must stop. If you don't, I'll go.'

'You were eating your heart out when I met you. Still are. Can't you see that?'

'I was just homesick. That was all.' She jumped up, picked up her clothes but hesitated before pulling them on.

'Do you want to take a shower?' She felt dirty, not from him – that would be impossible – but from her own perspiration.

'I think I'd better just go.'

He shook his head and pulled out a towel from the cupboard. 'Bathroom's that way.' She took the towel and walked out. He heard water running and after a while went to the bathroom and hesitated at the open door. 'I'm sorry. I shouldn't have said that. About Bernard.' No answer. 'But the fact is, what has happened has happened. I wanted it to happen. I think you did too. And I've seen how you two are together. It's like Paul Henreid and Ingrid Bergman in *Casablanca*. Bergman's totally loyal to the bastard, oh, but *he's* married to the Week's Great Cause, ridding the world of Nazis. He needs her for convenience. She's good PR, buys him more respectability, washes his dishes, probably bears him a dozen kids once he's through dealing with the Nazis. Whereas she's crazy for Bogey, and Bogey has completely ruined his life for the loss of her. And in the end, after she's allowed Bogey to persuade her to stick with him, he hasn't even got the bigness to acknowledge their sacrifice.' His anger had been waxing throughout this exposition, but his voice stayed calm and quiet. 'What's Bernie's good cause, Anna? What drives him? Fame? Vanity? What the fuck is it that makes him charge around the place trying to hold five jobs in one hand?' She came out of the shower and without making any attempt to hide herself from him, she began to dry her body as if they had been living together for a lifetime.

'Verne, I know you are only saying these things because you are angry, and because you feel unable to do anything about what has happened to us. But please, please, I'm begging you to stop.'

'Why the hell should I?'

'Because you are only hurting the two of us.' She was fighting to keep her voice level. 'And especially, you're hurting yourself.' He looked at her; his eyes prickled with unshed tears.

'You have to be the most beautiful creature ever created.' He went to embrace her. '*The* most beautiful.' He stepped into the shower. She waited, happy to be naked in the heat of the day and the steaminess of the bathroom. Through the shower curtain, she watched his outline as he soaped himself and then rinsed off the sweat of their lovemaking. She handed him a towel and enjoyed watching his large body as he dried himself. He was more massive than Bernard, perhaps not even quite so well proportioned, but he exuded something – she couldn't really say what – that she found irresistible. She did not know whether she would be able to give him up. One thing she was sure of: she would have to level with Bernard – whatever the outcome. She simply could not live with herself otherwise.

'Verne, what are we going to do?'

'You keep asking that.' He walked past her to his bedroom. She followed and began to pick up her clothes.

'Well?'

He knew there was no way they could have a secret affair. It wasn't his style. He suspected that she wouldn't countenance it either and besides, the risk of detection in such a close community was enormous. One or two pairs of eyebrows would already have been raised after tonight when they would be seen together, without Bernard, at the opera. 'We have a little time – not much, but at least it's something.'

'How so?'

'The kids are up at camp and Bernie doesn't get back before midweek. We have a couple of days to work things out.'

> That weekend was the best and the worst of my life, [Anna wrote]. Being with Verne, undiluted by anything or anybody, made me happier than I thought anyone could possibly be. It gave me a kind of strength that I had not recognised in myself before, as if some new life force were being driven into my sinews. But the guilt I felt, about betraying Bernard, and perhaps more, about jeopardising William's happiness, was almost unbearable.

On Tuesday afternoon, while Verne was in town collecting food for them both to eat that evening, this time at Tudor Avenue, there was a phone call from the owner of the summer camp.

'Say, Mrs Morfey,' he sounded apologetic but also guarded, 'I'm real sorry to bother you, but we're a little worried about your son, Bill.'

'What's wrong?' Alarm pinched her voice

'Now please don't get upset, I'm sure it's something every kid gets once in a while, but he was kinda off colour yesterday and has a nasty fever this morning. We've had the camp medic look at him and I guess he has flu.'

'Oh, I see.' Relief that it was nothing worse blended with alarm that he was ill at all.

'I'm sure you'll understand that we would prefer for you to collect him as soon as you can.' The camp owner's voice was solicitous, but he was delivering an instruction, rather than making a suggestion. 'He can come back when he's recovered, of course.'

'Of course.' She began to wonder how she could get all the way up there and back in the time. Would Verne mind her taking the station wagon so far? 'I'll leave as soon as I can.'

It was unlike William to be ill. Apart from the usual

measles, chicken pox and mumps he'd hardly even had a cold and as she pondered this her concern grew. She tried to ring Verne, forgetting that he was out shopping and would be coming on to Tudor Avenue later. By the time he arrived she was in an anxious state. He was calming. 'It's probably nothing at all,' he said. 'Relax. We'll drive up there right now. We can stay at that Howard Johnson's, and then collect him early tomorrow morning.'

'Do you mind coming? I could drive myself up there in your station wagon.'

'Anna!'

'But what if Bernard phones?'

'Call him first. Or leave a message at his hotel.' The Chicago hotel told her he was not in his room, so she left a detailed message and promised to phone later. But he called back within a few minutes, when she was at the point of leaving.

'Anna? Darling? What's going on?' She explained. She was surprised at his response. 'It's just a virus, nothing more. People are getting so litigious these days, the camp people probably just want to reduce the risk of being sued. I'll bet it's nothing more than a feverish cold.'

'How can you know?'

'Kids get 'em all the time.'

'Not William.' She could not keep the tremor out of her voice.

'Anna? It's not like you to overreact in this way.'

He hummed for a few seconds, thinking out his strategy. 'Want me to fly home, to take you up there? It's a hell of a way to drive on your own.'

'Verne Henschke has offered to come with me.'

'Oh brilliant! He's the salt of the earth, that man.'

'Bernard,' she struggled to keep her voice as normal as possible, 'when are you coming home?'

'Are you all right, darling? You sound funny.'

'Of course I'm not all right. How could I be?' She began to break down.

'Anna! Hang in there!' He added extra strength to his voice. 'It won't be serious.'

'How can you know?'

'Trust me. Have I been wrong about anything serious in the past?'

'Bernard, come home.' There was a pause. Perhaps it was the noise on the line, but she thought she heard a sigh, short, exasperated.

'I'll do my best to get back tomorrow.'

She fuelled the station wagon before collecting Verne, knowing that otherwise he'd have insisted on paying. The journey up to the Adirondacks was so different from Friday, when the car had been noisy with the excited little boys. They might have used the time to talk about their situation, but Anna was too preoccupied with William to concentrate on much else. When they pulled into the Howard Johnson's it was almost too late to want to eat. Anna had packed up a couple of sandwiches, some apples and a six-pack of Budweiser.

'We could eat in the room,' Verne said.

'Are we sharing one?' After Saturday afternoon, neither had mentioned it but both knew that they would not be having sex until they had got things worked out.

'Anna, don't let's make pretences.' Verne was not smiling. 'There's no way I'm leaving you on your own in this state.' She was too tired and too tense from worry to make any further protest. They ate and drank in silence.

Afterwards, she said, 'I'm going to shower.' He went into the bathroom after her and when he emerged, ten minutes later, she was lying in one of the two double beds, very still and very straight. He moved to the other bed. 'Verne?'

'Yah?'

'Would you come in here and hold me please? Just hold me.' They lay together in each other's arms. She cried a little and then calmed. He soothed her brow, stroked her back, held her close.

They arrived at the camp before mid-morning and found

the owner who took them to where the littlest boys were canoeing. Brad and Peter cheered and ran over to speak to them before they collected William.

'Go, wait by the car to say goodbye,' Verne told them, 'but keep your distance when we bring Bill over. OK?'

'OK, Dad!'

'Mom, I'm sorry!' William said, lying in his lonely bed in the camp's sick bay. Verne carried the boy to his car while Anna brought his bag. Seeing the anxiety on Anna's face, he gave her back a stroke. Peter looked from his father to Anna and back again.

'Are you two planning to get married?' he asked.

'Now, son, you know Mrs Morfey already has a husband.'

The little boy thought for a minute and then said, 'Can you only have one husband?'

'Boys, say goodbye to each other,' Anna said. 'We've a long way to go.'

In her cabin on the *Brisbane*, Anna had to stop typing. She had been at it for so long that her fingers had gone crampy and her back felt numb from sitting at the small desk. Outside, the tropical day was about to give way to a brief twilight before night. She had hardly been out of the little room for three days. The day after tomorrow, they would dock at Honolulu but she was undecided about going ashore. She so wanted to get this painful spell of writing behind her.

She decided to have a turn on deck before changing for dinner and went to tap on the Boys' door in case they might want some exercise. Ant answered the door. He looked haggard and untidy, as if he'd been sleeping in his clothes, which he had.

'Hello, stranger! Where've you been hiding yourself?' He yawned behind his hand and then pulled his sweater down over his waistband.

'Oh I'm sorry, did I disturb you?'

'One of my nastier headaches. Came on after lunch. Cedric

has no sympathy at all when I get them so I usually try to sleep them off.'

'I wondered if you'd like a walk. I've been cooped up in there all day, writing.'

'You're developing into quite a little swot, Anna. And what's more, you were missing at today's writing class.'

'I know. I had intended to go but I got hopelessly caught up in there.' She pointed at her cabin door.

'Well, my dear, I can tell you it was quite revealing.'

'Really? In what way?'

'Do excuse me one instant, Anna darling.' He ducked back inside, pulling the door partly to. She heard water sounds and drawers being pulled open and pushed shut and within seconds he was back at the door, fresher of face, with a canary-yellow pullover draped over his shoulders. 'Shall we?' He offered an arm.

'Thank you.' She held his arm, feeling a little awkward and was glad of an excuse to let go while he pulled on the heavy door that led to the open deck.

'Cedric went to see the film.'

'I didn't even check which one it was today.'

'*Casablanca.*'

'Oh!' Anna tried not to react.

'We know practically every line.' Inevitably, Ant began to quote. '. . . it doesn't take much to see that the problems of three little people don't amount to a hill of beans in this crazy world.'

'Ant, *please!* Don't!' It was almost a shout.

'I'm sorry.' Ant was concerned. He said no more. A morning of irrationality from Cedric had driven him to overindulge at lunch and what he had passed off as a headache had really been a teatime hangover. And it was happening more often. Cedric's insecurity manifested itself in various ways, but the most common at present was an obsessive concern about AIDS. So many of their close friends had succumbed to the vile disease that it had become almost like a club. If you didn't know anyone who had it or who was HIV positive, it was as if you weren't a proper queer. Ant had been promiscuous in his youth but Cedric, according to Cedric, never. And since Ant had, over the years, recounted almost every youthful liaison – or at least those that had lasted for more than a single evening – Cedric could never quite discount the possibility that Ant could have picked something up from someone, even though it would have been almost thirty years ago. Cedric also had difficulty in believing that Ant could have reformed from such promiscuity to a wholly monogamous relationship. Periodically, the paranoia surfaced, brought on perhaps by the presence of a handsome waiter or by the news of a friend dying of the disease.

'I'm sorry, Antony. It's just that, well, that film . . .'

'Painful associations? You can't get to our age, love, without having those.' He sighed.

'Sounds as though you've had a rough day,' Anna said, mainly to throw him off the scent. She would never feel able to share what she had written in her private memoirs. The class could have the diluted versions, the short stories, but no one would read her main work. Ever. She didn't think her writing was up to much anyway. Pullen had kept several of her stories and had not read them out to the class.

'It's only a silly domestic thing. It began after the writing class . . .' He faltered, changed tack. 'Oh, and à propos of that, you know that fellow Pullen . . . I'm not sure I should be telling you this.'

'What? Telling me what?'

Ant fixed her with an arch expression. 'After all, we don't want our budding Brontë to grow a swelled head. Wouldn't be healthy.'

'What *are* you talking about?'

'Well, dearie. As soon as Pullen realised you weren't going to be there, he set us to write something banal and excused himself, returning seconds later with a typescript. "Now, class," he said. "I'm about to share something with you and I'd like your opinion." And then he read us this story. I can tell you, I was riveted. It was a simple enough theme, but my God, the strength of that writing. The descriptive passages were so real. You were there! You could even smell it—'

'What? What story?'

'You'll find out if you let me tell the tale uninterrupted. When he'd finished, most people were pretty complimentary about it. That rad-fem cow said it was a bit derivative and that she was sure she'd read something like it by Fay Weldon. Well, you can imagine Pullen's reaction to that. The rest of us all said we loved it and gave stumbling reasons for our enthusiasm. Cedric asked who had written it. 'Aha, that would be telling,' Pullen said, 'but it was nobody in this class.' I decided that I had to know who the author was. So I gave Cedric the glad eye and got him to set up a diversionary movement. All Cedric had to do was touch him, and you can tell that Pullen is terrified of, well, you know, people like us, and so he was distracted for long enough to let me glance at the name.'

'Well?'

'Not one that I recognised.'

'Ah.'

'Not at first, anyway.'

'Oh.'

'But I got to thinking. And, the more I thought, the more obvious it was.'

'What was the story about?'

'Aha! That would rather give the game away, wouldn't it, Mrs – or is it Miss, or perhaps, yes, definitely *Ms* Annabel Murphy.'

'Oh!' Anna blushed. 'Oh, I say!'

'But watch it, Anna,' Ant said. 'I think that Pullen fellow is interested in more than just your writing.'

'What? Oh, for goodness sake, Ant, you do talk rot!' Anna laughed out loud. 'I mean, *really*.'

'Don't say you haven't been warned.'

Chapter Eleven

—————

Bernard didn't manage to get home until late on Thursday night. His plane was delayed out of O'Hare Airport, Chicago, making him miss his connecting flight from Rochester. Eventually, he shared a taxi to Purlin with three other people, arriving just after eleven. He must have sensed that much was wrong as soon as he walked in. I felt wholly unnatural – one stranger talking to another. Something even prevented him from kissing me, and we stood exchanging pleasantries like acquaintances at a social gathering before he ran upstairs, as much to escape the odd situation between us as to look in on William. When he came down to the kitchen, almost twenty minutes later, he was still strange. His face showed tiredness with dark patches, like bruises around his eyes, but there was more: a sense of unease, of fear, even. For the very first time, I detected a flaw in his aura of self-confidence.

'Bill's never succumbed to a virus like that before.' He had stood looking down at his son, sleeping but restless in his feverish state, the skin flushed and dry, hot to the touch.

'It's just his high temperature.' She needed to reassure herself as well as him. 'You know how dramatic these viruses can be with children.'

'If I'd known he was feeling this mouldy, I'd have come home.' His tone was reproachful. He meant, 'if you'd told me'.

'I did ask you to come.'

'What have you done so far?' He fired the question as though she had barely managed, in his absence, but now he was here and ready to take over, clean up the mess and get everything back on an even keel. He was tired to the point of becoming irrational, and hungry. He poured himself a large Martini, sloshing gin on the kitchen worktop.

'Well, obviously, Dr Steiner's been,' Anna said. 'She's pretty certain it's just a flu-type bug. Didn't seem especially concerned. She says she shouldn't need to come back, but to call her if there's a change.'

'Did she say whether there was much flu about?'

'I don't think so.'

'Don't you know? Didn't you *ask* her?' She took his empty glass and quickly sloshed more gin into it before getting a jar of olives from the cupboard. He took a sip even before she had had time to add vermouth. 'Well, didn't you?'

'No, Bernard. Not as a—'

'Then what's the point?' He waved his glass, sloshing out some of the liquid. 'I mean what the hell's the point?'

'Bernard, please don't shout at me. I've done my best.'

'Well perhaps your best isn't quite good enough.' He drained his glass and held it out for more.

'This isn't like you. Haven't you had enough?'

'I want to know what's going on.'

'What?' She glanced at him guiltily. She must not be caught out. She had to tell him, but in her own way, at the right moment. 'What do you mean?'

'With the boy, for Christ's sake. I have to know what the hell is happening. You obviously haven't managed to find out.'

'There's nothing to find out. He just needs a day or two in bed.'

'You think so? Come and look at him again.' He took her

hand and led her quickly up stairs, treading softly so as not to disturb the boy. He had turned over in bed since Bernard had last looked and his face was now lit by the brighter, whiter light from the landing rather than the reddish glow of his bedside night light. His brow was still hot but his breathing, though wheezy from a congested chest, was slow and regular.

'He's no worse than when Dr Steiner came,' she said. She stroked the boy's sweat-darkened hair and straightened the sheet. They stood looking down at their son for a few more moments before going back downstairs.

'It just isn't William,' Bernard said. 'He's never ill. You should have told me sooner.'

'Bernard, I did try.'

'Did you?'

'Perhaps if you'd been here, I—'

'What is that supposed to mean?'

'I just don't think you are here enough. I sometimes feel everything around me is falling apart. And now I *know* that it is.' She began to weep. 'I . . . give you support . . . I try so hard . . . but we can't be a family if a third of it is absent all the time. Even when you're here, you bury yourself in work. This is the recess, for heaven's sake, when most people are taking it easy.'

'You know, sometimes, Anna,' he said as he leapt up, swayed and clutched at the curtains, 'sometimes I simply don't understand you. You know perfectly well I'm doing all this precisely to keep the family going. All the time at Chicago I missed you and, and, the boy. Christ Anna! I just *don't* understand.' Then the lurch, the comic curtain fall, and William coming in, wobbling on feverish legs.

Later, after they had got him back into bed and to sleep again, Anna offered to make Bernard scrambled eggs. He refused, saying he felt sick, but he accepted black coffee. She sat with him, mostly in silence, while he composed himself.

'I'm calling Dr Steiner. What time does her surgery start tomorrow?'

'Nine.'

'Damn! I've got a meeting fixed with Ascher. I'll cancel it.'

'There's no need to call Steiner,' Anna said, a little calmer by now, 'unless there's change.' She looked at the dark lines round his eyes. 'But stay home tomorrow, darling. You look so tired.' How she wished she could sponge away the perplexed look on his face, but nothing would relieve the stress and she knew she was the author of it all. She had to talk about Verne.

'Was Chicago a success?'

'Mmm? Oh God yes! I'm going to co-author a new basic textbook. It's bound to get used on the best campuses, both sides of the pond.'

'That's wonderful.' To feign enthusiasm was impossible. 'I think we should look in on William and then go to bed.'

Under the covers, she tried to hold him, but his body felt tense. She turned over and tried to weep as quietly as she could. He lay, exhausted but unable to sleep, wondering what was happening to his little boy; what was making Anna so strange; what had made his life, at the very threshold of such astronomic success, go so jagged at the edges. He could sense Anna's misery next to him, but knew that in her present state he would be quite unable to help however much he might want to. At last he slept. Next morning, he felt better but she had been awake for the entire night and could hardly stand up.

'Look, you may be getting William's flu. Stay in bed, I can manage.'

'I'll be fine, once I've got dressed.'

'No Anna. Let me take over for a while.' He kissed the top of her head. 'And I'm sorry I was so intolerable last night.' To his dismay, this elicited more tears and instead of responding to his embrace she pushed him away, dragging herself out of bed to see William.

As she put on her dressing gown, he picked up the phone and dialled. 'Verne? Oh, hi! Bernie here. Say, you wouldn't care to drop over for a while this morning would you?' Anna, halfway along the landing by now, heard and froze. 'Bill is sick and I have to get to a meeting today with Ascher. I hate to burden you with all this, but I don't think Anna's feeling too brilliant. She could do with a little support.' She turned and went back to stand in the doorway of their bedroom. There was a silence while Bernard listened. Then he said, 'No, Verne. No particular reason, except that you are probably her closest friend, and you know how well Bill gets on with you . . . You will? . . . Thanks, Verne. You're a saint.' He hung up and looked at Anna. 'Extraordinary thing. He asked whether there was any special reason for asking him over.' Anna said nothing but went to William's bedroom. He was sitting up in bed trying to clip together the pieces of a plastic model aircraft. A Mustang. Morning sunshine on his tanned face gave the impression of health but his eyes still carried a feverish glitter.

'How's this boy?' Anna asked, forcing a cheery note into her voice.

'Much better, Mom, but I can't get this wing thing to fit.' He glanced up from his toy. 'Mom? Are you OK?'

'Never better!' What must she look like? 'I might get your horrible flu, but I'm fine at the moment.'

'Hey, Dad! Can you fix this?' Bernard had come quietly into the room behind her.

'You see?' he said to Anna, when he had kissed the top of his son's brush-cut head and gently mimed punching his chest. 'He's fine. I told you there was no need to get steamed up about it.' He turned back to William. 'Now you be good and stay put safely in bed until your temperature's been normal for a while.' He took the Mustang fuselage and wing, looked at the connecting lug and socket but handed the two pieces back. 'I think it's better if you sort that little problem out for yourself, now you're better, don't you?' William sighed and nodded.

'Are you going into the office?' Anna asked.

'I have to see Ascher. I promised. But I'll come straight back. Lunchtime at the latest, OK?'

'I'll do you some coffee and an egg.'

'No need.' He gave William another stroke, on the head. 'I'll grab a glass of milk, soon as I've dressed.' He kissed her and moved off to dress. She sat on William's bed watching him struggle with the model.

'Mom, please?' He held out the pieces

'Oh darling, I'm *hopeless* with that sort of thing.' But she took the toy and, with a sudden effort, snapped the lug into place. Their eyes met, a conspiratorial silence.

Verne arrived moments after Bernard had left. He kissed her – a social kiss to a casual observer, but intimate enough to make her freeze with guilt. He followed her into the kitchen.

'William's in bed. Let's go into the yard.' She poured out two glasses of orange juice and opened the back door. There was a wooden garden seat under a tattered striped awning.

'Anna, what's up?'

'Nothing really, I just didn't sleep at all last night and may be coming down with William's bug. Probably it's just tiredness, though.'

'Anna, Anna.' He kissed her again. She could not make herself forbid him.

'Verne, I have to tell him. I cannot live a lie. It just isn't in my nature.'

'Nor mine. But, Anna, I'm not going to lose you.'

'I don't know what to do.'

'We agreed to give ourselves time, you know, to decide what to do. But then Bill got ill and we never really did hammer things out.'

'Like what things?'

'Well,' Verne held her hand, 'practicalities. Big things, like whether you could leave Bernard. Little things, like where we would live, whether Bernard would oppose your having custody of your boy. Whether—'

'Oh, Verne, no! Stop it!' He turned her shoulders so that she faced him and held both her hands. She could barely see more than a fuzzy outline of his large head and shoulders. He took a handkerchief out of his pocket and dabbed her eyes.

As his face came back into focus he said, 'I am *not* going to lose you.'

'Verne, I don't belong to you. You don't have me to lose.'

'But I want you so much.'

'Like a possession?'

'Oh forgive me, Anna. That's absolutely the last thing I want you to feel. The very last. I've never known anyone treated more like a possession than you are by Bernard.'

'He's my husband, Verne. I promised to be faithful, before God, in a church.'

'You love me. I love you.'

'He's my husband.'

'Does he love you?'

She thought for quite a while before answering that.

'Yes Verne. I think he does. I know he does.'

'I won't ever stop loving you. Ever.' He stared so hard into her eyes she could almost feel his meaning, a physical sensation. 'Whoever should come along, whatever should happen to me – or whenever – I,' he swallowed, making a supreme effort to get the words out coherently, and started again. 'Whatever the future brings, I will be alone. Or. I – will – be – with – you.'

Each word had fallen like a blow. Chiselled into the bedrock of her being, never to be erased. They were silent for some minutes.

When Verne had composed himself again he said, in a relatively normal voice, 'I can't see Bernard having that level of commitment.'

'You don't know him.'

'Does anyone? Really?'

'He's William's father. And William needs us both.' More tears.

'Oh Anna, honey.' He held her. She nestled into his chest, feeling the warmth of his skin beneath his shirt and sensing the faintest but most seductive fragrance of his body. She wanted to stay like that, breathing him in, losing all her pain in the comfort of his warm frame, gaining strength from him. But William was upstairs and she had to find her courage from somewhere else.

She looked up at Verne's face, drawn with grief, his own eyes red, upper lip trembling. 'I've got to tell him,' she said. 'You do understand, don't you, Verne?'

It took a long time before he answered.

'I do. But I think you still have to make a decision, *the* decision.'

'I know.'

'It's a simple choice.'

'Is it, Verne? Is it simple?'

She had to move. With a lurch, she realised that William might have looked out of a window and seen them. 'I must check on the boy.' She ran to the house. He sat for some minutes before following her. He found William's room, following the sound of her voice, soft and gentle, and saw her sitting on the child's bed. She looked up, worry now creasing her brow.

'He was virtually better this morning, but his temperature's up again.' Verne came closer and took in William's flushed cheeks and glittering red eyes.

'Hey, soldier!' He took the boy's hand and felt for his pulse, massive, gentle fingers circling the fragile wrist.

'Mom, my head started hurting real bad.'

'I guess you tried to get up too soon, Bill,' Verne said. 'You need to rest up while your body fights off that nasty old virus.' To Anna, 'I didn't know there was any flu on campus.'

'Neither did I. This is unlike William to get so poorly. He usually shakes a cold off in twenty-four hours.'

'Yeah, but flu, if it's the real thing, can be pretty nasty. Both my kids had it last winter. They were out of action for several days.' He caught sight of her face. 'Hey, don't look so worried. He'll be OK. Just needs rest and plenty of fluids is all.'

'I know. It's just on top of everything.' She blinked, swallowed, kissed her little boy and led Verne out. As they came downstairs, Bernard returned from campus, looking refreshed and vigorous despite his short night. He greeted Verne, and kissed his wife.

'How's Bill?'

'Not as bright at he was first thing,' Anna said. 'He's trying to sleep now.'

'Then I'd best not disturb him. Verne? You'll stay for a drink?'

'Gee, I'd love to, Bernie, but I have to get back.' And he was gone. Anna had the feeling that his leaving may be one of the most significant events of both their lives.

Telling Bernard about Verne was the most difficult task I have ever undertaken. I couldn't think how to begin but I knew that I could not carry this awful secret any longer. It must have hurt him so much to hear, first, that I had started this thing with Verne and, worse – so much worse – that I had yet to decide which way to go. I wanted Verne so desperately that I could not concentrate on anything. I hungered for him. William's illness, and Bernard's obvious distress on that horrible day simply added to my burden, but did nothing to wipe out my desire for Verne, my love for him, my need to be with him. Yet, impossible though it might seem, I still loved Bernard. If anything, I loved him more, now that everything was open to question, than I had before. And the burden of knowing that whatever decision I made would cause so much damage to another human being was too horrible to bear.

Bernard was dismissive at first, assuming that Anna had, in her previous period of depression and homesickness, suffered some sort of flight of fancy. Gradually, as it sunk in, he changed his attitude, but to her surprise it was not to recrimination, but first to incredulity and then to concern. He could hardly believe that she would even want to be with anyone else. He demanded details, not to embarrass her but to get the whole thing clear in his mind.

'We've only been . . . well . . . only once,' she said. 'I stayed with him for the day when you went to Chicago.'

'You love him?'

She nodded. 'But I love you. That's the agony of the whole damn thing.'

'Do you consider him to be an honourable man?'

'I do.'

'Then why would he allow himself to coax you into an adulterous liaison?'

'He misunderstood our marriage.' She recounted the scene at Grackle Wood. 'He thought we were not, you know.'

'I'm sure I don't know.'

'Not absolutely fine together.'

Bernard thought for a while. 'I suppose he was right. We haven't been absolutely fine together since we came out here.'

'Since a while before that, I'd say.' Her back hairs were standing on end at the enormity of what she was saying, making her neck tingle, but she knew they both needed total honesty. After a long pause, he reacted in a surprising way.

'I am to blame,' he said, 'almost entirely.'

'Bernard. You don't have to say that.'

'Oh yes I do. I've been so absorbed with my career, feeling so bloody virtuous, telling myself that what I was doing was best for you, for William. If I put work first, all the time, it was really for the good of us all, or,' and here he coughed out a bitter laugh, 'so I kept telling myself.'

'You shouldn't blame yourself. Everything you've done is honourable.'

He repeated the bitter laugh. 'No, Anna. We both know that's rot.' He sighed, paced up and down the room and then came and tried to hold her. He wanted to express how sorry and how tender he felt, seeing her dilemma. But he could not find a way to unclench. Instead, with stiff arms held formally at her waist – like a timid adolescent at his first dancing class – he said, 'I *can*, er, understand what has happened. And Anna,' here he had great difficulty controlling his voice, 'I, I really don't feel I can issue any blame. Or, at least, I don't think you or, or Verne should be sole recipients of blame.'

She had to get the next sentence out, even though uttering it would be more repugnant than swallowing a toad.

'Bernard, I still love him.'

'I do realise that.' He looked as though he had swallowed the same toad. 'I'm not completely insensitive, you know.'

Their silence was shattered by the sound of retching upstairs. They both ran up, Bernard going into the room first. William was lying back on his pillows, his face flushed crimson, breathing in short gasps. Yellow bile had run down his chin and stained the bed linen.

Bernard took his son's hand, unnaturally hot and dry, in his and stroked his cheek. The boy whimpered a little and tried to take his hand away.

'Mummy, I feel sick and my head hurts.' The reversion into English was as startling as the symptoms. 'Couldn't you close the curtains?'

'They are closed, darling,' Anna said, fighting to keep her voice calm.

'It's too bright,' William whimpered again, more like a three-year-old than a boy within a few weeks of his ninth birthday. He tried to turn over, but seemed too weak and when Anna tried to turn him he cried out in pain for his neck was so stiff it could barely flex. Bernard took Anna out into the hall.

'I can't believe he's got like this so fast,' she said. 'You saw him before you left. He was almost better.'

'We must call Dr Steiner.'

Dr Steiner summoned an ambulance at once and within an hour of her arrival William was in the paediatric ward at the Minorca Hospital. The overworked paediatrician was abrupt. He told them, matter of factly, that their son probably had meningitis and that he hoped they would have caught it in time, but the disease had advanced pretty rapidly, which did not augur well. William would have to be treated with massive doses of antibiotics dripped steadily into his vein. There would be side effects. If matters improved over the next day or so, they could expect a full recovery, but in such cases improvement was a matter of luck. It depended on the individual patient.

Anna stayed, with Bernard, in the ward for the rest of the day and into the night. William seemed neither better nor worse. He was semi-conscious for most of the time and even when awake too drowsy, and in too much pain, to be able to talk. At first one parent had held each hand, but the contact seemed to be physically painful, so they sat as close as they could. Just after midnight, the charge nurse said to them, 'You folks look all in, and you're going to need your strength over the next few days. Why'ncha go on home for now. We'll call you if there's any change.'

They drove home in silence. Neither felt able to utter a word. She waited by the front door until he had driven the car into the garage. The night was close, with insects flying in erratic orbits round the street lamps. Bernard unlocked the door, pushed it open and stood back to let Anna through.

'If you don't want me to sleep with you, I can go into the guest room,' she said.

'How *could* you think I wouldn't want to?' Bernard was as close to tears as she had seen him since Cornwall, in an earlier age – another world.

'I just didn't want to make you have to reject me.'

They lay in each other's arms, but were not comfortable. Neither slept very much.

Next morning early they drove, red-eyed, to the hospital. They had to wait for several hours before the return of the paediatrician, Dr Rosen.

'I am asking you not to keep anything from us,' Bernard said. 'We would both prefer to hear the straight facts,'

'OK,' Rosen nodded. 'Bacterial meningitis is caused by a microbe called meningococcus which invades the meninges

– delicate membranes which cover brain and spinal cord. The body systems tend to go haywire. There may be kidney failure, a breakdown in circulation. Your kid has not responded, so far, to the antibiotic treatment, but then again he has not grown any worse. You should be thankful for that, but,' here Rosen sighed and adjusted his glasses, 'I think the kid has a way to go yet, before he's out of danger.'

During the day, William's skin developed a purplish rash. It began on his cheeks but gradually spread over his entire body. By noon, he had lost consciousness, and stayed comatose for the rest of the day. Within a relatively short time his kidneys failed and he was connected to a dialysis machine. After that, his breathing improved slightly for a few hours, but then his decline accelerated. He died just two days after having been admitted.

There were arrangements to make, but the Morfeys were too numb to take much in and responded to the various enquiries and instructions like automata. On their way home from the hospital, while Bernard drove, Anna tried to understand why she could not feel anything. She noticed, outside, the passing lights, the car lots, the cheap diners and fast food joints, the trees, lit a ghastly yellow by the sodium vapour street lighting. She watched the other cars, American monsters with fins and grinning radiators; she studied the neon lighting as they passed along the town's main street – Benjy's Delicatessen, The College Spa. The Lincoln Cinema, she noted, was screening *A Man for All Seasons*. She tried to remember what Paul Scofield looked like. Still she felt nothing. They crossed to Tudor Avenue, beginning the long climb to the gorge, and she waited for the harsh drumming whine of the car's wheels on the metal grid of the bridge. On the other side, the street lights had been turned off; when Bernard had parked the car in the drive and switched off his lights she could see stars, set in a blue-black sky. And still she could feel nothing.

Inside, they both walked slowly upstairs, too exhausted to eat, just wanting to escape into sleep. She had kicked off her shoes and was sitting on the bed when Bernard went out and she heard him cross the landing and open the door to William's room. In the silence, even on this balmy midsummer night, the house felt cold. She began to shake. Then she heard Bernard's cry. A low growl which steadily increased in volume and rose in pitch almost to a scream. She walked to the threshold and saw William's bed, still rucked up, almost still warm, the bile stains greenish-yellow on the pillow. The model fighter plane, now in two pieces again, lay on the floor beside his worn sneakers. Bernard was standing by the window, his forehead jammed so hard against the frame that the thin flesh between skin and skull must be bruising. He was silent now, but his face reflected in the glass was contorted with pain. Anna picked up the sneakers, held them to her nose, inhaled the salty smell of sweated canvas and rubber. Thus she knew that William was gone and that, very soon, the grief would come. But at this moment the agony of the man beside her was what concerned her most. She stood behind him and placed her hands on his hunched shoulders.

'Bernard. If you want me, I'll stay with you.' She tried to think of Verne. She knew she'd be grieving for him, too, but later. Just now, recent events were grave enough, on their own, to occupy her entire consciousness.

The *Brisbane*'s arrival at Honolulu was delayed. Throughout the previous day, the wind had steadily increased and Captain Maclean had opted to change course to avoid the centre of a tropical low pressure area which looked as though it was developing into something quite nasty. Cedric, now cheerful again after yesterday's mood, tapped on Anna's door to deliver the news.

'Late again, Anna,' he said, not without a certain amount of glee. 'That's the second port this cruise. Rumour has it we'll not get in before about two.'

'Oh?' Anna was disappointed. Hawaii was one of the places she had especially looked forward to. After Madeira and the

Caribbean, she had discovered that islands had a very special charm – a kind of personal identity that had all but disappeared from the continental cities she had visited. 'It hardly seems worth stopping.'

'And, just to keep the cheerful note going,' he said, this time with an even broader grin, 'there was another death on board last night. That brings the score to four. And we're not even halfway round yet!'

'Cedric!'

'I know, awful, aren't I? But I've got a bet with Ant that the tally will exceed half a dozen, and I think I'm going to win.'

'That's terribly unkind of you.'

'Oh come on, Anna! They don't know. Anyway they're all old biddies. And can you think of a better way of going than while you're having, quote, the cruise of a lifetime, unquote?'

'I was thinking of the people they leave behind.'

'Oh!' Cedric suddenly realised how tactless he'd been. 'Oh Anna I'm so sorry. I don't know what to say. How *awful* of me.'

'Have you breakfasted?' Anna wanted to smooth away his embarrassment. He shook his head. He had blushed, almost like a young boy, and could barely speak. 'Neither have I. Shall we?' This time, she offered an arm, just as Ant had before. 'Is your chum up yet?'

'You *are* joking. I told you, he never rises until some disgusting hour.'

While they took coffee and a sticky bun, up on one of the afterdecks, Captain Maclean's voice came over the ship's tannoys. 'Good morning ladies and gentlemen. No doubt you are wondering about Hawaii and I have to tell you that we will not arrive at Honolulu before two-thirty this afternoon. I do apologise for the lateness but I'm sure you would prefer to be a few hours late than to be shaken about in a tropical storm. In order to give you a little more time ashore, we will delay sailing until eleven tonight, so if you like, some of you will be able to dine on the island. And in the meantime, to help while away your morning, all the normal "at sea" activities will take place.'

'That means there'll be a writing class,' Cedric said. 'You can make up for playing truant the day before yesterday.'

'No mention of anyone dying,' Anna said.

'Well il capitano wouldn't, would he?' Cedric said. 'Not company policy to depress the passengers.'

Nine people attended Pullen's class. Anna's presence was noted with a curt nod. 'Missed you last time,' he said. 'Had you bothered to come, you would have heard quite an interesting little piece of writing.' She noted the arch look on some of the faces and open resentment on Elspeth Crampin's.

'I wasn't being idle, I promise,' Anna said. Pullen ignored her.

'Death,' he said, after one of his usual dramatic pauses, waiting for everyone's full and undivided attention. 'One of the more important events in anyone's life. Or, as Woody Allen once said, "it's nature's way of telling you to slow down."' Instead of the snigger he expected, he was met with an embarrassed silence. 'Oh, come on folks! This is the age when *all* taboos are taboo – especially if we want to be writers. We can talk about sex openly and, if we want to be writers, we have to face the nastier side – prostitution, corruption of children, oh' – here he looked directly at Cedric and Ant – 'and all the perversions. And death is another untouchable that must be touched.'

Elspeth Crampin glared. 'I don't think this is quite the—'

'The time? The place? Do you suppose death makes an appointment? Any of us could go. Today, tomorrow – any time.' Some members of the class stared, bug-eyed with anger, others were baffled. 'What the hell's the matter with everyone today?' Pullen asked.

In response, Molly Golby blew her nose, gathered up her papers and said, 'Mr Pullen, either you must be even more insensitive than I first thought, or you cannot possibly know that Mr Tanner passed away last night.'

'Mr Cabbage,' Cedric whispered, in Anna's ear. 'So that's who it was. Poor Mrs Cabbage.'

'Oh shit!' said Pullen. 'I . . . I think, in, er, in respect to Sylvia, we'll cancel the rest of the class but before we do, we'll have a minute's silence for her.'

That night, with the *Brisbane* tied up in Honolulu and most of the passengers ashore, Anna found herself dining alone. She had already finished her soup when Captain Maclean walked up to the table. 'I do hope you'll forgive me for joining you halfway through but the fact is I only have a little time. Ah, Joseph,' he signalled to the waiter, 'just the fish, I think, and a green salad.' He glanced at Anna. 'Will you have a little wine with me, Lady Morfey?' Without waiting for an answer, he said to Joseph, 'Ask Kate to bring a half-bottle of Puligny Montrachet, and let's have some fizzy water too.' Joseph gave his captain a half smile. Both men knew that section waiters were not supposed to deal with drinks. 'Pulling rank, I'm afraid,' he told Anna. 'Sometimes the passengers have to wait for ages before the wine waiters get to their tables. Smart alec accountants at head office are happy to cut down on crew numbers but they never seem to come on board and see how we have to cope. There'll be even fewer staff on the *Orkney* when she gets into cruising next year.' In moments, Kate, a harassed Mancunian with tangled ropes of straw-coloured hair, appeared from nowhere carrying their wine and water.

'Very sad news,' Maclean said, as they ate.

'I'm so sorry for Mrs – for Sylvia.'

'An object lesson to us all. Overindulgence can carry a high price.' Anna was shocked and a little affronted by what seemed a callous attitude. 'I've known them for ever. They cruise with us round the world every winter, or did.'

'Will Sylvia go home now?'

'Already disembarked. It will leave two vacant places here. I don't suppose you can think of any passengers who might liven this table up a bit?'

'Isn't it a little hard to be talking about that so soon?'

'I'm sorry, Lady Morfey. You're quite right. But you see, in this job, with the average age of the passengers and so on, one gets rather used to it. He's with the Good Lord now. That's something to rejoice at, surely?' Anna realised that what had seemed like callousness was simply faith. She envied his blithe confidence in the afterlife. But she felt awkward in the presence of such strong convictions and changed the subject.

'I do know a couple who are eligible, in a way. They've certainly travelled with you for years and years.'

'Really?'

'Mmm. They live next door to me on A Deck. Cedric and Antony.'

'The odd couple? Would you mind them here?'

'I wouldn't, no. But what about the others?'

'Perhaps it's time to stir things up a little. Let's give them a try. If it doesn't work out you can have a general reshuffle at Sydney when Wishart replaces me. He's bound to liven things up anyway. Always does.' Anna still felt uneasy about discussing the Tanners' empty places.

'How was Sylvia when she left?'

'Surprisingly calm, but I suppose the impact will be some time coming to her.'

'Poor woman.'

'She has this extraordinary notion that he would want to be buried on Hawaii. Apparently he made her agree, years ago, that wherever it happened he was not to be buried at sea.'

He lifted his glass. 'Cheers!' She followed suit. The chilled white Burgundy was delicious on her tongue, sharp, fragrant with a burst of flavours that changed as the wine warmed in her mouth. She looked around at the familiar dining room, the lights reflected in the polished brass fittings, the soft buzz of conversation, waiters moving among the tables, the whiteness of the napery, the even crisper cleanness of Captain Maclean's uniform, contrasting with his tanned features and bright blue eyes; and she thought of the cold, dark, numbing ocean.

They had floated over the deepest part and she imagined a body, sewn into a shroud, the last stitch traditionally through the nose, drifting inexorably down, down, down, while the unimaginable pressure increased all over the body, crushing, pulping, compressing.

'I can see his point of view.' An involuntary shudder passed over her body. Someone walking over her grave. She lifted her glass again. 'Let's drink to life!' Captain Maclean looked at her afresh. He could see, behind the bravely forced smile, behind the moistness of the eyes, a latent strength emerging.

'To life, Lady Morfey. And to you!'

Chapter Twelve

'Lisa darling, come to Mummy!'

'No!'

'I want to put a sun hat on you, sweetie'

'Don't want to.' Pink, shapeless toddler legs pounded away across the small back terrace at Tudor Avenue, stumbled a little where the paving ended and the coarse grass of the lawn began, recovered and pumped on towards the old apple tree from which Bernard had suspended a small swing. 'Wing, Mummy, wing!' She was too small to climb on to the swing herself.

Anna worked to keep her patience. Lisa was now almost two and had obviously inherited Bernard's brains and, Anna suspected, his particular brand of single-mindedness. Most babies when they begin to talk say Dada or Mama, but with Lisa – or so it seemed to Anna – the first articulated word had been 'No!'

'Mummy push, Mummy push!' Lisa shouted from the swing.

'Not until you've got your sun hat on!'

'Mummy PUSH!'

'No sun hat, no swing!' Anna called from the kitchen door. Lisa yelled again, stamped her foot so hard that she fell on her bottom. Real tears, now, of pain and humiliation.

When raised in volume, the child's voice had unbelievable

penetrating qualities. Anna felt sure William had been quieter and more biddable in every respect. And definitely more affectionate. When hugged, William would sort of melt into your arms, Anna remembered, with an inner pricking of grief and regret. She could still remember the smell, especially of the back of his baby neck just below the hairline when, fresh from his bath, she would hug him before getting him tucked up for the night. Lisa was spiky. When you picked her up, she was all arms and legs, pushing against any embrace, squirming to avoid Anna's kisses. If anything she was more spiky with Anna than with Bernard, who she utterly adored. After her birth, Bernard determined to get himself more closely involved with her upbringing than he had with William. He even, on a couple of occasions, changed diapers – as they were now known in the Morfey family – and was present, as often as he could be, at her bath times, or at least for part of her day.

Lisa's birth had been so much easier than William's that Anna regretted the hours, no, days she had wasted in periods of anxiety, and, at times during the last weeks of her pregnancy, sheer panic. Fear of pain, the actual discomfort of parturition and all the attendant indignities were not the problem. They were not to be taken lightly, but all mothers had them, and almost all mothers coped with their impending ordeals one way or another. But after William, Anna was afraid that she would never be able to shake off the terror that the unthinkable might happen again. As the tiny germ inside her grew and took shape, the seeds of anxiety germinated in her mind. Would it be all right? Would it have all the necessary parts in all the right places? How would she be able to prevent another fatal disease? How could she protect it from accident? She knew, of course, in the wakeful part of her mind, that these fears were irrational, groundless, stupid and self-destructive, but they were there all right, and they just wouldn't go away.

There was worry, too, that if this child did perish then so would their marriage. Cracks had been developing as imperceptible hairlines during William's early childhood in England, but had begun to gape on their arrival in upstate New York and then burst wide open after Verne, and after William's death.

When they returned from the hospital, Anna had made her decision without a moment's hesitation. Bernard's howl of despair, the sight of William's mussed-up bed, still carrying the imprint of his sick little body, and the taint of the boy's sweat in his old sneakers had done the trick, but there was still so much to repair and the cracks were so wide that they would take a great deal of filling.

Verne came, alone, to the funeral. 'I left the boys behind,' he said. 'I didn't think it'd be, you know, all that good for them.' His eyes looked terrible, puffy, half closed in the harsh sunlight of the summer afternoon.

The cemetery where William was to be buried backed on to the yards of the houses on the west side of Tudor Avenue. Not at all like an English burial ground, this was a place of natural beauty, more like a park with rolling, grassy terrain, trees – mostly cedars and hemlock spruces – and in places, rocky outcrops. Headstones were arranged with generous areas in between so that only a keen observer would note the religious segregation: Jews on the town side, Roman Catholics to the east, Episcopalians a little nearer to heaven, on the undulating upper slopes of the hill among the maturest and most beautiful of the trees. William and his friends, though discouraged by their parents, had often played in this parkland and sometimes Anna had sat on one of the benches, or a particular flat-topped boulder not far from their back garden, to look for birds. That William should be buried in this place was unthinkable. That he should be dead at all had still not properly sunk in. Even as they stood round this ugly slit in the turf, with the brown soil and bright flowers of the wreaths looking unnatural against the grassy landscape, she could not accept that this was to do with her son. It was more like another strange American social custom, with faculty people and their few local friends

looking uncomfortable in dark suits on such a bright, hot day,
eyes downcast as they waited for the Episcopalian minister to
begin running through the words.

'I'm grateful you came, Verne.' In that odd suspension of
emotions, she was able to converse in a perfectly normal
way. Horribly wrong, but she heard herself sounding almost
cheerful. 'He thought so much of you. And I quite agree about
your boys.' Your boys? Last week they would have been 'the'
boys and she'd have thought of them as 'our' boys, meaning
all three, of course. It came to her that William had been
seeing almost as much of Verne as of his father in recent
months – more, even. He and the Henschke kids had been
like brothers. Now it was over, she supposed that William, she
and Bernard would have to reconstruct their futures and . . .
What was she thinking? William's future had been snatched
away and so, therefore, had hers. The flowers, the new hole
in the ground, the small coffin – they pointed to the past, to
an ending. There was no future. Verne squeezed her shoulder
and, sensing that his presence was causing her too much pain,
he slipped away into the group of friends and acquaintances,
and then, as soon as the ceremony was concluded, out to his
car. That was the last time she spoke to him directly.

A day later, he wrote.

My dearest Anna,

   I expect you will have received piles of mail express-
ing sympathy for your loss. I cannot add any words here
that will help. We all know how much it hurts and there
is nothing more to say.

   I realise, too, that you have made your big decision.
I knew it as soon as I saw you and Bernie together
before the funeral and read your faces and, well, just
noticed the way you looked together. I know you will
have wanted to speak to me about it, and soon, and that
the prospect will have been filling you with misery –
or it would have if there had been room for any more.
Anna, I want to save you at least some of that hurt by

telling you that I understand. No one can ever replace you. Absolutely no one. But I understand.

Purlin, as you possibly know, has a department of marine biology situated at Key Pequeño, Florida. The department head down there, Eric Reinsdorf, retired at the end of last semester and I would be front runner to replace him. I've decided to go for that and, assuming I get the post, would move to Florida just as soon as I can get everything fixed here. I will still be on the Purlin faculty, of course, with tenure, but hundreds of miles away from campus.

Anna, it's best this way. No goodbyes. We don't need them. We will always have each other.

She read the letter several times but did not appreciate its noble sentiment until almost a year later when she redis-covered it, folded and slipped into a secret side pocket of her best handbag. At that stage she had broken down and, on being discovered in a state of misery by Bernard who had assumed it was a burst of grieving for William, had shown him the letter.

'You were right about what you told me last year,' he had said. 'Henschke *was* honourable.'

'Is!'

That, Bernard assumed, had concluded the whole affair. Certainly Anna never saw Verne again and, though she frequently thought of him, fondly and still with the same hunger, she was happy with Bernard. Happy because Bernard had changed, or rather reverted to a closer replica of the young man who had taken her to Cornwall in his old, open-topped Morris. But the reversion took quite a while.

After the funeral, there was the inevitable period of pain. Neither partner seemed able to share this, however, and thus the burden was doubled with each suffering in their own private hell. In bed, while their bodies were insulated from each other by poplin and nylon, they clung, hands on shoulders, in an almost formal embrace, for minutes after they had put the light out. But soon limbs began to ache from such unnatural positions, and they felt forced to separate and lie, back to back, each with their private grief. As well as aching for William, Anna thought frequently of Verne, alone now, almost certainly for the rest of his life. *No one can ever replace you.* She knew he meant it.

Then one Sunday morning, soon after the beginning of the fall semester, Bernard said, 'Let's go for a picnic.'

The day had started chilly with a light mist but by the time they had got to Kilmarnock Falls the temperature was balmy and the sky clear blue. Carrying a coolbox, they walked from the car park along the banks of Kilmarnock Creek, lit by dappled sunlight turned even more gold by the colour of the autumn foliage. There had not been a single vehicle in the park and it looked as though they had the entire reserve to themselves. Here and there, along the waterside, grew blue asters.

'Look,' Anna said, 'exactly the same as those Michaelmas daisies I got from Lizzie Branklyn in Kent.' Bernard put the hamper down for a few minutes to rest, while they enjoyed the view. A few golden, yellow or russet leaves – hickory and maple, mainly, with the occasional red oak – were floating on the surface, borne down on the swift stream. Whenever one fell to the water from the overhanging trees, a trout would rise in the water, investigate and then sink silently into the shadow of the deeper water. Bernard saw the sunlight shining on Anna's face, saw her open smile when she spotted the fish, caught her look when she turned to him, if not of joy, then of something pretty damned close.

'Glad you came, Mrs M?' She blushed a little, and looked down at the asters growing near her feet. He had not called her that since England.

'It's so beautiful,' she murmured.

They found a grassy area close enough to the falls to hear their constant hiss but far enough away that they could talk without having their conversation drowned. He opened the coolbox, pulled out a bottle of Chablis and two glasses. He drew the cork and poured. Anna tasted.

'Mmm. This is special,' she said. 'Are we celebrating?' Then a slight chill came over her. 'Bernard, you hadn't planned this?' He looked crestfallen, for a moment, and then a little indignant.

'I did not.' And to settle her doubts he said, 'The wine was a gift from the Aschers, if you remember, when they dined with us months ago. The idea of the picnic was a whim.'

'Cheers, then,' she said. About to lift her glass, she caught sight of his changing expression. He looked away, staring with concentration across to the falls, his back gone rigid. 'What, darling?' she whispered, but she knew what. Brad and Peter and William had practically learnt to swim in the shallow pool a little way downstream.

'Maybe this was a mistake.'

'No, Bernard. I don't think so.' He looked at her. 'We have to get back to normal.' He stayed still for a few moments while she returned his gaze. Then he lifted his glass. Sunlight sparked on the liquid, a pale amber flash from deep within the glass. Anna thought briefly of the *Rheingold* leitmotif and, inevitably, of Verne. She dropped her gaze for a moment but then lifted her eyes again. Bless Verne for showing her that wonderful music, and bless this man for helping her to be strong.

'What do we drink to?' Bernard said.

'To William,' Anna replied promptly, with only the slightest tremor. 'And to life!'

They ate little of the food she had hastily prepared and instead lay for a while, heads close together on the tartan travel rug brought from England. From time to time, he stroked her face or nuzzled her neck. She brushed her hands across his thighs and detected his erection pushing against the cloth.

'Bernard!'

'Do you realise,' he whispered, 'that we have not made love for—'

'Something like three months.' He began to unbutton her blouse. 'Bernard, we can't here. It isn't private enough.'

'Let's go home, then.'

They packed up the picnic things and walked back to the car. As the afternoon waned, the temperature dropped rapidly, not to a chill, but to a comfortable coolness so that they could leave both bedroom windows open, even after each had removed the other's clothes. There had been no urgency, at first, but as they stripped away the layers their hunger, not just for sexual gratification, but to be lost in one another, grew with such strength that they could barely control their movements. They wrestled, almost like contestants, not consciously trying to give pleasure, but whimpering with passion, clinging to one another for dear life. She kissed his chest, just as she had Verne's that one time, but it was the touch and taste of Bernard that fired her passion now. He cupped his hand behind her lovely neck so that he could reach her mouth, half open, ravening for his kisses. She needed him, now, to be truly united with her, the two of them becoming one single sentient being, but within seconds he let out a bark of combined surprise, pleasure and, almost immediately, exasperation.

'O Jesus, Anna, I'm so sorry!' He was almost in tears.

'Sshh.' She stroked the back of his neck, feeling the hair, tickling delicately behind his ears. 'It hasn't finished, my love. It's only just begun.' They lay very still while his breathing subsided to normal. She continued her stroking movements and kissed his ear. After some minutes he began to respond, almost imitating what she did to him, little nips, surprising caresses in areas which, on himself, he had not realised gave pleasure, the very verge of being tickled, but still giving a voluptuous tingling warmth. Gradually, they both felt their bodies had become so relaxed, but at the same time so aroused that every movement had a sensuous undercurrent. When he entered her for the second time she uttered a deep sigh of pleasure. This time he was in control of himself, and able, without thinking about it, to pace his movements to her needs. Sometimes, as they proceeded with their journey towards climax and release, an image of Verne would swim into her senses, but these were fleeting moments, too brief to interfere with the moment, the momentousness of his presence, his essence, his entire persona blending with hers.

Sitting now in her cabin, Anna wrote:

Nothing could ever again be so complete as that one experience. Everything in our future would hinge upon it. Even decades later, when our lovemaking became more perfunctory, and when the intervals between sexual union lengthened, as one would expect them to do with menopause approaching, and with the crippling pressure of Bernard's career, that Sunday was our benchmark. Not that we compared or evaluated each time with that as a basis, but rather each time we were as close together as it is possible to be, the memory of that first union since William's death was recalled and that particular special fire rekindled.

After William, since Anna had not conceived for nine years, she and Bernard had ceased to bother with birth control so when Anna missed two periods and a pregnancy test proved positive they were surprised and delighted. It seemed right, to Anna, that Lisa should be the result of that memorable union which she still privately called their First Proper Time. Their two spirits had joined so seamlessly that it was perfectly natural for there to be issue.

The anxiety had begun soon after the test had proved positive. Fear of miscarriage had soon given way to all the other neuroses, but as soon as her eighth month had begun, when in her previous pregnancy she had suffered toxaemia and been so ill and uncomfortable that she hardly slept, this time her anticipation of the birth was almost unbearable. When Lisa decided to arrive twenty-six days early Anna was terrified that it would be all up with the baby. When the child was born normal she wept with relief. Lisa had to spend a couple of weeks in an incubator, and perhaps that prevented the mother bond from developing as fully and as warmly as it had between Anna and William. With Lisa, right from the start, any bonding was with Bernard. Determined not to make the same mistake again, of allowing his career to put his family stability at risk, Bernard made an extra effort to spend as much time as he possibly could with his daughter, and with his wife.

Bernard's book, *Classic Economics, Theory and Practice* was published in 1968, soon after Lisa's first birthday. Though hardly a volume to enjoy high sales in main street bookshops, it was acclaimed worldwide in academic circles as the model textbook, particularly for beginners and intermediate students. Sales promised to be sustained for many years to come, and would provide a handsome supplement to their university income. His publishers, seeing his growing fame as a television guru, begged him to consider producing a more popular version, something that would spell out the simplest economic theory to ordinary consumers. *Sharing the Cake*, which he completed in a frenzied seven weeks, was published in time for the pre-Christmas rush and, after an orchestrated promotional campaign, not only in the USA, but also in Britain and Europe, sold more than a million copies in paperback. The book became an icon, to be found on the shelves of every thinking person, regardless of profession or political persuasion. It neither preached, nor exhorted any particular political ideal but described what happened to resources within an economy, and attempted to explain why.

The Morfeys were relatively rich.

The importance of being financially independent had not occurred to Anna before, but now she wrote:

Bernard's success was already well established before his books were published and as our means were already perfectly adequate for our needs I hardly noticed our money as it accumulated. There didn't seem to be much point in selling Tudor Avenue, since we were perfectly happy there, and, although Bernard paid off the balance of the mortgage and we spent rather a lot on refurbishing and redesigning the garden, having money made but little difference to our lives. Bernard still worked excruciating hours, and still chased around the country, and around the world now, but we were able to employ someone to look after Lisa when we went on short trips, and if we travelled for longer periods I took her with me.

Bernard never failed to find time for his family, however demanding his schedule might be, but one aspect of his success that threatened all of us was the publicity. I hated it when people would whisper and point, but found it even more irritating when they were so obsequious to Bernard. Some, especially those in his own field, were hostile, and not only to him. I remember even Professor Ascher, who had become quite a close friend, looking at Lisa when he came to supper on the evening of her second birthday party and saying, 'Well *she'll* be getting a pretty handsome share of the cake, even if she never learns to spell w-o-r-k.' It seemed an inoffensive remark, but it was said with a bitter tone – professor's salaries were not princely, even in the lushly financed days of the sixties – and as he spoke, his envy showed through.

Anna needed more fresh air than the small cabin could provide. She had been writing for too long and had pains in her back and neck. Tomorrow the *Brisbane* would be docking at Sydney where she would be alongside for two nights – an unusual event for a cruise liner. Anna had decided to get away from the ship for as long as possible, and had even considered moving to an hotel for the duration. She discussed this with the Boys when she discovered them, after a hard walk eight times round the promenade deck, near the stern swimming pool. One wandering albatross was still following the vessel, and she had stopped to watch its flight for a while before finding a lounger near them. It must be wonderful to be so free, she thought, and to go wherever you liked. It still had not occurred to her that she was and she could.

'An hotel? Anna, darling, how will we exist without you?' Cedric had said.

'I, um, I thought we might still do some things together, in Sydney,' Anna said, 'but I felt like a break from the ship. Unless you want to do things on your own.'

'We both want nothing better than to show you around,' Cedric said. 'Really and truly,' and he caught hold of Anna's hand and squeezed.

'The ship ties up right in the middle of town,' Ant explained, 'almost under the harbour bridge, so there's no need to move house. Oh, Anna, you're going to absolutely love it.'

'You needn't spend more than your sleeping hours on board,' Cedric chipped in. 'There just might be something divine on at the Opera House, and even if there isn't it's worth going, just to admire the building. And it is absolutely *de rigueur* to dine by the waterfront, so that will take care of both evenings.'

'By the by,' Ant said, adding a dab more archness even than usual, 'we've had a little invite under our cabin door.' Anna looked puzzled. '*A propos* of revised dining arrangements. And I suspect we have *you* to thank for that.' The Boys had grabbed a hand each and by this stage in the voyage their devotion was not feigned. 'I can't tell you what that means to us.'

'You've been such a darling to us,' Cedric said.

'Other way round, I think,' Anna replied.

Later, when Anna returned to her cabin, an envelope had been slipped under her door. She was invited to a farewell drink with Captain Maclean. She read it with a small pang of regret. She had grown fond of Maclean and had taken comfort from the small kindnesses he had shown earlier in the cruise,

when she was – what? A different person? She had to think
about that one. The sense of loss was still with her, sometimes
so strong it was intolerable – an anger, really, rather than
sadness. But, yes, she *did* feel different. She could write
now, without inhibition. She had written in the most careful
detail about the most intimate things and she was not afraid
of recalling those tranches of text on her computer. She could
even edit and adjust her English. Tears still flowed, especially
when the subject of William came up, but she felt a warm
glow when she recalled other memories and could refresh
them by rereading what she had written. 'Max,' Anna said,
aloud but in a quiet voice, 'you are something of a genius.
I'm sorry I ever thought of you as a charlatan!' She imagined
him flipping away her apology, thought of him saying, 'It's
what you pay me so much money for!' Then she glanced
guiltily around, as if someone might have noticed her talking
to herself. 'First sign of madness,' she giggled, and then said,
'Jeez, Anna, you smiled.'

She decided to test her strength once more. Her computer
had a clever device called a finder. By pressing a key
and typing in the word she sought she could make the
computer display the relevant text on to its screen. She
tried it now. Command: Find: Verne. Within seconds, up
it came and she was able to read through what she had
written about him. After browsing in the text for a while,
she lingered on that final letter. She had not seen it for
nearly thirty years, but when she had recounted the whole
affair she had remembered, word for word. *No one can ever
replace you. But I understand.* And, at the letter's conclusion:
*No goodbyes. We don't need them. We will always have
each other.*

Those words, it suddenly came to her, might have a new
significance now. But she dismissed the idea. They meant
just the same now as they had when written: that, like the
years with his first wife, the memory would always live, but
only as a memory. Looking back, fine, but no going back.
As Bogart says to Bergman, in *Casablanca*, 'We'll always

have Paris.' True, they would, but only as mental luggage to carry along to their separate destinies.

After the captain's private party – about twenty people attended – Anna decided to dine quickly and return to her cabin to write. She needed a break from her journal, which now ran to far too many pages, but she wanted to finish the current episode. Within a short time, she was at her desk.

Bernard would have been content to spend the rest of his career in America, using Purlin as his base, teaching to a certain extent, but also writing and lecturing around the country. Frequently, especially in those first two years after losing William, I would dream about Verne and felt such longing that I thought I would burst. But whenever I had those thoughts I would feel guilty. Those were the moments when I most needed Bernard, but whereas before he had been unable to decipher my language, now he would respond with understanding, even if it meant distracting him a little from his work. As for Lisa, he doted on her. Every evening, when he was home, he insisted upon feeding her; often he bathed her and at weekends he would expect to spend time playing with her in the garden or, if it was cold, playing games or even watching daytime television with her. He taught her to swim before she was five years old, using our own pool in summer, and taking her up to one of Purlin's indoor pools in winter. Most faculty parents made use of this facility, but none so regularly as Bernard.

But he seldom referred to William. At first, the subject was too painful, and neither of us could talk about him without breaking down. But later, as Lisa's birth drew near, I knew that he had forced himself to box up his feelings for his son and set them aside in a mental archive not to be revisited if at all possible. It wasn't because he did not care, but because his only way of dealing with such intolerable agony was to shut it off.

I suppose, looking back, it may have been a mistake to have buried William so near to us, but it comforted me to know that he was a short distance beyond our back fence and I often imagined him to be present, looking on, watching his baby sister grow. Every afternoon, I walked over to where he was buried, not to put flowers on his grave, or to act out a duty, but simply in an attempt to be near him. When Lisa could walk I began to take her with me into the park. Bernard disapproved.

Our lives, in mostly gentle harmony, crept on their petty paces, not just from day to day, but from year to year.

'I really don't think she should be burdened with all that, do you?' Bernard said one afternoon. He had come home early to prepare for a trip to Washington and had spotted mother and daughter coming through the back gate.

'She doesn't really understand about William.' Anna had recomposed her features when she had spotted him looking across the garden. 'It's just somewhere for us to walk.'

'Well, there's no need for her to get morbidly involved.'

Anna could not bring herself to discuss this any further. She knew that Lisa was bound to want to know about her brother one day, and could not see that she was doing anything wrong. But she also knew that Bernard's disapproval was all part of the 'boxing off' business. She wondered how he was so able to regulate his emotions.

One evening Bernard came back from work and said, 'Let's eat out. There's something I need to discuss.' He had a neutral expression, but Anna sensed something momentous brewing. The old signs of an extra excitement were there, and she suspected that he was fighting to keep whatever it was to himself until the right moment. They dined at Chez Solange in Collegeville, a new and rather pretentious restaurant which had, so far, been boycotted by faculty members because too many of the wealthier undergrads used it to impress their dates. Bernard wanted somewhere quiet where they would not be overheard, or at least not by colleagues.

'I'll come straight to the point,' Bernard said. 'I've been offered the Chair of Economics at Stoneford.'

'Stoneford? In *England*? That's pretty big, isn't it?' Everyone, even with the most tenuous connections, knew that the University of Stoneford had the most revered department of economics in the world. Many statesmen, not only British, but international, had studied there, and academics from Stoneford were on advisory bodies to the movers and shakers of some of the world's largest and most influential economies.

'The biggest, I'd say.'

'Bernard, that's absolutely wonderful!' She looked across the table at him. His eyes were glittery with excitement, but there was an edge, almost of nerves.

'It would mean another move. This time to eastern England.'

What irony, Anna thought. When I was so homesick I'd have leapt at the chance. Now I'm not so sure. Now she loved the clapboard house on Tudor Avenue. They had done such a lot to it, expanding the ground floor to include a large well-lit room at the back which opened on to the swimming pool – usable between May and September. Anna had developed the garden to be interesting all year and productive for most of the summer and fall. Tomatoes, peppers and melons would never ripen so well in England as they did here. She would miss it, and she would miss upstate New York. The winters were long and hard, but she could tolerate those, knowing that they were always followed by warm, hasty springs and dramatically hot summers. But mostly, she would miss her friends. As Lisa grew toward school age there were so many other mothers at playgroups around the campus, most having husbands who worked at the university. Moving, especially to an entirely new area, would be difficult. She felt the dragging sense that everything was going to start all over again.

'I presume you've accepted.'

'Anna!' He forced a grin. 'Would I accept before consulting

you?' Anna said nothing. 'But I guess there's nothing you'd want more than to go back home. We'll even be near Norfolk.'

'You want to accept.'

'I want to know what *you* want to do. I have tenure here and besides, with what I've done for this place, they wouldn't want to lose me.'

'But you really want to accept.'

'What I want is only half the equation.'

'It's a big jump upwards.' She was playing for a little time. Perhaps she was still testing his willingness to sacrifice for her.

'Mmm,' he made a poor pretence of being casual, 'in academic circles.'

'No, in every circle. This is your big chance. Especially if you want to move into politics.'

'*I* don't want to go into politics. Whatever gives you that idea? But you're right, it is big.' Bernard allowed himself to smile. 'Big in that I could end up working alongside politicians – chancellors, prime ministers perhaps – to clear up some of the messes they've made.'

'You could end up helping politicians to *make* messes.'

'Economics is an inexact science. Things happen, circumstances change, things fall apart. So!' He was becoming fractionally irritable. He wanted an answer. 'How do you feel about it?'

'Bernard, I'd love to go back,' Anna said, but as she spoke she thought of William. How could she leave him behind? Who would tend the grave? He would have nobody in America. It would feel like a betrayal. Could she bear to forgo her daily quiet moment by his headstone, standing alone while Lisa ran among the hemlock trees looking for squirrels? In her mind she caressed her son's head, feeling the American brush-cut hair under her palm. She remembered how she had fixed the wing on his model aircraft that last day before he went to hospital, their eyes meeting as the plastic lug snapped into its bracket.

'Anna!' Bernard noticed a tear. 'Anna, I know exactly what you are thinking.'

'Do you?'

'We won't be leaving him behind.' He took her hand. 'He's here, with us, all the time. Not back there.' She loved him for saying that. But she could not trust herself to follow that train of thought. This was a moment of triumph for his career. Another one, and she did not want to spoil that.

'Actually,' and here she pulled his hand towards her and kissed it, 'I was thinking how grateful I am that you consulted me first.'

Anna switched off her computer, determined not to touch it again until the vessel had sailed from Sydney in three days' time. She had gone straight to bed after leaving the dining room, so as to rise soon after four, work for a couple of hours and then go up on deck to watch the *Brisbane* sail into Sydney Harbour. As usual, Cedric was also up with the lark, and together, wrapped against a slight morning coolness, they stood on the ship's forward Observation Deck and watched as she slipped into the inlet, with the heads on either side, and progressed along the natural haven towards the city. Soon Anna saw skyscrapers and the harbour bridge, outlined against a cloudless sky, pearly pink in the rising sun. They passed various bays and coves, some of them tree-lined, while Cedric pointed them out.

'That's Woolloomoloo,' he said, pointing to an inlet presided over by a huge ship-building derrick. 'Then Farm Cove,' he indicated a small, rounded bay surrounded by trees and shrubs, 'where the first convicts grew food.' But Anna was staring at the Opera House.

'I can't believe it,' she said. 'Those amazing roof things, like huge white sails, or up-ended boats. They look pink in this light.'

'Ah, but wait until you get close.' He took her hand. 'Oh I do hope something good is on tonight.'

Within minutes, the *Brisbane* was sidling past the great

white building and beginning to slew round before being nudged, by a number of tugs, into her moorings at Circular Quay.

'See what I mean?' said Cedric. 'Absolutely plumb centre. Practically under the bridge.' At that point, Anna felt a hand take her other arm. 'Good God alive!' Cedric squeaked. 'This I do *not* believe!' Ant was standing with them, tired, shaky, unshaven, but up before seven in the morning.

'This is the hub,' Ant said. 'Trains, buses, big ships, little ferries – everything starts from here.' There was a tremor in his voice, caused by more than his being up at least two hours before he would normally open a single baleful eye. 'Ships that pass in the night, and ships that move away together.'

'It's a bit special for us, you see,' Cedric explained. 'This is where we first met.' And in front of a surprised Anna, he took Ant's hand and kissed it. She was not offended: it was unconventional rather than shocking, like spotting someone in jeans and a T-shirt at a formal dinner party.

'As I said,' Ant murmured, 'a hub. A place of departures. And of arrivals.'

PART THREE

ARRIVALS

Chapter Thirteen

They did go to the opera. As soon as the ship had been cleared, Anna and the Boys walked down the gangway and set off at a brisk pace in the cool, moist morning. Later it would be hot but now they were moving among early commuters, newly disgorged from ferries and trains, scurrying to their offices in the business district. The smell of fresh coffee tempted them to stop at a pavement café, where Ant disgraced himself by ordering a breakfast chop with scrambled egg.

'Ant, really!' Cedric protested, 'you'll end up the size of a house.'

'If you two tear me out of bed at such an unearthly hour, I need sustenance.'

After breakfast, they walked along the waterside to the opera house and, finding the box office already open, were thrilled to discover that *Così fan tutte* was to be performed that evening and that there were still some seats available. Anna insisted on paying for these, a token of gratitude to her friends, and then suggested that despite the increasing temperatures it would be fun to explore the city on foot.

She wondered why Bernard had not told her how lovely it all was. He had been often enough but had never suggested that she should accompany him on such distant trips. They visited the art gallery; they travelled to Darling Harbour on the new monorail that threaded itself like a giant caterpillar through shopping arcades and around buildings to the modernistic developments of the Aquarium and Maritime Museum. It was fun, just for the ride, like playing trains. They had drinks at the Wentworth Hotel and then spent an afternoon strolling in the botanic garden. Hearing high-pitched bird whistles in the palms of the gardens at Farm Cove, Anna had looked up to see a group of parrots with vivid colours – blue heads, orange throats, green backs and red wing flashes – feeding on the fruits.

'Oh look, Boys,' she called to her companions who had wandered ahead, 'they're gorgeous!'

'Parrots of some kind,' Ant said, glancing up.

'Rainbow lorikeets,' Anna said. 'I've only ever seen them caged, in bird parks before.' A flash of Charlie, her first bullfinch that Christmas morning. The pleasure of watching such dazzling beauty, here at the bottom of the world, almost took her breath away. When Bernard had gone, so had her love of nature. Interest had begun to revive on board, with the dolphins and sea birds, but now the love of wild things, and the sheer joy in their existence had come flooding back. 'I must get some binoculars,' she announced. 'Now, before we get back on board.'

'Opera glasses!' the Boys chorused.

'Mmm,' Anna said, 'I suppose they would do for that too.'

And they did. With a pair of field glasses powerful enough for ad hoc birdwatching, but small enough to fit into her handbag, she and the Boys walked from ship to Opera House, more slowly this time, so as not to perspire, as Cedric so delicately put it, into their smart duds. Mozart and the age of Viennese elegance, from a different epoch and from the opposite side of the earth, seemed to Anna ridiculously out of kilter in such a space age building, but as soon as the first chords of the overture were played she was lost in the music. She knew the story well enough but had not, until now, read its sinister sexual innuendoes. She

could see through the hypocrisy of the main characters easily
enough, but for her, infidelity and its consequences were far
too agonising to lampoon in this way. Or so she considered
until she rediscovered a new depth to the words, actions
and music which made her understand, as if for the first
time, not only the inestimable value of a single relationship
between two humans but how flippantly such capital can be
squandered. As this sank in, she watched the rest of the opera
with a chill in her spirits, as if a death's head shadow had
been projected on to the cyclorama – not obvious, not even
noticed by some, but insistently there.

The boys must have acquired the same feelings. Cedric
was quite touchy with Ant and when he suggested that they
might go to some of their old haunts in the Rocks area or
even take a cab to Oxford Street he retorted, 'How can you
possibly imagine that Anna would want to see *that* side of
your past?'

'Your past too,' Ant muttered.

'Not in the same way at all,' Cedric snapped. 'Never
like *that*.'

'Our past,' Ant insisted. Cedric snorted and increased his
pace, walking a few yards in front of the other two. Anna felt
embarrassed to be caught in the crossfire.

'I suppose he's told you that I was a bit of a lad, in
my youth.'

'No, Ant.' Anna did not want to get involved. 'You did.'

'*I* did?' He was silent for a while. 'Must have been in
my cups.'

'Somewhat.'

'God!' He was silent for a while longer. 'Hope I spared
you the details.'

'I'm not sure I'd have wanted to hang around for details,
Antony. Not back then, when you told me.' But now, she
thought, I think I would be interested. There might be a story
in it all. She even toyed with the idea of drawing him out a
little. 'Promiscuous, I think, was the word you used.'

'Ah.' He looked ahead, at the back of Cedric, walking

erect, shying fastidiously when a group of beery Australian men took up a little too much pavement. They looked like part of a rugby team and, when they passed, Anna noticed that although Ant did not exactly ogle, he managed to pass an appraising eye over them.

'Have you ever been tempted?' Anna asked, slipping her hand into his – a natural action for mutual comfort. 'I mean, it's a pretty big change if you were, you know, um, promiscuous before you met Cedric but – what's the word?—monogamous, ever after?'

'Tempted? Constantly,' Ant muttered, 'even now. But temptation isn't something you can control, it just happens to you. If you respond to the temptation, *that's* where it becomes wrong.'

'And Cedric confuses temptation with the actual sin?'

'I wish he could realise,' Ant's hand tightened on Anna's, 'that this kind of stupid paranoia could be enough to drive one away.' Anna knew he did not mean that. It would cause intense irritation, might drive him to drink too much, or to shout back, perhaps even to lash out, but not to leave. Paranoid was one thing Bernard never was, she thought.

'Shall we catch up with him?' she said. They quickened their pace and came abreast of Cedric. This time it was Anna and Ant who took one each of his hands. I never used to be the touchy-feely kind, Anna thought, but I don't object. In fact I love it, just as I love the company of this odd couple. Verne was a toucher and holder; Bernard not.

'Actually, Cedric,' she said, after they had been walking for a while in silence, 'I really would quite like to see a little more of the – you know – night life.' They were close to the harbour bridge now, with the *Brisbane* blocking out the foreground. It was natural for all three to slow their pace and move to the water's edge, to lean on the railings and look across at the lights on the other side of the harbour. The huge clown mouth advertising the funfair at Luna Park was lit up in an obscene gape, marring the scene, its reflected image shattered in the small waves on the water surface.

'Night life?' He was still cool, but it was an act now, rather than a true manifestation of his feelings.

'Pubs and things. The sorts of places I can't really go to on my own.'

'Cedric,' Ant said, 'let's take her to dinner, tomorrow, at the Waterfront. Then we can pop into a few places afterwards.'

'Not Oxford Street,' Cedric said.

'Definitely not Oxford Street,' Ant agreed. But while Cedric's head was turned he gave Anna a wicked wink. More than a gleam of conspiracy, there was enough excitement in it to help her understand why Cedric had so little faith in his fidelity.

Because she was travelling alone, Anna was invited to remain on the captain's table and since the Boys, who had only just begun to dine there, were also to stay, she accepted. The other new guests included a business man who was so similar to Mr Cabbage that Anna found it hard to believe the original had died. His wife was Australian, heavily dewlapped and even more heavily bejewelled, but with an ability to resort to coarse language without batting an eye. Anna christened them Cabbage Two. The numbers were completed by a retired Australian politician, who had resigned government office to escape too deep an investigation into allegations of corruption, had then undergone open heart surgery and was on the ship to convalesce. He was accompanied by a head-turningly beautiful young Anglo-Asian woman. Anna could not fathom what their ménage might comprise, but clearly they were not husband and wife, and she felt sure there would be more story fodder in the offing. She could not help calling them Bruce and Sheila. Outwardly, Anna remained as demure and modest as when she had boarded the vessel back in Southampton, but now that she was able to look at part of her own tragedy a little more objectively, watching the behaviour of others – often busy constructing their own tragedies – had become so compulsive to her that it was likely to become an addiction.

Captain Wishart was as different from Maclean as it was possible to be. Close to retirement, but looking young for his years, especially with his face sun-kissed, he was clean shaven but with craggy eyebrows and a mischievous twinkle in his dark brown eyes. He was a master of aimless small talk but took little pleasure from it, preferring to provoke more animated conversation. Thus, before they had begun their main courses on their first night out of Sydney, he had engaged every member of his table in friendly but lively sparring matches on a whole range of subjects from the genius of Noël Coward, with the Boys; which of Norfolk's flintstone wool churches is the finest, with Anna; why Gough Whitlam was the best and the worst prime minister Australia ever had, and, with Cabbage Two, why British business practices had to be adopted down under if they wanted to compete more effectively in world markets. Most people, trying such tricks, would have been condemned as wiseacres, but Wishart had a light touch and stimulated animated discussion from his companions so deftly that they did not realise they were being lured into action. Anna liked him instantly and during the evening frequently met his eye, her glances almost always returned with an impish wink.

By the end of their first dinner with him, everyone was at their ease – although, surprisingly, the Boys had seemed a little more subdued than usual – and laughter seemed louder and more frequent from his area of the restaurant. Afterwards, he apologised for having to leave them, explaining that it was unusual for a captain to dine on his first night at sea, and, taking Anna's arm as if they had been partners for decades, ushered them out of the restaurant.

'It's a great privilege to meet you, Lady Morfey,' he said. 'I was quite a follower of your husband's work when he was head of that special prime minister's group.'

'Not really head of.' Anna did not want even to think about it. 'Just an economic adviser. That was all.'

'Oh there's no need for modesty. Everyone knows he was one of the big brains behind that government.'

'Well, I . . .' Anna wanted to get off the subject. She tried to think of something else to say, but with increasing unease could only sense an undertow of memories tugging away at the sand under her feet.

'His policies were quite mad, of course. Mad and dangerous.'

She was startled out of her introspection and, without thinking, heard her voice develop an edge. 'Isn't that rather impertinent?'

'Highly,' said Wishart, and when their eyes met she was so caught by the wicked twinkle in his that she actually laughed.

'I think we'd better change the subject,' she said.

'I'll walk you to your cabin.'

'You don't know where I live.'

'Your cabin is A-twelve, but you live in Carborough, I fancy.'

'How do you—'

'In all my years at sea – and there have been a hell of a lot of those – I've made a hobby of getting to know the, um, the *distaff* side of famous people. Wives of – or sometimes, husbands of – are so much more interesting than the great people themselves, don't you think? In almost every case I've studied, and believe me, Lady Morfey—'

'Anna, please!'

'And I'm Bill. In almost every case, the big person would not be where he or she was without the partner, even when it looks as though it's in spite of.'

'In my case that simply is not so. Also, although my husband achieved a small level of fame, he was really an academic rather than a personality, and slipped quickly into the background again, particularly after the change of prime minister.'

'In fact, he seemed to be far more in the background during his period with the government than he had been before, when everyone was reading that book of his. Never seemed to be off the telly in those days.'

'From choice.'

'Really? Whose choice, his or yours?'

'Both.' Anna remembered how she had craved privacy, and how Bernard had hated seeing what being in the public eye was doing to her. 'But notoriety would have been a distinct disadvantage in his last job.' They had been strolling slowly along A Deck and came now to her court.

'That's for sure.'

'And luckily, the public has a very short memory. Captain Maclean obviously hadn't heard of Bernard. Neither has anyone else on this ship.'

'Oh I find that hard to believe.' He took her key from her, unlocked her door and held it open. 'One thing that does intrigue me, though, and that is, why you are travelling alone?'

The question felt like a dash of iced water down the back of the neck. 'Don't you know?' A strangled whisper, after a tense pause. 'You seemed to know so much about it.' Tears welled and began to smudge her eye make-up.

For the first time that evening, he lost his poise. 'Oh, I do beg your . . .' but she simply pushed him before stepping backwards and slowly, but irrevocably, closing the door, not quite in his face. Then the undertow washed away the rest of her footing. Blinded now by a mix of tears and mascara, she threw off her clothes and crept into bed, biting her pillow in an effort to make the pain go away.

Having cried herself to sleep at around ten, she was awake at four. As soon as her eyes were open she felt the lurch of unhappiness beginning and immediately berated herself for giving way to it. Get up, get dressed, get writing, she commanded. There must not be time for sliding back into the quicksand of depression. After such a happy interlude at Sydney and knowing, now, that she could still develop new and deep friendships with people like the Boys, she had felt much happier. So much happier that she had decided, more or less, to give up her memoirs and to concentrate on narrative writing – stories that would be fun to write, that could be shared with others. But all it had taken to knock her back down the steep bank made slick with the mud of despair was that fragment of conversation with Bill Wishart. After that, she knew that she had to complete her private life story. All of it. Her therapy would not be complete until every event had been probed, dissected and laid out as text, like specimens in an insect collection, their colours and shapes still life-like but at last controlled, dead and pinned in their places.

She decided to start afresh by washing her hair, scrubbing and rubbing until the water sloshing about her feet in the tiny cabin shower threatened to overflow and flood the floor. She rinsed, turned the shower on full cold for a few seconds before turning off the water and reaching for her towel. She brushed her teeth with as much vigour as she had used to wash her hair, making her gums bleed, and then brushed her hair as she dried, enjoying the caressing warmth of the hair dryer at full power. Finally, feeling clean and fresh, she sat down and switched on her computer for the first time since her arrival at Sydney. There was a short story she had written some days before and she made herself read and edit that before turning to her memoirs. It was sound. The language was fluent, the imagery worked well and, she felt, the plot was strong enough to impel a reader through to the end. She checked for spelling errors and then set the story to print while she opened the big document. She glanced at her watch. Five-seventeen. Since waking, she had not thought once of Bernard. She braced herself, and began to write.

After Kent and upstate New York, the East Midlands presented another culture shock. Stoneford itself was a perfectly ravishing town, with mostly grey or honey-coloured limestone buildings. The surrounding countryside, in spite of being close to the flat fenland of East Anglia and south Lincolnshire, had gentle undulations, well garnished with woodland areas and consisting mainly of grassland which was dotted, in

spring, with cowslips and later with blue meadow cranesbills and field scabious. I took to the area at once,
partly because its prettiness had surprised me so, and partly
because it was within easy driving distance of Norfolk.

Unlike Oxford or Cambridge, Stoneford was a very
small town with a modest collection of shops. For any
serious purchasing one had to travel twenty miles to
Carborough, a great city on the very edge of the Fens
whose centre, around its cathedral, was beautiful, but
quite ruined by huge developments, both residential and
industrial, all around its outskirts. The parkways and
by-pass roads reminded me of America, but the vast
estates of mean little houses, pretentious, ugly hotels
and soulless suburbs made the place difficult to like.
The university was set in a twenty thousand-acre estate
between Stoneford and Carborough. Originally it had
occupied the huge mansion built for one of Elizabeth I's
advisers but was then confiscated when his advice turned
out to be duff. During the growth of British industry at
the beginning of the nineteenth century, what had been
a small model school of political science and agriculture
for just over a hundred years was refounded, expanded
and, though known as a university, developed largely
as a school of economics. Its stature continued to grow,
and today, to hold the chair of economics at Stoneford
is more akin to being vice chancellor of a more conven-
tional university than simply a professor.

Anna glanced back through her work and wondered why
she was recording all this detail. Probably to put off the
next phase.

After all the publicity he had received in the USA,
Bernard decided, from the start, to assume a lower
profile. He declined interviews, refused to appear on
television and kept his public speaking to a minimum.
Instead he used the press to convey his mission. He

soon persuaded one of the broadsheets to carry a regular column, to be written under a pseudonym, in which he eroded every economic and quite a few political arguments presented not only by the current government but by much of the opposition. Under different names he also wrote for the *Spectator* and for the most popular Sunday newspapers, adapting his style in each to suit the special needs of the readers. He was determined never to repeat the mistake of becoming so caught up in his career that Lisa and I were deprived of his attentions, but the pressures on him, both in and out of Stoneford, were growing.

'Darling, you can do the house hunting,' Bernard said within a day or so of their return to Britain. 'Let's not go for anything too costly to maintain or to heat.' Meanwhile they rented a roomy cottage in Sufford, a pretty limestone village between the university and Carborough. It was late spring and Anna had already fallen in love with the large magnolia tree in full bloom in the cottage garden. She had made enquiries, in case the owners might be prepared to sell, but was somewhat coldly turned down, as if the very request had been an affront. She thought something similar would suit them all rather nicely. Their needs, in spite of Bernard's wealth, were pretty simple: a bedroom each plus one spare for guests; a good but not unmanageably large garden for her; a study for Bernard to work in at home and space for giving small parties. Big parties could be arranged at the university or, and this was the exciting part, in the flat Bernard had decided to buy in London. She viewed a number of period houses, looking out the attributes they needed, checking for interesting features, and gauging what she thought of as the spirit or atmosphere of each property rather than worrying about the asking price. When she had narrowed down her list, she suggested that Bernard should come with her to have a more detailed look.

Lisa, nearly nine, who had already started school mid-term

at Savernake House, could come along too. Anna felt it important that she should play a part in selecting their home, since much of her growing up would take place there. Lisa's personality was the antithesis of Anna's. The mother was retiring to the point of timidity; the child was brash. Anna was contemplative; Lisa was competitive. Anna mostly gave; Lisa, like any average child, took. As soon as she was eleven, Bernard wanted her to board at one of the best public schools for girls – Benenden, possibly, or Roedean, he wasn't yet sure – but Anna couldn't help feeling that missing out on so much home life might somehow deprive their daughter. Yet when she tried to feel regret that Lisa was soon to spend weeks on end away, she couldn't, and then felt guilty for not regretting.

Of the three country properties on Anna's shortlist, two would have done at a pinch but one, a small early nineteenth-century farmhouse, she had fallen in love with the moment she saw its chimneys above the trees. The approach lay along a narrow lane, not paved with asphalt but with a good stony base, so that even in bad weather it would stay dry and firm. The house stood within a sizable walled garden with room enough for long borders, a mature apple orchard and – enclosed by more walls and an old hornbeam hedge – a kitchen garden. This had once been a thriving family farm but in changing times, when rural incomes had plunged, almost all the land had been sold off to more successful neighbouring farmers. There was, however, a stone barn, with hayloft – perfect for Bernard to use as an office, or even to convert as an annexe for guests – and a four-acre paddock which she could imagine Lisa wanting to use for a pony if she should happen to develop a fondness for horses. Anna rather hoped she would.

She planned the house-choosing day so that they could view the other two properties in the morning and could then spend the whole afternoon looking over Boxwood Farm. Lisa had grown bored with being shown through successions of strange rooms during the morning, and elected to play in the derelict garden and paddock. Anna knew that Bernard would not be especially moved by the rural tranquillity or by the beauty of the landscape but she had planned to emphasise the practical strengths.

'This is a poky little front hall,' she admitted, having turned the key with some difficulty in the stiff lock, 'but I thought we could knock that wall out and have this door opening straight into the room which would become a sort of large hall.' She talked rapidly about all the plans she had been developing and refining for days. 'Two more big rooms here, and here. Back door there. No downstairs loo, but there's a perfect spot for it if we build on a small structure there. We could make it big enough to house a utility room and somewhere for kicking off muddy wellingtons.'

'It seems not to have been lived in for ages,' Bernard said. 'I wonder why.'

'I did too, but apparently it's been a family thing. It was left jointly to three sons and a daughter. They couldn't agree which of them should live in it, but no one would allow anyone else to sell.'

'That's a bit ominous.'

'Not really, I gather families – especially farming ones – can be a bit like that round here.'

'No, *that*.' Bernard was running his finger along a crack in the wall.

'Probably just the plaster.' She led him away to the upstairs. They looked out of the master bedroom window, down on to the garden.

'Looks a mess.'

'Lovely! Just what I need to get my teeth into. The walls make it warm and sheltered, and the soil doesn't seem too bad.' She walked over to a door in the bedroom. 'And Bernard, look! A small dressing room – begging to become our own private bathroom. *En suite*, as they say.'

Before coming to Boxwood Farm, they had lunched at a pub in a rather odd little village called Wychgate St Peters, made ugly by a group of council houses right at its centre and darkened by the shadows of a badly overgrown plantation of fir trees planted right up to edge of the village street. Anna had packed a Thermos and some rock cakes for tea and suggested, now, that they should sit under one of the old apple trees in the orchard.

'Well, you two?' she asked.

'I think it's lovely,' Bernard said. 'I don't know how you manage to see so much potential in such a, well, such a dilapidated-looking building.' He shuffled closer to her, on the grass. 'But it's obvious you're nuts about it, and I know you'll love doing it up.'

'Lisa?' Anna said. The girl had turned away when Bernard put his arm round Anna's waist and was gazing over the trees on the far side of a second paddock in which maturing lambs grazed.

'Won't it be lonely out here?' She bit into her rock cake, chewed with a dry mouth and took a slurp of tea to help it down. 'You can't see any other houses, anywhere.' Her American accent was already fading, yet they'd hardly been home a month. Anna wasn't sure she was happy with the intonations that were replacing the drawl. A lot of the girls at Savernake House tended to say 'OK yah!' rather a lot, and Lisa had already begun experimenting with the expression at home. Even Bernard had caught it; once she had heard them saying it to each other. Their intimacy had rattled her, perhaps because she knew, as they must have done, that it was an expression she would never have picked up.

'We're really much closer to that village than you think,' Anna said. 'It's only the other side of those trees. Easily walkable.'

'It's so quiet,' Lisa said.

'Peaceful,' Anna said. 'And I bet there'll be nightingales in that wood.'

'Scary,' Lisa said, with an ever-so-slightly dramatic little shudder.

'You'll get used to it, my sweet,' Bernard told her, but his own face had fallen at the sight of her bleak expression.

Anna's offer, made first thing Monday morning, was accepted without hesitation, even though it was considerably below the asking price.

Chapter Fourteen

The surveyor's report on Boxwood Farm was more damning than she had expected. There were structural cracks, signs of movement, every known fungus and pest infested the timbers, the roof was not very sound and there was doubt over the exact position of one of the boundary lines. Anna handed the report to Bernard as soon as he had brought Lisa home from her music lesson in Stoneford.

'That'll be why no one wanted to buy it,' he said.

'I'm sure we can put these things right.' Anna spoke without conviction. The place was a wreck and Bernard was never one to make a bad investment. She felt the weight of disappointment beginning to crush her spirit.

'There's so much wrong with it,' Bernard said, scanning the pages. Lisa looked over her father's shoulder at the report.

'Daddy, I don't want to live in a ruin.'

'Don't be ridiculous Lisa!' Anna snapped, noticing the two of them exchange glances. It was impossible not to sense a conspiracy.

'But I don't want to.' The child's voice was developing into a whine.

'Surely it doesn't matter if we have to rebuild the whole damned thing,' Anna persisted. 'We can easily afford it.'

Bernard caught the desperation in her voice and put his arm

round her shoulders. 'Of course we can.' He kissed the top of her head.

The estate agents played the next move, producing, from nowhere – in spite of several years without a single enquiry – another keen buyer who had, they explained with convincing sympathy, just made an offer which was higher, but only slightly, than Anna's.

'I don't believe it,' Bernard said. 'I bet it will be the farmer trying to squeeze a little more out of us.'

'We can afford it,' Anna said.

'Bad principle to be drawn into a Dutch auction,' Bernard said, but with reluctance he agreed that she should increase her offer. The agents took a whole week to come back to her, claiming that the vendors had gone away. Finally they telephoned on Saturday morning while Anna was out buying provisions. Bernard received the call. They told him that the vendors had instructed them to invite a further increase on the offer, since there was now further new interest in the property.

This he recounted to Anna when she returned with a car-load of groceries. She had spent much of the morning trying to force herself to concentrate on the shopping, but was so preoccupied with the farmhouse and all the improvements she wanted to make that she constantly forgot what she was looking for on the shelves. There would be room, if they wanted, to have chickens, so that they could enjoy truly fresh eggs, every day, just like in her childhood. With Bernard travelling so much, and with the planned London flat, they would have to have someone to look after the place: someone who could feed chickens, clean and dust, hoe the vegetables. She fantasised about finding another Dawn, about working with her, shoulder to shoulder, on the renovations, on the decorating, on the daunting but absorbing tasks they would undertake in the garden. Hot and tired, but feeling virtuous, they would reward themselves with glasses of homemade lemonade under one of the mossed apple trees in the orchard. Love – that was all the place needed, really, and she had plenty to give. It was too late in the year to tell, just then, but she had a bet with herself that there would be primroses and snowdrops growing in the turf of the old orchard.

'I've called the agents' bluff,' Bernard told Anna, as he carried the heaviest box of provisions from her car to the kitchen table. 'I've withdrawn the offer and told them that I'm no longer interested in that property or any other they might be handling.'

'Bernard, why?'

'Face it, darling, they're totally crooked – I bet there hasn't been an offer for that place in years. Besides, it's a ruin. Too far gone not to cost a fortune to renovate.'

'We could afford it. You said—'

'We'd have to spend far more than it would be worth when we'd finished.'

'Would we? Would that matter?'

'And I'm not sure it's right for Lisa.'

'Ah.'

'Poor darling. You loved the place already, didn't you.'

'Lisa would have got used to it. She's just too young to know what I plan . . . was planning to do with it.' Anna felt disappointment begin to grind down, almost a physical sensation on the back of her neck.

'She'll be in her teens in a very few years, Anna, darling, and she's going to need a healthy social life.'

Bernard came home during the following week to announce, with triumph, that he thought he had solved what he called 'our homelessness problem.' On his way to Carborough to catch the London train, he had spotted a workman erecting a 'for sale' board outside a rather grand Edwardian redbrick villa on, as he put it, the very edge of the city. 'It may not be pure country, Anna, but it's got this vast garden, five walloping bedrooms, a servant annexe and, get this, a huge conservatory.'

Sudden loud static from the loudspeaker in her cabin snatched

Anna back to the present. She never switched on the ship's radio station but important messages could, perforce, be fed into every speaker, invading even silent cabins. 'This is the captain speaking.' Wishart's voice sounded quite different over the public address system, but its sound brought a brief return of self pity, instantly repressed. That was last night. 'In fifteen minutes, at ten a.m., the ship's emergency signal will be sounded.' This was to be a full boat drill, a result, partly, of so many people having skipped the compulsory, and much briefer, muster drill the evening they sailed from Sydney. Life jacket in hand – for she knew, now, that one was not to don the cumbersome things until after arrival at the muster station – she waited for the seven short and one long blast on the ship's whistle. It seemed demeaning, she thought, to refer to such a deep-bowelled, resounding roar as a whistle, but there it was.

The Boys emerged from A10 just as she opened her own door and all three just avoided collision with what looked like a very junior officer, already wearing his life jacket. He wore a set, worried expression and Anna suspected that his pallid face was not the usual colour. They watched him tap on the door of the drunk's cabin.

'We'd better get up there,' Ant said. 'The alarm's gone already.' But he and Cedric were finding it difficult to tear themselves from the scene, sure that if they went they would miss something dramatic.

'Perhaps that young man needs some support,' Cedric muttered.

'I don't think so,' Ant said, guiding his companion firmly out of the court. Anna followed them to the muster station. The room, which had been the first class lounge in the *Brisbane*'s early days when she had made regular voyages bearing immigrants from England to Australia, was already full when they arrived. All the seats were taken, so they had to stand just inside the forward doors. One of the entertainments staff, a chorus girl whose dazzling smile on stage was replaced during the day by a constant sullen scowl, was showing newly joined passengers how to tie the tapes of their life jackets. A slight fracas at the door caused several heads to turn, but Anna and the Boys resolutely faced the other way, since they knew it was the drunk being ushered in.

'Thank you, young man,' he said. Anna couldn't tell whether he was being sarcastic or not. On balance she thought not. Obviously he was sober enough, at present, not to be a nuisance. The young officer excused himself but indicated the presence of his charge to the chorus girl. As she moved towards the drunk, she noted his incompetent fumbling with the tapes on his life jacket and took over.

'In a bit of a muddle, are we?' She took the tapes out of his hands and in smooth, brisk movements circled them round the back of his waist and was about to knot them in front when he snatched them out of her hands.

'Don't you dare lay your hands on me!' His voice rose in pitch and volume. 'I was at sea before you were born.'

'All right, sir!' The girl undid the tapes again letting them hang to the floor. 'Obviously, *you* know best.' She threaded her way through the passengers to the other side of the lounge. A moment later, one of the most junior purser's assistants, a slight girl barely into her twenties with dark, doe-like eyes which contrasted oddly with her blonde curls, walked through the door behind Anna and noticed the drunk still fumbling.

'May I help you sir?' The voice was slightly tremulous. This was her first voyage, and she had spent much of it working behind the scenes in the purser's office. Often she had overheard passengers berating crew members on duty at the purser's desk and had dreaded her own duty spells. Even now that she had served considerable time behind the counter, the accusing faces and aggrieved voices still upset her, as if everything that went wrong on board was her personal fault.

'No!' The drunk was trying to find his missing tapes. He might have been struggling with the Gordian Knot. She stooped to pick up one of the loose ends of the binding tape.

'I said no!' He snatched the tape from her but in doing so dropped the other. On a reflex of politeness, the girl stooped again to pick it up, catching her head on the edge of his life jacket. He reacted as if she had punched him in the stomach.

'Get your hands off me, you little slut!' he yelled, swinging his arm to fend her off but catching her a sharpish glancing blow on her temple. She gasped, staggered to her knees, recovered and ran through the door, colliding with the staff captain who had been about to enter to help the whole lounge full of passengers through their drill.

'Oh, I'm so sorry, sir, I didn't . . .' The girl burst into tears, a bruise already beginning to form at the side of her young face, and rushed through the door. The passengers in the lounge, especially those nearest to the drunk, were beginning to rumble indignantly. The staff captain whipped out his small two-way radio and uttered terse instructions into it. In a moment, the door opened again and two large seamen walked in with the head of security close behind.

'Yes, I thought it might be him,' he muttered, eyeing the drunk who stood now with head bowed. 'Take him to his cabin,' he instructed the men, 'and stay there with him. Don't let him move until I get down there after the drill. You're excused.'

'Will you come, sir?' The men were ready to take an arm each, but he simply nodded and walked out between them, one in front, one behind. Anna caught sight of his face. It was a mask, expressionless, but she was sure he was burning with shame and embarrassment beneath it and she felt not contempt for him, but pity. There was more hurting him than simply drink. He seemed to want to destroy himself, but couldn't quite succeed.

They stood waiting in the lounge for ten minutes before Captain Wishart's voice came over the PA system. 'Ladies and gentlemen, I do apologise for keeping you waiting. A small operational problem presented itself at an awkward time. We now have it under control and can proceed with our drill.'

The whole procedure lasted almost an hour. They were divided into boat groups, formed into processions, each with a hand on the shoulder of the passenger in front, and were obliged to walk up the stairs onto the boat deck and there assemble in double lines, women in front, men behind, awaiting instructions to enter the boats. Anna was reluctant to place her hand on the shoulder of the huge man in front of her and flinched at the pressure of the hand on her own, until she realised it belonged to Ant. She reached up with her other hand and gave it a little squeeze, returned by a flexing of the fingers on her shoulder. Once on deck, they watched the lifeboats being lowered, so that they could see more clearly what an emergency might be like.

At last it was over and they were free. Anna wanted to get back to her journal but as she arrived at her cabin door she remembered the incident with the drunk. With great trepidation, she knocked on his door. It was opened instantly by one of the men who had escorted him.

'Ah,' she said. 'I, um. I wondered if I might talk to Mr, er . . .' In all these weeks, she had not even learnt his name. That was shaming.

' 'Ang on a mo, madam, I'll ask.' He pushed the door to for a few seconds and then stepped out again. 'I'll be just outside, if I'm needed,' he said, holding the door open for her. 'I'm afraid I can't close the door, but I'll push it to, like.'

Inside, the small cabin was untidy, with clothes lying about on most of the surfaces. A large, open suitcase lay on the bed. He was sitting beside it. He looked smaller sitting down, his shoulders hunched, hands rather shaky, holding his knees. He regarded her with bloodshot eyes but could not hold her gaze and resumed staring at his knees. She could not think of anything to say. The silence looked as though it might last for a couple of centuries. She thought she ought to go again.

'Pathetic, isn't it,' he muttered at last. 'Pathetic!' She hardly knew how to respond.

'Is it?' She talked in low tones, careful not to be overheard. There was another lengthy pause. 'Had you thought of getting help?'

'What, me?' He flashed a bloodshot look at her. 'I'm talking about *you.*' He shook his head and snorted. '*Pathetic.*'

'Oh.'

'Don't you bloody well know a lost cause when it gets up and slugs you in the fucking kisser?' His voice was quiet, hardly more than a whisper, but he stood up. She stifled an impulse to giggle. Would he hit her? She had completely forgotten his minder outside. She was surprised that she didn't feel frightened.

'You use bad language as a substitute for physical violence.' It was an observation, only half meant for his ears.

'Get back to your own *pathetic* world. Leave me to rot in mine.' She noticed that the arrangement of bottles on his dressing table had disappeared. She assumed that the ship's company had confiscated them. Were they allowed to do that? Presumably he was also barred from the bars. She felt the giggle reflex coming back.

'Oh you can laugh.' He sat down again. 'But you and I are pretty much the same. We both fit on this ruddy boat about as comfortably as foreskins at a bar mitzvah.'

'You needn't bother to try to shock me,' Anna said. 'I'm too old for that.' She pulled the chair round from his small dressing table and sat facing him.

'Do sit down, dear lady.'

'And the difference between us,' she said, ignoring his mock politeness, 'is that you haven't managed to disguise your differentness.' She could hardly believe she was talking like this.

'It was an accident, you know. Just now. They had no right to—'

'That was no accident. You've been angling for something drastic to happen for weeks.' He threw her a look of hatred, then seemed to subside. His shoulders were sloping now, more rounded, Anna thought, than when she had first seen him. She remembered the sight of him drunk and naked at the beginning of the voyage. He wasn't so bad to look at, not really, but without booze to pump up his persona he seemed to have shrivelled. The wild corona of hair that had surrounded his bald dome was smoothed down now and his hands shook.

'They're throwing me off, you know. Day after tomorrow, at Cairns.'

'What will you do?'

He shrugged. 'Fuck off to the outback for a while. I hear that Alice Springs is a drunk's paradise.' Anna wondered whether she should talk about his getting help, joining Alcoholics Anonymous or something. He read her thoughts.

'I've not the slightest intention of changing my ways.'

'Looks as though you'll have to do without your crutch until Cairns.' She saw a look of fear pass across his face, a chill reminder of his predicament. Getting through the next forty-eight hours was going to take more doing than travelling to the end of his life. 'Can you?'

'What do you take me for?' Bravado in the voice belied the look. William on his first day at school in America, uncomfortable in his new clothes, surrounded by the local kids, fascinated to hear his accent. He had glanced back at her as she stood by the school gates, swallowed, then turned to the boy nearest to him, who had looked a little like Dave, his best friend in Kent.

'Hello,' he had said, in a soft voice, husky with embarrassment.

'Hi!' the kid had replied. 'What grade are you in? What's your name? Where d'ya live? Is that your Mom back there?' But William had shaken his head, puzzled by the accent and buckling under the torrent of questions. He had glanced back at Anna again, almost tearful. She had waved and had forced herself to leave the gates, to let him adapt on his own. She looked at the mess of clothes in the drunk's cabin.

'I'll help you to pack, if you like,' she said.

'I don't need any help.'

'I'd *like* to.'

'I don't give a . . .' The sight of her face prevented him from swearing. He sighed, shifted, and sat on his hands. She wondered how sharp his thirst was – was it a grinding ache, like her longing for Bernard? Why did people get hooked?

'Perhaps I'd better go, then.' But she sensed he wanted her to stay, even though he was too cussed to say so.

'I gather you write.'

'Well hardly. I, um . . .'

'I wrote a novel once.' He pulled his hands out from under his rump and folded his arms a little too tightly round his chest. 'Shortly after . . . well. It doesn't matter.' He glanced at her and looked quickly away. 'McHamish published it. They thought quite highly of it.'

'But that's wonderful.'

'Is it? No one reviewed it. Sales were dismal!' Another bitter laugh. 'Complete waste of time, really.'

'What did you do before?'

'Retailing. I had a china shop. Thirty-four years of grinding, crushing boredom.'

'If you hated it, why did you stay?'

He shrugged. 'I didn't know how much I hated it until I stopped. Does that seem daft?' She shook her head. 'The shop belonged to my father. There seemed no other possibility than to go into it as soon as I left school. At sixteen, I was wiping down Royal Worcester plates and laying them out on the display tables. And on my fiftieth birthday I was doing precisely the same thing. If I'd gone on much longer, I might have done something disastrous.'

'What stopped you?'

'What? Oh, Henry Gray – *the* Henry Gray Partnership. They wanted a chain of outlets in the Northwest and bought me out. Nice lump sum. I was set to retire at fifty. Well, fifty-one, to be precise.' He grinned at her, a tense rictus. 'Lots of dosh for lots of booze.'

'Have you always been on you own?'

The rictus froze. 'My business!' he muttered. His mood

had swung back to the antagonism of their first moments. 'I think you'd better go.' This time he meant it. Anna put her hand on the door handle.

'I'd still be happy to help you with your packing. You know where I am if you need me.' On her way across to her own cabin she smiled at the minder.

Back at her tiny desk she wrote:

I hoped I would get used to Carborough but, looking back over the nineteen years that we lived at Ketton House, I now realise that I never felt truly at home. The building itself was fine, though a little too grand for our needs. The rooms were large, most of them well lit with generous windows – Bernard had them all refitted with double glazing – and there was plenty of space for everyone to live, move and have their beings without getting in one another's way. The house was near the main London road, but set far enough back in its grounds to be quiet, with a front garden heavily planted with evergreens which dampened almost all the traffic noise. Out at the back there was a huge lawn and flowerbeds with weatherboard fencing to separate the garden from water meadows which sloped towards the River Nene. Plenty of space and a setting that was attractive enough, but I never really succeeded with the garden. The soil was a horribly sticky clay which stuck to my spade and my boots with such tenacity that I soon grew tired of trying to scrape it off. In summer, when it dried, it would set like concrete and then deep cracks would appear in the land. The front was thrown into constant heavy shade by the conifers and brooding laurels, necessary to reduce street noise and to ensure our privacy, but awkward for gardening.

Once Lisa had started boarding at St Etheldreda's, Bernard encouraged me to travel with him more often and leaving home so frequently made it difficult to be timely with the vegetable garden. After four – or was it five?—years, I abandoned the idea of growing food at all, and we blotted out the kitchen garden by installing a swimming pool and hard tennis court. Lisa loved it, and in summer the garden would ring out with the sounds of youngsters enjoying the water or playing mixed doubles. I seem to remember that summers were short at Carborough, apart from the year we moved in – the great drought of 1976 – but Lisa's first year at St Etheldreda's, 1980, seemed endless and we practically lived by the pool, grilling supper on the barbecue most weekends and accommodating a constant stream of teenage girls and boys. That was also the year that Bernard employed Margaret.

'Anna that's *brilliant*!' Margaret yelled when Anna returned her gentle serve accurately over the net so that the ball bounced inside the base line, just out of her reach. 'You're a natural.'

'Just a fluke,' Anna said. But she glowed with inner satisfaction when, after so many false shots, the ball had gone almost exactly where she expected it to.

'I think you're a fraud. I'll bet you've played before.'

'I swear I haven't. My brothers played when we were little, but I never even had a racket.' On the next serve Anna tried the same shot, but this time Margaret anticipated it and returned it to Anna's left. She was unable to do anything, even though the ball passed within a couple of feet. 'Oh *bugger*!' She giggled and put a hand over her mouth. Margaret walked round the net and came close.

'Next thing you have to learn is to play a backhanded stroke. Look, like this.' Gently, she took hold of Anna's right hand. 'No, relax. Just let your arm hang loose, and I'll show you how to take the shot.' Anna marvelled at the ease and speed with which she and Margaret seemed to have slipped into an almost intimate friendship. She must have been at least fifteen years younger but was so assured and poised that she made Anna feel as though she were the junior. With most people, particularly with other men, Anna would have felt uncomfortable with such close physical contact but now she felt perfectly at ease, allowing Margaret to hold her arm and guide it through several examples of sweeping backhand strokes. 'The angle of your racket is important. Get it wrong, and the ball shoots upwards. The knack is to keep it low, over the net, and give it as much speed you can.'

'OK, I think I've got it.' Anna was impatient to try these strokes out.

'Right.' Margaret returned to her side of the court, gathering half a dozen tennis balls on the way. 'Now, I'll serve them to your left side so that you can try some backhanders.' It took longer to develop the stroke than she expected and at first the balls went everywhere, or she missed them completely. After a while, though, she was able to return some of the more gentle serves, but never with enough force to make it difficult for Margaret to get them back, always pitched in the same place, within reach of her backhand. After about fifteen minutes her limbs began to ache and she began to grow frustrated.

'I think I've had it,' she said, after clouting a low ball with the metal edge of her racket, jarring her wrist.

'OK!' Margaret hit the last ball hard and high into the air, cursing when it fell outside the court enclosure and plopped into the swimming pool. 'Perhaps it's time we both rested.' Anna had left a jug of homemade lemonade – its top protected from flies with a beaded muslin cloth – with two glasses on the table beside the pool and as they walked over to sit down Margaret took the sweatband from her forehead and allowed long ropes of cinnamon-coloured hair to fall to her shoulders. She tossed her head from side to side, to allow the hair to hang more naturally, then wiped her forehead with the sweatband. Anna marvelled at how healthy she looked. Her own skin was milky, rather than tanned, with concentrations of small freckles on her upper arms and cheekbones.

'Shall I pour yours?' Anna asked, lifting the heavy jug.

Exertions with the tennis racket, one of Lisa's, had made her muscles ache, and the hand that held the jug was atremble.

'Please! Oh, hey, Anna! I don't suppose you have a shower in those changing rooms?'

'We certainly do!'

'Then, might I?'

'Of course! That's what it's there for. You'll find a clean towel and soaps and things in the wicker work cupboard. I would have laid them out, but Bernard hates what he calls clutter.'

'Doesn't he just! That's the first thing I've had to learn about him. I'd never seen such an empty desk.' Anna glanced up from her pouring and looked directly into Margaret's eyes, smiling eyes, startlingly dark green, with upturned crinkles at the corners and rusty lashes. It occurred to her that she had never discussed Bernard with anyone before – not since Verne.

'Do you know, I'd forgotten that you've been working for him for two weeks.'

'Almost two.' She watched the cloudy liquid rising in the glass. 'Hey! Watch out, Anna! You'll spill it.' A lemon slice slopped out of the jug into the glass, making it overflow. Margaret took a paper napkin and wiped the sides before picking up the glass and drinking half its contents down in a couple of greedy gulps.

'Nice?' Anna asked.

'Best I've ever tasted!' She set the glass down. 'Bloody good dinner last night too, if I haven't said so already. Who did you get to do the meal?'

'What? Oh, no one. I do all the food.'

'Really? *All* of it? The salmon mousse, those *amazing* desserts?' Margaret seemed impressed. 'No, that really is clever.' She pondered for a moment. 'Not sure I could do all that.'

'Ridiculous!' Anna uttered a little laugh. 'There really isn't much to it.'

One thing Ketton House was perfect for was dinner parties.

As soon as Bernard had spotted the vastness of the dining room, he had commissioned a Stoneford antique dealer to find him what he called a proper dining table. Within a few weeks the dealer located a dozen pretty Hepplewhite-style chairs and a well-made nineteenth-century mahogany table which could seat twelve comfortably and fourteen at a pinch. On routine days, he and Anna would eat in the large kitchen or in the breakfast room or, on mild summer nights, at the small glass and wrought iron table in the conservatory. But once a month, on average, any number of guests from four to a dozen would come to sip Pimm's in the garden, or to assemble for cocktails round the library fire if it were winter, before moving into the dining room. Anna would spend ages making small individual flower arrangements and setting the table with Irish linen cloths; sometimes, she would leave the beautiful wood bare so that the guests could enjoy the dull gleam of candle light reflected in its surface. She polished it once a week with beeswax polish, a smell that always reminded her of their first country home in Kent.

Last evening, their guests had included the Bishop of Carborough, the Member of Parliament for Stoneford East who had recently become a junior minister for education, and assorted locals. All the guests but two had dined *chez* Morfey previously and were familiar with the routine. The Turnbulls were new, but had soon been put at their ease by Anna who was a gracious, if slightly distracted host. Fiennes Turnbull, who for some reason liked to be called Pip, was something to do with making pet foods somewhere in Leicestershire and his wife, Margaret, had recently become Bernard's new part-time secretary.

'Quite a bit more than a secretary, actually,' she had explained to Anna, as soon as they had been introduced, 'but I can't stand that stupid term "PA". Makes one sound like a loudspeaker system or something!' Anna might have been taken aback by her breezy confidence. With any other female fifteen years her junior, such an attitude might have seemed cocky, but Margaret's open features and honest smile had appealed. It was extraordinary, really, but from the moment they had shaken hands, Anna knew that they were going to become great friends. If they had belonged to opposite sexes, this rapport could not have happened because their mutual attraction would be sure to contain sexual overtones. But without thinking any more about it, Anna knew that she had stumbled upon a soul mate.

At dinner, Anna arranged the seating so that Pip sat on her left and the bishop on her right.

'Would you like me to help with the wine?' Pip had asked, rising as he did so.

'Sweet of you if you would. You and Margaret must be the babies of the group by quite a few years,' Anna had said. 'Oh I'm sorry. I hope that doesn't sound patronising.'

'I think I'm just about old enough for that to be flattering,' he had replied, but Anna felt sure she had irritated him. Once he had sat down, the bishop began to raise the subject of morality among members of Pip's generation and Anna was able to relax while the two men slogged it out. She knew that conversation with the bishop was a challenge if you were male, and impossible if you were female. He simply talked at you. Pip held his ground reasonably well, occasionally managing a whole sentence without interruption.

After a while, when voices had grown louder and guests were less inhibited about heckling each other across the table, Bernard had piped up from the far end.

'Make no mistake, this new hike in interest rates is the price we've all got to pay for a generation of featherbedding.' To emphasise his message, he had waved the cheese knife at the guests on either side of the dinner table. 'Inflation, the balance of payments crisis – they'd been brewing for decades. Macmillan, Wilson, Callaghan, Heath – especially Heath – they're all culpable. Wilson knew when to get out. Callaghan must have known he'd inherited the poisoned chalice but it took three more years to get rid of that lily-livered crew. The country was run by the TUC, if you remember, not by the elected government.' The table had fallen silent by now, heads turned to Bernard.

'Ah, but Bernard,' the bishop piped up from the far end of the table, 'thousands of small businesses are going bust now. And that means millions are losing their jobs. How can anyone justify that?'

'Can't be helped,' Bernard said. 'There has to be a shakeout of the inefficient ones.'

'But in terms of human lives,' the bishop persisted, 'is what Maggie's doing really acceptable?'

'It's a bitter pill, Bishop, but no nation can afford to support lame ducks. All Mrs Thatcher is doing is pointing out that you cannot live on money you haven't got.' The bishop was going quite red. 'Can't you remember nineteen seventy-six? That *awful* humiliation?' He put down the cheese knife and imitated speaking into a phone. 'Hello? World Bank? Britain here. Look, we seem to have gone a teensy bit broke, can you spare us three billion quid? Just to tide us over, like.'

'Oh I don't think it was quite like that,' the bishop said.

'It was every bit like that,' the member for Stoneford East muttered. 'Everyone's going to have to do a hell of a lot of readjusting.'

'I say,' Margaret said, 'before we get too heavy, can I just say, erm, Anna, that your crème brûlée was quite the most divine I have ever tasted. I'd never have thought of having fresh peach in the custard. How on earth did you get it in without cooking it?'

Just the note Anna needed, a cue to usher the women out to the drawing room. 'Well, chaps,' she said, 'don't be too long.' She rose.

'Good Lord,' Margaret had said, as the other women began to respond by standing up. 'Do we still do that?'

Anna had hesitated while the rest of her female guests began to file out. 'Sometimes we do.'

'How hilarious!' Margaret muttered, following. 'Still, we can tell each other filthy stories without embarrassing the menfolk!'

Once Anna had dispensed coffee to the other women she had sat next to Margaret on one of the long chesterfields in the drawing room.

'What do you do when you're not giving dinner parties?' Margaret asked.

'Oh you know, the usual things. Gardening, the house—'

'No, silly, I mean work. What job do you do?'

'Well, with Lisa and this house and everything . . . I look after Bernard too.' She felt ashamed of admitting that she didn't have a job. Anna had often wondered about doing something more useful but had always sensed that Bernard would prefer it if she didn't. 'I don't really have to, you see.'

'Well obviously not.' Margaret sensed her new friend's unease about the subject and did not pursue it. Instead, both women enjoyed a long, uncompetitive conversation.

Now, two days later, sitting by the swimming pool in the June sunshine, Anna could hear the shower splashing. After a while, Margaret emerged, wrapped in a large yellow towel. She had placed a hand towel on her shoulders to take up surplus water from her hair.

'It's very private, in this enclosure,' she said. 'I dare say you could swim in the nude.'

'I dare say you could,' Anna agreed. She had never thought of doing so.

'So, do you want me to come over every Monday?'

I learnt to play a reasonable game surprisingly quickly and, by the time the first rains fell in September, I had become moderately confident. As I had known we would the moment we met, Margaret and I became close friends. We did everything together. We went on shopping excursions, not just to Carborough, but sometimes to London, staying at our flat in Bloomsbury and making excursions to Harrods or Harvey Nichols or spending ludicrous amounts on coffee at Fortnums. We went to films together, and to the theatre, often dining afterwards and nattering on and on until the restaurateurs would almost beg us to leave.

Bernard became almost jealous. 'Mind if I borrow my PA?' he said once. The three of us had gone up to town so that he could attend a spate of urgent meetings just before the Tory party conference. Technically Margaret was supposed to be working for him – she was full-time by then – but she had managed to join me for lunch at Wheelers, and then we had slipped off to see a rather odd French film at the Phoenix. He had wanted her to type a speech for the evening. But she had it ready for him, just, bashing it out while he had his bath.

Back in Carborough, Pip and Margaret almost always came to our parties or came to borrow the pool most weekends. Bernard spoke of building a structure over it so that we could use it all the year.

In September, not long before the Conservative party conference, Bernard was invited to a late-night meeting somewhere in North London.

'It's quite extraordinary,' he told Anna on his return just after two in the morning. He had tried to slip into bed without waking her, but she had been disturbed by the light and at once recognised his excitement, however hard he tried to suppress it. 'I've just had the most incredible conversation.' Anna knew that it would be quite a while before he was able to settle down.

'I'll make you some tea,' she said, sitting up.

'Absolutely not! I'll do it.' He filled the kettle at their bathroom tap and plugged it in. 'Oh, and I'm having a brandy. Want one?'

'Bernard, it's two in the morning,' Anna protested. But he had dashed out of the bedroom. He returned with a balloon glass in each hand. The kettle had boiled, so Anna had made tea and was now sitting up in bed, shivering a little because the night had turned chilly. She took the offered glass because it seemed easier than refusing. 'Well?' She waited.

'I've been having a long talk with the powerhouse. The epicentre. Margaret, of course.'

'Well, of course.'

'No, you goose, not my Margaret. *The* Margaret. Thatcher.'

'Oh.'

'Walters was there earlier – you know, economist Walters – and Young, Bibby, Morgenstein, Heseltine, Lord Kandinsky – all the real heavyweights. But later they left and I had this private, well, audience. It seems that I'm to form a small body, technically within the auspices of the party – but a somewhat unofficial one. Walters is to continue as chief economic adviser, but my role will be, in many respects, as powerful. I'm to sound out, to recruit, to act as a kind of intelligence, in short, to find extra ways and means of making things work. I can form a small team, and I can have whatever and whoever I need to make those things work.'

'What things?' Anna was too sleepy to absorb all of what he was saying.

'Everything. You might consider the things she's already done a bit radical, even in her first year, but believe me, we ain't seen nothing yet. This isn't going to be just a new government; this is practically revolution. A *total* reappraisal, not merely prodding the economy a bit to invite investment but of the whole of society. She despises privilege unless it's earned – can't stand Eton and Oxbridge types. Her first question to me was, "Where were you at school?" I felt almost embarrassed to admit that it was the Grammar at King's Lynn, but she seemed visibly relieved.'

'Didn't she go to Oxford?'

'Oh, but on merit. From very humble origins.' He began to pace the bedroom floor. 'No, what we're looking at here is a return to Adam Smith. A truly free enterprise economy. *Everything* will be provided by private businesses: phones, railways, electricity, water even.'

'But what exactly are *you* going to do?' She was growing concerned. He already had a very heavy schedule and had been showing signs of overwork lately. Anything extra might be too much for him. 'Revolutions need a lot of organising. How will you find the time?'

'I'll make time.' He giggled at the joke and then turned serious. 'Anna, this is the greatest. This is the opportunity I've been hanging on for – a chance to . . . to . . .' He finished his brandy while he groped for words. 'To bring pride back to the country. To help more people back to wealth – not those workshy bastards who draw dole off the backs of the real breadwinners, but small business people, self-employed chaps who are crippled with tax and bureaucracy. They're the ones who can make the country great again. And they're the ones who need the biggest tax incentives. They've been abused for too long.'

'It all sounds very political. Are you sure that's where you want to be?'

'Oh, this job is bigger than politics. What power does a member of Parliament have? Or a cabinet minister, for that matter?'

'She's a member of Parliament.'

'That is the least of her attributes.'

'You always said civil servants had too much power.'

'Oh poof!' He waved a dismissive hand. 'She's going to clip their wings anyway. And the legal system. It'll all get busted wide open.' He took her hand and placed it on his chest. 'No, *this* is going to be where it's at. A small handful of individuals behind the scenes. We're the ones who will actually make things happen. And believe me, there are going to be some tough fights ahead. The country is practically broke. Yet we have the brains, the resources, the know-how to outdo Germany and Japan put together.' He lifted his glass, noted it was empty and when she offered hers, untouched, took it without a word. 'That woman, my God! You know how I despise most politicians, but she . . . well, in one sense she's no politician. She's a . . . I don't really know what she is.' He sipped his brandy and pondered. 'A visionary. She talks in simple terms, like a housewife guarding her pennies, yet she gives the impression that, well, that she could do a pretty respectable job running the world.'

'Bernard, I think it's time you got into bed.' Anna knew he had to be up for his first meeting in a little more than a couple of hours. Now he was passing from light-headed to feverish.

'I'll tell you what, though.' He giggled again. 'She's the first prime minister with balls since Churchill.' He chuckled a little more at his joke, drunk with fatigue rather than with brandy, with only adrenalin to keep him on the move. He climbed into bed without cleaning his teeth. Anna pulled him to her and kissed him. The brandy in her glass had revolted her. On his lips it tasted fine.

'You're such a clever man,' she said. 'I can't imagine how you ended up with someone as ordinary as me.'

'Anna, how could you say that?' He kissed her breasts through the cotton nightdress and she felt him stroking the area just above her hip and round to the small of her back, exactly where she liked it best. It was natural for her hand to slip into the fly of his pyjamas.

'I love you, Bernard.' She encountered softness, in there, but that was all right. It was so late.

'I think I'm a bit tired,' he murmured.

'I know, I know.' She kissed him again. 'I think I am too.'

Chapter Fifteen

———

Leaning on the rail of the Promenade Deck as the *Brisbane* approached Cairns, Anna noticed what she thought was a short coil of old rope floating on the surface of the green sea. But as the ship moved nearer the coil unfurled itself and Anna saw that it was a large sea snake. She could even make out the flattened tail, speckling on the scales and the snub nose. It wriggled on the surface for a few seconds and then swam strongly down out of sight into the deep water. She remembered lines from Coleridge's *The Rime of the Ancient Mariner* about things crawling on a slimy ocean and shuddered. The mariner's punishment, eternal solitude, seemed harsh for a single act of thoughtless violence. After all, it had not been premeditated and at first his shipmates had seemed convinced that shooting the albatross had actually done some good.

Once the ship had docked most people, it seemed, were planning to spend the day on the Great Barrier Reef. Various boats had been organised to ferry people to one of the reef islands where they could swim, or explore the coral. Anna had decided to be more terrestrial. She was weary of seascapes, and had planned to take the little antique railway through the hilly rainforest to Kuranda, there to eat a leisurely lunch before returning to the

ship. But reading the literature about the region she
was reminded that the mudflats along the esplanade at
Cairns were one of the richest habitats for estuarine bird
species in the southern hemisphere. Ant and Cedric were
set on going to one of the reef islands, but she would be
perfectly all right, she had told them, left on her own.

She went to her cabin, to put field glasses, rain cape,
bottle of mineral water and the bird book she had purchased
in Sydney out on her bunk, ready to collect as soon as
they were able to disembark. Outside her neighbour's
door she spotted the large suitcase that she had packed
virtually unaided the evening before, and a smaller one
which she had not noticed. With a sense of guilt she
remembered that she still had not asked him his name
and, after conversing for so long, had felt unable to do
so without feeling embarrassed. He had been in quite a
bad way. Trembling and complaining of feeling sick, he
was unable to eat anything at all, and had seemed on the
brink of either rage or despair. She hovered at his door,
wondering whether to say goodbye. Eventually she found
the courage to tap, but there was no reply. She was about
to try again, a little louder, when Tony came quietly into
the court carrying a small folding trolley.

'Not there, madam,' he said, with his usual polite half
smile. 'Already disembarked.'

'But we've hardly docked yet,' Anna said.

'One of the first gentlemans to be taken off the ship.' His
smile broadened. She wondered how many times, without
complaining, he had had to clean up messes in that cabin.
Pissed-in beds, near misses round the lavatory. She hoped
his tip was generous.

'I see. Well, thank you, Tony.' She went to her own
cabin and found a note, in shaky handwriting, pushed under
her door.

I know your name is Anna, but we were not introduced. I'm not sure I want to know what you think

of me, but I do want to thank you for your kindness.

I may have been half cut all the time we were
neighbours, but it was still obvious that you were, and
as far as I can tell still are, grappling with something.
I know you will win because, unlike me, you have
strength, but I hope the winning does not damage you
more than the thing itself.

You are the only person on this ship who showed
me kindness. Thank you for that.

Stephen Cutler

Anna opened her cabin door to see if Tony was still
outside. He was in Cutler's cabin, pulling the sheets
off the bed. Hearing her door open, he looked up and
smiled.

'Tony, did Mr Cutler look after you?' She did a little
mime of feeling money, a physical cliché. Recently Pullen
had spent an entire class exhorting them to avoid clichés and
other signs of hack writing. Now she was constantly on the
lookout for unoriginality.

'No, madam.' The smile remained. 'I think in his hurry
he was forgetting.'

'I *am* sorry.' She thought of telling him that she would
double her own tip to make up, but did not want to make
him feel indebted. She would present the enlarged sum on
her last day as a nice surprise for him.

She had assumed that she would need some form of
transport to get to the mudflats, but at the gangway
she encountered Captain Wishart who said, 'You can
practically see them from here. Go through that shopping
centre thing and keep to the waterside. The mud begins
over there.' He eyed her bird book and the small field
glasses. 'You seem well equipped. Are you hoping to see
anything really special?'

'I'm afraid I'm very ignorant of the local fauna.' Anna
blushed. 'Just a bungling amateur, really.'

'Well, look out for one of my favourites, the Mongolian plover.'

'This late?' Anna began to thumb her book. 'Maybe, but not still in breeding plumage, surely.'

'Bungling amateur, eh!' Wishart winked and paced away up the corridor of D Deck.

Anna decided to avoid the shopping centre altogether by walking all the way along the waterfront. As she turned the corner at the end of the buildings she saw a large expanse of very still water bordered by an equally large foreshore of greyish-brown mud. The tide was about halfway out and falling, leaving the expanding area to the sea birds. Small mangrove seedlings jostled at the edge of the mud and, when she looked more closely at the small rills and creeks that were emptying themselves as the sea receded, she spotted hundreds of mudskippers – small fish halfway evolved to amphibians. They used their front fins as legs and seemed able to survive out of the water for a considerable time. At first glance, the place looked birdless and she felt cheated. Obviously no one was able to walk on this filthy ooze and come out alive, so if any birds did turn up they would need to be near the shore or they'd be impossible to see. And that was the other disappointment. When reading up on the region she had expected to wander alone in the salt marshes, leaving everything manmade behind. That was why she loved Norfolk so. Even in midsummer, there, you could lose yourself among the sighing reeds. But this was town. There was a paved path all along the waterfront, with park benches at intervals, formal trees, close-mown grass and people walking, cycling, jogging. On the ground, beneath a group of macadamia trees next to the public lavatory block, a group of Aborigines seemed to be having a noisy dispute. They were surrounded by empty bottles and litter. Some had dogs on rope leashes.

Anna quickened her pace, noticing as she passed that a large woman had a bleeding face and was weeping loudly and copiously. A rat-faced little man with a nose that seemed to have been split at some time and had healed splayed, without being stitched up, was shouting at her, but was being restrained by two younger men. She had never seen native Australians before and was struck by their extraordinary physiognomies. This group seemed to be as drink-oriented as her ex-neighbour on the *Brisbane*. They had obviously been there for ages – the litter and broken glass plus their possessions suggested that they practically lived there – yet there was nothing for them to do. She wanted to find out more about them, but dared not approach the group. She turned her head away and concentrated on the mudflats as she walked. A movement caught her eye and she realised that a kingfisher was sitting on a young mangrove plant less than ten feet from the edge of the mud. Its back was a soft blend of olive green and blue and there was a primrose band on its neck, a black eye stripe and the typical kingfisher beak. As she watched, it snapped up a mudskipper. Then, as she scanned the mud more slowly, she realised that it was teaming with bird life. There were low brown waders, large curlew-like birds, more kingfishers, a tiny heron which stood motionless for minutes at a time until its prey – mudskippers again – came within snatching distance.

As the tide ebbed, turned and began to creep back up the tiny channels and creeks, she made a slow progress across the whole bay, stopping at each of the park benches, watching, noting, sometimes gasping with delight, especially when she discovered a species familiar from the Norfolk waters. Greenshank, sandpipers and sanderlings almost moved her to tears, since they brought back such memories of marshland walks with Charlie. Charlie would stay so patiently while they squatted in reed beds or perched on a fence post waiting for the waders to move into the mudflats on a falling tide. He would ask her for his heavy binoculars occasionally, but mostly they hung round her neck and so she was the one who would scout the field. 'What've we got this time, sis?' She tried to make herself hear his voice in her ear, to conjure up the idea of him, sitting beside her, right here on a bench in Queensland. A schoolboy with shapeless grey flannel shorts, muddied knees and an ancient sweater, so patched and darned by Dawn that she'd once said, 'Tha's more hooly than roighteous, moi li'll ol' boy!' Anna smiled, finding comfort in these memories, and didn't mind the tear which she felt on her cheek. It was partly caused by the breeze blowing behind her binocular eyepieces anyway. Charlie had never given up. Healthy, careful with his diet, too conscious of the modern terrors of cholesterol and hypertension after their father had developed angina and died of heart disease before he was seventy-three, Charlie had taken frequent exercise and had always exuded a glow of rude health. But the tumour in his stomach had grown, undetected, and by the time he had suddenly begun to feel ill it had already released cancerous cells around his body. Metastasis. Liver failure finally killed him less than two months after that first diagnosis. He was forty-four.

The loss hurt almost as much as when William died. Bernard was wonderful. He cancelled engagements for a whole week so that he could spend time with her, dashing to the office for an hour or two each afternoon, but otherwise keeping close to her. It was so strange, too, that Charlie had never married. Such a warm, loving husband he would have made, and a wonderful father. Anna supposed his pupils would have been substitutes for children of his own. Certainly he was much loved at the school, and when the headmaster had spoken at his memorial service in the great school chapel she had noticed not only senior boys, but several of Charlie's colleagues weeping. But there must still have been a yawning gap in his life and she wished she had spent more time with him. He had barely met William. Now, with Bernard gone, she would miss Charlie more than ever.

She sensed that the flow of tears was about to increase. There were people about. She opened her book and stared intently at one of the pages, looking at illustrations of terns.

She must concentrate. She must not make a fool of herself. Fifty yards in front of her, a group of terns stood on a slightly raised area of mud, their heads facing into the land breeze. Caspian terns were easy to identify, they were so huge and had untidy coifs, but there were others. I must get these identified, she thought. I must keep my mind on the job. Charlie had once trodden on a tern's nest when they had gone with Father to Cley-next-the-Sea. Seeing the bloody mess of half-developed chicks among the broken eggshells, he had cried. Father had scolded at first, and then had had to comfort him.

'Having problems?' An English voice butted into her thoughts. A smell of sweat. She glanced up from her book and, out of focus, saw the outline of a man, his features fuzzed by an untidy beard. A small female was standing beside him. Both had field glasses round their necks and the girl carried an earlier edition of Anna's field guide.

'Oh, hello.' She fished for a handkerchief and dabbed. 'The breeze makes your eyes water.' She had developed a skill for composing herself quickly, these days, and had soon locked her memories away in the correct compartment of her mind. 'It's these terns. I can see Caspian, gull-billed, but what are those smaller ones?'

The young man raised his binoculars. 'Little tern. They're just going out of breeding plumage.' They talked for a while, the girl standing silently beside him, a polite smile fixed on her weaselly features. Anna was sure he was English, not Australian, but she also detected a slight American inflection.

'Where have you come from?' she asked after a while.

'Well, from Newport Pagnell originally, but we've been around a bit, haven't we, Karen?'

Karen nodded. 'Alan's a lecturer, at Hull, but we've been over here for six weeks, birdwatching everywhere.'

'And we had a year in the States before that,' Alan added.

'Oh,' Anna said. 'Where?'

'Various places,' Karen said, 'Florida, New Mexico, Boston.'

'But we were based in upstate New York, at Purlin University,' Alan said. 'It's beautiful,' he went on.

'I know it is,' Anna replied after a pause. 'My hu— We lived there for a while, back in the sixties.'

'Oh, you know it?' Their eyes lit up. 'Didn't you just *love* it? That glorious campus! The woods in spring!'

'Great for birds, too,' Alan said, tugging at his beard as he spoke. 'Did you used to go to Grackle Wood when you were there?' That name, on someone else's tongue, sounded odd. As if her privacy was being threatened. 'And what about Kilmarnock Gorge? Wasn't that marvellous?'

Anna nodded, not very sure of her voice. At length she said, 'Were you connected with the university?'

'Visiting lecturer,' Alan replied. 'As you probably deduced from the beard and sandals, I'm an ecologist.' He tugged his beard a little more and arranged his features into a wry smile. 'You should know that we're both vegetarians, too!' Anna liked him for this gentle self-mocking. But she could not tear her mind away from the images of Purlin that preoccupied her.

'Would that be part of the biology department?'

'Sure,' Alan's accent was thickening as he recalled his year. 'It was an exchange deal.'

Anna wanted to ask who was head of department, but she couldn't make herself. Verne's warm breath on her neck distracted her; she could almost feel, even now in steamy Queensland, his soft but rough flannel shirt against her cheek. 'I, er, I wonder if any of the people we knew in the sixties are still there.' The couple looked blank. 'No,' she said, 'I don't suppose they are.'

'Well, we didn't get to know *that* many professors. But in the biology department, well.' They both tried to recall the older faculty members. 'Spicer, of course, and that geneticist from Yugoslavia, Dr Brno.'

'Who was head?'

'Chap called Brownlow. Not especially popular.'

'Ah.' Anna tried not to sound disappointed.

'He was fairly new,' Karen explained, 'But his predecessor was still on campus, just working on research now. Sort of early retirement. Oh. Al, what was his name?' Alan shrugged. '*You* know,' she persisted. 'Lost his wife and brought up those two sons entirely on his own. Still lives by himself, near the lake. One of them's in the music school now, teaching composition – *you* know.'

'Haven't a clue,' Alan shrugged. He began to sweep the mudflats with his glasses.

'Oh well,' Anna said. 'It was quite a while ago. Doesn't really matter now.'

As the *Brisbane* sailed for Singapore, Anna sat in her cabin, preparing to continue with her memoirs. She wanted to recall the Falklands campaign and the miners' strike. Memories blur, but she could remember the row over the sinking of the *General Belgrano*, the horror at seeing film of the *Sheffield* burning and waking up to the news that the Task Force had retaken Port Stanley. The Falklands seemed to have united the country – a kind of endorsement, for Thatcher, that Britain was great again. Few chose to remember the diplomatic bungling that led to the war in the first place, or to question the morality of causing so many deaths for such a minuscule fragment of Empire. But it was the miners' strike that finally convinced her that the price of Thatcher's revolution was too high. She remembered driving down with Bernard to London very early one Sunday morning, during the strike, and seeing a constant stream, minibus after minibus, each one full of police officers heading north to the coal fields. There were hundreds of them.

'That looks more like an army than a police force,' she had said.

'Fighting for democracy,' Bernard had said. 'Union might has to be broken. Besides, Scargill is totally irrational.'

Bernard's workload increased even more after Thatcher's second election victory, but I had not realised quite how it would take over our entire lives. During the mid-eighties, I hardly saw him. I needed to stay at Carborough for much of the time, but Bernard lived almost permanently in London. After a few months he decided that Bloomsbury was too far away and managed to acquire a flat in Whitehall Court, five minutes' walk from Downing Street.

During that period Margaret Turnbull, who spent much of her time as a backstop for Bernard at Stoneford, was my greatest friend and ally. She was almost as busy as Bernard, but at least she was nearby, and was therefore able to come to Carborough more frequently even than Bernard. Of an evening, she would come over with Pip, or I would go over to their town house in Stoneford.

Anna never went to a theatre or cinema without the Turnbulls, or at least without Margaret. The two became so in tune with each other that they even thought together. Pip called himself the gooseberry when all three were together and on the rare occasions that Bernard was able to tear himself away from the office to have some leisure at home, he found that it was natural to team up with Pip and to leave the girls together. Thus the almost intolerable pressure of work on Bernard, and therefore on his relationship with Anna, was relieved by her friendship with Margaret. During the early years of Thatcher's reign, in many respects the two women were more like a couple than Anna and Bernard.

But Bernard always managed to find time for Lisa. 'She's away at school so much, poor love,' Anna would say. 'Do try to make time for her when she's home.' And Bernard did, to the extent that Anna felt jealous. If she was ill, or if she had been selected to play in a school match, he would rearrange his engagements so that he could at least make a brief appearance.

One day, soon after the resolution of the miners' strike, Bernard rang Anna from London.

'I can't go to Paris now, because I'm needed here, but since I've got tickets, and since Margaret needs to get signatures on a couple of legal documents, why don't you go with her?'

'Sounds fun,' Anna said, mentally running through a list of her commitments and beginning to work out how she could reorganise everything to have the time free. Within seconds of hanging up, the phone rang again.

'Fact is,' Margaret said, 'I've not got that much to do over there, other than to get signatures on these documents. I'm feeling, you know, sort of stale, but with you there, we could go *really* wild.'

'All right, but cancel Bernard's room. We can share.' Margaret hesitated for a moment before agreeing.

They met at Heathrow. Anna, who had racked her brains and ransacked her wardrobe in an agony of indecision about what would be correct wear for Paris, and who had not seen Margaret decked out for work for some time, was struck by the charcoal suit, gentian blouse and small peaked cap that barely contained the ropes of reddish hair. No doubt about it, Margaret turned heads, even in the business class lounge, where self-confidence oozed and conversation hummed in quiet tones.

'Heavens!' Margaret said. 'You've actually managed to look sexy!'

'Nonsense,' Anna retorted, but inwardly she glowed. 'I'll bag a couple seats while you get some coffees.' She sat down and watched her friend cross the lounge. Several more heads turned.

'Jesus, Anna. Look at that!' Margaret said, returning with two coffees. 'Yummy or what?' With her chin she indicated two young men who stood waiting while a stewardess opened a bottle of champagne. One was at least six foot three, black, with incredibly long legs; the other perhaps two inches shorter, but less willowy with broader shoulders, had tightly curled blond hair. They both wore fashionable loose-fitting blue-grey suits.

'What? Oh, they always do a buffet like that in this lounge.'

'Don't be a cretin all your life,' Margaret laughed, 'you know bloody well what I'm referring to.' Of course Anna knew, having experienced Margaret's ribald observations before. She found them refreshing, after the stuffiness of her neighbours in Carborough, but a little disturbing.

'Which one?' Anna asked.

'Which do *you* prefer?'

'Oh, I . . .' Anna was embarrassed. 'I don't really know' She really hadn't given much thought to that kind of thing. In spite of herself, though, she allowed a fleeting image of Verne to pass her vision, and for the millionth time relived the sensation of being held tightly in his arms. The shorter of the two men could, at a very long stretch, resemble Verne. When he turned she noted that his upper lip was full, like Verne's. He was barely more than a boy, Anna thought. Before she glanced away she met his eye and felt her neck hairs bristle. He coloured, half smiled and looked away.

'Oh yes you do,' Margaret said. 'I can see it written all over your face.'

'Margaret, I'm forty-seven.' Anna was silent for ages, thoughtful while she stirred her coffee and quiet until their flight was called and they had assembled themselves at the departure gate. Hearing a voice like liquid honey right behind her, she glanced round to see the young black man and his companion. He nodded and smiled, and Anna could see by the way his glance slid to Margaret's neat hat and reddish curls that she was about to be used as a means for an introduction.

'Off to Paris?' He was smiling at Anna but his question was obviously addressed to Margaret.

'No, Rio de Janeiro!' Margaret retorted. It had been a feeble opener. 'Where else do you think this flight is going to?'

'Oddly enough, I come from Brazil,' he said. 'My name is Eduardo and this,' he indicated his companion, 'is Benjy.' Anna thought the names were the wrong way round.

'Where the nuts come from,' Margaret said, with a giggle, but they continued to chat for a while. With the greatest of ease – too much ease for Anna's liking – Margaret let them know that they were staying at the Picard Hotel. Then it was time to board.

Margaret's work in Paris was completed by early afternoon. They had two nights and almost two days in which to enjoy themselves. Anna wanted to fit in a concert and to visit the Louvre. Otherwise, she was open to whatever Margaret suggested.

'We could be free and easy tonight,' Margaret said, as they changed their clothes, 'then we can do your Paris Conservatoire tomorrow. There's a Brahms thing on, I think.' When they went downstairs for a drink before setting off, it was hardly surprising that they should bump into Eduardo and Benjy.

'Fancy seeing you two here,' they cried, clicking their fingers for two more glasses. They were sharing a bottle of sparkling blanc de blancs.

'Let's jettison this muck,' Benjy said, when the waiter arrived, '*Nous voudrions, er, de champagne. Quelle, um, quelle marque avez-vous?*'

'*Laurent Perrier, m'sieu'?*'

'Oh fine. Er, *bon!*' The waiter took the bottle, still one-third full, away and returned with a new ice bucket which contained the champagne. He removed the foil and wire in a single movement and eased the cork which let the gas out with a smug sigh.

'Like a fart from a duchess,' Benjy said, and then, looking at Anna, 'Whoops! Rude! Sorry.' Anna giggled, in spite of herself. This was developing into an adventure.

'Are you two by any chance sisters?' Eduardo said, once the champagne had been poured and the women had been persuaded to down their first glass quickly, to catch up.

'Bloody cheek,' yelled Margaret, just a fraction too loud, and everyone laughed. A head or two turned. Anna was secretly flattered.

'Why do you ask?'

'Because we were watching you at the airport,' Benjy said, 'you seemed to, I don't know, almost to think together.'

'Benjy's a twin,' Eduardo said, as if this offered an explanation. 'He notices that sort of thing.'

'We spend most of our lives together, at the moment,' Margaret said. 'In fact, I work for her husband.' At which point Anna noticed that she had taken off her wedding ring. If you looked very closely you could just see the crease in her skin, like a faint shadow, where it had been.

It was natural that they should dine together, that the boys should accompany them back to the Picard where they enjoyed several digestifs. At last Margaret, who had been getting closer to Eduardo all evening, yawned and said, 'I'm ready for bed, is it far back to your hotel?'

'Oh, didn't you realise?' Benjy said. 'We moved our stuff over here.'

'Really? Whatever for?' Margaret stood up and wobbled slightly. 'Eduardo, be an angel and take me up. I'm too tired to walk all that way on my own.' Anna made to follow but Benjy, still seated, put his hand over hers. It felt pleasant. Large, dry, warm, a man's hand.

'Stay for a final one?'

'No thank you.' She caught his look. 'But if you want another, I'll stay and chat.'

He shook his head. 'I've had more alcohol tonight than I usually consume in a week.' Neither seemed inclined to move. He took her hand again and she could see the pupils of his eyes, dilated in the low light, making him look vulnerable. A rabbit in the twilight. There was quite a lot of Verne about him, the upper lip, the pale hair. She began to feel all the old pulses of desire beating out around her body, spiced with the extra excitement of being away from home, where the usual rules did not apply. That so young and handsome a man should be in the slightest bit interested in her added further fuel. After sitting hand in hand in silence for a while, he swallowed and said, 'I don't suppose you'd like to come to my room?'

'Benjy.' Anna took her hand away from his. 'I'm not at all like that.'

'No,' he said, after another long pause, 'I didn't really think that you were.'

'I should be rather insulted.'

'Insulted? Why?'

'What would you have thought of me if I'd accepted?' Benjy was unable or disinclined to answer. She hated making him feel mortified and seeing his puzzled face, wanted to grab him and kiss him. Instead, she patted his hand and said, 'But actually, I'm rather flattered.'

'Oh?'

'I must be nearly old enough to be your mother.'

'I'm thirty,' Benjy said, with a soupçon of indignation.

'Exactly.'

When she went to her room, Margaret had not returned. Nor had she next morning when their breakfast arrived. She finally bustled in at almost nine o'clock.

'My god, Anna, what a *gorgeous* creature.' She began to peel off her clothes. 'I'm dying for a shower.' She paused, standing in bra and knickers. 'His skin, Anna. Like . . . like—'

'I'd rather not know,' Anna interrupted, sounding a little arch, but not meaning to. Margaret spent ten minutes in the bathroom and then emerged, pink and steamy, her long hair wound up in a towel.

'By the way, how was Benjy?'

'We chatted downstairs for a while. Then I took myself off to bed.'

'Oh.' Margaret paused again, and then looked directly at Anna. 'You disapprove.'

'Do I?'

'Oh yes.'

'Margaret, it's not my business.'

'But you wouldn't.'

'I'm fifteen years older than you.'

'But you still wouldn't, even if you were thirty.'

'I don't say I'm not tempted.'

'Answer please! Teacher's waiting.'

'No.'

'Do you think Bernard would?'

'No.'

'Doesn't mean a thing, you know.'

'Doesn't it? Would Pip mind?'

'Mind? For all I know, Pip's having a tumble right now.' Anna could not see how that could work. 'Oh, he'd mind if I had an affair. Fell in love. But that,' she jerked a thumb at the bedroom door. 'Just a bit of harmless fun. Never to be repeated. Worst luck.'

Anna glanced closely at Margaret's face. She caught the wistfulness, even the start of a tear.

There must have been moments of tenderness during even that briefest of encounters, perhaps the pre-dawn glow of some kind of love even though they were strangers. He was certainly very beautiful. So was she. They must have created something more together than merely a lustful coupling – something beautiful, something that only two humans can make by becoming totally intimate. By taking off their clothes, by each laying body and soul bare to the other, even if just for the shortest of leases. But how could they have the strength to end it before it had really begun? Perhaps choosing not to begin had been the easier option.

Anna looked up from her writing. 'I had not realised until this moment,' she said, aloud, 'just how thirsty I was for . . .' she was going to say love, but that wasn't really it.

Her need was not merely for sex, but for physical love; for tenderness, compassion, and just to be close. Poor Bernard had become so totally absorbed with his career he simply had not had time. And even when they did get together, they mostly talked. Or rather he talked and she listened. He talked about everything: politics, economics, the antics of his colleagues, triumphs (lots), disasters (few) and he talked so entertainingly that one of her pleasures, in this constantly interrupted marriage, was to listen to him. When he recounted an event he turned it into a story, a ripping yarn that had a plot, a climax and a conclusion. When he opined his words flowed so smoothly that she was seduced, even if he was talking nonsense.

Reflecting, now more than a decade later, on Margaret's behaviour that night, Anna understood that there had been a good deal more than mere disapproval. She had said, at the time, that she hadn't disapproved, but she had, not because Margaret was deceiving Pip – if they had an open arrangement that was their affair – but because she was jealous. Jealous of Margaret's ability to indulge without problems of conscience, but also jealous of losing part of her. Her friendship with Margaret had been closer, deeper than perhaps was common between women, but what had not dawned on her until this moment, sitting silent and alone on a huge crowded ocean liner, was that in a way she had been in love with Margaret. At least she had cared so much for her that it was difficult to accept that she might spread her affections beyond Pip and herself. She'd known it all the time, really, but had not actually made herself face it. Now she found the recollection of her previous self distasteful, stupid, feeble. She was beginning to believe that her present friendless, partnerless state was, somehow, her personal fault – a pay-off for past weakness. This particular fold in the tangled cloth of her persona was going to take some unravelling and she wasn't sure how, or whether she could manage that. Not quite yet, anyway. Not while this monster of depression was creeping quietly about in her cabin, waiting for her to allow it to fold itself round her. Carrion comfort. She switched off her computer and felt under the bed for her deck shoes. Heavy physical activity, followed by more writing: that was the key.

As she tidied her cabin before leaving, she was struck with an idea. With a little name-changing, and set in a different location, the Paris experience would make a good story to hand in to Jack Pullen. She decided to go for a stiff walk to get the structure worked out in her head, and then attempt to bash it out in rough at one sitting, while the whole feel of the thing was fresh in her mind.

On deck, on her fourth circuit, she ran into Pullen, walking the opposite way. He turned and continued alongside her.

'Mind if I walk with you?'

'Of course not.' Actually she did.

'Are you working on anything at the moment?'

'A story idea. Love triangle, but a bit different.'

'Want to tell me about it?'

She did not. 'Of course.' She filled him in, making a few hasty changes to events. She noticed that he was losing his breath and quickened her pace, hoping that he might find the effort too demanding and drop out of the walk.

'Sounds . . . great,' he managed to say when she had explained her conclusion. 'Don't think . . . I could . . . fault that.' He had never, except behind her back, commented on anything she had written without criticism. Now she took pity on his breathlessness and slowed down to a dawdle.

'Let's take a breather,' she said. Side by side, they leant over the stern rail.

'I like your symbolism,' Pullen said when he had got his breath back. 'The interloper being black, and wearing a smart suit and all that – managing to outdress your protagonist, even though she's sweated blood to select the right duds for the trip.'

'I didn't see that as symbolism. It just came naturally. Part of the story.'

'That's what makes good writing. Subtext, semiotics and all that crap – you shouldn't need to work that in, not consciously. If the characterisation is strong and the story is good, that almost writes itself.' They watched the ship's wake for a while. Brown gannet-like birds had replaced the albatross in these waters, less majestic in flight, but still capable of impressive aerobatics.

'Wonder what those are,' he said.

'Boobies.' Inwardly she cringed, waiting for a crude Pullen-like reaction. Even the Boys had made remarks about topless beach girls, but they were inoffensive. Pullen always attached a yellow-toothed leer to his smutty references.

'Odd name,' was all he said. Then, a few minutes later, 'Can I buy you a drink?'

'That's sweet of you, Jack, but I'm wanting to go off and start my story now.'

'OK, I won't intercept the muse.' He turned from the sea to look at her. 'But can I beg a big favour?'

'Of course.'

'Could I have that story, when it's done? Without sharing it with the class.'

She was puzzled. 'That will make it your fourth since we sailed. I don't quite understand.' He was silent for a while. She thought he looked slightly guilty and wondered if he might be wanting to steal them, then immediately told herself not to presume that they were anywhere near good enough for him to plagiarise.

'The fact is,' he found it hard to meet her eye, 'I think you write a lot better when you know you won't have to share with an audience. Your class stuff is coming on all right, but when you've written just for me, it's been, well, more relaxed, if you see what I mean. Less inhibited.'

'Oh.' She was unconvinced by his explanation but valued his appraisals so highly that she felt it might be better to agree. Would she be writing much after getting back to England? Probably not, she thought, pushing ideas of going back home out of her mind. 'All right, this one will be for your eyes only.'

'Better get cracking, then,' Pullen said. He squeezed her wrist a fraction too hard and left.

Chapter Sixteen

The big changes in our lives began in 1987. Looking back, the series of mishaps that year should have seemed portentous. The Zeebrugge ferry disaster, in March, was an awful beginning. Two hundred terrified passengers lost their lives, clinging first to the fixed tables and chairs as the vessel capsized, then getting lost in the darkness, the confusion and finally, the numbing cold of the winter sea.

Anna glanced out of her porthole at the Indian Ocean, glistening darkly in the lights from the ship, and shuddered. There had been increasing talk of greed, not only about ferry operators who cut corners in safety procedures, but in society. Wealth had been redistributed, just as Bernard had said it would, but Anna was not sure it had yet gone to the right places. She was still seeing lines of homeless sleepers under Hungerford Bridge every time she walked from Embankment Station to their flat in Whitehall Court and, unless you could afford private medicine, you still had to wait, sometimes years, for surgery. Beneath the new, zesty prosperity of the capital, where noisy young career people lunched on Bollinger and sandwiches in the City wine bars, Anna sensed incredulity. As if no one really believed it could last. Almost every week, some egocentric chef or other would open a new restaurant that sold a dissected tomato or a fragment of fish for a sum that would take a registered nurse or a postman days of work to earn. And every week, instead of being outraged at the swindle, people would flock to eat at such places, anxious to be seen dining on chic scraps of nutriment. It was the nearest thing Anna had seen to the emperor's new clothes.

Instead of a St Luke's Summer, that year, the autumn weather began with a gale that ruined houses and tore whole forests out of the ground. Its epicentre was the heart of the prosperous southeast. Stockbroker country: not the new breed of financiers, with their gelled hair, red braces and nasal whines, but the older establishment, the weekday worsted, weekend tweed brigade. Within a couple of days – the symbolism was apt – came the stock market collapse. And the bright new blood in the city, those young adventuring traders, became villains overnight, too young and too brash to handle something as delicate and unpredictable as the world's finances. Almost as if by conspiracy, they had sliced billions off the value of the weekend tweeds' pensions, and off quite a few other capital accounts.

'I hardly know how to explain this,' Bernard said, 'and if it gets out, it will be extremely embarrassing, but as a family we have rather lost our shirts on this crash.'

'Oh, we'll survive,' Anna said. 'We always have.'

'We'll survive all right, no problems there, but I think I should tell you that we are worth rather less than half what we were last week. And it is not going to get better.'

'Everything's been going up and up. It had to come down. It's only on paper, anyway.' Anna found it impossible to worry. Their capital ran to more than a million pounds, Bernard had told her recently, so if that was halved, or even quartered, she could not see how they could possibly need any more income than they enjoyed already. Bernard was earning a reasonable salary at the university, and his job as head of the special group also paid generously. Yet he seemed quite agitated.

'I think we should start to be more careful,' he said.

'Bernard, I'm always careful.' Anna assumed that he was more worried about the fact that as one of Britain's leading economic gurus he should have been able to save himself from such losses than he was about the financial crisis.

'No, no. I've thought hard about this. I'm going to start salting away some special funds in different places.'

'I thought you already did that.'

'Well, yes, but I mean a kind of extra evasive action. Against any more problems caused by those yuppies at the City.' Anna could not understand why he seemed so agitated.

'You've rather blown your cool over this, haven't you?'

'I've got a feeling that things are going to get worse. A lot worse.' He began to pace. 'There's all this talk about a "soft landing" but I think we may be in for a nineteen-thirties-style depression. It happened last time when there were millions of small investors and I can see parallels today.' He fidgeted with his cuffs. 'I'm, um, I'm going to open a new bank account tomorrow, and start moving some funds around.'

'You don't have to tell me all about that sort of thing.' She wished she could make him feel more comfortable. 'It's your money, really, anyway. You've earned it. I don't have any right to tell you what to do.' She shrugged and smiled. 'Don't worry.'

To her surprise, he took her hands and said, 'Oh but I do worry. I worry a great deal. And I am *not* prepared to put you or Lisa at risk. Ever.' He sighed. She was sure he was more troubled by this whole thing than he need be. 'The fact is, we are joint signatories on virtually everything, but I want to start this new account in my own name. I need to be totally versatile. It's the computers you see. I need to be able to act instantly, whenever the opportunity arises.'

'Bernard, of course.'

'It's mainly for Lisa. You understand? I want to make sure we pass as much as possible on to her.'

Things did get worse. There was widespread talk of recession. Bankruptcies increased, house prices collapsed and there seemed to be more poor on the streets than ever. Furious demonstrations against a poll tax that nobody wanted – other than well-heeled householders – amplified the growing discontent among the huge underclass who hadn't been able, or hadn't bothered, to board the gravy train of the enterprise culture. Violent crime was on the increase, caused, the liberals said, by the desperation of unemployment; caused, the Conservatives said, by a collapse in moral values and decline of the family. And in London and the major cities, beggars haunted almost every street corner. As well as the usual drunks there were youngsters, teenagers sleeping on pavements, in shop doorways, in 'cardboard cities' not even substantial enough to be called shanty towns. Bernard's economic philosophy had suddenly grown less glamorous and soon there was talk of the need for profound changes in policy. Bernard was still working excruciating hours, mostly in London, while Anna 'held the fort' as he called it at Carborough. Margaret had begun spending almost as much time in London as at the university and, with winter coming on, time began to hang rather heavily on Anna's hands.

One dull November afternoon, she returned from a drive over the Fens – she had taken to birdwatching along the lower reaches of the River Nene and had been on the lookout for the first of the winter migrant ducks – to find a message on her answering machine that Bernard, contrary to expectations, would be coming home that evening, and would need meeting at Carborough station. She cursed, having garaged her car, but was delighted at the prospect of having him home, and went directly to the deep-freeze to fish out a package of sweetbreads, which she knew he loved, and some raspberries which she would use with one of the meringue 'hats' she had made the previous day. There was a fresh lettuce in the cellar; while she was there, she selected a bottle of Meursault, and then grabbed a second, just in case. With deft movements and concentrated thoughts, she had set the strategy for an impromptu dinner party *à deux* by the time she had come back up the cellar stairs.

Thirty-five minutes remained before needing to leave for the station, so she set to work developing a sauce for the sweetbreads, making a salad, setting potatoes to boil so that they could be creamed immediately on their return. She sliced a huge tomato, sprinkled olive oil, diced garlic, black olives and a crumble or two of feta cheese over the slices to serve as an appetiser and quickly laid the table.

Bernard was not on the train. Once she had found a parking place, having outstayed her brief standing time outside the station doors, she tried to contact him on his new mobile phone. A recorded voice advised her that his phone was switched off.

He'll just have to ring me when he's arrived, she decided, remembering that she had left the potatoes simmering, and drove the short distance home to catch them before they boiled dry. For comfort, while she tried to put supper on 'hold' and replan the evening, she turned on the television in the sitting room, to hear its sound from the kitchen. News was being relayed of a fire in the Underground station at King's Cross. No one knew how many had been killed, but the heat was so intense that it was hard to imagine anyone on the crowded escalators managing to survive.

'Bernard!' Anna gasped his name out loud. Bernard never took the tube. Never. He was a taxi man, but supposing he had just this once? She tried his mobile phone number again. Apparently it was still switched off. But if he had it with him, and had been burnt – did a burnt phone behave exactly as a switched off phone? She tried to calm herself. He was constantly being held up. Unexpected arrivals, capricious demands from Downing Street: delays were frequent and unavoidable.

Then she remembered that odd, agitated little speech of his, soon after the stock market crash. 'I think we should start to be more careful.' And she knew that sometimes, to prove a point, he would take unnecessarily extreme action. Once, after a medical, when the doctors had advised him that he was eleven pounds overweight, he had fasted, taking nothing but water for two whole days. Thereafter he took neither milk nor sugar in tea or coffee. Anna knew that tonight he had taken the tube. It was exactly what he would have done, in his present frame of mind. The news bulletin had broadcast a phone number for relatives to ring, but the line was too busy for her to get through. She tried it half a dozen times and then gave up. By now it was almost eight-thirty. When the phone rang she snatched it up so violently that she knocked the whole instrument on to the floor, disconnecting the call. She replaced the receiver and held it, trembling, waiting for it to ring again, waiting for the inevitable.

The relief I felt when Bernard finally telephoned was so intense that I burst into tears, right there on the phone. He was almost crying too, I seem to remember, when he realised how worried I had been. He had been delayed at Whitehall, and had heard nothing of the fire until he arrived, by taxi, to see the chaos at King's Cross, and had told the driver to take him on to Finsbury Park to take a train from there. His portable telephone had developed a fault and discharged its battery. As the weeks went by, and the awful stench of burning began to fade at King's Cross, I remember one particular aspect of that fire more vividly than any other. Long after the hundreds of withered bouquets had been cleared away from the pavements near the subway entrance, even after much of the rebuilding had been completed, a small bill was posted all over the station requesting information about one of the victims. The face on the poster was male, a reconstruction extrapolated from the charred remains, but the message was that no one had missed this man, and no one knew who he was. It seemed such a pathetic end, terrible enough to be burnt alive, but what was the value of a life that no one missed?

After their emotional reunion they settled down to a late supper in the kitchen. The sweetbreads were still just about eatable but neither did more than pick at their plate. Now, half an hour, and half a bottle of Meursault later, they were beginning to relax.

'Anna, this whole thing has really made me think.'

'Let's skip this, and go on to pudding,' Anna said, taking their plates over to the sink.

A little later, as he swallowed the last spoonful of raspberry meringue, he said, 'Things are getting sticky.' He placed his spoon on the plate at exactly ninety degrees to the table side. 'In fact you could say that I'm fighting for my life up there with that lot.'

'You're working far too hard, anyway,' Anna said, pouring his coffee. 'I know how important the whole job is to you, but I think you need a break. Perhaps even a spell of gentler work.'

'We can have that when I retire,' Bernard retorted. 'And in case you think that is ages away, it is actually less than eight years, now. If I finish at sixty.'

That did seem an age to Anna. Eight more years of Carborough dinner parties, entertaining what Bernard called the Good and the Great – people who were at the sharp end of things, people who knew so well how very important they were. Some were kind, some flirtatious, some paid her compliments that made her feel good about her role as hostess, but most were unable to do that without patronising. Some of the women were worse than the men, addressing her with tones of mild pity, suggesting she must be frightfully bored when Bernard was up in town, attempting small talk with her about children, schools, cooking. When they were not there and she was alone in the large house with its high ceilings and heavy-handed Edwardian atmosphere, she would spend endless evenings playing records of Mozart, Brahms and Wagner or watching indifferent television. When that grew too bad to watch, she would struggle with a difficult novel; she read the whole of *Moby Dick* in a week, but gave up on

Ulysses after dozens of fresh attempts. Bernard would ring in at roughly the same time each evening when he was away, but occasionally, because she missed her so much, away at Cambridge, she would telephone Lisa, but whenever she did she always hung up wishing the call had gone differently. She hated her being away for such long periods, but whenever they spoke the abrasiveness in their relationship seemed even more gritty when there was neither eye contact nor body language to read. They never said goodbye in anger, but Anna never felt able to convey or to receive the sense of warmth or love that they both needed until the receiver was back in its cradle. Then, on the second, she began to feel guilty. I should have asked her more about her work, I should have told her what Bernard was doing at that moment, I should have . . .

Even now, looking back to those years, Anna felt a pang of guilt for letting Lisa down so often. She resolved to send her another fax, as soon as she finished her current writing spell. She got up to stretch her legs and give her eyes a rest from the keyboard. Looking through the cabin porthole, she was surprised to see a tiny fishing boat, less than a hundred yards away, miles out in the middle of the Indian Ocean. She wondered how the ship's crew could see such craft at dead of night. The *Brisbane* could run one down without even feeling the shock. She imagined being in such a boat, bobbing on the swell, deafened by the sound of wind in the ears but then looking up to see the vast prow of the liner towering above, seconds before the impact. She sat at her tiny desk again and dragged her mind back into the past.

Rereading what she had just written, she felt the recollections had been a little too negative. There was what Bernard would have called an 'upside'. Some of the celebrities she had met were fascinating, wonderful people who she quickly admired and one or two of whom had kept in contact for years, though now with Bernard gone she supposed they'd desist. There had been so many special, memorable evenings: dining at the House of Commons restaurant with political friends, riotous late-night tipples with Margaret and Pip at the Groucho Club, West End cinema visits, also with Margaret and Pip, eating afterwards at a Covent Garden bistro or racing to King's Cross for the last train to Carborough. A day with Bernard on the river, drinking warm lager as they cruised to Greenwich. But these were highlights, dotted sparingly through a life that lacked shape or purpose. Bernard was the doer, the 'go-getter', and she had been content to help and support him in whatever way she could. She was going nowhere. But that was fine, while Bernard was cutting and thrusting and hewing his career in London, always fighting on the fringes of politics, but never getting his feet wet – or dirty. One day, he would be back. Meanwhile she would continue to wait for her share of him, as she had waited for a quarter of a century.

Sitting at that table, on the night of the fire, she realised suddenly that she had sat brooding for too long. She looked across at Bernard. 'Well, I'd be happy to have a little more of you. On your own, all to myself.'

'I'm here now.' He got up and walked round to her side of the table, putting his hand on her shoulder and stroking her neck. 'I'm here whenever I can be.' It was late; the room had grown chilly since the central heating was set to turn itself off at eleven-thirty, but she could feel the warmth of his body through his clothes. Hungry for contact, she rested her face against his stomach and allowed her hand to caress the inside of his thigh, moving upwards. He cradled her head, still holding her to him, but almost caressingly took her arm and guided her hand to a safer area, around the small of his back. It had been a gentle invitation, graciously refused. They were both very tired.

'I'll never get used to this frenzied life.' Her words were muffled by his clothing.

'You enjoy the glamour.'

'Do I?' She reflected that it was fun. She looked up. 'I'd give it all up tomorrow, happily, if it meant I could have you back. Properly back.' She felt her voice wobble slightly as she spoke. 'I bet you see more of Margaret than you do of me, now she's gone down to London.' Bernard took himself gently away, and returned to his place.

'Maybe.' He stirred his coffee. 'But that's part of the job.' He put his spoon in his saucer and drank. 'This is not going to last. The bastards have already got the knives out for Maggie. Can you believe that?'

'Yes.'

'Oh, can you?'

'Bernard, she's building up a pretty big storehouse of enemies. All those colleagues she's destroyed – you can't treat people like that and expect them to love you.'

'But her policies are faultless. So are her decisions.'

'Poll tax? Westland?'

'She snatched us back from ruin. And she defeated the tyranny of the unions. You must remember that.'

'Oh, I do.' Anna offered him more coffee. He shook his head. She noticed that the lines above his brow were deepening – had been deepening more noticeably in the last couple of years. She knew how much deft side-stepping he had to do, how much rapid thinking was needed to keep, at all times, one step ahead. Throughout his career he had embraced every challenge with delight, pining only when things grew quiet. But now he was different; more haunted. Something else was troubling him.

'And I *am* a realist.' He met her eye, held her gaze for a moment and then looked back at his coffee cup. 'If they do ditch Maggie,' he murmured, 'you must realise that I will have to go too.'

'That much is pretty obvious.'

'But they may get rid of me sooner.' Anna knew that too. In spite of his ducking and weaving he still had rivals among the coterie of advisers, spin doctors, movers and shakers.

'What will you do?'

'Resume my chair at Stoneford. The poor old place deserves a little more attention from me anyway.'

Bernard's job did last. Exactly as long as Margaret Thatcher. In fact he resigned on the same day that she did, shortly before Christmas in 1990. And things seemed almost to get back to normal. Margaret slipped back to working part-time for Bernard at Stoneford and for the following summer we resumed our Monday tennis meetings. Bernard, who had lost far too much weight during his spell at Westminster, now concentrated on getting his body fitter and his mind more relaxed. He too played tennis, often in mixed doubles with me, Margaret and Pip. His game improved so quickly that soon he was better than all of us, in spite of the others' relative youth. When he and Margaret teamed against Pip and me it was hopeless. We almost always lost in straight sets.

Lisa spent most of that summer at home. After completing her degree and spending an extra year working for a special diploma, she had decided on a change of direction and needed space and time to work out her future. Her history qualifications, she claimed, would not help much with her career plans and she wanted to go on somewhere – possibly Purlin – to take a master's in business studies. She and Bernard got very chummy during that summer, making up for all the lost time when she had been away at St Etheldreda's and he had been so busy in London. The only time they had a cross word was when he allowed her to beat him at tennis.

'You did that on purpose,' she yelled, when after the score had returned to deuce goodness knows how many times in the last game of a best of three match, he had hit the ball hard over her head, right out of the enclosure. 'In fact you've been bloody well giving me points all afternoon. I don't *need* you to do that.' If she could not win in her own right she did not want to win. How like her father she was, Anna thought.

'Advantage, spoilt brat,' he announced. Then in a simulated rage he served with all the force he could muster smack into the top of the net. The second ball followed, possibly even faster, fizzing into the white cloth band that held net to cable. A double fault. 'Game, set and match to the younger generation,' he said, now beginning genuinely to lose his patience.

'I don't have to take this!' Lisa hurled her racket against the enclosure netting.

'Temper temper!' he taunted. She flounced off to the changing room by the pool. Moments later he heard a heavy splash followed by the slooshing sound of her confident strokes as she swam, fast as she could, back and forth, back and forth.

Clash of the Titans, Anna thought. She had been hand-weeding a long, thin border that ran along the side of the tennis court. Both father and daughter seemed unaware of her presence.

'I'm getting a small group of writers together,' Jack Pullen said on the evening before they docked at Bali. 'The idea is that we hire a minibus and driver and take four or, at the most, five people deep into the interior. Get away from the beach resorts and up into the hills. Want to come?'

'I was going to do something similar with the Boys,' Anna said. They were standing at the Cricketer's Bar. 'But I'm sure we could join forces.'

'The boys?' Pullen looked confused for a moment, 'Oh, them!' He stifled a shudder and looked awkward.

'They have been very loyal to your classes.'

'Mm. I hadn't really thought of them.' He seemed embarrassed. Before he could say another word they came into the bar. Ant wore a vivid Hawaiian shirt, with tropical foliage all over it in the most unlikely orange and green and Cedric a very correct soft cotton affair in beige with a small silk scarf at the neck in forget-me-not blue. Both wore knee-length navy shorts and expensive loafers. Pullen, who seemed to have a limitless wardrobe of worn, black denim, glared at them, flashing yellow teeth.

'Ah, Boys!' Anna called. 'It seems that Jack here has had the same idea as we have. I've suggested that we join forces.' The Boys hesitated for only the briefest of moments.

'Only if we can still wear our sarongs,' Cedric said.

'And I'll have nothing on under mine,' Ant said, rolling his eyes ever so slightly at Anna. Pullen's face barely concealed his disgust.

In the end, no other member of the creative writing class seemed very interested in joining the group, so the four of them caught the first tender ashore and, by nine o' clock were running the gauntlet of street vendors pestering them to buy fake Rolex watches, wooden carvings, paper fans and designer perfumes. They selected a driver, checked out his vehicle to make sure that it was air-conditioned, and set off for the hills.

'I can't believe how beautiful it is,' Cedric said as the vehicle cleared the small town and began to climb. Soon they began to pass small rice paddies in various stages of development from young plants freshly set out in the water to mature crops, ripening on the drained fields ready to be cut, stem by stem, with a small sickle. Anna was impressed by the neatness of the farming, the vivid emerald of the young rice plants, reflected in the still water in which they had been planted. In one tiny field, less than a tenth of an acre, an elderly man was hand-weeding, up to his knees in the mud which underlay the few inches of water, pulling weeds with his toes, transferring them to his hand to throw them to a growing heap at the side.

The driver took them to a village whose long street was a series of terraces with small houses on either side and a long house at its centre. This was a raised stage, open-sided and covered with a thick palm thatch: a meeting place where men could gather on special occasions to converse. On either side, the family houses had tiny courtyards, many made cool with wells, or small pools of water and with shaded seating areas. Some advertised sarongs and ceremonial clothes made from cloth woven on the premises. As they strolled, as slowly as possible because of the heavy humidity and tropical heat,

Anna felt herself affected by the serenity of the place. The villagers were beautiful, not necessarily because their appearance was handsome – though often it was – but because of the openness of their smiles, and their apparent gentleness. They exuded a kind of innocence. Further up the hill, they passed a stream where people were washing themselves and their clothes. Men, women and children, all naked, enjoying the cooling waters of the stream together, quite unashamed.

'What beautiful people,' Ant said.

Later, when they had piled back into the car and been driven to a seaside restaurant for lunch, Cedric said, 'Let's jump ship and finish our days here.' He was joking, of course, but his face carried a wistful expression. Across the blue-green water of the bay they could see the *Brisbane* at anchor in front of the island's volcanoes which rose behind into white clouds.

They ate prawns in a spicy sauce, and drank bottles of local lager. Afterwards, the Boys wanted to snooze on the beach but Anna decided to walk, to see more. Pullen insisted on accompanying her.

'So?' he said, when they had walked for a few yards along the beach, 'what do you really think of this place?'

'Ravishing.' They walked on in silence. Anna never quite felt at ease with Pullen. 'Peaceful. Every citizen seems to be an artist of some kind – they're so expressive, but at the same time so incredibly modest.'

'And?' He seemed to want more.

'But I couldn't stand living here.'

'Mmm. It's pretty poor. I notice the natives were washing uphill from the village. I bet the shit all comes out at the downstream end.'

'Oh it isn't that. My needs are very simple and with practically any Western income one could live very comfortably here. It's the religion. These people all look so beautiful and serene and peaceful, but their every move seems to be governed by religious rules. I mean, twenty-five thousand temples – isn't that what they've got here? It isn't that religion plays an important role in their lives but rather that their lives are entirely supplementary to it. They're living sacrifices.'

'My God, that's what I like so much about you Anna!' Pullen took her hand. She hardly liked to snatch it back, but she was uneasy. 'You've got eyes and a mind.'

'Isn't it obvious to everyone? All religions are tyrannous, but this one, gentle as everyone keeps saying it is, seems more than usually so. I mean look at the time and money they spend on these Barong dances and all those religious festivals. There seems to be one practically every day.' They had rounded a bluff in the coastline, putting the restaurant behind them out of sight.

'You must admit, though, the women are lovely. Those people bathing. You must have noticed them – the men anyway.' He leered. She recalled images of golden-skinned people, mainly small children, happily splashing about in the clear, cascading water.

'I noticed the children the most.'

'But . . .' he seemed to want to say something, but couldn't quite get to the point. 'Do you still, you know, *like* men? I mean, would you ever think of finding another partner? Marrying again?' She took her hand away and increased her pace slightly to create a little distance between them. He matched his gait to hers, staying close.

'It's still less than nine months since I lost . . .' She swallowed. 'Really, I have no idea. And I'd rather not discuss it.'

'But you're not tied to where you are. You could up sticks to . . . I don't know . . . anywhere.'

'I suppose so.' She wasn't ready for this kind of talk. He seemed too near, in this tropical humidity. She could smell tobacco on his breath and a trace of sweat on his cotton shirt. The black must absorb the heat horribly.

'Your Paris story, by the way. Bloody brilliant.'

'Really? You think so?' She felt a buzz of excitement. She had so wanted to impress him.

'Best thing you've done so far.' She stopped, and turned

to face him. She could see his yellow teeth, tapering towards the receding gums. The ones in his lower jaw were angled in several different directions, like gravestones in an old churchyard. 'A really professional job. You could publish that.' She was so delighted she wanted to leap, to shout, but they resumed walking at a dawdling pace.

'I'm not sure what'll happen when I get back home, but I'm determined to go on writing. It's what I should have been doing for the last forty years.'

'And you can. Bloody hell, you're the nearest thing I've seen to a natural—' She held her hand up to stop him.

'Don't. You'll give me a swelled head. But thank you for all the guidance and help you have given me.

'Gerrtcher!' He shrugged. She couldn't know how difficult it was for him to suppress his envy for her talent.

'Anna, there's something else that I . . .' He looked behind him and snorted with frustration after spotting the Boys rounding the bluff. 'Damn it to hell!' He hesitated, taking short breaths, fingers clenching and unclenching, then said, 'Well, I don't suppose it matters now. Here come your pansy friends.' She was puzzled by his sudden anger.

By the time they had all walked back to their vehicle and were sitting in the relative comfort of its air-conditioning, Pullen's brief rage had subsided. Without the Boys noticing, she pressed his hand, once, making him turn his head to wink. She tried not to shudder at the lasciviousness of his gesture but read it as some kind of a pay-off.

Pullen turned again, to look out through the side windows, barely noticing the verdant landscape. She must have been a bloody fantastic wife, and, if the sensuousness of her Paris story was anything to go by, he dared bet she would still be OK in bed, despite her age. Or, at least, she'd still be interested. He wondered why she seemed so unable to appreciate her own talent. It was she who should be teaching him, for Christ's sake. She had an instinct for working a good plot and more, she had a deftness of touch that he could never master. He sighed, outwardly relaxed, but hating himself inside just a little more. How could he be so pathetic as to envy some poor old bag who hadn't even published? Yet compared with her prose his was shoddy. Clichéd, even. On the whole, he told himself, taking the rough with the smooth, at the end of the day, in the final analysis, when push came to shove, life was a bit of a bugger really.

Chapter Seventeen

After Bali, the *Brisbane* crossed the Indian Ocean calling at Singapore, Colombo and Mombasa before following the African coastline to Cape Town and the colder, more treacherous Atlantic. Fully adjusted to shipboard routine after more than two months at sea, Anna was surprised at how quickly and easily the time seemed to slide by. Each sea day, she walked two miles round the Promenade Deck but avoided the organised strolls which met early in the morning and moved much too slowly for her even to get breathless. She preferred to give herself a spell of solitude in which she could exercise her body while making herself think hard about developing plots and characters for her stories. Since sailing from Southampton, besides her memoirs and a lot of rather sub-standard stuff, she had completed five short stories which, she felt, were beginning to be respectable. Pullen still had four of them, though she could not understand why he would not give them back, and two she had read aloud during the routine sessions. The writing class had expanded to around ten; every time new members turned up he would make a point of giving them a critical drubbing to see whether they had staying power. Few did, but those who survived his verbal attacks kept coming back.

'They're mostly driven here by boredom,' he told Anna one afternoon, when she had stayed on to discuss an idea with him.

'They've fallen out with their bridge groups or with Hawaiian dancing classes by now, so I'm all there is left to try. And I have to admit,' he added, 'I get pretty bloody bored myself, by this stage in the cruise – or at least I would have, if you hadn't been here.'

One of his most surprising pupils – though his attendance was anything but regular – was Captain Wishart. Whenever he turned up, the discussion periods were much more animated than usual and Anna felt she learnt rather more, during those noisy sessions, than when Pullen spent the whole period trying to wring contributions from the more reticent of his pupils. Only about half the class members were willing to read their works out loud, and of those few were able to hold the attention of the rest of the class. Pullen was still publicly very hard on Anna, though Wishart flew eagerly to her defence every time he was there, but by now she had more or less managed to come to terms with his harshness, making herself believe that it was doing her writing a lot of good. She felt far too insecure about her own abilities openly to criticise the others – unless very gently – but increasingly she was able to recognise weakness in their work; more to the point, she noticed that they kept making the same mistakes and continued to miss opportunities every time they wrote something new. She found herself trying to reshape their tales as they read, or trying to think up better, more telling imagery. With some, she resorted to awarding imaginary scores for clichés and howlers. 'General consensus of opinion', for instance, won ten points, 'gales of laughter' five and there were single penalty points for every superfluous adverb. Euphemisms about sensitive subjects were her especial *bête noire*: 'she felt his manhood close to her' cropped up in one class member's work almost every week but when once she wrote, 'he drank in the twin peaks of her loveliness' Anna uttered a snort of protest and was about to comment when she realised that, had she not been exposed to Pullen's scorn for beating about the bush, she might still have written like that herself. Well, perhaps

not like *that*, but she had at least learnt to call a spade
a spade.

The computer file that held her memoirs had grown enormous and she decided to divide the opus into three smaller,
more manageable documents. Each needed a title, for no other
reason than to identify it on the screen, but she agonised over
this for some time. Part One she called 'Departures', that was
relatively easy, but it took a deal more cogitation to come up
with 'Crossing The Line' for Part Two. Part Three she simply
called 'Three' in the computer index, deciding to name it
when it was complete. There would be no Part Four.

Interesting though the ports of call were, she was becoming
so absorbed with writing that every day not spent at work she
felt was being wasted. She had looked forward to Singapore,
but hated it. Bernard had praised the place so highly whenever
he had been that she felt sure its cleanliness and order would
suit her, especially after the chaos of Indonesia.

'We should all look to Singapore,' he had often said. 'A
shining example of how enterprise can really work.' Usually
he would add, 'And they have no problems with law and
order.' Bernard supported the concept, not only of caning or
flogging criminals, but also of capital punishment. 'Anyone
who takes life should forfeit it.' Anna expected to feel safe
in the streets, and to see a clean, well-run city state. But far
from feeling secure, she sensed eyes boring into her wherever
she went. Even in the public lavatory a sign warned her that
failure to flush the thing would result in a fine of two hundred
Singapore dollars.

She had decided to travel around the city on her own,
but in the magnificent new orchid gardens, at the centre of
Singapore's huge botanic garden, she bumped into the Boys
who were enthusing over the plants.

'This is quite amazing,' Cedric was saying. 'It's only just
been opened and look! Have you ever seen so many priceless
flowers in one spot?' Anna hadn't. And she wasn't sure she
liked them very much. They had an arrogance of colour and
a sophistication of shape that made her uneasy. She much

preferred simple flowers in gentler colour combinations. Some of these glistened with a waxiness that made them look plastic, others had the appearance of genitalia, not necessarily human, but suggestive, fantastically mutated and presented without shame.

'They look a bit like, um, reproductive organs,' she said.

'Well, dearie, that is exactly what they are,' Ant replied.

They left the orchids after a while and wandered slowly among the trees. Later, Cedric said that they absolutely had to drink a Singapore Sling at Raffles Hotel. They would have time, since the *Brisbane* did not sail until nine p.m. Anna fell in love with the old colonial building even though she knew it had been gutted and rebuilt. They elected to drink in the Long Bar, where fans turned in the ceiling and the floor was littered with peanut husks. It was like a dramatisation of something by Somerset Maugham. Anna half expected some 1920s rubber planter from up country to come bursting in, driven mad with jealousy because he had discovered that his wife was, at that very moment, being unfaithful. He would drink himself into a stupor at the bar while she canoodled with an evil neighbour, a German emigré who had grown up in – yes, that was it, – the Dutch East Indies, and had neither scruples nor good looks nor the faintest inkling about personal hygiene. Later, full of alcoholic remorse, the planter would drive back all the way to Johore, or Baru or wherever, and shoot her, her servant and then himself, leaving the way clear for the unsavoury neighbour to pick up his plantation at a knockdown price. Oh, and of course it would turn out that she was pregnant, but only after years of their longing for a son, of having given up hope of her ever managing to conceive. Perhaps her unexpected pregnancy was the final clincher on his suspicions – and that would impugn his manhood too.

All the while, through the action of the story, the monsoon rain would pour endlessly, making gutters gush, dampening every inch indoors and out, filling the air with sweaty humidity. All their treasured European possessions would become covered with a mould that developed in the damp atmosphere overnight. This mildew would be a symbol of his jealousy, covering everything that was good and clean, with its contamination, until all was destroyed.

'Good God alive!' yelled Ant, bringing Anna out of her reverie with an uncomfortable jerk. She stared at him, thinking some tropical creepy-crawly had crawled up the leg of his immaculate white drill trousers. 'Will you look at that!' He was holding the bill. Three Singapore Slings had cost them more than thirty pounds.

'Perhaps we'd better have our second one somewhere else,' Cedric said.

At Colombo, shore leave was cancelled. There had been a bomb scare – something to do with the Tamil Tigers – and she had been disappointed at not, after all, visiting Kandy and the Temple of the Sacred Tooth, but happy to be granted an extra day for writing. She had been exercising her mind over the Malaya story and had begun to think of several ways in which to make it original. But she knew that she must first work on her memoirs. She brought Part Three up on to the screen with reluctance, half fearing what would appear in print. The next section was going to be the most difficult to write. For the thousandth time she asked herself: do I really need to do this? As she asked, the sensations began to well up. Her throat turned dry, but her mouth began to salivate as nausea churned in her stomach. She blew her nose, poured a little mineral water – long since turned flat and warm – into a glass, and drank. At last, with hesitant fingers, she began to type.

It is very difficult, now, to write about Lisa with any sort of objectivity. There's no doubt that the older she grew, the better we were with each other. I cried for days when she first went to boarding school, yet when she was home for the holidays, despite all my strongest intentions, I would find myself losing patience with her. She was, if anything, even stronger willed than Bernard, and, even when she did not defy me openly, I knew that she found it difficult to accept most of my decisions. Once she had travelled through puberty and become a young woman, her relationship with Bernard went through a profound change. They behaved like two children, giggling together over some mistake I might have made, or planning expeditions together, to which I might or might not be invited. One Saturday, when Lisa was home between completing her postgraduate business course and beginning her career in the City – the eve of Mid Lent Sunday – Bernard suggested that he should do the weekly shopping, a chore which he knew I loathed.

'Bernard, you can't possibly do it,' Anna said. 'You haven't a clue what we need.'

'No, but Lisa will know exactly, won't you, poppet, and it's Mothering Sunday tomorrow.'

The infuriating thing was that they got it almost exactly right. Nothing was forgotten. Lisa had even persuaded Bernard to resist such unnecessary impulse purchases as chocolate creams – which the family never ate – a jar of olive oil containing a whole truffle from Perigord and half a side of smoked salmon, all of which he had suggested would be 'good investments'. Anna's larder held several time-expired items from Bernard's previous, infrequent trips into what he called 'the world of retailing'.

Lisa brought breakfast in bed too early for Anna to surface and thank her graciously; Bernard heaped praises on the way she had prepared the tray, on how clever to have found a few primroses in the garden, in spite of the beastliness of the past weather and even how crisp and aromatic the toast smelt. It was obvious to Anna that the two of them had planned this some time ago. She felt awkward, now, and looking at the fresh, clean features of her daughter's face, felt herself to be sluggish with sleep, creased and unattractive. She wondered how William might have looked at twenty-five. He would almost certainly have lost the roundness of his face, just as

Lisa had, but would he have developed Bernard's aquiline stare that could so unnerve people, especially if the eye glinted with anger? She thought he might, but that he would have been gentler – not weaker, but more sympathetic.

It was inevitable that, once locked into this track, her mind would run along all the well-worn grooves. Would they have had Lisa if William had not died? If they had, how would Lisa have been with a much older brother? She could hardly have been more difficult, as a child – difficult for her, never for Bernard – but Anna would never know whether the problems with their relationship stemmed from her, or whether they were simply inborn in Lisa. It had been impossible, especially in their early years, for her not to make comparisons with William; often she suspected that this had affected the mother-daughter bond. For the first decade of Lisa's life, Anna was constantly wondering why, when William had been so easy to bring up, so willing to try his best at everything and above all, so loving, Lisa should have been so difficult. William had been gorgeous to cuddle, right from babyhood, but Bernard had not liked to be too physical and had kept his distance. With Lisa it was the other way round. Anna had wanted to cuddle her when she was tiny, but sensed the child was uncomfortable. With Anna she had squirmed, but with Bernard she had clung with her arms round his neck like a baby monkey. It troubled her too, sometimes, that Lisa had not shown more interest in her dead brother. Anna often wished she had asked about the brother she never knew. Instead, whenever Anna had broached the subject, wanting to keep his memory fresh, neither Lisa nor Bernard wanted to be involved. Lisa would change the subject with an impatient retort; with Bernard a troubled expression would appear and Anna would refrain from pressing on, sensing that she was causing too much pain.

'Penny for them.' Bernard was looking at her.

'Thank you, darlings both,' she said, at once wishing she hadn't made it so obvious that she knew they had connived. She did not mean to sound disapproving.

Later, they told her to put on a smartish frock as there was a surprise in store. Bernard and Lisa sat in the front of Lisa's new Golf while they drove to Carborough Business Airfield. 'What exactly is going on?' Anna asked from the cramped back seat. She was beginning to be rattled by the conspiratorial atmosphere.

'You'll find out soon enough,' Lisa chortled, looking directly at her father. They walked through the tiny wooden airport building and out across the tarmac to one of a half-dozen small aircraft which were parked neatly on the grass. Lisa pulled a set of keys, like car keys, Anna thought, out of her pocket and unlocked the door.

'You put your foot on here, Mummy,' she said, as she reached out a hand to help her mother into the cockpit of the aircraft. Anna hated everything to do with flying. The impression of freedom one might have had, watching light aeroplanes soaring and dipping like swallows in a summer sky was entirely spurious. The reality was that you were strapped into a tiny claustrophobic cabin and which bucked and surged, making you feel sick the moment it left the ground.

'Who's going to fly us?'

Lisa and Bernard exchanged glances so smug she could have hit them. Then Lisa climbed into the left-hand front seat. She turned before strapping herself in. 'I didn't want to tell you, while I was learning,' she said, 'because I didn't want you to be worried. But now I'm qualified, and I've done the hours, well, I thought you ought to know.'

'But your father knew.' Daughter and father exchanged another glance, this time not so confident. 'Wouldn't he have worried too?' Bernard shook his head.

'I had total confidence in her. A mother always worries.'

They flew for an hour and landed in another tiny airfield somewhere in the Cotswolds. There, Margaret and Pip were waiting.

'Don't tell me *you* knew about Lisa being able to fly as well,' Anna said, close to tears.

'Lisa fly? Did she?' Margaret looked in amazement at the

girl's cool handling of the aircraft door, watched her locking it and slipping the key into the small briefcase she was carrying. Then she uttered a short ironic bark of laughter. 'Precocious brat,' she retorted, giving her a swift kiss on the forehead. The action almost concealed the scorn on her face. 'What you need, my girl, is a lovely man to sort you out. Help you get your priorities right.'

They walked over to a stretched limousine and climbed in while a capped chauffeur stood by the open doors.

'Burford, is it, sir?' the driver asked.

'Close by,' Bernard said. 'I'll direct you when we get close.'

The restaurant had been open for less than six months. Its proprietor, a chef made popular by a television series, had been lionised in both tabloid and quality newspapers and was therefore able to charge exorbitant prices for very small – though artistic – portions of food. Anna began to scan the menu that was placed in front of her while a waiter quietly opened a bottle of Dom Perignon.

'That's just for interest,' Bernard said, looking over her shoulder. 'I've organised the ordering and things already.' Anna hoped that some of the things she liked the look of in the menu would turn up for lunch, but all the dishes came as a complete surprise and seemed unrelated to what she had seen listed. It was a classic lunch. She would never forget the out-of-season cherries, warmed, rather than poached, so that their fresh juice gushed on to the tongue as she bit them. They had come with a garnish of fresh basil leaves – also out of season – and the plate had been decorated all round the outside with strands of spun sugar and fresh purple violets. The sweet-sour taste of that desert would stay with her for the rest of her days. Even now, writing in her cabin, she could recall without effort the extraordinary blend of aromas.

After lunch, the limousine took them to a riding school where for an hour they watched a demonstration of dressage on four beautiful white horses. Lipizzaners, Lisa said, were the breed used in the Spanish Riding School at Vienna. These horses were so perfectly coordinated and so in tune with their riders that they might have been automata. Their graceful leg movements, slow cantering, half passes, pirouettes and bows seemed so effortless that Anna was surprised when she noticed how deeply and rapidly they were breathing and how flared their nostrils were. Soon, one of the stallions stood very close to the small gallery where they sat, and she could see that the animal's coat was damp with sweat, and that a network of veins pulsed just beneath the sensitive skin. The carriage of the head, the look in the horse's eye and the wild flowing forelock were strangely disturbing, a concentration of masculinity, of brooding strength, but also of nervousness and sensitivity. A noble, graceful animal, to a casual onlooker, but Anna understood that every move it made was directed by the rider who, with minimal movements of rein and spur, achieved complete domination.

At dusk Lisa flew back to Carborough from where Bernard drove mother and daughter home. Anna's spirits, which had been declining throughout the afternoon, fell more sharply as they approached Ketton House. She had so wanted to express her admiration for Lisa's achievement in learning to fly, but she felt too left out. Not knowing about the lessons had deprived her of sharing her daughter's experiences, from the first terror-filled flight through the period of gaining confidence, developing her skill and finally winning her spurs. She knew that Lisa would be wondering why she had not expressed more enthusiasm for being flown, and why she had not been more open-handed with her praise. That worried her, but not half so much as did the envy of her daughter's breezy competence, not just in flying but in whatever she undertook. Anna knew that it was wrong to be jealous of her daughter's capable ways, but the feeling just wouldn't go away.

'I know it's a bit naff,' Anna said as Lisa followed her into the drawing room, 'but I'd really sooner have a cup of tea than alcohol.' On cue, Bernard came in bearing a tray that had to have been prepared before they had left that morning.

'Earl Grey,' he said, setting down the tray before her and glancing at Lisa.

'You've thought of absolutely everything.' Anna was close to tears now.

'Of course,' Bernard said. He winked at his daughter. Anna intercepted the exchange and felt rage and hurt building up.

'I am able to think, you know. I mean, I have got a mind of my own.' Tears were flowing. 'What's left of a mind, anyway.'

'Aren't you being a little ungrateful?' Bernard's voice was hardening.

'It's been a lovely day. I couldn't have asked for more.' Lisa handed her mother a handkerchief. She looked at it, noticed its quality and rummaged in her handbag for a tissue. 'It's just that I . . . I want . . .'

'I think I'll do a bit of work,' Bernard said, putting his cup back down on the tray and walking from the room. They heard his study door bang. Anna cried for a while and Lisa put her arm round her.

'It's not as if I'm ungrateful,' she said, when she had recovered a little. 'I don't even have to be in control. But I like to know what I'm doing.'

'Mum!' Lisa stroked her mother's hair. 'We wanted to give you a lovely surprise.'

'A bunch of violets would have done the trick.' Anna stayed silent for a while. Later she said, 'Lisa, I wish you'd told me about your flying.'

'I didn't want you to be worried.'

'That's not the real reason, is it?'

'I, well, I wasn't sure whether I could do it. I was so terrified at first.'

'But you did do it.'

'Yes. Eventually.'

'And you still didn't tell me.' A longish pause.

'No.'

'But you told Dad.' An even longer pause.

'Yes.' Fresh tears from Anna. 'Oh, Mum, please!' Lisa

herself was close to weeping. 'I didn't mean to hurt you like this. I don't see how I *have* hurt you.'

'No.' Anna dried her eyes. 'I don't suppose you do.' She decided she wanted to be by herself, but felt she could not ask her daughter to leave her alone. Lisa sensed hostility and moved away from her mother, placing a few inches between them on the large sofa. After a longish pause, Anna said, 'I suppose I shouldn't be so selfish. You and Dad did so much for me today. But I just wish you'd . . . I don't know . . . *confide* in me a bit sometimes.' They continued to sit for some minutes, neither at all sure of what to say to the other.

'I think Dad's a bit upset,' Lisa said eventually. 'I couldn't bear it if you two fell out, especially if it was over me.'

'We won't, darling, I promise.' Anna got up. 'I'll go to him.' She left the drawing-room door open behind her — a sign that she did not want to exclude her daughter. She knocked and walked into the study. He was playing with his computer. He did not look up.

'Thank you, Bernard.' She walked round to his side of the desk and kissed the top of his head. 'Thank you for a wonderful day.' Still sitting, he put his arms round her waist and held her to him while she fiddled with his hair. 'You've got a tiny bald patch,' she said, parting the hair, 'just here.' She kissed it before he could reach up and straighten his hair. 'Oh, and sorry for the tantrums. Put it down to the menopause!'

'You can be such a goose sometimes, Anna.' He put a gentle hand under her chin and tilted her face upwards to plant a kiss on her mouth. 'You know, for a fifty-five year old you are in cracking form.' She studied his face. The lines round the eyes and slight hollows in his cheeks, if anything, added to his appearance of strength.

'You don't do so badly yourself.' Inevitably her mind drifted back to the autumn picnic at Kilmarnock Falls. Never before and never since that late afternoon when they had hurried home to make love had he let go quite so completely. 'You know, darling, what would make a perfect end to

Mothering Sunday?' She reached under his jacket and tugged at his shirt until she could slip her hand inside and stroke the small of his back above the hip, just where he liked it. Yes, he knew.

'You go on up. I'll just finish this little job here. Half an hour – forty-five minutes tops. Yah?' She took her hand out of his shirt and glanced at the computer.

'Must you?'

'I need to get this thing finished, now I've started.' He read disappointment in her face, tinged with exasperation. 'Darling, it's work!'

'I know.' She wanted him so badly now. Not necessarily for sex, but to be held, to be the single focus of his attention. She wanted him to make her feel important, to help her to repair her self-esteem. 'I know.' She tried to sound matter-of-fact, but it didn't work.

'Hang in there, love! I'll be retired in a couple of years. *Then*, we'll be able to do anything we like, whenever we like.'

She went to have a long bath and to watch television in bed while she waited for him. By the time he came upstairs it was past midnight and she had fallen asleep. Seeing her, lying with covers to her chin mouth slightly open, breathing regularly, he wondered how much she really cared these days.

A few months after the Mothering Sunday treat, Bernard found out that he was to receive a knighthood. He made little of it, even when the press nagged him for comments after the Queen's Birthday Honours list had been published. 'Nothing more than a routine handout,' he said, and refused to discuss it any more with anyone. But I knew that he was secretly thrilled, and also relieved that after all he had not been forgotten by the politicians he helped the most.

Lisa's behaviour went through an abrupt and inexplicable change. Just after Whitsun she rang me to announce that she intended to chuck in her job. I was staggered. Up to that moment, she had told us, constantly, how much she loved her work, how exciting it all was, and how lucky she felt to have come so far in such a short time. When I asked her why, she simply told me I wouldn't understand. When I quizzed her more intently, she told me it wasn't really my business – and then immediately began to cry on the phone. I felt she was heading for some sort of breakdown and begged her to take time off to consider before throwing such a valuable job away. It was probably boyfriend trouble. I hoped it was nothing more sinister than that, but knew that in spite of her almost unbroken record of success, she had had relatively little experience in the love department. No doubt she'd had her head turned, or had been jilted by some male or other. I asked her to come up to Carborough for a rest. She refused. 'I don't feel I can quite yet,' she said.

'What is that supposed to mean?' Anna asked.

'I don't feel I can say.' Lisa sounded so odd that Anna felt sure there was more to this.

'What are you concealing?'

'Am I concealing anything?'

'Yes.' Anna waited. There was no further response. She could hear Lisa's breathing, jerky and irregular, while she tried to gain control. 'There's someone, isn't there? A man?'

'What?' She sounded scared. Then relieved. 'Oh, yes, sort of. Look, Mummy, I'll talk all about it as soon as I feel I can.'

Anna told Bernard about the odd phone conversation and was, if anything, even more surprised by his reaction.

'I have to say,' he remarked, 'I'm not altogether surprised she's gone a bit off the rails. I don't think she's quite cut out for the City, after all. You need to be tough.'

'She's hard as nails.'

'Maybe. Maybe not.'

'Bernard, you're not being totally candid either. You know something.'

'Do I?' Bernard looked hard at Anna. 'Do I?'

Eventually, after nearly three weeks during which Anna repeatedly phoned, receiving little in response other than monosyllables, Lisa agreed to come home to Carborough for a weekend. At first things looked as though they would be all right. Lisa, if not quite her old self, was more communicative.

'I'm so sorry Dad's not here until tomorrow,' Anna had said when she picked her up from the station. 'He seems to be working harder than ever at the university.'

'Has he ever not overworked?' They both laughed at that, but Anna noticed a sadness in Lisa's eyes that she had never before detected.

'Darling, you look different. You've lost weight.'

'Have I?'

'You were skinny as a reed before, but now I think you're a bit too peaky.'

'Mum! Stop fussing!'

'Anyway, Dad will be home tomorrow around midday. Some economic meeting in Oxford tonight, and then he's dining with a pal at Balliol.' She waited for Lisa to say something.

'Ah.'

'And then on Sunday, I've asked Pip and Margaret over.'

'What?' Lisa sounded alarmed.

'I thought you'd like to see them.' Anna noted distress on Lisa's face, even though it was instantly concealed. 'But I can put them off if you'd rather.'

'I'd love to see them.' Lisa found it difficult to feign enthusiasm. Anna knew her daughter too well not to read a subtext.

'It isn't Pip, by any chance, is it?'

'What isn't Pip?'

'Your, um, your man.'

'My what?' She seemed genuinely confused. 'Oh! Of

course not!' Then suddenly she was angry. 'Jesus, Mother! What sort of a shit do you think I am? Jesus!'

When the Turnbulls arrived on Sunday, everything was more or less normal, but Anna could still detect something odd about Lisa's behaviour. She elected not to play tennis when they suggested it, even though Bernard had just had the lines on the court painted for the season. Instead she watched for a while as Margaret and Bernard teamed up to trounce Pip and Anna. Anna's wrist was still weak from a late winter sprain and she could hardly return the gentlest of backhand shots. Lisa seemed uninterested and at one point, when Margaret had played a particularly forceful shot to Anna's left side, and had then apologised, showing genuine contrition, she got up and walked away.

Later, in the early evening when blackbirds and song thrushes were scolding neighbourhood cats in the deepening twilight, Anna had been putting finishing touches to their light Sunday supper in the kitchen and was on her way to her bedroom to bath and change. As she passed the study, she noticed that the door was open and went to close it when she heard low voices.

'I can't, Daddy, I simply can't.'

'Oh yes you can.' Bernard whispered, but with such strength that the sibilants were distinctly audible, even through the half-closed door. 'Yes you *can.*'

'But—'

'And if you *do* weaken, remember what I said.' Anna heard Lisa sigh.

'You don't mean—'

'That's not a threat, Lisa, that's a promise.' Bernard's voice was softer now, but stern. Anna pushed open the door.

'Oh sorry, you two,' she said. 'The light was off, so I thought the room was empty.'

'It's OK darling. We're just coming out,' Bernard said. 'She just needs a little career advice, that's all.' He placed a paternal arm on her shoulder to guide her out, but angrily she pushed him away and ran out of the room. 'Says she's going to

France. Got a temporary job at Chartres, well, at Maintenon, actually. Helping to run the new conference centre there.'

'Yes, she told me earlier, when you and Margaret had finished annihilating us out there.'

'Good for her language, I suppose.' He was trying to make himself jolly. 'But she'll find something much better soon, mark my words if she doesn't.'

Hearing familiar voices outside her cabin, Anna pulled open the door and looked out while staying seated at her desk. The Boys were peering through the court windows at the sea. She smiled at them. Cedric came over, looking conspiratorial, followed by Ant.

'Heard the rumour?' Anna shook her head. Cedric glanced quickly over both shoulders before whispering, 'There's illness on board.'

'Possible typhoid,' Ant said, also in a stage whisper. 'I heard from one of the junior officers. Eight cases already!'

'Are you sure?' Without thinking she had lowered her own voice to a whisper – ridiculous, since she was neither alarmed nor credulous.

'Oh yes. Ant says his source is impeccable. Have you had your jabs?'

Anna nodded. 'Are either of you going for breakfast?' She wanted to steer the subject somewhere else.

'We've had coffee. Ant's still got this fitness thing. We're about to tramp the decks.'

Anna excused herself and quickly checked her hair in the mirror before locking her cabin door and walking slowly down towards the restaurant. Infectious disease on board, she decided, in such a confined area where people lived cheek by jowl, could be interesting. She thought of Thomas Mann's story, *Death in Venice*, and Albert Camus's *The Plague*. What would a modern writer make of being in the thick of such drama? I must get the facts and research the thing, she decided, and without a single thought for herself – for she cared not a toss whether she caught typhoid or, for that matter, any dangerous disease – she walked briskly along the corridor to the restaurant.

Up in the bridge, with a mildly troubled expression on his face and his hands clasped a little too tightly behind his back, Captain Wishart watched the peak known as the Lion's Head and the curious flat summit of Table Mountain emerge above the waves as the great ship edged towards Cape Town.

Chapter Eighteen

After breakfast, Anna walked slowly up to the Observation Deck to watch the ship dock at Cape Town. The day was bright and clear, with a deep blue sky, but Table Mountain carried its 'cloth' of white cloud which seemed about to unroll itself down the sides. The mountain looked too flat-topped to be natural, as if there had once been a summit which had been bulldozed off. Most of her acquaintances had booked on one of the tours that took parties up to the top but Anna had no desire for that, preferring to explore the city and to travel inland.

The Boys, who had visited the Cape frequently, suggested either a trip to Paarl or Stellenbosch, to try some of the local wines, or a coastal drive.

'The sea might be a bit rough for swimming,' Cedric said, 'but there is some gorgeous scenery. We could hire a car. Ant could drive.' Cedric had a driving licence but scarcely ever sat at a steering wheel. Ant refused to be driven by him, ever.

'I don't mind sharing the driving,' Anna said. 'I lived in America once, so I'm used to driving on the wrong side of the road.'

'Oh they drive on the left, here,' Ant said. 'No, let me drive – you must enjoy the scenery.'

'But hey!' Cedric said. 'You're a garden freak, aren't you Anna?' She nodded. 'Then we'll call at Kirstenbosch.'

Ant groaned. 'Not another botanic bloody garden.'

'Just a flying call, Ant, dear heart! It's the most divine scenery. Then we can run through Constantia and, I'll tell you what: lunch at Hout Bay – my treat – then a quick whiz along to Chapman's Peak and a glimpse at the Cape of Good Hope itself, if we've time before we get back on to this bloody ship.'

The great garden at Kirstenbosch took Anna's breath away, not so much because of the huge collection of such alien plants – it was the wrong time of year to see those at their best – but mainly because of its setting, below the rugged mountains which Cedric thought were called the Twelve Apostles. The lower slopes were clothed with trees whose foliage was so silver it looked metallic.

'I think they are called silver trees,' Cedric said. 'Same family as those great coarse flowers.'

'Proteas,' Anna said. 'These must be leucadendrons. I've seen them at Tresco, on the Isles of Scilly, but never like that.' She had not realised how ravishing the scenery was, with Table Mountain to the north and across the great city to the east other mountains known as the Hottentots' Holland.

It was hot in the gardens by the time they were ready to leave, but Constantia was leafy and beautiful, cool under the forest trees with expensive-looking properties set a long way back from the road and well hidden. At Hout Bay they drove to a small dock area and stopped for lunch at a harbourside wharf, converted to a fish restaurant. Anna ate yellowtail, plain grilled, but the Boys went for kingclip. They drank a pink wine called Blanc de Noir, not sweet, but with a softness on the palate and a delicious mix of warm, fruity aromas that she had never experienced from anything French.

After lunch, because Ant had consumed more than a third of the bottle and had concluded with a South African brandy, Anna drove while he directed. Trees gave way to wild heathland reminiscent of the north York moors as they neared the Cape. There were zebra grazing and strange antelope known as bontebok whose black and white faces

looked as though they had been painted with clown make-up.
Once they had neared Cape Point itself they saw baboons
feeding on the ripening fruits of the sprawling fleshy plants
known as Hottentot figs. There were few wild flowers among
the low vegetation at this time of year, but here and there
sizable bushes of blooming proteas.

'If you come here in August and September, you see
whales along this coast,' Ant said. 'They come to the inshore
waters to mate and to calve. The young are less likely to be
attacked by great white sharks which are also common here.'
Anna, who had read Verne's book, knew this, and now she
thought of him. As his image grew stronger in her mind's
eye she was struck with a powerful surge of regret and
longing. Even though she was growing stronger, through
her writing, and more used to being alone, these sudden
hunger pangs – for something more sustaining than mere
food – had an almost physical strength. At these times,
she would suddenly feel famished for human comfort, for
someone to hold, to be held by, someone with warmth and
strength, a need so sharp and urgent that she almost cried
out aloud. And always, that 'someone' took Verne's shape,
his particular feel, his voice, his presence. She took a few
steps away from the Boys, pretending to look at a plant
growing at the edge of the car park, but really she needed
a few moments to recover. She must think rationally. Birds.
What were those gulls? Hartlaub's gulls. And kelp gulls
– just like British greater black backs. She remembered
the young couple birdwatching at Cairns. It had to have
been Verne that they had described, still living alone. How
hurt he must have been when she . . . Whichever way you
looked at it, he must have felt betrayed. But what could she
have done?

'I say, Anna, are you all right?' Ant had come over to
her. He had been watching her standing rigid, motionless,
half leaning into the cold breeze coming off the sea.

'I think we ought to get back to the ship,' Anna whispered.
She let him drive.

'That then,' said Cedric from the back of the car, 'was the Cape of Good Hope.'

'And the sea over that side,' Ant added, 'is the Atlantic. Our last big ocean before entering the English Channel.'

Was it Anna's imagination, or did the sea on that western horizon look greyer, despite the sun?

'It's cold down there,' Ant continued. 'Chill waters up from Antarctica. That's why the locals always swim that side, in the Indian Ocean; it's several degrees warmer. The waters around the Cape are treacherous too. Remember the legend of the Flying Dutchman? Apparently there are more wrecks along this coast than anywhere in the world.'

'Why the hell do they call it Good Hope, then?' Cedric asked.

Anna, silent, struggled with her feelings. Seeing the Atlantic stretching away to a leaden horizon – the weather *was* different over there – filled her with dread. In less than three weeks she would be back in England. To what? To return to the aching emptiness? The sessions with Max? Occasional duty visits from Lisa? She must not be a drag on Lisa's marriage. She wondered what the point was of going home at all. This place was about the most beautiful she had seen anywhere, why not jump ship and stay here? Why should she give a damn about the threat of an unstable future when the New South Africa's honeymoon ended – as end it would, as soon as Mandela quit the stage? Why not stay, why not wait through the winter for spring to bring forth all those floral treasures for which the Cape is so famous? Why not stay, to observe this brave nation's progress as a disinterested outsider, and to create stories about the human struggle that would have to continue here, perhaps even for decades after the obscenity of apartheid had ended? Why not? Her pulse began to race and her scalp to tingle as plans began to form, but she said nothing, keeping her eyes fixed, staring at, but not seeing the Cape of Good Hope.

Back in her cabin, she switched on her computer. The need

to work through the memoirs was so urgent now that little else mattered to her when she was on board.

As Bernard's retirement approached, he seemed to be working harder than ever. He could have kept the chair at Stoneford for much longer, if he had wanted it, but when he had almost killed himself with overwork during the Thatcher era, he had promised Lisa and me that he would retire at 60, come hell or high water. We had plenty of funds, even though the stipend from Stoneford was hardly generous, and in spite of having lost so much in the 1987 crash and subsequently, during the recession of the late eighties and early nineties. Bernard's books still generated respectable royalties and he was writing regular columns, still under pseudonyms, for the *Spectator* and the *Telegraph*, so there was plenty in the bank in spite of our living quite high off the hog at Carborough.

During those last years of his career, I grew even more discontented, not only with Carborough, but particularly with Ketton House. Its solid, uncompromising Edwardianness had never charmed me but now that Lisa was hardly ever there and we felt less and less like playing tennis or swimming in the pool, the place seemed to expand around me until I felt continually dwarfed by its oppressive character. I rekindled my interest in the garden, trying to coax the stiff, unyielding clay into better heart, but I never really succeeded. If the borders looked promising, a dry spell would make the ground open up in cracks and the plants all wilted, or, if it were wet, shrubs and perennials would rot away at the roots and die. In the front garden, the sound of traffic on the main road behind the tall evergreens seemed to get louder each year. I began to suggest to Bernard that we ought to move somewhere more manageable, but I knew he loved the house.

'There's no point quite yet, darling,' Bernard had said. 'Wait until I retire. Just another two years, and then we can move away to wherever you like. I don't mind where we live. London, Kent, if you like – abroad, even. You name it and we'll go.'

'Norfolk?'

'Anywhere!' But she had detected the half beat pause before he responded. One of his few weaknesses was an inexplicable embarrassment about his origins. He would love to have been born into an old, landed family: totally illogical for one who preached the virtues of free market meritocracy wherever he went. Norfolk might have been a little too close to his humble roots.

'Not near Lynn,' Anna had quickly added, 'but I thought somewhere up the coast, away from the Wash. Burnham Market, or Stiffkey. Cley, perhaps.'

'Wherever you like.' He had hugged her and twiddled her ear. 'As long as I'm with you, I don't give a stuff where we are.' He had made to move away but she had held him tightly, squeezing until she felt him relax.

'Bernard, why do you have to be away so much?'

'My job, I'm afraid.' The body stiffening. 'As you know.'

'But you should be winding down by now, Bernard.'

'Just be patient for a bit longer. When I retire I promise . . .'

'Bernard, I want to start house-hunting. Now.'

'Just be a little patient, Anna. Really, it won't be long. Besides, this is a hopeless time to sell.'

'But an excellent time to buy. We could afford to buy a smaller place and still have this one.'

'But there's no point.'

'A good investment.'

'Properties aren't going to increase in value at all. Not for a while yet.'

'But it would give me something to do. Something to – oh I don't know – something to work towards.'

'I'll think very hard about it, darling.'

'Oh and there's something else.' She knew she had to bring

this up with care. 'I wondered if you'd mind if I borrowed Margaret.'

'What *can* you mean?' He was rigid in her arms.

'It's not for long. But I was hoping she might be able to come away with me in October, when you go over to New York for the conference at Cornell.'

Bernard thought for a while. 'Might be tricky. I'm certainly going to need a PA, giving all those papers and the extra jobs while I'm there.'

'But you've got that new girl in the office. She's a bright lass. Couldn't you take her? It would be a great break for her.'

'I'm not sure she's experienced enough quite yet.' He caught the appeal in her eyes. 'But I'll think about it.'

Later, when she had the chance, Anna decided to try to exert a little more pressure on Bernard through Margaret herself. She rang her to invite her over for coffee the following Saturday while Bernard was out looking for a new watch.

'Sorry, love, but I'm a bit tied up here.'

Anna was disappointed. 'You know, Margaret,' she said, 'you don't come over half as often as you used to. It's an age since we sat and chewed the fat together. We don't even play tennis now.'

'You know how long it took your tennis elbow to cure last year. I don't want you to hurt yourself again. As for not hanging round so much, blame your husband, Anna, love. He has me doing so damned much for him.'

'That's what I wanted to talk to you about. I've got an offer.'

'What sort of offer?'

Anna summoned up her courage. 'I was wondering whether you might consider, instead of going to New York with Bernard, coming with me.'

'To New York?'

'No, to Prague.'

'Prague? What the hell for?'

'I've got a spare ticket for a cheap deal. Lisa was coming

with me but apparently she's been summoned back to Maintenon to do some freelance work for a while. Do come, Margaret.'

'Mmm. I'm tempted, but I don't really see Bernard letting me off, do you?'

'Couldn't you let what's-her-name – Marion – go? It might give her a chance to prove her mettle.'

'Anna! You can be pretty naïve when it comes to business politics. Next thing you know, she'll be replacing me!'

'Margaret! Bernard would be totally at sea without you. You're indispensable to him.'

'No one is indispensable, Anna. Absolutely no one at all.'

'Which is why I'd so love you to dump my husband, for once, and come. We get to see some opera – something I've never done enough of – and a tour of the city is included.'

'Anna, poppet, I *am* tempted.' Margaret paused for a few seconds. 'I'll see what I can do about your old man.'

But Margaret, in the end, was unable to go. When Anna tried to coax Bernard he was quite adamant, even when she attempted one final time to persuade him later that evening.

'Bernard, she's my greatest friend, and I don't see nearly enough of her. It's such a waste, with Lisa not coming now, and I don't really feel I want to go on my own.'

'Then don't go.'

'But I've been looking forward to it for ages. After all, I hardly go anywhere these days.'

'Darling, you do! Besides, we can do all the travel you want when I've retired. Even go on a world cruise, if you like.' He wanted to comfort. 'But this is work, Anna, it's very important. I daren't let anyone down and I will need Margaret.'

Anna understood. Anna always understood. Always accepted. But she was disappointed. To comfort herself, she decided to talk to Lisa anyway. Perhaps something might have happened with Maintenon, so that she could come after all. She dialled Lisa's London number. A male voice answered, cheerful but quiet, with a sexual charm which she found slightly disturbing.

'Jamie?'

'Lady Morfey!' Being addressed by her title still surprised her and made her feel uneasy. It was all Bernard's honour. She had nothing to do with it at all.

'It's Anna, *please*! What a surprise to hear you.' She struggled for something else to say. 'I thought you and Lisa had—'

'So did I, um, Anna. But, well, here I am. In fact it's rather more than us merely being together.' He faltered. 'Um, perhaps you should speak to Lisa.' Anna heard a hasty, muffled conversation, a hand half held over the mouthpiece. Then Lisa's voice came over the wire, breezy, but with a defensive edge.

'Mummy? Hi!'

'Lisa, darling. What's going on?'

'Oh, you mean Jamie. I've, um, we've got some news for you.'

'I can guess.'

'Well, I expect you can.' Both women were silent, both gripped hard on the hand set at either end of the wire that was failing to tug them together. 'We're actually going to get married.'

Anna was quite fond of Jamie. He was attractive enough physically but she had always felt she detected a certain effeteness, well hidden of course, behind a businesslike manner. He was a wonderful talker and could charm anyone with the lightest touch, caressing them with oblique flattery, seeming to pay extra special attention to whoever was in his sights. Yet there was something she didn't quite have full confidence in. The strength he seemed to exude, she suspected, was manufactured to disguise a special weakness of some kind.

'Darling, that's wonderful. I'm so glad for you.' She wasn't sure what to say next. The prospect of wedding arrangements, reception plans, guests and so on hadn't sunk in. 'When?'

'Haven't decided yet. We'll let you know.' Something was beginning to nag at Anna. It identified itself as a question.

'What about Dad?' She forced herself to continue. 'I suppose he knows already.'

'Oh, Mummy!' Lisa sounded contrite. 'I wanted to tell you both at the same time, but—'

'What did he say?'

'Don't be thick, Mother,' Lisa said. 'I haven't been able to tell you both together because, well, because Jamie's just gone and dropped this clanger. Here and now!'

'Really?'

'I would never have told Dad first. You know that!'

She couldn't think of anything more to say, yet there was so much she wanted to express. 'I'm very happy for you both, my darlings.'

'Hang on, Mum, Jamie wants to say something. I'll say goodbye then—'

'No, wait, darling. I wanted just to check about Prague. Are you still having to go to France?'

'Oh that! No, I've cancelled, mainly because of Jamie. I don't totally need the Maintenon thing. Not now, anyway.'

'Then do Prague.'

'Oh, Mother.' Lisa's voice went flat. 'Are you sure you really want me?'

'Lisa! You're my only child. Of course I really want you – in Prague or anywhere.' But she had caught the vibes, and without a single further thought for herself continued, 'But I said "*do* Prague", not "come to Prague". With Jamie, I mean. He can have my ticket.' Lisa, this time without covering the mouthpiece, told Jamie what Anna had offered. He came on to the line.

'That really is very generous, Anna. I think you're going to make one hell of a ma in law.'

After a few more moments of small talk Anna said goodbye, hung up and sat by the phone wanting to cry. Why, she wondered, am I always the last to know anything? She wished Bernard was there. Then she remembered that he would be away in London all next week and would need at least seven clean shirts. She went to the old scullery of

Ketton House where the old copper-bottomed boiler had been ripped out and replaced with an electronic washer, tumble dryer, ironing board and airing cupboard. The window was tiny and darkened, outside, by the current season's growth of ivy; for some reason Anna's small transistor radio refused to work properly in there, particularly in winter when the central heating boiler seemed to cause constant static interference. Ironing was a chore that she hated, even when relieved by familiar voices on Radio 4. The weight of the iron, the smell of hot cloth, the slow pace at which the pile of clean, pressed clothes grew and the even slower rate at which the mountain of creased garments eroded was guaranteed to bring down her spirits. But Bernard always said that no one else ironed shirts so well as she, and she appreciated that. Once she had even tried the laundry but everything came back smelling wrong. Anyway, laundries were ruination as far as decent cotton was concerned.

Reaching to do the sleeves of the third shirt made her back twinge just below the shoulder blades, and she began to wonder whether Bernard would need quite so many smart clothes after he had retired. She hoped not, and comforted herself in her labour with thoughts of how their life would change. More travel together would be fun, and finding a house in the country was something she was hugely looking forward to. In fact she had already begun to glance more purposefully than before at the front pages of *Country Life*, and into estate agent's windows. But the absolute best thing, which flavoured most of her thinking moments and provided a constant undercurrent of warmth and joy, was the notion that she and Bernard would be together, on their own, not with heavy activities, not with any object other than just being. That state of relaxed togetherness, feeling him always by her side or if not, never far away – that was something that could take place anywhere, city or country, day or night, summer or winter and that was what she longed for most.

The *Brisbane* sailed from Cape Town into heavy weather.

Departure was delayed by almost eight hours, after a heavy steel cable from one of the tugboats had become wound round the starboard propeller shaft. While frogmen operated underwater cutting gear, the wind steadily increased. Sailing had been scheduled for seven in the evening but the passengers dined while the ship was tied up. The view of Table Mountain, floodlit from below, so that it seemed to have a luminescence of its own, lasted for the first couple of hours of darkness, but later, as cloud built and the Cape's first autumn rain began to fall, the lights in Table Bay were blotted out and the ship was enclosed in a swirl of rain and sea spray mixed by the wind.

Captain Wishart was too busy with the repairs to the propeller to dine with his passengers, which disappointed the Boys who wanted to find out whether there was a grain of truth about there being typhoid on board. All day long rumours had burgeoned and now, with the ship's delay, had changed emphasis. The crew had been so badly affected, one woman – an acquaintance who smiled and chatted during deck hikes – told her, that they were running with just over half the usual complement of hands. When Anna asked where the sick ones were, the woman couldn't say. 'In 'ospital, I suppose.'

'Would there be room?'

'They live cheek by jowl down there,' she said, 'under the waterline. You can imagine 'ow disease can spread – 'alf of 'em are nancy boys anyway.'

One of the Crow's Nest regulars remarked that the ship was likely to be put into quarantine. That was why she was delayed. To check that she was not imagining the frogmen, Anna walked there and then to the stern to see the lorry still parked on the quay and lights coming eerily from under the surface as the submerged repair men worked. She had always imagined diving to be among corals, with colourful fish darting about. The thought of being down there in the dark under the huge bulk of an ocean liner gave her the creeps.

Much later, warm in bed, Anna woke with a start, knowing that the ship had sailed. She got up to look through the porthole and saw the lights of the harbour gradually getting sparser and weaker as the vessel slipped out towards the open sea. She began to sense motion in the deck, a gentle heave beneath the feet which promised that a rough spell was round the corner. She saw from her watch that it was a little after three, but having retired very early she felt refreshed and unwilling to get back into bed. Their return to the Atlantic, after sailing three-quarters of the way round the world, was to be stormy and Anna felt unable to sleep through it. The fear of her impending return to Britain was also growing and her unease threatened to undermine the sense of stability she had been managing to develop over the past few weeks.

I must conclude my story, she thought, but she had no idea what was going to happen after it had ended. She could relate events now, even painful ones, without feeling the cold hand of depression on the back of her neck, but thoughts of the future, even when lightly touched upon, were so sharply uncomfortable that she was prepared to do almost anything to avoid them. Previously she had managed to stave off any thought at all of the future, partly by immersing herself in her journal and partly because so much of the cruise seemed to be stretching out in front of her. She had discovered how to use writing as an escape and, as long as she was beating about in her brain for ideas of plots, for apt imagery or to make her language flow, she found comfort. But when images of the future came into sharper, more terrifying focus, like a gaping empty maw, she would resort to revisiting the most painful parts of her memoirs. Often she would amplify the effect of the counter-irritant by forcing her eyes to run across the print on the screen, and to go on reliving those recorded events. There remained but three ports before Southampton – Dakar, Tenerife and Lisbon – and the few sea days remaining left too little time in which to prepare. And to prepare for what? She turned on her computer and, while it was booting up, cleaned her teeth and washed her face before settling down to pull the memoirs closer to the present day. By now the ship was moving so much that at times she had to hold on to the tiny desk, a protective hand on the small computer to prevent it from sliding to the floor.

Lisa's wedding happened so quickly that I could hardly believe I had a son-in-law. Within a couple of months of Jamie answering the phone that day, they were man and wife. Lisa had never had much truck for religion and when they had arrived for Sunday lunch the weekend after their announcement, I had asked her what style of wedding she had in mind. She and Jamie had exchanged glances before she had said, 'Well, none at all, really.'

'The fact is, um, Anna,' Jamie had explained, 'we don't really believe in all that white lace and bridesmaids bit and so we'll probably just get hitched at Camden, in the register office.'

'Why?' I wanted to know why they were bothering to get married at all, if there was no religion involved. They could have just gone on living together.

'Why not?' Lisa retorted, in a voice that discouraged any further discussion. I was anxious not to start a family row – we were all three so seldom together these days that I did not want to spoil things by causing dishar- mony. I looked to Bernard to take up the discussion. He winked at Lisa and looked directly at me.

'I think that's an answer, Anna. Don't you?'

Jamie was concentrating hard on his Yorkshire pudding, Lisa was smiling at her father.

'I hope you'll be very happy, the pair of you,' I said. But I wondered how thoroughly they would feel committed without an act of worship. The vows they made, at the civil ceremony, seemed hollow when they were not a part of the sacrament.

They were married in Carborough, rather than Bloomsbury, and apart from Bernard, me, Jamie's mother – his father had suffered a fatal coronary in 1990 – the registrar and a couple of witnesses, the room was empty. Afterwards we had a rather embarrassed lunch in a Victorian country house turned restaurant on the shores of Rutland Water.

Months passed. I felt unable to visit Lisa in London, now that she was married, without phoning first. That loss of spontaneity turned out to be harder to bear than I had expected, and I always had the feeling that it applied more to me than to Bernard. But I grew accustomed to Lisa being an occasional guest at home, rather than a family member, and whatever my reservations might have been about Jamie I loved having them both to stay whenever they could spare the time. Jamie turned out to be a keen and knowledgeable plant enthusiast, and whenever he came to visit he would bring some little treasure picked up at one of the Royal Horticultural Society flower shows in Westminster. 'Mother's useless, now she lives in a flat,' he would say, 'but when we have our own garden, at last, I shall expect cuttings or divisions of all these plants.' I felt duty bound to make them thrive, if only to be able to let him have bits of them later, but I longed to get away from Carborough, and to find somewhere with decent soil.

I wanted to begin house-hunting before Bernard retired, but for some reason that I could not fathom he seemed set against it. 'Far better to wait until just after the finish date,' he said. 'After all, I'll have plenty of time then and we can do it together. Wouldn't that be better?' And I was so happy that I overlooked the fact that in the past, Bernard had merely paid lip service to my involvement, but in each move – Kent, America, Carborough – he had made his own decision on our dwelling and hardly consulted me at all. I was keen for him to be involved in the purchase of what might turn out to be our last joint home, but I really didn't want to be steamrollered. Not this time.

'I wasn't intending to dash out and buy a house on the instant,' Anna said, as she handed him his coffee one weekday morning. 'I just thought I might explore a few possible areas. Margaret's on holiday next week and has agreed to come over with me to help look. We thought we'd go to Norfolk when you're away in Aberystwyth, to see how some of the areas I used to know have changed.' Bernard's response was a sarcastic laugh.

'When you and Margaret get together, you'll be gossiping too much to concentrate. You're like a pair of schoolgirls.'

'Probably, but I'll be getting ideas about which bits of Norfolk we don't want to be in, and which bits might do. Anyway, what does it matter if we have a little fun? Margaret's so full of fun and we get on really well. We might do a little antique shop browsing too.'

'As long as you don't leap to any big decisions – on the housing front, I mean. Don't make any offers or anything, even if you find the place of your dreams.' He got up from the breakfast table, picked up his briefcase and walked to the door, which she opened. 'I want to stay here until I actually retire, and there's still a year to go.'

'Eleven months from tomorrow,' Anna corrected. She noticed a look of concern on his features, no more than the briefest flash. She knew that in ending his career, he was making a considerable sacrifice. They might not need for money, but his work was his life. Was she expecting too much of him? 'You know, darling, you don't *have* to retire.'

'Oh don't I?' he muttered. They kissed – a perfunctory exchange – and he left.

As the retirement date approached, each season became a landmark in their progress towards their new lives. Christmas came. Bernard, always scornful of those who took more than the two official days out of work, usually arranged his diary so that Christmas Eve was as busy as a normal work day and invariably returned to work the day after Boxing Day. 'Last time, promise,' he reassured Anna, who wanted to invite people to lunchtime drinks on 27 December, rather than on Boxing Day. 'Next year we can take a whole month preparing. And on New Year's Eve I'll take you somewhere really exciting. How about Lake Louise, in the Canadian Rockies?'

Spring was feeble that year, starting prematurely, with soft, balmy days in late February, then turning treacherous with April frosts and biting easterly winds. Bernard would complete his work at Stoneford shortly before the longest day and Anna, with support from Lisa and Jamie, had been developing the idea of a large summer retirement party.

'We could put up a marquee in the garden,' Anna suggested. Neither declared it, but this was a way in which they could compensate for the absence of what Anna would have called a 'proper celebration' at Lisa's wedding the previous year.

'If you're going big,' Bernard agreed, when they consulted him, 'you'd better go over the top. We won't be able to have huge parties if we move to a smaller house. Let's have hundreds of guests.'

In the months that followed, Anna busied herself with preparations. Margaret was deputed to help, particularly with invitations and the administrative side. 'I think it's much nicer if people can sit down and be waited on,' she told Anna, 'rather than one of those awful buffets where you need a third hand and there's nowhere to perch.'

'Then we should organise a seating plan,' Anna said. 'We can both do that, but will you get cards made up?'

'Piece of cake,' Margaret said. 'We can do most of it on the university computer system. We need to make sure there's plenty of mixing and matching. Get the dons to sit near the rich and famous. Most of them are wetting their knickers to get on TV anyway, so we'll sprinkle some producers and other BBC types among them.'

A week before the party, the marquee was erected over the tennis court. They had to take down the surrounding netting and posts but, as no one played tennis any more, this had become tatty and run-down anyway. The tent was lined with apricot silk and Margaret had ordered a thousand rose blooms in exactly the same shade. These were to be arranged all over the place, but each table was to have dark maroon rosebuds and petals scattered on the cloth a few minutes before the guests were due. There were to be no speeches – that was one of Bernard's conditions – but the party was to conclude with fireworks. Anna had managed to persuade the local authority to allow this, on condition that the whole display was staged in the water meadows behind the house, and that the general public would be allowed to witness it from the other side of the fence. They would not know that the display was being financed by, and given for, Bernard. Very few of them would know who Bernard was, but Carborough's charity for homeless people had publicised the display in advance and would use it as a means of raising funds. Anna hoped to keep this final detail from Bernard, who had rather odd views about homeless people.

The party was a huge success. Everyone drank Bernard's health in champagne – he had refused to countenance any-thing cheaper – and a great many new contacts had been made, to the mutual benefit of the guests. The firework display had gone on for more than half an hour and had astounded guests and local residents. The final set piece was a vast red sun, a fireball that somehow managed to keep itself suspended in the darkened sky. Then, before it faded, a huge pall of black smoke welled up, blotting it out. Viewers thought the smoke was a mistake, until golden drops of fire began to fall out of it like rain. These increased in density and gradually changed colour to silver, after which the cloud dissipated revealing not the red sun, but now a huge silver moon.

Standing unnoticed in the dark just behind a small gaggle of academics watching the display, Anna heard someone mutter, 'Blood in their suns.'

'What's that?' his neighbour said.

'Dylan Thomas. A poem,' he explained, since his neigh-bour was a scientist. 'It's got a weird first line, um, "A process in the weather of the heart", er, "Turns damp to dry; the golden shot" er, then there's something about weather in the veins, um, "Turns night to day; blood in their suns/

Lights up the living worm." The fireworks just made me think of it.'

'I don't understand it,' the scientist muttered. 'But one does wonder why this particular golden shot is retiring so soon. I mean he can hardly be more than sixty and with his record, he could do anything he wanted.'

'Love, they tell me. Apparently he wants to spend more time with his wife.'

'Get away!' the scientist retorted. 'How often have we seen him and Anna together?'

'That's what he told me.'

'She must have put the pressure on, to make the poor sod give up. And she must have something up her sleeve to use as a lever.' The scientist's voice dropped to a low mutter. 'I wonder what she's got on 'im.'

'I don't think that's it at all,' a third voice chipped in. 'He's got other plans, it would seem. Wants to go into politics. Properly this time. That's what I hear, anyway.'

Anna allowed herself to melt into the darkness. She had heard enough tittle-tattle about Bernard, over the previous thirty years, to be able to ignore this lot. And she knew exactly what he thought of politicians. She acknowledged to everyone that he was sacrificing a great deal for her, but she knew, too, that they would be so much happier together once he had finished his work and had started to enjoy a period not so much of rest as of recreation.

Someone had tipped off the gossip columnists and on the next morning but one, several tabloids and *The Times* diary carried short pieces on the retirement of the previous decade's most contentious economic guru. No one in the family however – apart from Jamie – read those pieces, or the profile on Bernard in the following Saturday's *Independent* which gave an objective, if acerbic account of his career. Jamie cut them out to save for later, but in the weeks that followed there never seemed a right moment in which to bring them up.

The morning after the celebrations, events – momentous,

catastrophic events – crashed into Anna's life. At the party, Bernard was there – Bernard was everywhere – cheerful, hearty, marginally tipsy, making introductions, leading lonely-looking guests into the livelier of the groups, calling for champagne to be brought to the faster of the drinkers, joking, back-slapping, finding chairs for elderly guests, directing nauseous youngsters to the lavatory, or to quiet corners of the garden, flirting with the middle-aged and never keeping still for a moment.

Forty-eight hours later, Bernard was gone.

The second day after the party, when workmen were dismantling the marquee and employees of the catering firm were collecting up the last of the debris, restoring the garden more or less to its former condition, Anna spent every daylight hour sitting by herself in the small second guest bedroom. A cold room, this, on the north side of the house facing the cypress trees and other evergreens that screened the garden from the road. Downstairs, while Lisa kept an eye on things in the garden, Jamie stayed by the back door and repelled possible invaders. He and Lisa had driven home the morning after the party, but on hearing the awful news had had to come straight back to Carborough.

'No,' Jamie said to no fewer than forty-six potential query raisers that day, 'I'm afraid Lady Morfey is not able to speak to anyone today. She has been taken ill. She'll contact you as soon as she is able.'

Lisa was not doing a very good job outdoors. She tried to concentrate but her mind kept swinging back time and again to the phone call. She still tried to tell herself it was some kind of a vicious prank; that Bernard would come striding up the garden with an open smile on his face; that he would emerge, any moment now, with her mother on his arm, both of them radiant with some new success or other; that he would ring to say he had lined up some special retirement treat for Anna, and that the foregoing, if tasteless, had been a hoax to keep everyone off the tracks.

But Bernard never played hoaxes. Never. He had never practised anything but total openness. She busied herself, trying to exercise her mind, trying stop herself wishing uselessly that it had not happened. She watched the morning wear on, watched the workers finish their cleaning up, and wondered what she and Jamie could do next and what Anna would do. How would she get through the next few hours, the next few days, the rest of her life?

The last pieces of marquee had been rolled up, packed and stacked on to the lorry parked in the front drive. Lisa heard its engine roar as it crept away in bottom gear, negotiating the gateway with difficulty. Upstairs, sitting rigidly upright alone, shaking in the chill of the little room, Anna heard nothing. Downstairs, Jamie went to the front porch to check that the lorry did not collide with the gatepost – it was what Bernard would have done. Lisa, from a seat by the swimming pool, stared at a catering worker scurrying after the last of the litter blowing across the garden before disappearing round the side of the house to join her colleagues in the van which had replaced the tent lorry in the front drive. She noticed that a number of napkins had blown into the pool and supposed her mother would want to empty it to check for broken glass. Then she realised that it didn't matter since no one would be swimming in it now. She didn't think her mother would go on living here much longer anyway, now that she was alone.

Try as she might, she could not push the memory of that awful sound out of her mind. The alien sound of her father's voice on the phone. So strange, as if he did not know her. Not a phone call. Merely a formal declaration.

'Lisa. I've just written to your mother to inform her that I have left her. She's bound to be in need of comfort, so you'll probably want to go back up to Carborough.' Lisa had gripped the receiver hard and pressed it to her ear until it bruised. 'I think you have the intelligence to understand the circumstances. It is better for everyone this way, though it may seem a bit hard just at the moment.' And he had rung off.

Chapter Nineteen

———

Anna had been writing her memoirs non-stop for four hours and yet it was still dark outside. A mountainous sea rose and fell, sometimes seeming to come right up to the porthole, other times falling away and disappearing altogether in the darkness. The ship was both pitching and rolling and from time to time she could hear the crash of something not made fast falling on to the deck. The bulkheads groaned and shuddered and she fancied she could actually see the cabin changing shape in the deepest of the rolls. Her CDs, books and other odds and ends had fallen from their shelves and she had crammed as many objects as she could fit into the various drawers and lockers. She felt tired. Unable to write much more but not wanting sleep, she lay on her bed and pieced the rest of her story together in her mind so that when the time came to write it up, she would have the mental strength to go through with it.

The news, which Lisa broke to her before she had opened the letter, was impossible to comprehend. On the morning after the party, Bernard had driven to the office for one last time, to collect the rest of his things and to make sure there was no outstanding mail. He had been perfectly ordinary.

'You can manage here all right, can't you?' he had said to Anna.

'Of course. Most of the clearing up will be done by the

caterers today and tomorrow. The marquee goes tomorrow so, by the weekend, that should be it.'

'Bye, then,' Bernard had said, and had driven off in his Scorpio. But at lunchtime he had phoned to say he was fixing something on a final project which looked as though it would take much longer than he had first realised, and would be gone overnight. Anna, after a lifetime of unexpectedly prolonged absences and unscheduled departures, was disappointed but not in the least bit worried. Won't be many more absences like that, she thought, and decided to spend her day sorting the china, glass and cutlery that had been used for the party. She wished Lisa and Jamie could have stayed a little longer, especially now that Bernard would be gone overnight, but knew that they would be busy.

Lisa received her father's call just after midday and decided to drive, at once, back to Carborough. Jamie felt obliged to stay by his wife. 'I'm not sure what your ma really thinks of me,' he said, 'but I get the impression you're both going to need me along too, yah?'

'As long as you let me drive. I need something to occupy my mind.' She had not owned her little red Alfa Romeo for more than a few weeks. As usual, she drove fast and with precision. Halfway back, just before she negotiated the first of the Bedfordshire traffic islands on the Great North Road, Lisa suddenly shouted, 'Oh Jesus. Oh what a bastard. Oh Jesus fucking *hell*!' She began to cry, without reducing her driving speed. Jamie massaged her shoulder.

'Don't cry,' he said. 'Or at least, don't be too long crying. Your ma's going to need your strength.'

'But don't you see? He'll have known I would drop everything and go straight back to Carborough.'

'Obviously.'

'But she won't know. She can't have received his letter.'

'Unless he sent it with a runner. Perhaps he did that.'

'Oh no. He'll have posted it from the office and he'll know that I would get there first.'

'Perhaps that's as well for your ma.'

'But don't you see? It means that I'll have to be the one to break it to her. He'll have arranged it to happen like that. The *bastard*.' She drove on, her mind working hard, trying to think of the best way of telling her mother. Bernard had obviously done absolutely nothing to prepare her for this. No increasing coldness, no alienation, just this thunderbolt, like a fatal coronary. And what the hell had he been thinking of, sanctioning that bloody great party? It must have cost thousands of pounds, and for what? A final fling? A huge practical joke? Did he hate her mother that much? Or was it the usual thing with males – here she glanced sideways at Jamie – weakness? Had Bernard, for all his apparent courage, simply bottled out of telling her what he must have been planning for years? Could he have been living a lie, laying out the foundations for a new breakaway life, but unable to tell her? She glanced at Jamie again. His eyelashes were deliciously long, clotted rather than curved like a girl's and his lips sensuous, with a permanent upturn at the corners, like the beginnings of a smile. Bless his pretty face, she thought. But her father, weak? Never! She cried a little more. She wondered if they could put off breaking the news until the next morning, at least to give Anna one more night before . . .

When they arrived at Ketton House, Anna was surprised to see them, but not at all alarmed.

'If this is another of Bernard's damn silly surprises, I'll throttle him!' she said, laughing. 'I suppose you don't know, but he's not here tonight.' She was taken aback by their grim faces and faltered. 'Something's cooking, of that I pretty sure.'

'Oh Mummy, Mummy!' Lisa wailed, and threw her arms around her mother.

'What? What is it my pet?' Anna had never been very good at comforting Lisa. She thought of William. He had been such a glutton for cuddles, but she felt her tears start in sympathy for her daughter. 'Tell Mum, what it is.' But as Lisa managed to spit out the news, and then to repeat it, twice, she felt her body gradually chill down to freezing. She tried, without success, not to believe what she was hearing. Throughout their life together, one thing Bernard had never been was predictable.

'Can you leave me alone for a minute, darling?' she said at last, in a voice that was perfectly calm, level and reasoned.

'Um, we'll make some tea,' Jamie said, and went out to the kitchen. He found the local physician's telephone number on a list pinned to a cork pad on the wall by the kitchen phone. Dr Jenner was out, apparently, but his rebarbative receptionist said that she would inform him as soon as he was in. 'I think we have to get her off to bed,' Jamie said. 'She'll want to opt out for a while – maybe a couple of days. Let it sink in.'

'How do you know?'

'It's how my mother was when *my* dad died.'

'Mine hasn't died!' The retort was sharp.

'Really?' Jamie looked at her. 'Seems to me it'd be a lot less messy if he had.' She slapped him, hard, twice, across the face. Forehand, backhand. He stood facing her, tears from the smarting blow moistening his eyes, cheeks reddened, the suggestion of a tremor in his tense muscles. She stared into his eyes. In the low light, their pupils were dilated, his more than hers now, because of the adrenalin. She had never seen a man look more beautiful. He had the masculine grace that she loved – had loved – so much about her father but in him it was refined, made gentler. Her father had moved her with his drive, his force for success, but this man was full of love, as well as physical grandeur, and now she recognised its value.

'I'm sorry,' she said, still staring. Her voice was expressionless.

'You're not. Don't be,' he muttered. She began to cry again.

'Don't, Lisa.'

'I'm not crying because I'm sad. I'm crying because I'm so fucking angry.' She was angry with men, possibly all men. She wanted to smash Jamie's face again, to break the skin, to damage the beautiful line of his nose and brow, to make a mess of his wonderful face; but she wanted to smother it with kisses too. He could do it too – anyone could – she recognised that well enough, just the same as her father. That was what was making her so angry.

'You see, the trouble is, I knew,' she said. '*Have* known for ages. Don't you think that is despicable?' He was silent. 'I mean I knew that he was having it off with . . .' She blew her nose. 'For years.'

His eyes widened with disbelief. 'You didn't say anything to anyone?'

'I couldn't.'

'You mean you carried on *living* here, when you knew? Helping your mother wash up, playing tennis with her, flirting with your father – oh I've seen exactly what you two were like together – when you actually knew what he was doing to her?'

'It's not like that at all. You can't begin to understand.'

'No? It's what anyone decent would have done.'

'You *don't* understand. I found out, you see. And I shouldn't have.' Jamie turned away from her and looked out of the window. 'I tackled him about it, but he said that if I breathed so much as a word, a single solitary word, not just to Mum, but to anyone, absolutely anyone, he'd . . . he'd . . .'

'He'd what?'

'He said he'd leave Mum. Just like that, for good. And he would have. I know him well enough to understand that once driven he follows everything to its absolute conclusion, even if the consequences are self-destructive. If I had spoken, I would have ruined their marriage. I couldn't have borne that. I thought he was just, you know, having a bit extra.' Now Jamie had turned from the window to look at her again. 'I mean, if his appetites were still keen, and Mum's . . . well, you know how it must be when people get older. I just thought, if he's getting his rocks off a bit, it will help, not hinder. I thought he'd be more content.' She was starting to shake. 'I realise now he must have been planning to do this for years.'

'Oh my poor honey.' Jamie pulled her to him.

'"And remember, Lisa."' Within the limitations of the female timbre, and in her emotional state, Lisa imitated her father's voice rather well. '"That's not a threat. That's a promise."'

'Sshh.' Jamie hugged her closely, stroking her back for comfort.

'And the absolute worst thing, that I keep thinking, is that if I'd blown his gaff, I might have put a stop to it all.' She cried some more, Jamie comforted, brushing the top of her head with his lips and making shushing sounds.

'She'll get over it,' he said, after a bit. 'People always do.'

'You don't know how they are – were. You can't know. She existed solely for him. Far more than for me.'

Captain Wishart's voice was bellowing over the ship's PA system, distorted to a squawk outside on the sun deck but so soft as to be barely audible on some of the lower cabin decks. 'Rumours of typhoid, cholera, plague and other deadly afflictions on this ship are grossly exaggerated. But to set your minds at rest, I thought I would give you a short report from the medical centre.

'There are no dangerous illnesses on board, ladies and gentlemen, that's *no* serious illnesses. That we have had an outbreak of mild food poisoning, entirely among the crew, is correct, but almost everyone has recovered from that, and I hasten to add that it occurred among our deck hands, and has not affected restaurant staff. Among passengers in the ship's hospital, there are five in-patients at present, and I'm glad to say that they are making a speedy recovery. Two broke their arms yesterday, when the ship was moving about so much, and one has a perfectly common affliction which the ship's doctor expects to clear up in a day or two. The remaining two are a little more poorly, and we will be flying them home from Dakar, later this week. You will understand, I'm sure, that in a seaborne community of nearly two and a half thousand people, to have so few unwell shows what a remarkably healthy lot you all are! Rumours which have absolutely no foundation are often spread on ships, especially towards the end of a long voyage, but these can cause unnecessary fear and distress. I do ask you therefore, ladies and gentlemen, to think before you pass on what may seem, at the time, to be an item of hot gossip.

'And finally, may I congratulate you all on the way you coped with the bad weather yesterday, and the night before last. I realise how boring it will have been for you all to have been so cooped up, but by keeping still, and staying in your cabins for the worst of the storm, we were able to keep injuries down to the two unfortunate passengers I mentioned earlier.'

The members of Pullen's class waited for a moment after the end of the announcement before gathering up their notebooks and papers. Pullen held up a hand to prevent them from leaving.

'In the couple of minutes remaining,' he said, 'what would we say about truth?' The class members looked puzzled. 'I mean, I don't want to create more uncertainty, but do we buy that? Do we swallow the story? What makes a story credible? How do we look for cracks and imperfections that shake that credibility?' There was, as always with Pullen's open questions in class, no reaction. He began to draw answers from individuals. 'Cedric?'

'Well, you can usually tell,' Cedric said. 'I mean it all adds up.'

'Detail,' said Suzanne, a new recruit who boarded the ship at Cape Town and who had published several stories in magazines in South Africa. 'We had the broken arms, the numbers given were low, we were told the food poisoning was limited to crew.'

'Good,' said Pullen. 'I read your stories, by the way. I really enjoyed them.' Suzanne smiled, flushing slightly. Anna could tell that he had not been particularly impressed.

'There was also much that remained unsaid,' Anna piped up

now. She felt more at ease, nowadays, contributing far more to classes than she had at the beginning, but she still found it difficult to voice criticisms, even when she felt strongly about her classmates' efforts. 'We weren't told what was wrong with the other two patients, but to have to ship them home must mean it's pretty serious. And to bother to make an announcement at all suggests that there is strong concern. I would say there's a pretty substantial subtext to this which we are not being told about.'

'A nasty suspicious mind,' Pullen leered at his favourite pupil, 'is, I would say, an essential quality of a good writer.'

'And *I* would say,' Mr Bunn – another recent arrival, who had fallen out with other members of the bridge club – called out, 'that we're being pretty irresponsible talking like this. For heaven's sake, the captain's just warned us about rumour-mongering.' Anna had been so caught up in the exercise that she had forgotten for a moment that they were dealing with a real situation.

'I'm so sorry,' Anna said, looking round at the other class members, 'I didn't mean for one instant to—'

'An exercise,' Pullen said, 'nothing more. But it has demonstrated several things: the need a writer has, not merely to express, but to investigate, to delve, to find out. If we want readers to suspend their disbelief, we must be accurate on facts and painstaking on detail – that way, we buy credibility. But above all, if we have the power to attract an audience or a readership, then we have a great responsibility too. The power of the pen is not merely mightier than the sword. It is what forges the sword in the first place; it is what shatters the same sword in other times, moulding the fragments into ploughshares.'

Pullen asked Anna to stay after the class so that they could talk over a project idea, but she felt she needed air.

'OK, take your walk,' Pullen said. 'I won't overcrowd your thoughts. I know when I'm not wanted.'

'Jack,' she dared lay a hand on his denim-clad arm,

'you've been more help to me than you can possibly know. But . . .'

'But you need your exercise. I probably couldn't keep up anyway. But I do want to talk to you, in private, not in class.' Anna felt uneasy about this. 'Oh, don't worry. It's purely work-related.'

'You're going to give my stories back?'

'Of course. We'll talk about that.' Did she imagine it or did he look shifty as he said that? Clearly, she did have a nasty suspicious mind. But that was something she had recently acquired.

She walked two miles, fast, and then went to her cabin to shower. Nine days remained of the voyage, two of which were shore days, and she had much to write. Since about the middle of the Indian Ocean, she had decided that she needed to finish her whole journal before getting home. The project had become talismanic, and if she did not draw the story to its final conclusion before the *Brisbane* entered the English Channel some sort of disaster would strike. It was childish, but it kept her from brooding on the future. And she was learning to speed up – chasing her first deadline.

She was about to put on her towelling dressing gown when a note was pushed under her door. She was requested to call at the purser's desk between three and three-thirty that afternoon. Mild panic clutched at her. What could they want? She felt unable to concentrate, now, and didn't even turn on her computer. Instead she dressed in a cotton skirt and a T-shirt that was too large and went up on deck. Three days after the storm the sea was oily-looking, almost black when you looked towards the sun, with a flat surface that made it seem viscous. Every few minutes a gentle swell would move the great ship, kissing up her bows so that her stern dipped lazily and then rose to settle to another period of motionlessness. The wake seemed to stretch for miles; all along the sides of the ship flying fish would clear the water with rapid fin beats, like birds, then glide over the surface.

Anna found the Boys, and joined them for lunch at the

buffet on deck. 'Don't you want a drink?' Ant asked, since Cedric had volunteered to go to the bar. She shook her head. Some minutes later he returned with two glasses of white wine. Time crept by. She felt self-conscious, playing with her prawn salad while they tucked into smoked trout with gusto. By the time they had finished, Anna had barely eaten two prawns and was now shunting a fragment of lettuce leaf around in the salad dressing that had gathered in the edge of her plate.

'Off your tucker?' Cedric asked.

'It's this heat,' Anna said. 'I can never get up an appetite when it's so hot.'

On the stroke of three, Anna went to the purser's desk. 'Good afternoon, Lady Morfey, would you like to come this way?' The girl disappeared through a side door, and then appeared apparently out of the woodwork, on Anna's side of the desk. 'It's a bit complicated.' She opened another door, in what Anna had always assumed was simply a bulkhead, as Cedric said it must be called, and stood back for her to enter. She stepped from plush, passenger accommodation into a different world. A terrestrial world of clacking typewriters, office desks, papers, the jumble of people and things on the move that signify work in progress. The purser came out of a small side office to greet her.

'Lady Morfey, I've the captain in with me at present.' He held the door of his inner lair open. Wishart was sitting in the chair at his desk. He leapt to his feet.

'Anna, please forgive us for summoning you to the office, and all that, but I wanted the pleasure of telling you myself.' Wishart beamed. 'Someone rather special is going to join you for the last few days of the cruise. Boarding at Dakar.' All she could do was gape. Bernard? No! Bernard deciding the whole thing had been a terrible mistake, after nearly nine months – a pregnancy of doubt giving birth to a recantation, a penitential return? Anger began to well up in her throat. Images of Bernard, like a montage, slipped in and out of vision in her mind's eye. Bernard arrogant, scornful of failure, intolerant of anything deviant. How dare he? But among these images she saw his perplexed, hurt stare, when she had tried to explain about Verne; his cry, like a hurt child, and the poor bruised forehead where he had pressed it against the window frame after William's death. Recalling the smell of canvas and rubber mingled with sweat on the little boy's sneaker actually made her nostrils twitch. She saw their picnic at Kilmarnock Falls soon after losing William, and afterwards, when she felt their spirits had moved together again, in the bout of lovemaking that like a healing draft had begun to rebuild their marriage. It was too painful, to lose all that was more than she could bear. But she knew she could never accept—

'Anna? Are you all right?' Wishart's voice broke in on her confusion. His face, with the purser standing behind him, swam into focus.

'What? Oh, I'm sorry.' She was getting better at composing herself. 'I don't eat much lunch in the heat. Occasionally, that makes me feel faint. I'm fine now.' She had to think what to do, but not here.

'Anyway, I expect you'll be delighted to have Mrs Burroughs join you.'

'Mrs Burroughs?' She was so confused she forgot her daughter's married name. '*Lisa?*' She felt relief and frustration whirled together in a sickening mix.

'She has actually booked on a shared cabin basis,' the purser said, 'and we thought the two of you might like to move in together. Obviously, since your own accommodation is single, we'd be delighted to upgrade your cabin too. I do have one of our verandah suites which we could move you into.'

'I'm not sure,' Anna said. A sinking in her spirits. If Lisa came, lovely though it would be to have her on board, she didn't see how she would get her journal finished before the end of the cruise.

'Of course if you prefer,' the purser went on, 'we could put your daughter into the single cabin opposite yours, in your court.'

'Mr Cutler's? Yes, that might be better.' They could be close, then, without interfering with one another's privacy. But what on earth was Lisa thinking of, flying out to Senegal merely to return with her mother? Perhaps she had business to do in Dakar. Yes, it must be business. If it were holiday, Jamie would be with her.

After the first shock of losing Bernard, Lisa and Jamie were wonderful, particularly on that first day. They put me to bed and when the doctor came they were tactful enough not to tell him precisely what had happened. They said I'd had a bereavement, and was in a state of shock. Which was true, really, though it was not what he thought. He knocked me out with something that kept me under for what seemed like a couple of days. I really can't remember what was going on or how long I was like that. I couldn't cry or anything, that was the problem. I just felt numb – as if my whole body had been frozen like a dentist's injection before doing root work. I knew that the thaw would come, and then it would really hurt, but at the time I felt nothing.

Sweet though Lisa and Jamie were, during those first days, I felt I had to talk to someone else. I needed someone who knew me well enough to give good counsel, but unrelated, and therefore able to be objective. It had to be Margaret, I decided, but when I rang her I found I could not tell her what had happened. The right words simply wouldn't come out. Nevertheless, she was able to interpret my stammering overture and understood exactly what had happened.

'Why don't you talk to Pip?' Margaret said. It was an unexpected suggestion.

'You're my closest friend. My only friend,' Anna replied. Margaret was silent for a while, making Anna feel that she wanted to avoid contact. As if, somehow, Anna's predicament was a disease and that she might get contaminated from being in contact with her.

'Right,' Margaret said. 'I'll come today. Get the gin out.' She was there by mid-morning.

'Are you sure you want gin this early?' Anna had taken Margaret at her word and had set out a chunky Waterford decanter, two glasses, a dish of ice and several small tins of slimline tonic water.

'Christ, Anna!' Margaret pushed past her, into the room. Usually they would have pecked each other on the cheek. 'You still take trouble with niceties at a time like this?' She picked up a glass, tossed the ice tongs on to the silver tray with a clatter that made Anna start, grabbed a handful of ice, dropped it into a glass, sloshed in an enormous measure of gin and handed the glass to Anna. Anna shook her head. 'Drink!' Margaret said. It was like telling a dog to sit. Anna found herself lifting the glass to her mouth. The rank vapour from the spirits made her gorge rise. But she sipped. The gin was warm on her tongue, burning, but soothing.

'Christ, Anna! What a bloody mess!' Margaret poured herself a similar-sized drink. Anna was relieved that Margaret obviously knew what had happened, and that she would not have to explain. She sipped again. Margaret swallowed a large mouthful of neat gin, taking a small fragment of ice into her mouth with it. This she crunched.

'I don't know what to do, where to begin.' Anna sipped again.

'No,' Margaret studied her with a cool expression. 'I don't suppose you do.' They sat in silence. Anna would quite have liked her to do something physical at that stage. She felt that a held hand, a squeezed shoulder might have helped to thaw the frozen sensation, or at least eased the pain of being so clenched. The gin helped ever so slightly, thawing the chill in her guts. She sipped again and then thought that perhaps it was better if, after all, she stayed frozen for a bit longer.

'I don't know what to do,' Anna repeated.

'I feel sorry for you, Anna,' Margaret said, 'I'm going to

try to be truthful, and that will certainly hurt. But really, I *do* feel sorry.' She slipped off her shoes, put her feet up on the sofa and began to speak with care, as if the words might almost have been rehearsed. 'If you can't see how you have managed to lose him, I think you may be beyond help.' She thought for a bit, watching the words sink in. Then, 'Where do you suppose you belong, today? I mean, how do you imagine you fit in?'

'Fit in?'

'As a person – a single person. What is your identity?'

'I don't understand what you're saying.'

'Then perhaps you don't have an identity. Perhaps Anna no longer exists, except as an extension of Bernard.' Anna kept silent. 'Perhaps that individual, that woman called Anna, disappeared years ago, sucked up, absorbed, digested into a marriage.'

'Isn't that what marriage is about? A joining of souls?'

'A merger. Not a takeover. You threw your individuality away.'

'Did I?' Anna thought of Verne. The first time they went birdwatching, she got muddled and went to the wrong door of his car. *Oh, do you wanna drive? It's a European stick shift but I guess you'd be used to that.* He had loved that little car more than any other possession, but even though he hardly knew her, he was willing to share, to respect her ability. He had loved her from that first moment in the English Garden. *When daisies pied and violets blue –* Margaret's voice, strident and tense, intruded.

'Did it occur to you that your marriage had become in-grown, sterile? Did you think – *really* think – how it would be, when he retired and you were constantly under each other's feet?'

'Yes. No.'

'You'll have practical decisions to make now,' Margaret said, after a bit. 'Could you get a job?'

Anna didn't suppose that she could. What would she do? 'I don't see why not,' she said.

'Doing what, do you suppose?'

'Well, I could . . . I could . . .'

'What qualifications do you have?'

'I can type.'

'Oh? And what word processing system do you know?'

'I could learn.'

'You don't even know what a PC is.'

'You don't have to be a genius to learn.'

'So what are you good at?' Margaret finished her gin. She was feeling sick, but determined to work through to the end of this impossible interview. She owed that at least. They had, after all, been friends.

Anna wondered what she was good at. Even her garden was substandard, in this hateful soil. She came up with nothing and simply shook her head. 'Aren't you being a little cruel?' It was a low whisper.

'Anna, you are on your own now. You have to decide what you are going to do.'

'I can't, yet, it's too soon . . . I don't know.'

'Which is why you have to decide, first, what you're good at – really good at. Until you find that out, you won't find a way out of this.'

'I'm not really good at anything.' Anna was coming to understand that she was of very little worth. Her life had been, if not subservient, at the very least supplementary to Bernard's. Their marriage had never, until this moment, seemed quite so lopsided. She had been there for him; to do everything in her power to help him to succeed, and therefore to make their marriage happier. But if, after all, he had felt the need to opt out, and at this late stage, the whole thing had been for nothing. And now she was left, too old to change anything, too young to die. The thaw was beginning. She knew that soon the ice would melt inside her and that the real pain, no longer able to be deferred, would be flooding over her.

'Women have to be survivors,' Margaret muttered. 'Your generation' – it was the first time she had ever alluded to their age difference – 'is inclined to be deadbeat.' She poured herself another gin. 'I feel sorry for you. All of you. Not the men, of course. They've had it good since the beginning of time. But you.' She swigged, and as another boost of alcohol made the quick transit across her stomach lining into her bloodstream, she felt her inhibitions subsiding. They gave way to a kind of rage, not necessarily directed at Anna, but at everything. 'I do feel sorry for you Anna. You're a dinosaur. A relic of the stupid spineless sixties, no, you're worse, you're hampered by cute fifties' morals. "Love and marriage, love and marriage, go together like a horse and carriage." Fancy devoting an entire life to one man! Worse, fancy allowing him to gobble up what little talent you had, so that without him, now, you can't even survive. You couldn't even breathe without his say-so.'

'I can't bear this.' Anna did not think she could hold off her tears for much longer. 'I want you to go.'

'I will in a minute. I said this would hurt, but it's got to get worse for you before it gets better. This much I owe you.' She put her shoes back on and put the glass on to the floor at her feet.

'There's a side table there,' Anna said.

'Fuck the side table,' Margaret yelled. Then she resumed speaking in her former, softer tones. 'You couldn't even get the best out of Bernard. What happened, after Thatcher fell? *You* let him sit it out at Stoneford. You let him persuade himself that he wanted to retire early.'

'Not true.' Anna was weeping now. 'He was getting exhausted. The work almost killed him.'

'Really? You forget that I worked alongside him. Day after day, hour after hour. He was never more alive than when he headed that team.'

'You never saw the exhausted wreck that came home all hours.'

'And that other thing,' Margaret's tone softened further, 'in such a great marriage, how has your sex life been?'

'That's *our* business!' Anna had risen.

'Really?' Anna saw the arched eyebrow. 'Might he have

stayed if it had been better?' Anna was reminded that they had actually had sex infrequently, during the last few years. She had felt that she hungered for it more than he, but had put it down to advancing years and overwork. But as these things passed through her mind she was reminded, too, that the most vexed of questions was still unanswered. Right from the moment of Lisa's tearful news – a bald announcement without explanation – followed by the arrival of that awful, terse, formal note, *I am very sorry to do this to you at this stage, but sudden death really is better*, amid the tumult of feeling, of confusion, of hurt, the most urgent imperative had been to stop it. Reverse the clock. Make it unhappen. But the huge question was why? He mentioned nothing – why? Obviously, Lisa had been privy to his reasons but not her – why? And gradually, she had realised that she had failed him – but how?

'You've no right to even mention that,' Anna said to Margaret.

Lisa, just back from a visit to the corner shop to collect milk and bread, spotted Margaret and froze in the doorway, her hand still on the handle. 'You? Here?' Her eyes were wide with surprise.

'No right?' Margaret said, ignoring Lisa and staring intently at Anna. 'Better ask your daughter.' And Anna knew, then, that the answer was even more ugly than she had feared.

'You?' She felt she could no longer breathe. 'Bernard and . . .' Margaret neither nodded nor shook her head. She met Anna's gaze and held it. Anna looked down at her feet. She walked to the door as if Lisa was not there. Lisa stepped aside to let her out, made as if to follow, but then turned back to Margaret. They heard the back door close quietly.

'How *could* you come here?'

'It's hard to explain.'

'I'll bet it is.'

'I had to come. For Anna's sake. You don't know how fond of your mother I am.'

'Was.'

'Am.'

'Doesn't ring true.'

'Lisa, I assure you, we were the closest of friends. Even closer than some people would consider normal. I loved her. Pip actually wondered if we didn't have something going.'

'Poor, foolish bloody woman.' Lisa was close to tears now. 'She thought the sun shone out of you, certainly.'

'But Bernard . . .' Margaret sighed. 'It just sort of happened.'

'How long were you at it – before I found out – how long?' Lisa wanted to know but Margaret shook her head.

'He has such talent, Lisa. He hasn't begun to realise his full potential yet. When he gets into politics.'

'You can't know him that well,' Lisa said. 'He despises politicians.'

'Of course. That's why he wants to get power. He'll be on the fast track, with his record. He's still relatively young.'

'I think you'd better leave.' Lisa wanted to find her mother.

'I think I better had.' Margaret walked a little unsteadily towards the door where Lisa still stood.

'Go out the front way. Mother's in the back garden and I don't think she'll want to see you again.' Looking at Margaret, Lisa noted the green eyes, moistening now with tears but still exhibiting her usual cool strength. She took hold of the younger woman's rigid shoulders and, before she could prevent it, kissed the forehead and then turned to let herself out. Lisa went to find her mother sitting on the seat by the tennis court. She sat down beside her.

'There are weeds coming through the asphalt,' Anna said after a long silence. 'Have you noticed?'

Later that day, Jamie returned to London to resume his work, leaving Lisa to stay with her mother for a while longer.

'Mum, do you want any supper?' she said, peeping into the sitting room in the early evening. Anna was sitting on the sofa, a copy of *The Times* on her lap. She shook her head.

'I think I want to go to bed early.' The silence and composure was disconcerting.

'You'll have to eat something soon,' Lisa said. 'I'm having an Indian takeaway. Let me get you something.' But by the time she returned with the food, Anna had retired and, when she peeped into the bedroom her mother was already sleeping. After she had eaten, and then watched a late film on television, Lisa went to her own room, undressed, showered and was about to climb into bed when she thought she heard a muffled grunt. It seemed to be coming from her mother's room, so she crept along the passage and listened at her door. At first it almost sounded like a couple having sex – a kind of heaving grunt, interspersed by a muffled roar. Thinking that someone had broken in and was attacking her mother, she flung open the door. Anna was alone, sitting hunched up on the floor, her knees under her chin, rocking back and forth, back and forth, too far gone to weep, but grunting in her agony like an animal that has been injured. Lisa rushed in and took her mother's shoulders but Anna threw her hands off.

'You knew,' Anna gasped, with each swing of her body. 'You knew. You knew.'

'Mummy, don't!'

'You . . . didn't . . . tell . . . me . . .'

'Oh Mummy.'

The rocking stopped 'I didn't even know today.' The rocking resumed, harder. 'She . . . was . . . my . . .'

'Mummy, don't!' Lisa felt her own composure dissolving. 'Mummy, I couldn't tell you. I absolutely couldn't.' Now Lisa almost attacked her mother, putting hands under her shoulders, anxious to lift her into the large bed. 'I couldn't tell you, Mummy, don't you see?' She tried to unbend the stiff body, pushing her down as gently as possible, wanting her to unclench. 'Mummy, Mummy, you *have* to see that.' At last Anna lay still and Lisa slipped into bed beside her. She had never felt truly comfortable in close contact with her before, but now this was not her mother but a human beyond the limits of tolerance. Sensing her coming into the marriage bed, Anna turned and pummelled her daughter on her face, her shoulders, her breasts, beating with rapid, shallow blows like a drummer learning to do a roll. Lisa wrapped her arms around Anna, holding her tightly to reduce the force of the blows. She would have bruises tomorrow, but she would not let go. 'There, there, Mummy,' she breathed into her mother's ear. 'There, there, Mummy. Sshhh.' And at last Anna's arms stopped pumping, her fists relaxed, she unclenched her arms, and then clasped her daughter tightly, holding her close, thinking of everyone she had lost: Charlie, William, Verne, Bernard, Margaret even. Lisa smelt clean and soapy, but as Anna howled in her pain, her daughter's breast became Dawn's, and with her mind set back in her childhood, the musky, milky body odour of Dawn entered her nostrils and began, at last, to calm her as she cried herself to sleep in her daughter's arms.

Chapter Twenty

——•——

During those first weeks after losing Bernard, I tried to escape by revisiting my childhood. Dawn, who had been closer to me than a middle-class mother might have been, returned to dominate my thoughts. I wanted her earthy warmth and to heed her wisdom, uncluttered by intellect. I started to make enquiries, but Bernard's connections with the area meant that whoever I contacted asked about him and I found it impossible to explain.

Dr Jenner referred me to Max. I thought he would be a waste of time but he hooked me with his casual approach. 'Take it or leave it. *I* should care if you don't want help.' But when I decided to try one session, and we spent the time talking about my childhood, I was hooked. It was somewhere to escape from the hateful present. Max's office was near University College, and, since Lisa had taken me to Fitzroy Street soon after that horrible night, it seemed sensible to lodge with her for a while, and to begin visiting Max weekly. Lisa and Jamie were very kind but I could sense that I was beginning to get under their feet, even though their flat was quite roomy. So I began to commute down once a week, to stay overnight with Lisa and then to return the next day. It was a crazy arrangement, but I managed to make the whole exercise fill nearly two days a week for months. The other days were empty, sterile, useless.

For the rest of the day, after she had completed the next section of her journal, Anna kept herself cooped up in her cabin. She even cut her class that morning – first time in weeks – but felt she could not write any more. She read for some time, dozed and listened to her personal stereo, but by the end of the day she was becoming frustrated and tetchy, hungry for fresh air. In the early evening, Jack Pullen phoned her cabin.

'Missed you today.'

'Yes?' She really didn't want to talk. 'I was feeling a little tired.'

'I've got a fax here. I think it might interest you. I also have something to explain.'

'Oh?' A silence.

'You don't sound terribly interested.'

'I'm sorry. I'm really not myself.'

'You've been brooding too long.'

'No.' Her emotions were fragile. Tears waited not far below the surface.

'Let's meet on the Lido. It'll be dead quiet there now, everyone's in their cabin, changing for the captain's formal night.'

'Oh damn! I forgot it was another of those stupid reception things.'

'So, will you? I think you'll be glad if you do.'

'All right.' Anna looked at her face. The eyes were streaked, the skin blotchy. She washed in cold water, tipping some ice into the basin from the bucket that was refilled every morning. Minutes later, she inspected again. She still looked a fright but, realising they would be meeting on deck, took sunglasses with her. Jack Pullen was sitting almost alone at a table near the stern rail. The steward was about to close the bar but when he raised an enquiring eyebrow Anna smiled and shook her head.

'You might feel like a drink when you hear what I've got to say,' Pullen called from across the deck.

'A white wine, then.' That was what the Boys drank at lunchtime.

'I bring it, madame,' the steward said. She walked over to Jack's table.

'I don't know whether to show you this, or to explain first,' Pullen said. There was an envelope on the table with M&I's monogram on its flap.

'Never apologise, never explain!' Anna said. 'Those were about the first words I heard you utter.'

'Touché!' He raised his Scotch. 'Cheers. Those stories you wrote. The breadnut one, and those other three.'

'Yes. Are you going to let me have them back?'

'You don't need them. They'll still be in your dinky little computer.'

'Yes, but the printed ones. I should rather like to have them back.' She felt she wanted to know exactly where they were.

'Well that's it, you see.' Pullen gazed out to sea. 'I say, what a sunset! Have you ever seen the green flash?' The man could be insufferable. She used to dislike him, then she feared him. Now she could have punched him, but she had almost grown to like him. Apart from the clothes.

'The what?'

'The green flash. Supposed to be a flash, seconds after the sun has dipped below the horizon.'

'Really?' She knew that if she pressed too hard he would prevaricate more. He loved playing with people. She resisted the urge to ask and sat in silence, sipping the sharp wine.

'I haven't got them.' He had returned to the subject more quickly than she expected. It must be something moderately important.

'Haven't you?'

'You know, Anna, the sunset would look far better if you took off your dark glasses.' In the half light, she felt she might dare do that. She removed them and looked at him. 'You've been crying,' he said.

'Nonsense!' Anna looked away. This man really could be a bastard. 'It's . . . it's hay fever.'

'Five hundred miles from the nearest land. Priceless!' He saw her gazing a little too fixedly at the orange sky over the rail. The small clouds were violet. 'Anna, I do care, you know. You mustn't mind me teasing.'

'I don't really.' She did mind. A lot.

'Fact is, I sent your stories to someone I know back in England. Name of Maddox.'

'You did what? How dare you?'

'How *dare* I?' He noticed that the dead look had gone. Now her eyes were angry. 'Well, at least I've brought you to life again. Welcome back.'

'Don't patronise me.' She glared at him for almost half a minute. 'How could you even think of sending things, my first stories, without even asking me? How *could* you? What makes you think you had a right to do that?'

'Woah there – steady!' He held up a hand. 'First, I didn't mean to patronise you, simply to cheer you up. You were pretty low when you crawled up on deck and I reckon a spot of rage is better than plain doom. Secondly, I sent them off because I knew that if I had asked, you would have refused. Thirdly, I think you have a very special talent and I feel – thought this will probably piss you off more than somewhat – that I have every moral right, as your teacher, to help you to exploit that talent.'

'And how will sending my first shaky efforts to some crony of yours improve my writing?'

'It won't. But your first efforts are anything but shaky, as you bloody well know. And for the record, Cecil Maddox is not exactly a crony. He's a relatively important part of Baverstock, Maddox. In fact, since Baverstock died in nineteen sixty-nine, he's the most important part.'

'Sounds like a solicitor.'

'Literary agent. Mine, as it happens. I do a little scouting for them, for talent, and believe me, many are called – few chosen. They pay me a small retainer.' He picked up a towel that was on his chair back and put it over his shoulders. 'You warm enough?' Anna nodded. It was still hot, as far as she was concerned, but the sinking sun seemed to have initiated a refreshing breeze. Pullen didn't have nearly enough flesh on his bones.

'What exactly are you talking about?'

'Here.' He handed the envelope to her. She removed the flimsy fax paper and read.

Dear Jack,

Hope the cruise is doing you good.

I showed the five stories by Annabel Murphy to Thelma Robinson at Sirius. She thought they showed great promise but returned them, so I then let Douglas Day at Vintners have a look. He's thrilled with them and wants to meet your author as soon as possible after her return. He says, and I quote: 'this is precisely the sort of talent we are looking for at present. Sensitive, acutely observed, with a strong feeling for structure – we feel that the quality fiction market is hungry for this sort of material. If the author has another five or six similar tales up her sleeve, we would like to get to work with her right away. But we would want to talk about the obvious next step which would be something longer. If she were interested, we might be in a position to consider such a work as one of our lead titles for, say, 1999.'

Well spotted, Jack! I hope you will pass on my warmest greetings to your protégée and tell her how very much I would like to make her acquaintance on her return.

Yours aye
Cecil

Anna could not take it in. Then when she could, she was suspicious. 'It's a trick.'

'No trick, Anna! I told you you could become a writer. Now you are one.'

Her talk with Pullen made her late. She began to change hurriedly but then told herself that it was pointless to arrive on time anyway, and she slowed her pace, showering in water at blood heat to allow her body to cool. She took extra care in her grooming, taking out the one dress that she had not so far worn. This was black, a simple sheath with mid-length skirt and thin shoulder straps, designed for a youngster, but because it was so well cut, and because her figure was still trim, it suited her. Her shoulders had if anything developed a little more flesh and a good deal more muscle tone after so much energetic walking, and the tan skin also helped to disguise signs of age. She had a silk square, printed with huge peacock-blue and acid-yellow flowers, giving relief to the black accessories. When she arrived at the reception all the passengers had gone in and she stood by the door, looking for someone she knew. Cedric was in a small group not far inside and, when he glanced round, seemed not to recognise her at first. But when he did he broke away from the group and came over.

'I know it's what one is supposed to say, Anna,' he took her hand, 'but for once it is sincere: you look absolutely bloody marvellous.'

'Thanks,' Anna said.

'Not just your clothes – that is *not* a cheap dress – it's . . . it's you! You look as though you've just won the pools.'

'Do I?'

'Something's happened. You've heard good news. Perhaps you *have* won the pools.' Cedric brought her to his group, but stopped just short. 'Come on, Anna, sweetie, what is it?' Anna was not keen to let people know about her writing. She had hardly absorbed the news herself yet and still suspected it could turn out to be a false dawn.

'My daughter, Lisa,' she dissembled. 'Coming on board tomorrow at Dakar.'

'But that's wonderful news,' Cedric said. 'I must dash and find Ant.' And he was gone, leaving her the centre of the group's attention. For five minutes or more she chatted about Lisa's talent, about how charming Jamie was, about how they lived in London; gradually she relaxed, warmed by a glass and a half of fake champagne. For the first time since boarding the *Brisbane*, on that cold January day, she was enjoying the flickering warmth of attention from people she had barely spoken to over the previous weeks. Soon Cedric was back with Ant, who whistled at her outfit and then led her off to the bar.

'Lisbon,' Ant said. 'We must do something wild in Lisbon. Lunch up in Sintra, perhaps.'

Lisa's flight was not due until midday, and she would probably not board before mid-afternoon, so Anna decided to take a short trip ashore to the island of Gorée. The slave trade had developed a headquarters there, where, before abolition, Arab merchants dealt in human misery. The fortress depressed and disgusted her, even though the events had taken place centuries before. Among the various stories the guide relayed, one moved her almost to tears: dead, dying or sick slaves were simply pushed through holes in the wall of the fort, to fall into the sea below where they drowned or were eaten by sharks. Among these would be pregnant women not considered strong enough to survive the voyage across the Atlantic to the Caribbean. Within yards of the fortress she spotted two little boys sitting on the dirty pavement. With a piece of charcoal, they had drawn chequers on to a sheet of cardboard and were playing draughts with bottle tops. Coca-Cola versus Heineken. What a setting, Anna thought, for a story.

When she returned to her cabin, she was surprised to find the opposite door open and Lisa's suitcase already waiting outside. Moments later Lisa arrived, led by Tony who, grinning from ear to ear, hefted her case into the cabin.

Anna followed them. Daughter kissed mother, a little stiffly in front of the steward. Tony withdrew.

'Mummy. You look so well! I can hardly believe it!'

'I am well, Lisa.' Anna thought her daughter had lost weight. Her eyes had black lines beneath them, exactly the same as Bernard's when he was tired, and her mouth was different – downturned, trembly. Something was up. 'Lovely surprise, darling, but what brings you to Dakar? Business?' Lisa shook her head. Not entirely to Anna's surprise, her eyes filled with tears. Those are not for me, she thought, instantly hating herself for thinking that. 'Here,' she said, 'give me a proper hug.'

'Oh, Mummy!' Lisa flung her arms round her mother.

'There, there! Sshhh!' Anna held her, stroking her back, whispering softly into her ear, thinking that not so long ago it had been the other way round. After a bit, they sat side by side on Lisa's bed. Outside, on the quay, hawkers were selling cheap objects – carvings, shell necklaces, pots, acetate scarves, baskets and leather belts. The first few members of a brass band had arrived with their instruments. Later, they would play ragged march tunes while the ship edged her way out of the harbour.

'Is it work?'

'No, that's fine. They've given me extra holiday, to get this sorted out.'

'It must be Jamie, then,' Anna said. She had always known that someone as pretty and as charming as Jamie would constitute a risk. Women couldn't keep their eyes off him.

'A horrible irony,' Lisa said. 'But in a way, it's me. I mean I know it's me, but I can't make myself stop and I can't bear what I'm becoming.'

'Darling, you're not making much sense. Why don't we get you unpacked, watch the ship sail and then we'll have ages to talk. I can get Tony to bring us drinks to the cabin. Supper if you like.'

'Could you bear it if we talked now? I've bottled this up since just before you left, and it's got worse and worse. In fact, it's been ever since Dad . . .' She found it difficult to mention Bernard's departure, in case it hurt her mother.

'Let's unpack and talk at the same time.' Anna felt it would be better for them both to be active. Lisa sniffed, and bent to undo her suitcase. The task was over in moments. Anna helped her to put clothes into drawers and hung her silk dressing gown on the back of the shower room door.

'This is lovely.'

'Jamie gave it to me.' Another sniff. Anna handed her the box of tissues from the dressing table, sat in the chair and waited.

'Well?'

'I don't know how to begin.'

'How about the beginning. Oh, and Lisa. I want it all. The whole thing.'

'You won't think much of me.'

'I'll cope.'

She hesitated, trying to decide where to begin. 'Those first days, when Dad . . . you know. I was so preoccupied looking after you that I didn't sort of realise, until later, quite what an effect it had had on me.' Anna kept silent. She felt that showing any kind of response at this stage would probably lend itself to misinterpretation.

'I'd always been a bit worried about Jamie,' Lisa continued. 'It's not altogether his fault, but, well, with looks like that, women do tend to be drawn to him. I was always a little uneasy when he was away on business or when I was away and he was home. I liked to be able to account for his movements. I was never happier than when I could tell, chapter and verse, exactly where he had been and who he had been with.'

'With the example you were set, that is probably understandable.'

'But when Dad actually, you know, *did* it, I grew more obsessive. I found myself checking Jamie's pockets for evidence of infidelity. I was looking for ticket stubs to theatres, sniffing his suits to see whether I could detect strange perfumes. If I found something that needed an explanation, I could not relax until I had extracted one. At first my questions were guarded, disguised. But gradually the obsession grew stronger, and I could hear myself quizzing him. "Where are you lunching? What happens between seeing your lunch guest off and the end of the afternoon? If I ring the office will you be there?" and so on.'

'You were probably going through a bad patch after Dad's surprise.'

'I think Jamie understood that, at first, but I got more and more persistent, trying his patience until he blew his top.'

'Lisa, I've only been away for eleven weeks. You were blissful when I left. Isn't this only a phase? After all, we've all had to get used to . . . different circumstances.'

'Eleven weeks? Eleven hours is plenty of time to ruin a marriage.' She wept a little. Anna waited. 'It came to a head when you were in the Pacific. He said he was coming home early to cook supper. He wanted a serious talk. He made a steak and kidney pie. Delicious – he's as good at cooking as everything else – and as we ate he started. "You don't trust me," he said. "Since your father did that, you think I'm like all other men, capable of the same behaviour." I kept silent, I knew I had been irrational. I wanted to tell him that I knew it was unreasonable of me, but I couldn't get the words out. And I didn't expect what was coming next. "You treat me like a criminal," he said, "but you haven't found a scrap of evidence. And I can tell you now that you never will. I'm too clever and too careful, and if I feel like having a bit on the side, I will have it; but you will never know, and I will never tell." "How do I know you haven't already?" I asked him. "You don't know," he told me. "And I may as well tell you that as far as I'm concerned, if you see some bloke into whose knickers you are dying to get, well – that's your affair and I don't want to know about that either." And I said, "Do you really mean that?" And he said, "Do I mind going where other men have been?"—well actually, he said, "where other men have come" – and then he said, "No, I don't think I'd find that too difficult to live with." And, Mum, looking at him, across the table, with such an angry expression, I realised that I had hurt him terribly. But I knew too that I had made a bad mistake.' Lisa began to weep afresh. 'You see, I said that I gave and expected total commitment. One hundred per cent. That was what he had from me. For life. That was what I promised when we married. And that was what he promised in his vows and what I expected from him. But he said . . . he said,' she was finding it difficult to speak between sobs, now, 'he said that the vow meant love, not sex and that being a monk was not his style. And so I, I left him. Last week, actually.' She cried for a while, soaking Anna's blouse.

'Shhh! Darling, don't take on so.' Anna stroked her head. 'You're incredibly clever, you're very young. You've got years in front of you, decades. You'll . . .' What was she going to say? You'll get over it? You'll get together again? You'll find someone else? 'Darling, I'm sure there'll be someone.'

'But Mummy, I don't want someone. I want Jamie. I can't bear to lose him, but I can't stay with him unless it's total. It absolutely has to be total.'

'I think we should watch the ship sail,' Anna said. 'I'll give you five minutes to wash your face. I'll be in my cabin – it's that one over there. Next door there's a gay couple. They've become great friends of mine and they can't wait to meet you. Five minutes.'

Anna returned to her cabin. So. The same mess, the same pain. She knew that she would have to give her daughter good counsel. But she also suspected that Lisa would have a pretty clear idea of where she wanted things to go. Once she had recovered from the emotional storm, brought on by confiding in her mother, a rational proposition would be presented. Anna rather feared, particularly if there was to be a permanent bust-up with Jamie, that she would be figuring in Lisa's plans for the future. She was, at last, developing some ideas of where her own future, such as it was, might be going, but she still had much to consider, much to plan.

Whatever happened now, she must weigh her advice to Lisa very carefully.

Lisa knocked on her door and together they walked up to the Observation Deck. Anna glanced at the bridge, whose windows were above the deck, noticed Captain Wishart's outline against the glass and waved. The wave was instantly returned. Departure was not due for another five minutes. Lisa seemed calm now and there was just enough time, Anna decided, to clear the air on a question that had nagged her for months.

'I don't want to force an answer, but I would appreciate one if you can bear to talk about it.' She checked her daughter's face for composure and continued. 'How long, exactly, had you known about Margaret?' Lisa turned paler and stood in silence for a while. 'It was years, wasn't it?' Lisa nodded.

'Just after he resigned from the Team. When they slung out Thatcher.' Five years – more! In all that time Anna had been so happy in Margaret's company, confiding in her, hanging on her words, flirting with her admirers. She wondered whether Margaret had been any more faithful to Bernard than to Pip, but she presumed not. Perhaps they had a similar kind of arrangement. Poor Pip! These so-called open relationships carried their morality in layers. A clandestine one-night stand was venial – wrong, but forgivable. If undetected, she'd been told, it could strengthen, not weaken the marriage – so would that make it all right? Anna thought of Paris, Margaret's adventure with that Brazilian Adonis, Eduardo. How wrong had that been if Pip was not averse to doing something similar? Right and wrong didn't come by degree: it was either one thing or the other. That was what Anna had been taught from the cradle. That was what she had believed until she boarded the *Brisbane*. Now it all seemed less clear. Immorality, she now realised, took on more subtle guises, especially where relationships were concerned. If a marriage amounted to possession, one of another, however carefully dressed and disguised it might be, the relationship was nothing more than a form of enslavement – legitimised by the marriage laws, but as tyrannous and reprehensible as buying and owning another human.

'You were blackmailed.' Anna knew that her daughter wanted to be absolved. Being cruel to her would achieve nothing. 'In your circumstances, I'm not sure what I'd have done.' Anna was pretty sure she'd have risked breaking the silence. Conspiracies, she knew, grew like fungus, spreading millions of filaments into wholesome tissue, corrupting and consuming as they grew. A shout from the quayside below attracted their attention. A man at the forward end had just cast off a huge rope which was now being wound on to a winch in the bows. Within a minute, the strip of water between the ship's side and the quay began to widen. The *Brisbane* had sailed.

'Lisa, a couple of things you should know.' Anna wanted to set out their terms over the next few days. There was much to consider and decisions to be made – decisions that would have profound consequences. 'I've taken up writing. I've even bought a word processor. I rise very early in the morning, to work, but I take late sitting breakfast.'

'Fine.' Lisa looked at her mother. 'What sort of writing?'

'Well, it started with these memoirs. But I've done some short stories. They've been sent home and accepted by Vintners.'

'Vintners? Good Lord, Mother. That's amazing.'

'Isn't it.'

'I'm so pleased for you.'

'The fact is, I want to finish this memoir thing, and we've only a few more days at sea. So I hope you'll understand if I lock myself away in my cabin for a while. It should only be mornings.'

'Mum, darling, of course I don't mind. I think it's wonderful that you've found something to do. I'm dying to read the memoirs. Have you got them printed out yet?'

'What? Oh no, not quite yet.' Anna wasn't at all sure that even Lisa would be privy to them. 'But I'll let you read a couple of the stories.'

'And we can talk in the afternoons, can't we?'

'For as long as you like.' Anna patted Lisa's hand. 'Ah, here we are!' Her voice brightened at two approaching figures. 'Here come the Boys. Cedric, Ant – meet Lisa. Lisa, it's Ant – *never* Tony.'

Next morning Anna was up, as usual, soon after five. She realised that her story had almost reached its conclusion. She had a decision to make. Well, several decisions, really. 'But first, I must record my thoughts, right up to the end,' she muttered.

Lisa knocked on her door at lunchtime. 'Cedric tells me they have to winkle you out of here about this time, or you go all moody,' she said. 'Come and have lunch, there's a buffet thing at the back somewhere.'

'I know. I've been on this ship for almost three months, remember?' Anna seldom ate lunch, but sat with Lisa as she shelled and ate barbecued prawns. Her bikini, Anna noted, was a looser fit now than when she had last seen her in the summer. She had certainly lost weight.

'What are you going to do about Carborough?' Lisa asked. 'It's far too big for you.'

'I'd stay if I wanted to, but I don't. I hate the place. Always did.'

'Really?' Lisa wiped her fingers. 'I thought you enjoyed its stateliness.'

'There's nothing stately about Ketton House. It's simply a suburban villa built for a rich burgher in an ugly age.'

'Have you thought what you'll do?'

'Have you?'

'Actually, Mum, yes, I have.' What a cool little person this was today. The harrowed weepiness of the previous day seemed to have been left behind. 'I phoned Jamie late last night.'

'Aha!' Anna knew there was something different. 'Do you know what it costs – that satellite phone? Eleven pounds a minute!'

'Mummy, there *is* rather a lot at stake.' Lisa thought for a minute. 'Do you know, I hadn't spoken to him for eight days.' Anna saw the love in her eyes.

'Isn't this a bit different from yesterday?'

Lisa ignored her comment and pressed on. 'He says he was boorish. He was very tired. He didn't make proper allowances for how hurt I was, over you and Dad. He asks to be forgiven, and suggests, when this boat—'

'Ship!'

'Mother! When this *vessel* gets back to Southampton, that we get together. "Convene and consult" were his precise words.'

'And in all this conversation, at eleven pounds per minute, did he concede the bit about total commitment?'

'I'm getting some pudding, Mum. Do you want anything?' Lisa sprang up and carried her empty plate away. A deck steward reached out a hand to take it from her, but she seemed too distracted to give it up. Within a few moments she was back, carrying a large handful of black grapes.

'Nothing lah-di-dah like a plate or anything,' Anna said, with only the gentlest hint of reproach. Lisa ignored her mother and began again, before her neat bottom had come into contact with the plastic outdoor chair.

'The thing is, Mother, that Jamie and I had sort of hatched out this rather clever scheme. Obviously, if you sell Carborough, you'll need to move somewhere else. Well, the solution is so simple. We've bought this ruinous barn, down in Kent. You didn't know.'

'Scheme? Barn?'

'Near Canterbury. We got it pretty cheaply. Someone bought it to develop but then the property slump came and they went broke. Full planning permission, everything. It could make a fabulous house – huge!—and it's so pretty in the countryside down there.'

'You hate the country.'

'Mother! I've never lived in it. That's all.'

'You mentioned a scheme.'

'Well, all we could scrape together was enough to buy the thing. You can't get mortgages on ruins. Besides, we're still paying off Fitzroy Street. It'll be ages before we can afford to convert it. But now, with everything, you know, as it is, we have a perfect reason for getting on straight away. There's a separate outbuilding that could make a divine granny annexe. You could move in there. It'd be lovely having you close; Jamie's quite potty about you anyway – God knows why, ha ha ha – you'd be able to have your privacy, and when we travel there'd be a presence at home. Oh, and Mum, I'll need so much help and advice with the garden. It could be superb – there are walls and things – but it will need a loving touch.' Anna sat quietly, listening to her daughter. The initial temptation was strong. Security. Peace of mind, a friendly hand to hold in the night when she got frightened. But there was a complicated agenda. She would be a housesitter – no problem there. It would be fun developing the garden with them and life in rural Kent would be fine. But she would be in the way, worse, she would be keeping an eye on Jamie when Lisa travelled. A spy. That would be more onerous than creating the entire garden by herself. And she would not be independent.

'Lisa, that is very sweet of you. And of Jamie too. But how will you raise the money to do up the barn?'

'We could sell Fitzroy Street and get a loan. Or we thought, that if you were selling Carborough, you might like to, well, you know, help a bit.' Anna sat in silence. She could see that Lisa was impatient for a reaction.

'There's a lot to think about, darling.' Anna got to her feet. 'If you've finished your grapes, how about a walk round the deck?'

'OK.'

'The Promenade Deck is best, you can go all the way, round and round.' They walked in silence, one, two, three, four circuits. Eventually Lisa could bear it no more.

'Well?'

'Darling, it's far too soon for me to say anything yet.

And I think it's a bit soon for you too. Give me a day or two.'

The *Brisbane* entered the River Tagus at 6 am. As with most of the ports, Cedric and Anna were up to watch, but Ant, and now Lisa, were deeply asleep in their cabins.

'Our last port of call,' Cedric said. 'It's always so sad when the cruise comes to an end. But it's also such a huge relief. I can't wait to get home.' As always on these occasions nowadays, they were arm in arm.

'I shall miss you two,' Anna said.

'Not half so much as we'll miss you. And your heavenly daughter. My dear, if I weren't, you know, I'd—'

'Cedric! You don't have to heap compliments. We know each other too well by now.'

'But you're the dark horse. I'm damned glad Lisa filled us in. Fancy keeping all that business so quiet. We presumed you were a widow.'

'I am really. Good as.'

'We guessed there was something terribly wrong when we first saw you, but if only we'd known what it was. We'd have done more for you.'

'You couldn't have done more.'

'I don't know what I'd do if I lost Ant.' Cedric looked rather bleak. 'I mean, I know he's a lecherous old bastard. He's always slipping up to the West End on some pretext or other, and I'd rather not know what he gets up to, but if I lost him, I'd be done for.'

'One thing I have learnt, Cedric, is that there is no such thing as a certainty. If we're lucky enough to have a loving relationship, we should rejoice in each moment of it. But I'm not sure we have the right to book it for the full journey. One partner might decide to change direction. And perhaps the hurt is less if we do grant our other halves the privilege of freedom.'

'You reckon?'

'If we're joined, Cedric, perhaps we should be freely

joined. By love, but also by mutual respect. Not by bonds woven out of religious dogma.'

'Jesus, Anna. You have given it some thought.'

'A little,' Anna said. 'Of course, Lisa's arrival has helped me to crystallise my feelings.'

'And your writing.' Cedric felt the need to change the subject. 'We knew you had something there. We shall want a signed copy of the first edition, remember.'

The ship moved past the tiny riverside fortress known as Belem and the memorial to the Navigators. Soon they had sailed under the great suspension bridge where Anna looked up to see cars and lorries passing over the metal grids, showing their undersides. The buzzing sound was the same as vehicles crossing the gorge on Tudor Avenue at Purlin.

Ant had talked Tony into organising a picnic lunch for the four of them and as soon as the ship had docked, on that bright, spring Sunday, they disembarked and hired a taxi for the day. The road out of the capital was congested and in Sintra, where the air was cool and moist, it seemed that the whole of Lisbon had come to eat Sunday lunch. Every restaurant in the hilltop village was full, but the group took themselves to the ruined gardens of Monserrat where they carried their lunch in white paper carriers, down through the woods, past a vast wisteria in full bloom and onto a sloping lawn. There, in a discreet corner behind a persimmon tree – for picnicking in the garden was forbidden – they drank vinho verde and munched hardboiled eggs and chicken legs. After a while Anna said she would like to walk. Lisa jumped up, but the Boys elected to stay and rest.

'You've made your decision, haven't you?' Lisa was never one to beat about the bush.

'I was going to talk to you tomorrow, on our penultimate day at sea,' Anna said. She didn't want to spoil their short visit to Portugal. 'I know these gardens are ruinous, but it is lovely here, isn't it?'

'It's "no", isn't it?' Lisa could not help a catch developing in her voice.

'You really want to talk about this, don't you?' Anna said. They had come to a low wall below the great wisteria. 'Let's sit here.'

'OK.' The young woman sat beside her mother. There was a pause while Anna marshalled her thoughts. She had hoped for a conference the next day, when she had had more time.

'Lisa, I want to pay for you to convert your barn.'

'You do? Oh Mummy that's *wonderful*.' Lisa hugged her mother and kissed her cheek.

'I'm not sure what it will cost. I'm not a millionaire, but I can afford to help. If nothing else, it will enable you to hang on to your flat in Bloomsbury which I love anyway.' She took a deep breath. 'But I won't be living with you.'

'Oh Mummy!' Lisa's dismay was genuine enough. Anna was relieved. She had nursed a nagging fear that all they wanted was the capital. A nasty, mercenary little thought, she told herself now.

'I have spent almost forty years in total subservience, Lisa. In fact, if you look at my life, even with my brothers, as a tiny girl, I was supplementary. If I move in with you, I would be like a spare appendage. I'd be there to pick up the pieces, to make do and mend. And worse for you, I would get in the way of your marriage.'

'Mother, of course you wouldn't.'

'Hear me out, Lisa. You and Jamie have a great deal to iron out. He has weaknesses. I could spot them the moment I first saw him, but he is also a kind, gentle and – not that this means anything whatsoever – a very beautiful man. You have huge strengths and more than your fair share of talent. You're going to have to work things out between you, or you'll have to part. Now there is nothing, absolutely nothing that anyone other than the two of you can do to help. It is your problem, and yours only. But listen to this: in my marriage, I gave and I expected one hundred per cent.' Anna wondered whether Lisa had ever had any inkling about Verne. Bernard confided in her about most things. 'There was a particular time when this was put so sorely to the test that it nearly destroyed three lives. But until the day your father walked out, every ounce of my being was directed towards him and to our family.'

'Mummy, I know that.'

'And look, Lisa. Look where it got me!' Anna felt a surge of self-pity welling up in her breast and thrust it aside angrily. 'It got me nowhere. In fact, when you put me on that ship, I was as good as dead. A useless, dismembered limb – like the severed tail of a lizard. It wriggles, it has life for a while, but it is nothing but carrion.' Lisa took both her mother's hands into hers.

'I never thought that about you.'

Anna ignored her. 'I've decided what I'm going to do, now. I will be sixty soon. I do not regard that as impossibly old.

'I shall buy a cottage in Norfolk, probably near the coast, somewhere between Sheringham and Brancaster. I will write. I will go birdwatching. I will travel. Oh, and another thing. I will almost certainly be getting myself a small waterside dwelling on Lake Kanantuka in upstate New York, where I will probably spend pretty long periods. Your birthplace, Lisa darling, and I hope my grandchildren,' here Anna stroked Lisa's tummy in small round circular movements, 'will want to spend some of their summer holidays there.'

'You'll have to wait a while for those,' Lisa retorted, wondering why on earth her mother would want to go back to America.

'Not too long, I hope. The world can hardly be kept waiting for such beautiful people as you and Jamie are likely to beget.'

'Mother!' Lisa tried to put a brave face on all this, but she was put out. Seriously put out. 'You seem to have got everything absolutely sorted.' They got up and walked a little more, peering into the windows of the derelict house at the centre of the garden. Anna knew that Lisa was piqued, but that she would be relieved when she had had a chance to think it all through.

'You will come and see me in Norfolk, won't you?'

'Mummy! You don't even have to ask!' They walked back

to the lawn and found the Boys fast asleep. 'Looks odd,' Lisa said, 'seeing two grown men holding hands like that. It must be very difficult for them, having to hide their affection all the time.'

'They manage,' Anna said. 'In fact, in their way, they're a damn sight more affectionate than half the husbands and wives on board.'

On the last morning at sea, Anna rose extra early. Most of the passengers seemed to have done their packing already but Anna planned to do hers an hour before the heavy bags were to be collected, at midnight. She had given Tony his tip, and had included the tip that the drunken man Cutler should have given. She had placed it in an envelope but within minutes of Tony having taken it, when he called with her morning tea, he had returned, almost in tears.

'I'm very sorry, lady. You have given me too, too much.'

'Tony, it's from me, *and* from the man over there.' She pointed to the cabin door where Lisa was now sleeping.

'Such generosity is not necessary.' She took his hand and looked in his eye. He was so young to be working so long away from home.

'I am asking you to take it. If you are troubled about having too much, give some to your church at home.'

The previous morning, after they had sailed back out of the Tagus and on, up the Iberian coast into a grey, cold, choppy Bay of Biscay, Anna had set about rereading her memoirs. She reckoned there must be fifty or sixty thousand words of them, maybe more. She had got about three quarters of the way through when the craving for exercise and fresh air had driven her out on to the blowy decks. This morning she had to finish writing the last entry, and then to resume her reading to the very end. She recorded her most recent conversation, with Lisa, in the gardens of Monserrat and their return to the ship. She had made a fairly momentous decision about the memoirs too.

For the sake of completeness, she gave the third document

the title ARRIVALS. She fiddled with the computer for a while, closing her eyes and jiggling her mouse so that when she opened each of the three parts of her memoirs, a random page appeared on her screen. She told herself that there was some significance to where they opened, but really she did not believe in superstitions of that kind at all. Part One opened in the rectory garden, in frost, while she tried out Charlie's Christmas binoculars. Part Two opened boringly, on a blank page, inadvertently included by her striking the wrong key. She scrolled with her eyes closed and then opened them to read: *that bastard doesn't give a shit about you*. Quickly she shut her eyes, then opened them again and made herself read on, hearing Verne's soft voice in her ear. Finally she opened Part Three to find herself on the mudflats at Cairns, talking to the younger English birdwatchers who had been to Purlin and who described the semi-retired department head. Still single. And that reminded her, again, as she was so often reminded, of the closing words of Verne's last and only note: *No one can ever replace you. Absolutely no one. But I understand.*

Now, swiftly, before she could rationalise or over-analyse what she was doing, she put the cursor from her mouse on to the icon of each of the three documents and dragged them over to the little garbage can at the corner of the screen. The can grew pot-bellied, to show that it contained the data. Now she went to her menu marked 'special'. Down came the menu, and she selected the command 'empty wastebasket'. At once a warning sign came up on the screen, immobilising the computer until she had responded. 'The trash contains three items. They use 1.2 megabytes of disk space. Are you sure you want to permanently remove them?' She pressed the return key. The disk whirred for a moment, the trash can icon went slim again and Anna's memoirs were no more. Wiped out. Gone for good. She wept a little, of course. Anyone would who had destroyed almost two hundred hours of concentrated work at the push of a button. She remembered seeing a film on television about an American Indian artist who spent months collecting coloured stones and grinding these into powder to create pigments for making sand pictures. As the final moment approached, and his picture was complete, he became intensely emotional as he ritually destroyed his work. What sacrifice! Well, for better or for worse the whole sorry story was gone, the entrails wiped away leaving behind an almost empty disk. Now she really could start up a brand-new existence.

As the *Brisbane* bucked her way across the cold, angry sea, closing on the entrance to the English Channel; after Anna had packed her computer, papers, books, CDs and clothes, she sat down at her desk to complete one final writing task. This would be on the ship's headed paper with Lisa's London address at the top. She did not know exactly where her Norfolk cottage would be, but she was pretty sure that her American summer home would be close to Grackle Wood.

My dear Verne, she wrote.

You cannot possibly know but . . .